THE CONSCRIPT

THE CONSCRIPT

Charles Schultz

Paperback ISBN: 978-1-972291-08-5
Ebook ISBN: 978-1-972291-09-2
Imprint: Independently published

For my beautiful wife Erin who consistently allows me to continue to pursue my dreams. I wouldn't be who I am without your love and support.

For Hunter, Sayler, and Charlie you inspire me every day to be a better man and father. I hope my dedication to continuously pursue big things gives you strength to one day pursue your own big dreams.

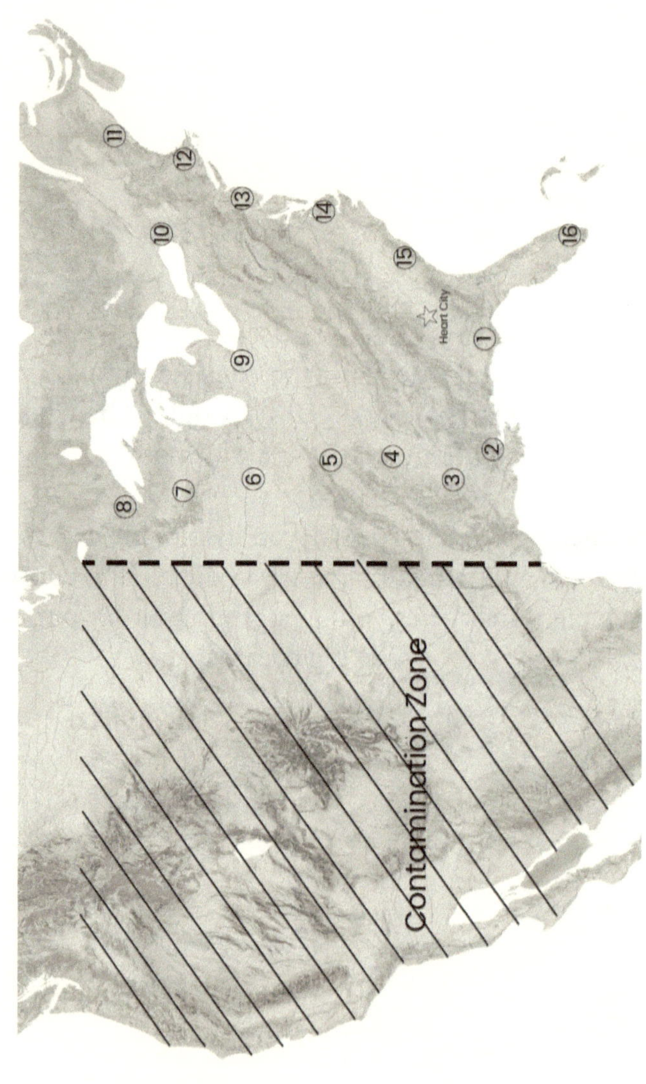

Heart City
Contamination Zone

CHAPTER 1

A large crash shook the floor and rattled the walls, waking me from my slumber. My eyes snapped open as I shot upright in my bed, my windows still rattling. I often woke up to the sound of construction within the dome and, no matter how many times it happened, it always took me back to the mine collapse. The mines were all located several miles outside the dome, but when there was an accident it shook the walls of the dome and everybody felt it.

It was hard to believe it had been almost three years since the last collapse. That was the day I lost my father. Nightmares still haunted me on most nights. Yet there was a sense of peace for most within the dome. Even a little hope.

I swung my feet over the side of my bed, rubbing my eyes. I took a deep breath, settling myself; today was a big day.

Today would be my first day outside the dome. I'd heard stories of the charred and burnt wasteland that resided beyond.

Section Eight only taught us a small amount about what was really beyond the dome. We were all told of the war that ended America and the emergence of a virus, which is why the domes were needed. They also taught us that the domes protected us from the Reapers. But for some reason they never explained what the Reapers were or where they came from.

Still, even with what they taught us in school there were many theories about what was really beyond the dome wall. Some said the bombs had killed everything. Others said the radiation had created mutated, vicious animals. The craziest rumors were those aimed at what the Reapers really were: not quite human, but something different, something evolved—or maybe more primal was the right word.

I thought they were all fools. There was obviously something useful out there and the Reapers weren't that much of a risk. If there were nothing worth salvaging outside of the dome, they wouldn't send us out there.

My morning routine passed in a blur. The excitement of starting work must have had me moving quicker than usual. I traversed the winding streets, finding my way to my transport depot. There were few people among the living at this hour. At a quarter to five in the morning, most people were still at home in bed. It was dark outside, but the light from the full moon illuminated the streets through the clear ceiling of the dome. The temperature was a regulated seventy-two degrees. I heard stories that outside was another story. This time of year it was usually in the mid-twenties.

I was the first to arrive at the work depot, and I made my way into the building to get prepped for my first day. Even though nobody was in yet, the hallways were lit, guiding the way to the locker room. At the end of the hall, I walked through the door and found my way to a set of lockers. Printed clearly on the very last one was my name: DANTIN CROSS. I took a seat on a bench positioned in front of my locker. I examined my name plate, wondering what my father would think about me getting to start work today.

The thoughts slowly faded and my vision focused on the contents of the locker. In the locker was a pair of long johns, grey sweatpants, and a grey sweatshirt. And one bright yellow hazmat suit. The bonus of working outside the dome was getting to look like a big walking banana. I guess the virus is still an issue. I let out a long sigh as a few people started to join me in the locker room. The conversations were minimal as we started to get dressed.

I slipped into my long johns. As I reached for my sweatpants, a large hand grabbed my shoulder.

"Dantin? Is today your first day?"

My eyes shot over my shoulder, making contact with a man I'd known for several years. He was good friends with my father and grandfather.

"Make sure you bundle up; it's been extremely cold the last few weeks," he said.

"Crick, is that you?" I asked as the man nodded. "Yeah, today's my first day. Are you on this detail too?"

Crick smiled. "Sure am. You stick with me and you'll be OK."

I finished getting ready, putting everything on except the mask for my hazmat suit. I walked down the ramp to the transport vehicle with the rest of the hazmat bananas. A large group of us piled into the back of the first rover. Crick sat beside me, a deep, low moan escaping him as he found his seat.

He nudged me. "I'm getting too old for this." He smiled and let out a low chuckle.

As the vehicle surged forward, a voice crackled over the PA system, running through a set of expectations for the trip: "Attention, lumber detail. Your time today will be spent in search of usable lumber. Your team will work together and remain as a group. We will be dropping off several groups at multiple locations. You will be required to work until your transport arrives again to pick you up. Your team leader will remain with you should you have any further questions. Good day."

Good day? I'm still not sure what is good about it. I'd heard so many stories of work beyond the walls of the dome. The morning briefing couldn't have sounded any more rehearsed or less sincere. *Maybe the stories have some truth to them?*

As the announcement ended, the group began to put on their hazmat helmets. I followed suit. The helmet snapped into place and I was now breathing filtered air. I looked up as we passed through the first gate of the dome, which led us into a small glass tunnel that was about a hundred yards in length. As we reached the second gate we came to a stop. I watched the first gate close, sealing us from the inside of the dome.

There was a hissing sound, as if someone were blowing through a straw, and the second gate opened. We started forward again into the wasteland that lay beyond. The ground was charred. There were no signs of life. Dust blew across the scorched earth. I could feel my eyes widen and jaw drop as I surveyed the destruction. I knew the war had taken its toll on our homeland, but this was more than I could have ever imagined. It had been years, yet the earth looked as if it had just burned yesterday.

I looked back, staring through the window at the dome. It was the first time I had seen it from the outside. It really was something spectacular. The half circle rose from the edge of the wall, arcing perfectly through the overcast sky behind it. I felt awestruck by it. It was baffling to think we were capable of such incredible structures when inside the dome we lived like primitive beings.

As I watched the ruins pass by, a reflection in the window froze me. My father, with his dark hair, blue eyes and muscular jaw, was staring back at me. I blinked hard, focusing on the reflection. This was the first time I realized how much I looked like my father. Other than the small amount of grey that had been starting to appear in my father's hair, we could have passed as brothers.

My thoughts returned to the worthless stretch of land that we were traveling through. *What could we possibly salvage from this wasteland?* The transport shook over the pothole-ridden road.

After a half hour of shaking and rocking, the truck suddenly felt as if it were floating on air. I looked out to see that the landscape had shifted. Large trees lined the road and countryside as far as I could see. The vast forest looked untouched by the war. There were no signs of destruction, bombs, or fire here.

After another ten minutes the truck squeaked to a halt.

"Everyone out," a voice crackled over the PA.

One by one, we filed out of the vehicle. I followed Crick as we walked single-file into the woods. There was a fresh layer of snow on the ground, and judging by the overcast sky, it look as though there may be more in the future. The only snow I'd seen was the manufactured snow that was produced inside the dome from time to time during the Christmas holiday. This stuff was different. Softer, whiter, and significantly fluffier. It was so light that it appeared to jump out from under our boots as we walked.

I turned back as the transport rover pulled away, leaving behind a large wagon with a smaller tow transport for any lumber that we were able to produce during the day's labor. Our small work group broke into two crews and got to work. I went with Crick as he grabbed a two-person saw. Crick pointed at one of the medium-sized trees, and without a word we started sawing. *I think I'm going to like this kind of work.*

I had a good feeling about working outside the dome. It was nice to be away from the dull apartment buildings. The constant grey. The green of the woods, the feeling of the brisk air–even though it was through a plastic suit–and the sounds of the wildlife invigorated me. It didn't take long for me to find my stride within the group.

"Timber!" Crick's voice echoed through the woods over the cracking sound of the tree we had been sawing at beginning its fall to the earth.

A successful battle against my first tree. The young elm settled into the ground, and a small group of workers hurried into position. Like a colony of ants, each member grabbed onto a different part of the tree, dragging it to the trimming station. It was then hoisted onto the carrier to be trimmed down. Small branches were discarded, and the trunk was cut into segments and then loaded neatly onto the transport wagon.

There were no private vehicles within the dome. Gas was not available for private use. The only way to get the timber back to Section Eight was by government vehicles. I could only imagine how much easier this must have been when gas was available for machines. My grandpa had told me stories about chain saws that could cut small branches off a trunk in seconds. With all the work being done by hand, a good day was getting five trees back to the dome, according to Crick. Especially with winter coming on.

The days were getting shorter. The temperature was quite cold today. Crick had told me that there were days when the snow was so thick they were lucky to come back with a single tree.

The woods where we worked had once been part of a state in old America called Minnesota. Now, they were just referred to as the woods outside Section Eight. It was a place with extremely harsh winters, and this year it looked like winter had started early.

It was only the beginning of December and already the temperatures were in the teens. Snow had started to come down hard. Based on what I had learned in school, usually, the harshest temperatures didn't occur until late January and February.

The cold and snow slowed our progress. We had only gotten two trees down by lunch. The short break was great while it lasted, but we didn't have time to waste, so it was back to work.

I was making my way back to the tree we had left half-cut when we heard the first cry. It sounded like a strong wind whistling around an apartment building back in Section Eight. Every worker froze. Staring through the falling snow, my eyes darted from side to side trying to locate the source of the howl.

"Can anyone see it?" Crick asked the group.

I couldn't see anything. The snow was starting to pick up and the wind was blowing swiftly out of the north. The strong breeze could easily have been enough to play tricks on us. The whistling and echoes sounded like they were coming from all around us. Whatever it was could have been several miles off. Or it could have been just a few yards away. There was really no way of telling.

"I don't see anything. This snow's too thick," George called from the edge of the worksite.

Another screeching howl. This time closer. The workers were now at full alert. Everyone moved slowly, staring into the mess of flying snow. Still no sign of what was making the sounds; however, there was little doubt that they were getting closer.

I looked at Crick. "What is it?"

Crick's eyes were wide with fear as he looked at me. "Nothing good."

What does that mean? How do I fight off "nothing good"?

I grabbed Crick's wrist. "What do you mean?"

"Just get ready to fight. Whatever it is, it's coming!"

"What's the holdup? Why aren't we working?" Torrey, the worksite Overseer, called out, joining the group. Torrey was a large gentleman with dark hair and pale skin. In the cold, I could see even through his hazmat mask that his cheeks and nose were starting to turn pink.. The Overseers' hazmat suits were white, to differentiate them from the workers, and they always carried a gun. Torrey carried a small automatic weapon that he wasn't afraid to let us know he had.

Truthfully, this wasn't much different from their normal appearance. The signature white military-style uniforms stood out like sore thumbs inside the Sections. They looked like ghosts in heavy black boots. Everything was military grade, from the cargo pants to the jackets and tops they were required to wear. "No identifying marks" seemed to be their motto. The only thing other than the white was the black logo, a symbol of Natio, printed on their left sleeve.

"Wolves or Reapers," Crick responded. "And they're getting closer."

Reapers? Are the stories true? I watched Crick closely as he backed up, staring in the direction of the howling sound.

Torrey waved his gun. "I don't give a damn about any damn—"

That's when it happened. A screaming man wearing torn and tattered clothing emerged like a shadow out of the blizzard, jumping on Torrey's back. I stood frozen as the man dug his teeth into the side of Torrey's neck and listened as Torrey let out a bloodcurdling scream that echoed through the trees. The next sound gargled from his lips, like he was already choking on his own blood. He looked dead as the man tore at him and then dragged his limp body deeper into the woods.

The group scattered, everyone running in different directions. I tried to follow Crick, moving swiftly, pulling an ax from a nearby stump. I could see a few of the other figures now sprinting through the trees. There was no way I was going to outrun them; there were too many, and they were fast. I cut back toward the wagon. As I passed the stump of one of the trees we had cut down earlier that day, I saw George get tackled by two creatures. His screams lasted longer than Torrey's as the Reapers pulled at his flesh, ripping him into pieces.

My heart pounded as I sprinted through the snow. I wasn't moving fast enough, though. I could hear the footsteps closing in on me. The Reapers howled, barked, and growled like wild animals. They were everywhere. I looked over my right shoulder, catching two more moving through the woods in pursuit. They were moving rapidly between the trees, and it was only a matter of time before I would be caught. I needed to come up with something quickly. That's when I saw it.

The tree about twenty-five yards ahead of me had a good set of branches about twelve feet up. However, I wasn't going to be able to reach them without some help. I was closing in on the tree quickly; I was only ten yards away now. This was my last hope. In a full sprint I cocked my arm back, firing my ax at the tree. The ax spun, slamming into the trunk and sticking to it perfectly. The head of the ax was about three and half feet off the ground.

I took three more strides and, pushing hard off of my left foot, I hurled myself at the tree. My right foot caught the head of the ax, boosting me up higher into the branches. I could hear the sound of jaws slamming shut right behind my feet. I threw my right arm up over the lowest branch, my ribs slamming hard into it. A surge of pain shot through me as the air was forced from my lungs. I hung for just a moment before throwing my foot up over the branch as the second Reaper jumped at my dangling leg.

I wrapped around the branch as the two crazed creatures tore at the tree below me. They screamed, first at me and then at each other. Then they ripped at the tree again, pulling bark off as they attempted to climb up to me. In the midst of all their thrashing they knocked the ax out of the tree. They jumped, only just missing the branch I was on.

I was safe for the moment, but I wasn't going to be able to stay here for long. If I got stuck out here all night I'd freeze to death. I climbed a little higher into the tree, sitting much more comfortably now. I was still pinned, though. It was only a matter of time before I would have to make another run for it.

What am I going to do? Terrible plans filled my head. I couldn't focus or calm myself down enough to think. Every plan ended with me most likely dead. Even in my agitated state of mind I knew that much. I squinted, trying to peer through the falling snow. *Is there anyone left?*

What am I going to do?

Two gunshots echoed through the trees. A small, pathetic howl followed. Someone must have gotten their hands on Torrey's gun. The two Reapers circling my tree screeched and then sprinted off, leaving me behind. I looked down, scanning the woods for any of my crew.

A figure moved through the trees. I couldn't quite make out who it was. The figure moved closer, scanning the woods. It was Crick.

"Is there anyone out there?" Crick asked as he searched the woods, aiming the gun wherever he looked.

He was about fifteen yards off as I started to make my way down the tree. "Crick, I'm over here." I slid down off the branch, falling the twelve feet to the ground.

"Dantin, is that you? Do you see anyone else?"

"No. I took off and tried to make it back to the wagon. I knew I wasn't going to make it, though, so I shot up this tree here. What about you? Have you seen anyone else?"

His look said it all before he spoke. "Only parts. They got Torrey, George, Clark, and Beagle." There were only five of us on our team. That meant Crick and I were all that were left. We needed to get to the wagon and regroup with the other teams.

"The wagon's just up ahead. We should head back while we still can." Crick pointed through the trees.

Crick and I dragged our feet through the snow, making our way back to the wagon. The keys were still in the transport vehicle that was attached to it. Thank God for that. Crick had driven the wagon before, so he handed me the gun as he put the vehicle in drive. As the wagon surged forward, he looked back at me and grabbed the gun back.

"It's probably best if you don't have this. You know how the Overseers are about us having weapons."

He was right. I'd seen someone shot in the town square for having a knife. It wasn't even a big one. I think it was a family heirloom pocketknife. Still, in the minds of the Overseers it was a weapon. Maybe it was best if Crick carried the gun, but maybe it was even better if nobody did.

"Maybe you shouldn't have the gun, either. Throw it over. We're moving now; we'll be safe without it."

Crick pondered my suggestion. "I'll ditch it when we get closer to the other teams. Just in case we need more protection."

I didn't like this idea, but it wasn't my place to argue. Crick had been doing this much longer than I had. I wasn't about to challenge him on this. Besides, he was right: we might need more protection. It was very possible the Reapers would attack again before the day was over.

"What were those things?" I asked, even though I was pretty sure I already knew the answer.

"Reapers," Crick said, his eyes focused on the path in front of us. "They used to be like me and you, before …" His voice faded off.

"Before what?" I questioned.

"Before the virus turned them."

"You mean Bloodfire?"

Crick's eyes shot at me. "Yes."

Bloodfire was the virus that had wiped out all but one percent of the world's population. It was the reason we lived in the domes. It still popped up from time to time, and people would be purged from the domes to die in the wasteland beyond.

It was what had led to the last civil war and the end of the United States as well as the rise of Natio. *But how did it do that? How does a virus cause so much damage?*

"I thought Bloodfire just killed people."

Crick shook his head. "Not everyone. Some were cursed with a worser fate. Some now roam these lands raving mad, bloodthirsty and cursed to avoid the sun. They are no longer able to reason. They don't feel. They just hunt. The virus killed most people, but some it turned, some it made stronger, more primal. Some became Reapers."

"How?"

Crick shook his head. "Nobody knows."

We rocked through the woods for nearly an hour, making our way to one of the other teams. Neither one of us said another word. I was starting to question if Crick knew where he was going. Maybe he was just making a run for it, breaking free into the unknown wilderness. I had heard others talk about it, but usually the fear stopped them. Now I knew what they were afraid of.

As we approached the other teams, I could see that they hadn't been hit by the Reapers. That was a relief. We pulled to a stop next to Cordy, the Overseer of Team Two. He looked over at us and his brow furrowed. Cordy rose to his feet, staring into the transport wagon containing Crick and me. His eyes suddenly widened and his gun snapped up, aiming at Crick.

"Get out of the wagon. Down! Out of the wagon."

Crick and I threw our hands up as we tried to maneuver our way out of the wagon. We crashed down into the snow. My legs buckled from the fall and I dropped to one knee. Crick let out a small grunt upon hitting the ground. We both had our hands raised as Cordy moved around the wagon, gun still fixed on Crick. Cordy aimed his gun at Crick's chest. *I knew we should have ditched the gun.*

"Where's the rest of your team?" His eyes narrowed as he studied the both of us.

Crick spoke. "Reapers, sir. We were attacked and the rest are gone. We were lucky to escape ourselves."

"Throw the gun! On your knees; you know the law."

Crick dropped to his knees, tossing the gun away as I attempted to protest. "He only has the gun for protection," I told Cordy. "If it wasn't for that gun, we'd both be dead too."

Cordy glared at me, not taking his gun off Crick. "Don't talk unless spoken to. Do you hear me? Go wait in the transport."

I was about to speak again, but as I caught Crick's eye, he shook his head. He knew there was nothing I could say to help him. I put my head down, heading in the direction of Team Two's transport vehicle. I looked back over my shoulder just as Cordy cracked Crick in the skull with the butt of his gun. Crick fell face-first into the snow. I felt enraged, but what could I do?

Nothing. That's what.

I kept moving forward. I wanted to stop and turn back, but that would only get me in trouble. There was nothing I could do. That was probably the worst of it, though. Crick would wake up with one heck of a headache, but it could be worse. Then two gunshots rang out through the forest. My head snapped around as I looked back at Crick. His lifeless body collapsed into the snow, blood staining the ground around him.

Why did he do that?

Cordy walked up to me. "There was a cut in his suit. He was infected by the Reapers."

No he wasn't. You just murdered him. I felt my head nod as I stood there in shock.

I fell asleep on the ride back to Section Eight, my body crashing as the adrenaline finally subsided. Dreams consumed me, one in particular: Reapers had me surrounded. I had nowhere to go. All I had was my ax. I raised it, getting ready to fight as one of the Reapers charged. I froze as Crick's raging face closed in on me. My eyes shot open and I let out a small yell. I could feel everyone looking at me as I squirmed in my seat.

This was the first time I had ever felt unsafe. The Overseers were there to keep us safe, but was there more to it? I knew they enforced the laws of Natio, but why did they just murder Crick? Why didn't they murder me? Or was I next? Maybe they would finish me off later. I felt so confused about everything: the land beyond the charred wasteland, the Reapers, the Overseers, and Bloodfire. There was so much I didn't understand. So much I needed to know.

CHAPTER 2

Back in the dome, a blizzard raged as huge gusts of wind tore through the streets, shaking the windows. Snow began to pile up along the sides of some of the buildings. In a few areas the snow had surpassed six feet high. I pushed through the streets, making my way back to the apartment. I buried my face in my jacket, unable to look up without being blinded. Each step found my foot submerged in snow up to my knee. *What the hell? They couldn't have waited until I got home?*

Anytime the Overseers handed out "justice," they would release a storm immediately after. It was their method of crowd control. Word of Crick's death had clearly reached the capital already. Cordy had tried to convince me that Crick was infected, but his hazmat suit was intact when we arrived at Team Two's worksite. This was an execution, not some attempt at preservation. However, the dome had become quite efficient at defusing potential situations with storms like this. Honestly, it was a pretty good strategy. In the last three years I couldn't remember there ever being any retaliation for Overseer punishment.

The normal fifteen-minute walk from the Capitol Building was going on thirty minutes now. I still had about three blocks to go. I wasn't at all dressed for this occasion. My normal dome outfit–long brown pants and a lightweight, long-sleeved brown shirt–didn't stand a chance against these blistering winter-like winds. My feet were numb from the snow seeping into my shoes. I wasn't sure if that was good or bad at the moment.

I finally reached my home. The windows on the lower level had already been boarded up for extra support. The doorway was blocked by a snowdrift that was up to the doorknob. I pounded on the door three times to let my family know I was home. Also, I was hoping to solicit a little help prying the door open. After waiting a moment to see if anyone came to help, I grabbed the knob, leaning back. My fingers slipped from the knob and I fell backward. The fall lasted half a second as my butt landed in a pile of snow the size of a chair.

Stupid door. Grandpa had told me that before the war all front doors opened inward. The resistance thought it would help prevent break-ins by switching them around. It's true that pushing something in versus pulling makes a difference, but today I wished they hadn't changed the doors.

I fumbled around for a second, trying to get to my feet. My butt was stuck, making it hard to get my footing. I finally made my way back to the door for another go at it. This time, over the sound of the howling wind, I could hear my grandpa on the other side. He was counting. It sounded like he said three. My mind registered what was about to happen as I grabbed the knob, giving a quick jerk. The door swung open as I lost my balance once again and found myself back in my snow chair.

My grandfather stood in the doorway. "So, you gonna come in out of the cold or just hang out in that chair you've made?"

"Real funny, Grandpa. You want to give me a hand?"

Grandpa took a couple of steps into the snow, grabbing my outstretched arm. A strong pull and I was up and through the door. Inside the house, the fire was burning. I could smell dinner cooking. The wind shook the windows behind the boards, then howled as it circled the house. I couldn't help but think of the Reapers as I kicked off my shoes. Fumbling my way to the fireplace with immobile, frozen feet, I crashed on the floor.

As I plopped down onto the floor I tossed my feet up near the fire. The warmth felt good. I could hear Grandpa and Mother arguing in the other room. I pondered for a moment just how much I should tell my family about today's events—or if I should just keep my mouth shut. Grandpa and how he reacted the last time we talked about the government made me nervous to say anything more. While I contemplated what to tell everyone, my feet started to ache as they began to thaw and regain feeling.

At dinner the conversation started as any normal dinner conversation: usual topics, similar answers. However, with it being inspection week and me going through my first week at work there were a few new topics on the docket. I'm not sure which of the two were the ones to set Grandpa off, but he was feistier than normal.

"So, Dantin, you didn't tell me, how did your first day go?"

I finished the carrot I was chewing before replying, "It was pretty boring, actually. We didn't do a whole lot. Besides, I already knew of all the safety procedures. I also knew how to wield an ax and a saw. So those tests were super easy. I had a little trouble with the rules and regulations of travel beyond the dome. I didn't realize how much you aren't allowed to do. They let me get away with a lot more before I turned eighteen."

My grandpa nodded. "They always do crack the whip a little harder the older you get. The less rules they let slide and the more they perceive you as a threat!"

My mother looked at him with shock and terror. "DAD! You watch your mouth. Are you trying to get us in trouble? You know you can't say that. Especially in front of the kids."

I wasn't sure what Grandpa said that had set her off so much. Things were strict in the dome, that was true, but we were safe from the virus that had destroyed most of the world and we were all given enough to survive. Sometimes the Overseer punishment went a little far, like today, but usually they didn't resort to the death sentence.

Maybe there really was a cut in Crick's suit.

No, I saw his suit, there was nothing wrong with it.

Why did they shoot him, then?

Grandpa shot a look back at her. "Dantin's not a kid anymore and Micca's smart enough to not repeat what I say here. Aren't you, sweetheart?"

Micca just nodded her head. She wasn't much of a talker outside of the house, anyway. I wasn't worried about her slipping up.

My sister had long, dark hair, almost always in a ponytail, and big blue eyes. Her hair and eyes were the only things we shared. She was only half my age and still, without a doubt, the smart one in the family.

I knew Micca wouldn't say anything to get herself or the family in trouble. Still, it was risky to be talking like that. This was one of the few times that I'd heard Grandpa speak out against the government so openly. I'm not sure what brought this on, but perhaps that's what he and Mother were arguing about when I came home.

I attempted to change the subject. "So, Grandpa, how was the first day of inspection week? Anything interesting?"

There was usually something of note during inspection week. Not normally on the first day, but it happened. Oftentimes, someone tried to sneak products from the factory for use at home. That was the most common crime. However, every now and then there was something juicy. Today wasn't one of those days. Grandpa simply shook his head, dismissing the question.

The rest of dinner was consumed in silence. Apparently, Grandpa's comments about the government were enough to get everyone a little flustered.

I never did see why there wasn't more dissension within Section Eight. I mean, outside of a few days in the stockades or maybe some time on probation, there was rarely more severe punishment. Yet the majority of people kept their heads down and mouths shut. Apparently, most people felt that keeping quiet was the best decision.

After dinner, Micca scurried back up to her room to continue reading. She always had her nose in a book. I sat on a chair next to Grandpa in the living room. Mom went into the kitchen to clean off the dishes from dinner. I looked at Grandpa and he just stared at the boarded-up window.

"Grandpa, why were you so upset with the government today?"

The question seemed to catch him off guard. He looked over at me. His dark eyes matched his hair which, even with his age, had only just begun to turn grey. His face still looked youthful as well, even after all he'd lived through.

"There was a time when we were more than just a workforce for the elites in power," he replied. "When people had freedom to do what they pleased with their lives. To be what they wanted to be. To pursue their own dreams. A day like today where you get *placed* into a position just gets me fired up. I just want more for you. You were meant for more."

I looked at him. I never knew he felt this way about the way we were forced to live. I also never knew that there was a time when we had so many freedoms. They didn't teach us about that in school. All they talked about was how people had tried to destroy themselves while our government saved us by stepping in. I'd always felt like there was more to the story than that, but that's what we were taught.

"How do you know so much about the way things used to be?"

Grandpa smiled. "Well, remember, I'm really old. My dad was actually around during the outbreak. Even though he was young, he made sure to tell me about the way things used to be and the truth about what really happened. The truth about Bloodfire and why we live this way now."

I had never heard Grandpa talk about life before Bloodfire. Honestly, nobody ever talked about what it was like before the outbreak swept the world.

"Please, Grandpa, tell me!" I could see that he was pondering whether to tell me more about what had happened.

The only details I knew about Bloodfire, and old America, were from school. Bloodfire started like any other virus, slowly spreading and attacking those with weak immune systems. Then somewhere along the way it mutated and began to infect more and more people. There was no cure, and those who got it died quickly. There was fear and panic, which led to government shutdown, looting, and rioting. It wasn't just in America, either; it happened worldwide. When it was all over the virus vanished, leaving just around one percent of the world's population alive.

Then the war started, which led to the eventual bombing of America. Finally, after lots of fighting among survivors, a group of militia formed a new government and put an end to the war. They called themselves Natio. They were the ones who constructed the domes. The virus was still out there, but inside the domes everything was safer. Half of America was deemed uninhabitable either because of the virus or the war. People were quickly moved into these safe havens.

When I was twelve another war broke out. The civil uprising began small, with a few people who didn't like the way of life inside the domes. Then things escalated. My father chose the side against the government. The war lasted three years before the capital's advanced weapons and vehicles became too much. After that things became a little more strict in the domes.

Grandpa's eyes came back to mine. "Not today," he said. "I'll tell you more when you're older. For now, you don't need to know. Besides, your mother would kill me if she knew that I had told you this much."

I went to protest but stopped. I knew I wasn't going to get anything out of him. He wasn't much for begging, so instead I just broke his gaze and looked toward the window. The storm had calmed. I moved over to the window and removed the boards, revealing the pitch-black streets. Curfew was marked by a loud siren that echoed throughout the dome. Anyone outside now would be punished, although I wasn't sure I'd ever heard of anyone being caught after curfew.

Grandpa pushed off of the arms of the chair he was sitting on, rising to his feet. "Well, time for me to head out."

My brow narrowed as I glared at him. "Where are you going? It's after curfew. Why do you always wait until after curfew to go out?"

"Don't worry 'bout me, son. I won't be long. I just have a quick meeting I have to attend. Pleasures of inspection week."

Grandpa was a terrible liar. I knew immediately that this meeting had nothing to do with inspection week. I shook my head, letting him think he had fooled me. I watched as he made his way to the door and grabbed his coat off of the hanger. As he opened the door I decided to speak my mind.

"When are you going to tell me what you really do after curfew? I know this has nothing to do with inspection week."

Grandpa froze in the doorway. He slid the door shut and moved back into the small apartment. I was now standing as he looked at me.

"You're a smart young man. I should have known I can't lie to you. I just want you to forget about this for a while. I promise when I can I will let you know what it is I do. Until then, just stay strong for me. OK?"

"When will I be old enough to know? I'm old enough to work. I'm old enough to go outside the dome. How old do I have to be?"

Grandpa grabbed my shoulders. "Be patient. The time will come. Until then, just remember, we all enter as one into the Kingdom of Lions."

Then he went back out the door and disappeared into the night. I stared blankly at the closed door. The line he said I hadn't heard since my father died. It was one that he would say to me whenever I had difficult questions that he couldn't or wouldn't answer. It didn't help me any then and I was just as confused by it now. What did it mean?

We enter as one into the Kingdom of Lions.

Later, I lay in bed thinking about all of the events of my first day of work. My head felt clouded as all the thoughts attacked me at once. Then, like the calm following a thunderstorm, my head cleared. One thought remained: *We enter as one into the Kingdom of Lions.* This single line repeated in my head as I fell asleep.

*****

It's amazing how much can happen in a day's time. Yesterday, I was going through first-day orientation and excited to get outside the dome for work. Today, I was in agreement with Grandpa about how much I didn't trust the government—not to mention, after one day of work, the amount of death I'd already seen.

Breakfast was just about ready when the emergency broadcast signal rang through the apartment.

The emergency broadcast system had been put in place by Heart City. It was where the remainder of government officials resided. Sort of like old-day Washington, D.C. This system for reports was the "first installment" of the technological advancements by Heart City. They said there would be more to come, but in the three years since the end of the war this was all we'd seen.

Five evenly-spaced screeching sounds buzzed over the dome's PA system. Then the voice of our Head Overseer cut through the speaker as the screeching echoed in my ears.

"Ladies and Gentlemen of Section Eight, this is a Level Three report. Due to the nature of the events yesterday we will be suspending all work today. A member of our community was exposed to Bloodfire and we will be shutting down all operations for your safety. All citizens are required to remain indoors. Anyone caught outside will be taken immediately into custody and held in quarantine. This will continue until further notice. Again, this is a Level Three report. No immediate action is needed. Thank you."

A Level Three report meant there was a slight threat to the population. The highest we'd ever experienced that I could remember was a Level Four. That was following the escape of a man who was apparently infected with Bloodfire and then attacked several Overseers of Section Eight. That was probably about two and a half years ago now. We were required to stay in our homes for three days while they searched for the man. They went door to door, tearing through everyone's apartment.

My grandpa frowned slightly as the announcement set in. Guess no meeting for him tonight. Even he wouldn't risk it in a Level Three There would be too many Overseers on patrol. Plus, he probably knew that if he got caught out tonight there was no amount of bullshit that could get him off. Instead, he just moved over near the fire, sitting down in the chair next to me.

"So, what events do you suppose they're talking about?" He looked at me as if he already knew that I had the information he was seeking.

"Well ..." Before I could go into any more details, my mother called us to the table.

"Food's ready; you boys can talk after!"

Thanks, Mom. This would give me enough time to determine just how much I should tell Grandpa. I didn't want to get him too worked up, but I really needed to talk to someone about what I'd seen. About the Reapers, about Crick, about how I was the only one left from my team. I started to worry more the more I thought about everything. *Will the government kill me next to keep me quiet?* I mean, I technically didn't see anything, but Crick was alive when we reached camp with the other teams yesterday.

I avoided Grandpa for the remainder of the day. After dinner, I pulled up my usual spot on the floor next to the fire. The memories of what had happened yesterday raced through my head. I needed to decide what I was going to do soon; Grandpa was done with dinner. He exchanged a few words with my mom before coming over to take a seat in his chair next to me. I sat staring at the fire, hoping he wouldn't push the conversation. My hope was misplaced.

Grandpa cleared his throat in an attempt to get my attention. "So, tell me about yesterday, Dantin."

"Well, it all started when the Reapers attacked ..."

Grandpa cut me off before I could even get started into the story. "Reapers attacked? How did you get out of there? Those things out there are dangerous. I'm going to get you reassigned to another job."

"You know about the Reapers?" I questioned, kind of surprised by Grandpa's reaction. "How do you know about them? What are they, really?"

Grandpa glanced into the kitchen and then leaned in close, whispering, "They are those who survived Bloodfire but have mutated. Bloodfire killed almost everyone, but a small percentage of the population didn't die. Instead, they changed. They turned into mindless, ravaging beings. They are sensitive to sunlight but have heightened senses. They are stronger and faster, with improved hearing, sight, and smell. But they can't control their primal urges and they are in a constant state of rage. They're dangerous. You can't go back out there."

"Grandpa, stop. I'm fine. I wish I could say the same for the rest of my team," I said solemnly.

"Tell me what happened."

"Torrey, our project Overseer, was the first victim. I saw him get dragged to the ground before I took off running. The Reapers also got George before I made it up a tree. Somewhere in there they took out Clark and Beagle. If it weren't for Crick, I'd still be up in that tree."

Grandpa sighed a little. "Well, I'm going to make sure I thank Crick next time I see him." Grandpa and Crick were old friends, and I knew it was dangerous to tell him about what happened to Crick, but I didn't have a choice.

"There's more, Grandpa. Crick had picked up Torrey's gun. He had shot two of the Reapers before we were able to escape."

"Well, good."

"No, Grandpa, let me finish." I lowered my voice, just barely above a whisper, as if someone were outside our apartment listening to what I was saying. "When we got back to base camp to regroup with the others ..." I paused, knowing that what I was about to say would send Grandpa into a fury. "… Crick still had the gun. So they forced him onto his knees. I saw them hit him in the back of the head"—I took a deep breath and swallowed hard—"then I heard two gunshots. The Team Two Overseer came over to me and said Crick's suit had been ripped and he had been exposed to Bloodfire, but I don't think that's what really happened."

I braced myself for a full-on explosion of rage. After a couple of seconds I looked up at Grandpa. As calm as I'd ever seen him, he looked at me. "Who?"

I was confused. Did he want to know who had shot Crick? Why? What was he planning to do? I knew he could see the concern in my eyes. "Why, Grandpa, wha—"

"Who, boy?" The calm was gone, replaced by the anger I had initially expected.

"Cordy, Team Two's Overseer."

Grandpa rose from his chair, pacing quickly back and forth through the living room. He was moving so quickly that I thought he might wear a trench through the small space. I knew he was furious, but what could he possibly do about it? It had happened outside the dome, not to mention you didn't challenge an Overseer unless you wanted to be punished too. That was just the way it was.

The only good thing I could think of was at least tonight's blizzard would force Grandpa to stay indoors. Hopefully it would be enough to let him cool off so he wouldn't do something stupid. This family couldn't handle another loss. I rose to my feet, meeting Grandpa halfway through another one of his laps. My right hand landed on his left shoulder, pulling him to a stop. I gave him a small shake and a good squeeze.

"I know you're upset right now, Grandpa. I know Crick was your friend; he was mine, too. There's one thing I want you to remember before you do anything: this family needs you as much as Crick's needed him. Don't do anything stupid, Grandpa. And if you're set on being dumb, you'd better take me with you."

He shot me a glance. I smiled the mischievous smile that I had flashed him so many times before—I was quite the hellion growing up, before Dad died. Grandpa's face lightened up as he let out a soft laugh. I think it calmed him a little, too—at least for the time being. I knew that once the snow subsided he'd be just as furious as he had been moments ago. I tapped him twice on the shoulder, then disappeared out of the living room to allow him to grieve in peace.

In my room, I lit a candle. The light danced off the walls as I dropped onto my bed. Reaching across my body, I grabbed my rubber ball from my nightstand, rubbing it between my hands. Yesterday's events replayed through my mind. I couldn't break free of the images of the Reapers, the way they had screamed and torn Torrey and the others apart. Then there was Crick. All he'd been trying to do was keep me safe, keep himself safe, and now he was gone. It was wrong. I hated Cordy and the Overseers for what they had done. I felt resentment toward the government for the first time.

I felt the anger that I knew burned inside of Grandpa. I felt the betrayal our government had committed. The wind howled around the apartment. The sound made me think of the predators that threatened us, how the dome with its high concrete base walls was supposed to keep them at bay. To protect us. *How helpful is a wall if all it does is lock us in with the biggest predator of all?* For the first time, I felt like the mice we were. At the mercy of a cat, with no escape.

Images flashed into my mind. Being toyed with. Tossed around. Just until they'd had their fun with everything—then, just like that, they could end it. There was no escaping this feeling. It consumed me. Helpless, hopeless. I used to think things would get better, that it was just a matter of time before Heart City came up with a solution. One that would free us from this life. Lead us into the next stage of our development.

I bounced my ball off the ceiling. The words of my father echoed in the sound. *Remember, we all enter as one into the Kingdom of Lions.* For the first time, the words had more meaning. This life was just the beginning, and in the end we would all face judgement in the Kingdom of Lions. When that time came we would be on our own, with only our actions to defend us. I wasn't sure if that was what he had meant. I wasn't even sure if that was close to being right. But on this night, after yesterday's events, it was all I could think about.

CHAPTER 3

It was hard to believe it had been three weeks since Crick's death and the incident. Nobody had said a word to me about it. It was business as usual, and the trips beyond the wall continued despite the loss of an entire work group. Back in the woods, the winter had continued to progress more violently. The cold winds whipped through the trees and the clouds blocked out the sun, destroying any greenhouse effect the hazmat suits provided. My teeth rattled as I went to work on the first tree of the day.

I was halfway through when I heard the first scream. It came from the east. Then another scream from the west. My heart raced as I squeezed my ax. I placed my back against one of the nearby trees. Another scream, this time closer. I froze with fear. *Not again!* My heart pounded as another scream echoed through the forest. I turned in the direction of the scream as a Reaper jumped out from behind a bush, tackling me to the ground, knocking my ax from my hands. I struggled, but it was no use. The Reaper tore at my suit, ripping it open, then bit at my throat.

I shot upright and my eyes struggled to focus. My bed was soaked with sweat, my heart raced, and my breathing was short and strained. It was just another nightmare. They had been ruining my sleep for the last few weeks now, though this one was worse than some of the others. I started to shake as the adrenaline faded and a chill came over my body from the sweat. I took one long, deep breath as my heart rate slowed and I felt myself begin to calm. The sun had begun to rise already, and a second panic arose. *I'm late!*

I jumped out of bed, then remembered. *Relax! No work today.* Today marked the first day of Remembrance Day. Every year, we got the last week of the year off of work for a big celebration to remember how we were "saved." Each day had different events and celebrations. One day to show our appreciation for the Overseers. One day for the heroes of the war following Bloodfire. So on and so forth, leading up to Remembrance Day, which celebrated the day Natio was formed and Heart City was named capital of the sixteen Sections.

Heart City was named after the commander of the armies that stopped the war following Bloodfire. His name was Nathanial Heart. He was by all accounts a charismatic leader and the reason the human race had survived. He had led an army that had brought peace to our lands and had also directed the construction of the domes. Ever since, his family had ruled from within Heart City and dictated what happened within the sixteen Sections.

The biggest event of Remembrance Day was The Conscript, which occurred on the last night after the Section's big feast. This year's celebrations were set to be the biggest ever. This year was the fiftieth anniversary of The Conscript and the hundredth anniversary of the founding of Natio. The Conscript was created fifty years after Natio was founded, as a way to unify the sixteen Sections. Two of the most promising young people in each Section were picked to travel to Heart City. There they would be trained and developed into the next generation of Overseers and Section leaders.

Leadership inside the government believed that by integrating the various Sections it would bring the people closer together and give them something to connect them to Heart City. The problem was that those who were picked to attend this training never returned. It was part of the reason why a small group began to question the validity of The Conscript. They didn't believe their loved ones were actually being trained and given a better opportunity; they suspected something far worse was happening. This unrest was what led to the three-year war.

Really, though, I wasn't even sure you could call it a war. More like an uprising that never really gained any traction. A small group of people from Section Eight rebelled against the government over The Conscript, trying to put an end to the yearly draft. I thought this was why my dad had always sided with the rebels. He knew one day I'd be eligible for The Conscript and didn't want to see me taken.

In the end, even though the uprising lasted three years, nobody ever felt that the rebels had the upper hand. Everyone involved—and a few that weren't—ended up dead or banished from the dome. My father was one of them. He was killed when one of the rebels accidentally set off a bomb inside the mines. This essentially ended the rebellion.

The years of the uprising were the only years that nobody was taken from Section Eight. They must have figured the 134 dead was enough. It was quite a blow to the dome and the morale of our Section. Ever since the conflict, people were more inclined to keep their heads down and mouths shut. I couldn't blame them. I still had nightmares of my father's death.

Following the war, Heart City made adjustments to Remembrance Day and The Conscript. Each day they would play videos of those who had been taken from years before . The videos showed how they were faring in their new lives, the new jobs they were performing and the new skills they had acquired. Something about them felt weird, but I couldn't put my finger on it. Maybe that was just me reading Grandpa's reaction every time they came on. He would curse under his breath and walk away. Everyone else seemed to enjoy seeing the success of those who had been chosen in previous years.

I gazed out my bedroom window toward the town square, where final preparations were being made for the start of the festivities. The snow mixed with the decorations made for a very inviting scene. Things were looking good.

It used to be that I looked forward to Remembrance Day. It was the one time of the year that everyone went to bed with full bellies. Plus, Heart City always sent new technology, developments, and entertainment for the party. Last year, they sent a generator that absorbed sunlight throughout the day then at night was able to reproduce light ten times brighter than any candle. It was quite impressive.

This was a fun time in Section Eight, assuming you weren't eligible for The Conscript. While it was deemed an honor to be selected, there was always a little apprehension around it. Maybe it was because it meant saying goodbye to your home and loved ones. This was my first year being eligible. It was the first time I found myself hoping that when the week was over I would have another year with my family. It was hard knowing that there were two people who wouldn't ever see their loved ones again after the end of the week. I tried to shake the thought, tried to focus on the activities the capital had planned for the celebration.

When I finally made it downstairs, Mom and Micca were sitting in front of the fire playing some sort of game. It looked like they were having fun, which was nice to see. Micca was usually upstairs doing schoolwork; she was a real bookworm. However, with the festival scheduled to start today, there would be no school, so for once she got to be a kid for a little bit. Having your head buried in a book is no way for a nine-year-old to spend her days. Playing games and having fun: this was more like it. This was one of the reasons I enjoyed the weeklong celebration of Remembrance Day. Most people would be in a good mood.

"Hey, Mom! Hey, Micca! What are you guys doing?"

Micca smiled. "Dantin, come join us. We're playing a game. Mom just showed me how to play."

Micca waved me over to where she was sitting. Her love of learning would serve her well as she got older; she'd be able to land a good job when the time came for her to go to work. I sat on the floor next to her, leaning in to see what they were doing. It was important to spend as much time with family this week as I could—just in case.

Mom smiled, watching Micca's excitement. The smile was short-lived, though, as she caught my eye. Reaching for my hand, she grabbed it, giving me a squeeze. "How are you doing? This will be your first real Remembrance Day."

I knew why my mother was worried. At the end of this week I could be gone forever. I hadn't really thought about it. The thought of not being in Section Eight, not being able to look after my family scared me. I didn't want to think about what would happen if I got taken. Grandpa would still be here, but for how long? He was here but always so preoccupied and into his own things. I needed to be here for them. I shook the thought from my head, trying to act strong for my mother.

"I'm doing OK. It should be a fun week, and at least we know we'll be eating well for a change!" I tried to flash her a smile, but I was sure she could tell it was forced.

"Dantin, Dantin, look!" Micca was pulling on my sleeve, trying to get my attention.

"OK, I'm watching. Show me."

Micca held her hand over a wooden cup, shaking it up and down. What sounded like rocks rattled against the cup and her hand. After about five or six shakes, Micca removed her hand, sending six cubes rolling out onto the floor. The small squares bounced off the floor, tumbling to a stop as Micca examined her pieces. She turned, smiling at me. "I win!"

I laughed. "I don't even know what we're playing. How do I know you're not cheating?"

Micca frowned. "I don't cheat! I'm not a cheater. Look, see! If you have an even score, you win. If you have an odd score, you lose."

I bent down, looking at the cubes. Each one was marked with either a single dot or two spaced dots. Her cubes still lay where they stopped rolling. Four cubes showed two dots and two cubes showed one dot.

I let out an approving sigh as I examined the pieces. "I see. You did win!"

Micca smiled again, going back to playing her game, not really concerned with me continuing to play with her. She was someone who didn't need others in order to enjoy her time. She could always entertain herself if given the right tools. She placed the cubes back in her cup, shaking them up again.

I climbed up off the floor. Moving over to Mom, I kissed her on the forehead. "I love you, Mom. I'm going to go lie down. This week at work was exhausting."

"But you just came downstairs. Don't you want to eat first?"

"No, I'll have plenty to eat the next couple of days. I'm just going to lie down. Thanks, though."

In my room I fell onto my bed. The hard mattress had never felt so good. Every part of my body ached from the work I had put in this week. The long hours and rushed effort to bring in as many trees for the festivities had worn me out. Thoughts of The Conscript flooded my mind as I eyeballed the ceiling. I wasn't entirely sure how they chose each person, but one year I was pretty sure I heard the screams of one of the families whose child had been taken that day. The sad cries had echoed through the city streets.

I did my best to push the thoughts from my mind, but no matter what I tried to do, they found their way back in. It was the first year that I truly appreciated the significance of The Conscript. I was afraid. I wasn't ready to leave my family, I wasn't ready to start new somewhere else. No matter how much Natio claimed it was an honor, I just didn't believe it. I shut my eyes so tightly my head started to ache. Then I relaxed as I focused on calming my breathing. Moments later, I fell asleep.

A few hours later I awoke to the sound of music. Still foggy from my nap, I wasn't sure where I was. That was some of the best sleep I'd had in weeks. I must have been more tired than I'd thought; these last few weeks it had felt like the morning whistle went off earlier each day. I rolled out of bed and made my way downstairs. The apartment was empty, but there was a note on the kitchen table.

> *Dantin,*
>
> *Grandpa, Micca, and I have gone into the city center. The festivities were about to start and we didn't want to miss the first round of food. You seemed very tired so we let you sleep. Come find us when you wake up.*
>
> *Love,*
>
> *Mom*

Normally, I would have been upset at being left to miss the beginning of the Remembrance Day celebration. However, today I wasn't in a rush. Besides, the real party wouldn't begin until tonight. That was when the official announcement from Heart City would be given to start the party. Everything up until then was designed to get people out into the streets. Music, food, and some games. It was usually the same every year.

I slid on my boots and reached for my jacket. I cracked the door, checking the weather. It was a sunny day and the wind was calm. A perfect start to the week. The snow from earlier had melted and it was now quite pleasant, so I left the jacket as I exited into the street. The street echoed with music from the city center. The music was lovely this afternoon, creating a light mood. It was nice to see smiles on the faces of the people of

Section Eight. It had been a long time since people had been happy here. Come to think of it, there wasn't a whole lot to be happy about these days.

As I got closer to the city center, the lyrics of the song were becoming clearer. The woman singing had a beautiful voice. As I reached the edge of the city circle, I could see Laurna, who was a year younger than me in school, on stage singing to the crowd. Her voice was like an angel's. I couldn't stop my feet as I was drawn across the open square to the stage. I'd never heard Laurna sing before, but it was quite lovely. Her eyes met mine and she smiled, starting into the chorus one last time:

I can see it, you can too. Just how great, me and you.
Fear of things that aren't safe. Trust in me, a little faith.
Take my hand, I'll lead the way. I know it's hard for you to say.

A soft farewell to all you know. A gentle kiss, away we go.
Unknown place, a foreign dance. All I need is just one chance.

A tug at my right arm shook me from my daze. The tugging at my sleeve intensified as I glanced down at Micca. She grinned at having finally gotten my attention. I glanced back up at Laurna. She smiled again and I felt my jaw snap shut, forming a smile of my own as I was dragged quickly through the crowd to where Grandpa and Mom were waiting.

"We're over here, silly. Come on!" Micca was leaning with all her might, trying to pull me through the crowd.

Laurna began another song. I was awestruck by the pure beauty of her voice. Nobody really sang in Section Eight, so it was a true treat to have someone who could perform like this. Usually the singers that performed during the celebration were from Heart City. None of the performers over the last few years were anywhere near as good as what I'd just heard.

At the far side of the city center, Grandpa, Mom, and a few others sat at a picnic table. Food was spread from end to end and everyone's plate had more food than we usually ate in a week. Most of the food had a couple of bites in it and everyone held their stomachs.

It was funny to see so many people in pain from eating too much food. It happened every year. People piled their plates full of all kinds of Heart City food only to barely make it through a couple of bites.

I forced down as much food as I could manage before my stomach felt like it was going to bust open. There were pancakes with syrup, fresh fruit, juice, waffles, and some chocolate muffins. The food was so filling and so good. I couldn't help thinking that this was what the people in Heart City got to enjoy every day.

But could things really be that much better in the capital than they were here?

The music died down and Overseer Hawkins, who had been Section Eight's Head Overseer since before I was born, took the stage. He was responsible for everything, receiving his orders directly from Heart City. Hawkins was beginning to show his age, moving slowly across the stage with a slight limp, his grayish hair matching his salt-and-pepper beard. His outfit was all white except for a crest of Natio—an eagle standing on a pile of rubble with a small half circle behind it—on his chest.

They had taught us about the crest in school, but I couldn't entirely place its meaning at this moment. It was supposed to be an eagle of old America standing on the remains of what used to be a great nation, with a new day dawning on what was now Natio. A better world.

What a load of horseshit.

It was interesting to think that this was the first time I'd really paid any attention to our nation's symbol. They only flew the nation's flag on the Capitol Building, but I never cared to look that close. The only flags in Section Eight that I really noticed were the ones outside at the gates signifying that this was indeed Section Eight. I always found that amusing, that in case for some reason we thought we had stumbled into Section Seven we could be reminded of where we were.

Hawkins cleared his throat into the megaphone that was anchored onto the stage. "Ladies and gentlemen of Natio. People of Section Eight," he boomed. "Today marks the start of a week in which we remember. We remember what once was. We remember what could have been. We give thanks for what we have and appreciate what it took to create this great nation.

"Bloodfire took many things from us, but out of the ashes rose Natio: A place of equality and justice. A place where all people are equal. The future is bright within this great country. The opportunities to survive were given to us. This week we look back on the heroes of the past, at our great leaders, and we celebrate this new life. Enjoy the food, enjoy the festivities, and always remember!"

There was a small round of applause as Hawkins slowly made his way from the stage. That speech had been repeated for so many years now that I had actually found myself saying it along with him. No wonder that even at his age Hawkins never needed any cue cards. I didn't think the speech had ever changed. I guessed that was fine, since nobody really cared what he had to say on that stage unless he was giving a special report. That was the one time that everyone in Section Eight actually listened.

I walked around the city center. There were booths set up throughout the square, each one with a different purpose. Some had games where prizes could be won. A few booths told of the history of Natio. Another booth talked about Grand Overseer Colton Heart, the leader of all of Natio. He was the great-great-great-grandson of Nathanial Heart.

It was the same every year. In my earlier years I would spend hours at each booth, learning as much as I could, winning prizes, and enjoying every moment of the celebration. As I got older I spent less time playing.

I finished my walk through the square. At the booth where I had started my walk, I found Laurna. She was bent over next to her little sister helping her play a game. I watched as they threw a bean bag at three milk jugs that had been stacked: two on the bottom and one on top. The trick was you had to knock them all down with one shot.

The girl's throw missed. The game seemed easy, but people always had trouble with it.

I walked over to the booth. "Looks like you could use a little help," I said, flashing Laurna a smile.

Laurna jumped, startled. But when she realized it was me, her eyes met mine and she smiled. "Yeah, I'm not much help on this game."

I chuckled lightly, holding out my hand. "Hi, Haimi, can I help you win a prize?"

Haimi, who was just a little younger than Micca, grinned as wide as she could and handed me the two remaining bean bags. "Yes, please."

"OK, let's see what I've got."

I wound up, letting the first bean bag fly. The bag spun out of my hand, making contact with the right bottom jug. The jug disappeared, flying off the platform as the top jug dropped down, making contact with the one on the left. The weight pushed it off-balance, sending it off the platform, scattering the jugs on the ground. I smiled with surprise. *How about that?*

Laurna let out an excited scream as Haimi jumped with joy. Laurna squeezed my arm, then slid past me to give Haimi a hug. Haimi's excitement made me smile. It was the first time I had felt at ease today.

The booth operator placed a small stuffed bear in her hands and she hugged it tightly. She turned, taking two quick steps toward me and wrapping her arms around my leg in a strong hug.

"Thank you, Dantin." And she was off running through the crowd.

Laurna stood watching her sister's excitement. "Thank you. I would have never won her that bear. You just made her festival."

"Well, I'm glad I was able to do something good this festival. I mean, I'm not going to entertain anyone with my voice, so the least I can do is throw a bean bag at some jugs." I smiled wide, watching Haimi disappear.

I turned, glancing at Laurna as her dark brown eyes pierced right into me. Her smile was almost enough to make everyone else fade away. She almost looked as if she were blushing a little, too, but that could have just been the cool air on her cheeks.

"Oh, that wasn't anything special. It's just a silly hobby."

"No, it was beautiful. The best singing I've heard in eighteen years of festivals." My comment caused a frown to come across Laurna's face. I paused, placing my arm on her shoulder. "What is it?"

"I just realized that you're up for The Conscript this year." Her eyes showed sincere concern. I didn't know what to make of this because I knew Laurna, but we weren't exactly close.

Nobody liked to see anyone leave. We all knew it was goodbye for good at that point. But this felt different, like she would be truly saddened if I were to be chosen.

I smiled, trying to lighten the mood. "Don't worry about it. The odds of getting picked are still so small there's next to no chance I'll be the one this year. Besides, if I am, I'll be the first to return home. Just you wait."

I didn't really believe this statement; nobody ever returned. I was just trying to ease Laurna's worry. Instead all I did was increase my own. I didn't want to leave; I wasn't ready to be gone forever. There was still so much I wanted to do, needed to do. I shook my head. There was no use worrying about it now. I was either going to be chosen or not.

I locked eyes with Laurna and she gave a half-hearted smile, trying to act strong. However, she knew my size made me a prime prospect for The Conscript. I knew this too. I doubted she really believed that if I were picked I'd make it back to Section Eight either. But she did seem a little less concerned, which was my ultimate goal at the moment.

"Well, I better get going. Good luck." Laurna wrapped both arms around my neck, giving me a squeeze. "Thank you for your help on the game." Then, like that, she was gone, into the crowd headed in the direction her sister had taken off.

I stood motionless, watching Laurna disappear into the crowd before drifting back on my path to our picnic table. Grandpa, Micca, and Mom still sat, alternating between picking at food and holding their bellies. They looked miserable, which made me smile. They were so full from all the food that they were completely uncomfortable.

I loved seeing everyone so happy. I wished every day could be like this. Not so much the festival, but full, without always being worked to the bone or fearing starvation.

As the sun started to drop, a huge fireball exploded in the center of the city square. The flames soared two stories high. We could feel the heat even from our table on the outskirts of the plaza. Every year, there was a different way for the party to last all night. It seemed this year that a huge bonfire was the answer. Then small lights flickered, dancing with life, floating on strings running in all directions. The lights dangled, looking like fireflies lighting up the entire plaza.

I'd never seen anything like it. The lights seemed to remain on without any fire or flame of any kind. Small glass shells encased each one. The wires ran in all directions, creating a very soft, pleasant glow. I reached up, grabbing one of the lines that floated just above my head. It was absolutely marvelous. There hadn't been accessible electricity in the domes since

Bloodfire. We all knew Heart City had access to power, but they hadn't shared it until now.

On stage, Head Overseer Hawkins took to the mic again.

"Ladies and gentlemen, let the real fun begin," he said. "This year we are given the gift of light from Natio and our beloved capital, Heart City. It is because of these feats that we are no longer in the dark. Natio has led us out of the darkness and into the light once again!"

My grandpa chuckled under his breath, "Led us into the light. Pssssh."

I looked over at him, his arms crossed and eyes narrow. As I watched the scowl come across his face, my curiosity got the best of me. "What is it, Grandpa?"

His eyes widened, surprised anyone had heard him. They fixed on me. "It's nothing, Dantin. Enjoy the party."

I leaned in closer, speaking softly. "No, Grandpa, I want to know."

Grandpa paused, looking around the plaza. It was way too loud and busy for anyone to hear us even if they tried. He threw his arm up around my shoulder, pulling me in close. "You see these lights here? These lights used to be used in celebration before Bloodfire for a thing called Christmas. It was a time that people gave gifts to one another. They were kinder, happier times. The season of Christmas was one of joy and worship. Now these lights are tainted by the stink of Natio. These lights used to have real meaning. Now they're just a means of distraction against the true reality that we live in. It's just a shame!"

I had read about Christmas. It was covered in our studies during school. There wasn't any time for worship anymore. There were still a few who hung onto their beliefs, my family among them; however, the majority of the population didn't even know anything about religion or church anymore. Grandpa's anger over the lights and Christmas were a shock to me, even though lately he appeared to be more upset than usual.

The rest of the night flew by; so did the week. Just like that, in what felt like a blink of an eye, it was the morning of the last day. The Conscript had arrived. By the end of the day today there would be two fewer people in Section Eight. The early morning light reflected off the dome, shining through the city streets. I always loved dawn and dusk as they were the only times the city held any color. The rest of the time the dreary grey washed out every building, giving Section Eight a lifeless feeling.

I made my way downstairs. Mom and Micca had left early to make their way to the city center. Grandpa sat rocking in his old chair next to the fireplace. He must have heard me as I tromped down the stairs. I could hear him stop rocking as I reached the bottom step, calling out to me without looking, "Dantin, come here, son, and have a seat."

I crossed the small living area. There was a seriousness in Grandpa's voice that I rarely heard. I moved quickly, pulling up a seat next to him. The heat from the fireplace warmed my back as I crouched in close, preparing myself for what Grandpa had to tell me. He leaned forward in his chair, resting his elbows on his knees for support.

I could see concern in Grandpa's eyes as they penetrated mine, digging deep into me. "Dantin, I need you to listen to me." I nodded my head, not breaking his gaze. "No, matter what happens today during The Conscript, you must remain strong. I know this can be a very stressful time. I also know that you are a special young man. They will know this too. You stay ready, be strong, and don't let this break you. Remember everything I taught you over the years and don't be afraid. And if ... if you are picked, keep your head up and walk tall and powerful."

Grandpa paused a moment, losing my gaze. As I was about to get up, his arm shot out, landing on my shoulder with a vice grip squeeze. "You listen to me, boy! You do what it takes. Be stronger than the others. Be faster. Be smarter. Outlast everyone and find your way home! You find a way home! Do you hear me? Always remember one thing! Remember, we enter as one into the Kingdom of Lions!"

I nodded as tears begin to fill Grandpa's eyes. Squeezing them shut, he pushed up off of my shoulder. Turning quickly, he made his way to the door, disappearing into the cold. I sat motionless, staring at the spot where Grandpa had just been before turning slowly to stare at the fire. It danced as the words from Grandpa echoed in my head.

I had known today would be tough. I knew there was a good possibility I would be taken. Apparently, it was more likely than I had thought. At least in Grandpa's mind.

His words continued to echo in my head, but what did they mean? *Outlast everyone? What does he know that I don't?* I sat in front of the fire for several more minutes trying to figure out what Grandpa had meant by his message. In the end I didn't fully understand, but I knew one thing for sure: I had to find my way back home. No matter what!

I made my way back to the city center, working my way through the small early crowd. People were slower to make it into town on the last day of the festival. The partying from earlier in the week had begun to take its toll. Only a fraction of the people who were there on day one had made their way to the city center by the time I arrived. Another reason for the slow start was that many families, especially those with older children, spent the morning saying their goodbyes. Just in case.

Grandpa was still one of the first, having pulled up a spot at the same picnic table we'd sat at all week. I sat down next to him, piling food on my plate for breakfast. The smells invaded my nose, causing my mouth to water. Laurna began to sing on stage at the center of the square. Her voice echoed beautifully across the plaza. Grandpa's eyes were still red and the concern still on his face as he peered off in the distance at Laurna.

I scanned the crowd for people eligible for The Conscript. My eyes bounced around, stopping briefly on each person before locking on Laurna. Non-eligible. At least not this year. Next year would be a different story. Perhaps that was why she'd acted the way she did earlier in the week. I hadn't had a chance to talk to her since. It felt as if she were avoiding me, but that didn't really make sense.

I continued to stare at Laurna as she sang. It felt like she could feel my gaze as she searched for me across the city center. At least that's what I wanted to believe, but I was too far away to be noticed.

"Pretty girl," Grandpa said, smiling at me. "Talented too."

I felt myself blush a little, but he was right. Laurna was quite beautiful, and her singing only added to her elegance. There was something special about her; it was a shame I had never noticed until now.

"Yes, she is. Yes, she is," I said, my voice drifting off as I continued to look her way.

I finished eating then made my way into the town center. The day was going to be full of a lot of people wishing me luck, people I hardly talked to or didn't even know giving me hugs and saying they hoped I wouldn't be picked. Everyone would be putting on fake smiles and fake concern. It was a day where you knew nobody would say what was really on their mind. A few pats on the back, a couple of hugs for luck, and deep down everyone really hoping that it wasn't someone they truly cared about who was chosen.

I knew what to expect because I had watched my family do it for others in the Section for years. Those who appeared to be at higher risk always had more people coming up to them. Those eligible for The Conscript could always tell just how good their odds were by how many people were saying their goodbyes. By the time the ceremony happened, the people chosen all but knew it was going to be them. I always felt bad for them; this year I just hoped it wasn't me getting all the attention.

As I continued to make my way through the crowd, people I hadn't talked to in years approached me to wish me luck. Everyone stopped to shake my hand. I couldn't help but think that this was what everyone eligible was dealing with. I appreciated everyone's concern for me, yet their visits only made me more anxious for the events I knew were only moments away. At least I was starting to assume I was about to be chosen.

Halfway across the plaza, I ran into Mom and Micca. Micca was at one of the booths playing a game. As I approached, she turned and ran, eyes welling up with tears, jumping into my arms. Her arms squeezed tightly around my neck with everything she had. I could hear the small sobs as she tried to remain composed. I was sure Mom had told her to be strong for me. I could feel the tears filling my eyes, so I buried my face into her hair. I, too, wanted to be strong. If not for Mom then definitely for Micca.

"Have you seen Grandpa yet?" Mother asked as Micca loosened her grip.

"Yeah, he's back at the picnic table," I said, nodding my head in the table's direction.

"Have you had a chance to talk to him?" Mom asked.

"Yeah, he stayed at the house this morning to talk. We're good." I smiled, trying to ease the fear I knew she was feeling.

Mom joined us, wrapping her arms around the both of us in an old-fashioned group hug. I hadn't been a part of one of those since Dad died. The thought of Dad added another dimension to the jungle of emotions I was trying to navigate. Who would take care of my family if I were gone? I had to find a way back to them. It was the only way I could be sure they would be OK. Mom pulled away, grabbing Micca's hand.

"You make sure you see everyone you can today. I'll see you later." My mother's words had never felt so ominous. I really did hope I was going to see her later.

I continued through the plaza. Jaxon and Harper, two friends from school, ran up to me, punching me in the arm as they greeted me. They still had one more year before they were eligible. Jaxon was probably a good candidate, though. He was just a little smaller than me. Harper was probably safe. Everything about him was average. That was something I wished for on a day like today. Our visit was short and I continued on my way.

I was walking along the outside of the plaza when a young girl wrapped her arm around my leg. I looked down at the blonde hair that covered her face. After a second, she pulled her head back, looking up at me with a crooked little grin.

"Harley, how are you doing?" I asked.

Harley was Crick's youngest daughter. She was a cute little kid. I hadn't seen her since the funeral. I tried to visit a couple of times, but she was never there. It was hard seeing Crick's beautiful family knowing that he was no longer around.

Harley was five years old. I looked at her and smiled; her blue eyes stared back at me. "Where's your mom at?" I asked.

Harley lit up, displaying a full set of white teeth, and pointed to my right. I turned my head as Rain made her way over to me. Gretchen, Crick's other daughter, who was seven, held on tight to her mom's hand. It was sad to think that they no longer had a father because of the actions of a power-hungry Overseer. I wished I could tell her the truth about what happened, but it wouldn't do anyone any good. Rain finally reached Harley and me. She tried to force a grin, but I could see that these times were tough.

"Hi, Gretchen, how are you?" I asked, bending down to her level.

Gretchen turned, burying her face into her mother's leg. I smirked, rising back up to my feet as Rain smiled—for real this time. "She's a little shy. Unlike this one over here," she said, grabbing the top of Harley's head. "I know what today is for you, and I'm sure you're tired of everyone wishing you the best of luck. I wouldn't feel right without at least stopping by to say something. So, be safe and be strong. Crick always talked so highly of you. We will all be thinking of you today." She gave me a soft kiss on the cheek.

I nodded, forcing a shy grin as Rain grabbed her two girls and continued through the crowd. She was right: everyone was wishing me luck, but the truth of it was that luck really had nothing to do with it. It wasn't like the people were chosen at random. Everyone was picked for a reason. There was a purpose to The Conscript. By this point, I was either chosen or I wasn't. I would find out soon enough. It was starting to get late in the day.

I turned, staring at one of the educational booths. My attention was torn away by someone yanking on my sleeve. I turned my head to see Haimi. She yanked on my sleeve again, forcing me to one knee. "I named my bear after you!" She said, wrapping her arms around my neck and giving me a strong squeeze.

"Thank you," I said softly. "As long as I'm still in Section Eight you will be safe." I pointed to the bear. She giggled and then ran off back into the crowd.

As I rose to my feet, Laurna's eyes met mine. "She's taken quite a liking to you. Thank you for being so good with her."

"Oh, she's a sweetie, there's no effort there." I smiled. Laurna frowned slightly, unable to fake a happy expression for me.

"What is it?"

"I know what today is. It just makes me sad is all. Be safe! I do hope this isn't goodbye!" Laurna hugged me. I wrapped my arms around her. I let go as our eyes met one last time. Then she turned, disappearing into the crowd.

I sighed, watching her leave my sight. The sun was starting to get lower in the sky. The selection was going to begin soon.

It was funny how things had evolved over the years. My father used to tell me about when they first started The Conscript: people in hoods would come and grab you off the street. They'd break into homes and even fight those who tried to protect you. Now it was treated more like an honor to be chosen. There was a big celebration and your name was announced in front of the entire Section. I didn't know why they changed or why people didn't talk about the old ways, but today I wondered more about it.

The Natio anthem began to play. Head Overseer Hawkins was standing on the main stage. The eligible draftees moved in close to the stage as the rest of the Section filtered in behind them. There was excitement in the eyes of a lot of the eligible kids. Some families saw being chosen as an honor. An opportunity for a better life. A chance to make your family proud. While there was sadness in the dome for those who may leave, there was also excitement and joy for the opportunity that came from being chosen.

My family saw things a little differently. Maybe it was because my father died in the last war, or maybe it was because growing up Grandpa was constantly blaming the government for nearly everything that went wrong. Either way, it wasn't something I was looking forward to. It wasn't something I was excited to be a part of.

Head Overseer Hawkins took the microphone.

"Ladies and gentlemen, tonight we have an opportunity to send two young, promising people to Heart City to be part of the next generation of Natio heroes. The two people chosen tonight will have a chance to train, learn, and grow from the best our great nation has to offer. I still remember my time training in Heart City. The lessons I learned there and the opportunities I got have led me to the position I'm in today. I'm excited to announce the next to begin this journey. May you both become more than you ever dreamed possible."

Hawkins held up an envelope that had the Natio seal on it. Sliding it open, he pulled out a card. "Lancaster Rose!" Hawkins paused as a small cheer broke out from the back of the crowd. Lancaster made his way to the stage next to Head Overseer Hawkins.

"And Dantin Cross."

CHAPTER 4

A huge lump filled my throat. My heart pounded and my body felt like I had just been punched in the gut. I stood frozen as the people of Section Eight cheered. My vision sharpened as I broke through the haze of the moment, being escorted toward the stage by those around me. Everyone was patting me on the back and smiling. I forced a smile, but inside my heart was breaking because I knew it meant my mother and my sister would never see me again.

Up on stage they positioned me next to Lancaster as the applause continued to roll in for this year's chosen. Lancaster waved, but all I could do was stare out into the crowd, frantically searching for my family. Finally, I met eyes with Micca. She waved with tears in her eyes. I forced back tears of my own and tried to smile as I waved to her. I didn't want her to think this was the end. I had to believe I could make my way back home. Maybe if I did exceptional work I could get back home someday.

Lancaster and I were escorted offstage and toward the Capitol Building. I imagined this was where they would process us and prepare us to ship out to Heart City. While leaving Section Eight was not on my bucket list, I was excited about getting a chance to see Heart City. Everything I had read about the city was incredible. They were blessed with all the latest technologies and luxuries that the Sections didn't have. It would be interesting to see how many of the stories were true.

Once inside, the Section Overseers escorted us toward the back of the Capitol Building. I'd never ventured deeper than the main lobby. There were so many doors and hallways. The building appeared so much bigger inside than it looked from the outside. It was impressive how much was going on behind the scenes that we never knew anything about.

We had been walking for what seemed like several minutes when we reached a large wooden double door at what had to be the back of the building. One of the Overseers fiddled for a second with the lock and then swung the doors open. They opened up to another huge hall that looked similar to the entry hall.

I would have never guessed that this building was so big. We continued across the massive room to a door on the far side. As we walked, we traveled across a seal in the middle of the floor of the open hall. It was a circle with words around the outside: THE GREAT SEAL OF THE STATE OF MINNESOTA * 1858. Inside the seal was an image of a man on horseback next to another man pushing what looked like a plow, with a waterfall in the background. The seal must have been a remainder of the history of old America. Natio must have repurposed the building after the reconstruction of the new world.

At the other side of the hall the Overseer holding the keys once again began to fiddle with them. Lancaster and I watched as he fumbled with what appeared to be at least thirty keys before finally sliding one into the door. A soft click and the door swung open. A stairwell lay ahead, leading us down into what must have been the basement of the building. The Overseer lit a torch and then proceeded down the staircase into the dark.

We descended further into the depths of the Capitol Building, the temperature cooling with each stair. It felt like we went down at least fifty steps before reaching a narrow passage at the bottom. We continued for several minutes, the only light coming from the torch of the lead Overseer. *There's no way we're still in the Capitol Building.* The temperature continued to drop and I felt myself start to shiver.

I was sure Lancaster was freezing. He was a skinny kid, much smaller than me, and extremely pale, which gave him the look of someone terminally ill. His sandy hair was long and it looked like he hadn't had a haircut in months. The shaggy hair fell over his ears and covered his forehead, hiding his grey eyes. Even through all the hair and in the dark I could tell he was distraught; the joy he'd displayed earlier was gone now.

At the end of the long hall was another door; this one had a large lock on it. The Overseer passed me the torch.

"Hold this."

Should I hit him?

No, don't be stupid, you'd just get lost down here and die.

I didn't know why I had that thought. Finally, after several attempts, the man placed a large key in the hole. The lock clicked and the door swung open. We were greeted by five more Overseers holding torches.

I emerged from the tunnel as the cool night bit at my nose. My breath lingered on the frozen air. We were well beyond the wall. The snow was thick, and each step crunched under my feet. We were ushered forward, then placed in one of the outdoor transport vehicles. There was just barely enough room for the six of us as two of the Overseers climbed up front to drive. Lancaster and I pressed up tightly next to each other.

As the transport jerked forward, everyone inside slammed into one another. We were moving quickly; however, part of me still expected this trip to take a while. I'd only been outside the walls for work, but I remembered my history classes from school, and Natio wasn't a small country. If we were going to drive all the way to Heart City, it was going to be a long trip.

Then, just as fast as the ride started, we slid to a halt. The sudden stop sent Lancaster falling onto the floor.

The side door of the transport flew open, revealing a small station that resembled the bus depot where we met for work every morning. There were a few differences, though, first being the set of metal rails running on the ground. It looked like train tracks, but according to the schoolbooks, trains didn't run anymore. Heart City prohibited inter-Section travel for all citizens.

I had never seen a train except for the few pictures in the old schoolbooks. This engine looked like a bullet, sleek and new. This didn't look anything like the old steam engines they talked about during history class. It shone as the lights from the torches bounced off the metal siding. We were escorted off the transport, up to the doors of the train. There was a small hiss and the doors opened without any assistance. When I looked at Lancaster, his eyes said what I was feeling.

It was like nothing I could ever have dreamed up. Doors that opened without assistance, lights that weren't fire—Heart City really was well advanced beyond anything we ever saw in the Sections.

Why don't they share these things with us? I wonder what else I'm about to see.

I studied everything I could as I stepped through the doors onto the train. There was so much I couldn't process it all. I didn't even know where to begin.

On the train, the halls were illuminated by lighting similar to what had been revealed at our party: small glowing lights situated behind glass shells. It was like something we would see in books about the history before Bloodfire.

In school, we learned that these "luxuries" (computers, cars, the internet, electricity, and cellphones) led to the eventual downfall of America, spawning the acts of terrorism that led to hatred and war.

Lancaster and I were ushered through three cars before we reached what looked like private quarters. About halfway through the car, our guide stopped, spinning around. He grabbed two doors opposite each other and slid them open.

"You, here." He pointed at Lancaster then gestured to his right. "And you here," he said, guiding me to his left. "Get some rest. We'll be in Heart City in the morning."

Once I was in my room the door slid closed, leaving me alone for the first time in hours. The light inside the room illuminated a small sleeping area the size of a couch, and a chair in the corner. I crossed the small quarters, taking a seat in the chair. *Heart City by morning.* I didn't believe it was possible. The train whistled, surging forward. It was smooth and effortless. A few small tremors and the train was floating along with ease.

The scenery passed outside the window so quickly that it was hard to make anything out. Trees blurred in and out of focus. White from the snow was the only constant. I stopped trying to figure out what direction we were heading. I knew Heart City was to the south; I just wasn't sure exactly how far or where, specifically. They didn't actually teach us that in school.

I moved from the chair and collapsed onto the bed. It was much more comfortable than my bed at home. The soft mattress absorbed my fall as if landing on a pile of feathers. The blankets felt smooth and silky under my fingers. Even so, I wasn't sure how I was going to sleep tonight with everything that was going on and all that lay ahead.

CHAPTER 5

I jolted upright as the sound of someone pounding on the door startled me awake. Light poured in through the window. It looked like it was at least mid-morning. The stress of the day before must have wiped me out more than I'd realized. The door rattled again as the knocking continued.

"Mr. Cross, are you awake?"

"I'm awake!" I called out.

"Get dressed. Breakfast will be served in fifteen minutes in the dining car," the voice on the other side of the door announced.

Outside the window there was no longer snow on the ground. The grass was green, the sky a bright blue. It looked like a spring day from back home. This was odd, being that it was winter back home. The trees were off, too. They weren't your normal evergreen trees from Section Eight. No branches to climb, no limbs at all until the very top. It looked like one of the stripped logs from the Lumber Yard with a green fuzzy hat. Everything about this landscape was off. It was the first time I truly felt uneasy.

Inside the dining car, Lancaster was already seated, waiting for breakfast to be served. I pulled up a seat next to him. In the car with us were two Overseers at each door and someone else I had not seen before. The man was wearing very nice clothing. His skin and hair shone in the light from the dining car. He made a gesture toward one of the Overseers, who disappeared into the next car. Turning back to us, the man began to talk.

"Good morning, gentlemen. My name is Stanton Landry. I will be coordinating your arrival to Heart City. I have your itinerary here so we can get you where you need to go. Heart City is large and hard to maneuver so I will make sure we don't get lost. If there are any questions, I'll do my best to answer them for you."

Two men entered the dining car carrying large portions of food and placed the trays on the table. It looked like another feast from our festival: eggs, bacon, pancakes, waffles, fresh fruit, and juice. Syrup sat in separate containers on each tray. There were also muffins and sweet, gooey cinnamon rolls. The events of yesterday mixed with the anxiety of today had made my stomach shrink. Apparently it hadn't affected Lancaster, as he dug right in.

Mr. Landry began to speak again. "We have two hours before we arrive, so enjoy breakfast, then head back to your room where you will find a new uniform to wear. Once we arrive, stick with me and I'll make sure we get where we need to go. I'll see you shortly." Mr. Landry dismissed himself, sliding away from the table and exiting the dining car.

Mr. Landry seemed unexpectedly pleasant. I wondered what all he would be able to tell us. I also wondered how much he knew about our situation. I wanted answers. I needed answers.

I watched as Lancaster stuffed his face, putting more food in his mouth before swallowing the previous bite. The sight made my stomach queasy. I looked away, staring out the nearby window. The sun was still shining brightly. I glanced back at the piles of food on the table, thinking I needed to eat something. I didn't know when I'd eat again today.

I put a small pile of eggs, a little bacon, and some fruit on my plate. The food was delicious, full of flavor and fresher than we usually got in Section Eight. I thought I was eating slowly, yet before I knew it my food was gone. I debated grabbing more. Lancaster sat back, holding his belly. He looked miserable, which was enough for me to refrain from a second plate. I pushed away from the table, getting to my feet.

Lancaster watched as I moved to the exit of the dining car. "What do you think they'll do with us?"

It was the first time he'd spoken to me. "I'm not sure. I guess it could be any number of things." I debated telling him what my Grandpa had said about surviving, but held my tongue.

"Do you think we'll ever see Section Eight again?"

I looked down at the floor. I knew that answer immediately: nobody ever saw Section Eight again.

"No." I slid open the door.

"Didn't think so," Lancaster dejectedly said under his breath as I exited the room.

Inside my room was a new uniform lying on the bed. It was extremely plain. There was a pair of grey cargo pants and a grey shirt. I slipped out of my Section Eight clothes, grabbing the new uniform. The clothes fit surprisingly well, and they were very comfortable. The shirt had a number printed on the chest: Fifteen. I assumed this was their way of telling who each of us was. There were no other identifying marks on the outfit.

Outside, the landscape was starting to open up. The train seemed to be running parallel to an old road that looked like smooth rocks. There were several holes in the road where it looked as though it had been dug up and grass had begun to grow in the cracks. This must have been a mode of transportation left over from old America. A sign appeared in the distance, next to the road: "Atlanta, 13 miles."

I wasn't sure what exactly that meant. Inside the dome everything was so close that time was used to convey distance.

Thirteen isn't too large of a number, we must not be too far now. I'm not sure if that's good or bad. Part of me wanted off the train, but another part of me was afraid of what was going to happen next.

A few moments later, the train began to slow. I returned to the window, staring into the distance. A city rose into view, large buildings spread out across the landscape. As we neared the city I noticed that the buildings were in ruins. Large pieces were missing from a number of the structures. Windows were broken out of others. Some of them looked as though they might be smoking. A couple of the buildings looked to be only a fraction of the size they used to be as the top of the buildings had been completely taken off.

I leaned in closer to the window, trying to get a clearer view of the buildings. But the train suddenly changed directions and descended down into a tunnel, leaving me looking into the dark. No more light, just black nothingness. The train traveled in total darkness for a few minutes, and when we finally returned into the light I had to cover my eyes. As my eyes adjusted to the new light source I didn't believe what I saw.

A huge city appeared before us. There were buildings everywhere, built with amazingly white stone. The sky was a perfect blue, and the city looked as though it stretched on forever. I had never seen anything so incredible. As I continued to explore the new surroundings I noticed tubes that shot out of the tops of several of the buildings into the sky. Then a light shot up one of the tubes, vanishing into the sky. *What? What was that?*

That's when I noticed it. We were still underground. The sky was a projection on the roof of whatever this enclosure was made of. The whole city was underground. More projections appeared on the sides of buildings, flashing into focus and then disappearing. Roads traveled in all directions through the city. Vehicles traveled the roads without making contact, hovering just off the ground. It was like another world, like nothing I had ever seen before. The train came to a stop in a large city square. Buildings surrounded us.

I pulled myself away from the window, exiting my quarters. As soon as I stepped into the hallway I found myself face-to-face with Lancaster, whose uniform was the same as mine with the exception of a number Sixteen on it. Yet again his eyes displayed the shock that I was feeling. He was definitely someone who wore his emotions on his face. He, too, was in awe of this place. We pushed forward through the car to the exit, stepping out onto the station platform.

I looked up to the ceiling, estimating that it was well over a couple hundred feet high. The buildings flashed images of people, gadgets, and food. Each image was followed by some kind of slogan describing what was on the screen. My eyes were finally starting to adjust to the extreme white of the buildings. We were marched forward through a large building that seemed to be the focal point of the square.

It was brilliant. The white stone was pristine. Four large pillars held up the front entry, each bigger than any tree I'd ever cut down working in the Lumber Yard. The intricate detail at the top and bottom of each pillar was masterful. There were two large doors at the entry, four steps up from street level. They were so big that they looked as if they were built for the gods. Giants could enter this building without ducking.

Inside the building the amazement continued. A large domed ceiling with some kind of artwork graced the lobby. More of the large pillars supported the dome at four points. The walls held more artwork, which looked like rugs with extremely detailed scenes depicted on them. The floor was marble, reflecting the brightness of the large room. We crossed the threshold to a set of doors on the far side of the lobby.

We moved deeper into the belly of the city. After we had descended another two levels below the building, another large lobby appeared. There were already a number of people waiting in this area. Half of them were wearing uniforms matching those of Lancaster and me. We joined the group that was already there, and Mr. Landry moved to the front of the group.

He started talking with a group of men who were all dressed similarly to him. They must have been the people from the other Sections who were assigned to get everyone here. I scanned the room. The majority of people in the room appeared scared: eyes down, slightly defeated look. There were already more than twenty people here.

As I continued to scan, I met the gaze of another kid at the other end of the room. He glared straight back at me. No fear. Didn't budge as I sized him up. He was slightly taller than me. Well-fed. Muscular and strong. His eyes narrowed as I continued to look at him. I didn't know what it was, but that guy rubbed me wrong. That's when my gaze was interrupted.

A medium-sized boy stood in front of me. Extending his hand, he said, "Hello, my name is Goby."

He was the epitome of average. He was of average height, weight, and build. His brown hair was medium-length. He had brown eyes and light-colored skin. His uniform had the number Twenty-one on it. I reached out, grabbing his hand and giving it a firm shake. Even his grip was average at best; he grimaced under the pressure of my handshake. He must have been one of the smart people, like Lancaster.

"I'm Dantin. What Section are you from?"

Goby pulled his hand away, rubbing his palm, trying to work out the pain. "I'm from Section Eleven. The number on your uniform indicates where you're from."

I looked at my number. *How does fifteen indicate Section Eight?* "Oh, that makes sense," I said, acting as if I knew what he meant.

"Look, there are two people here from every section. So, numbers One and Two are from Section One; you are Fifteen so you are from Section Eight, right?" Goby explained as he pointed at the numbers on the different uniforms.

I studied my number while the math worked through my head. I looked back up, trying to locate the guy who had been locked on my gaze a few minutes ago. "Have you met many of the others?"

"Yeah. Well, I've tried to. Some are more receptive to introductions than others."

I nodded, searching for the guy from earlier. His uniform had an eleven on it. "What about the guy from Section Six with the eleven on his shirt?"

Goby looked where I was looking and then snapped his gaze back at me. "Don't stare at him, he's the worst one I've met so far. He's the reason I have this." He pointed to his lip, which I just noticed was swollen a little with a tiny cut in it. "I went up to him to introduce myself, but apparently where he's from they greet each other with a punch in the mouth."

Goby smiled at his attempt to make a joke. I didn't pick up on it at first as I continued to watch Number Eleven. I realized that Goby was waiting for some kind of response so I forced a smile and small laugh. I could see that Goby was starting to feel a little uneasy.

"Don't worry, we just use a handshake where I'm from," I said, flashing him a more genuine smile. "Here, let me introduce you to someone else." I reached forward, grabbing Lancaster's shoulder. "This is Lancaster, the other guy from my Section."

Goby reached out, shaking his hand. The two started into a conversation right away as I tuned them out. It didn't surprise me that they'd hit it off. They were very similar. I could tell that Goby wasn't physically intimidating by any means, but he was well-educated. This was much like Lancaster. Education wasn't really my strong suit. I wasn't dumb, but I never really approached learning like Micca did. Micca. I really did miss her right now; she would be so impressed with this place.

I continued to scan the room. More people had joined the group, and the room was starting to fill. A man standing at the front of the group started to wave his hands to get everyone's attention. The group began to quiet down as the man spoke.

"Welcome, this year's Chosen Ones. You are lucky to be a part of this group. As the Chosen Ones, you are here for Heart City's special program. It is here where your future can change forever. Today will be orientation, and tomorrow will start your training. We will start in just a few more minutes by passing as a group through these doors"—he pointed behind himself—"where you'll be shown a short video and then directed to your quarters. Please hang tight while we get everything set up."

A couple of minutes passed. The man appeared back in front of the crowd as the doors opened behind him. The group was ushered through the doors into the back of a large auditorium. The rows slowly dropped down to a large white screen at the front. We were walked halfway down the length of the theater and then directed into the rows. There were enough of us to take up three rows.

Everyone settled in as the lights dimmed. The screen lit up and images flashed. A small countdown ran starting at three ... two ... one. The film started by showing the height of the United States: streets full of people, cars rushing from one place to another, everyone talking on cellphones and sitting in front of televisions. This was over 150 years ago now. Then, on March 14, 2014: Bloodfire.

It was first discovered by Dr. Bryce Young, a biochemical engineer who worked for the United States Health Department. He was studying the effects and spread of a virus that had appeared in Europe when he realized that Bloodfire had the potential to wipe out the world. The virus started by targeting the respiratory system, causing a cough, which helped the virus spread rapidly. Shortly after the cough it would move into the nervous system, causing catastrophic system failure. Balance, muscle control, and vision loss were first, then blood flow disorders led to most people dying of heart attack or stroke within a few weeks of exposure.

There was no cure, and as Dr. Young worked frantically to come up with a vaccine, he became exposed to the disease and died before finishing his research. The disease had a secondary effect that was unexpected as well: Reapers began to appear. People would go mad and change into raging beasts that couldn't control their most primal instincts. Later it was discovered that the virus's reaction to people taking any kind of anti-depressant was what triggered the Reaper response.

At this point, the world was thrown into chaos. People started pointing fingers, and war broke out across the globe. Those who were still alive fought with everyone to try to prevent the spread of the disease. The United States was thrown into the most turmoil as they fought with Canada, Mexico, and among themselves. A civil war broke out while fighting with Mexico and Canada that brought the whole of the United States crashing down. All major cities were gone, and America was thrown into a new stone age.

Then, from the ashes of what was once America, rose Natio! Natio, which is the Latin word for "nation," grew to power using the motto "That which has been born." The new government divided the country into sixteen Sections and declared that all goods, work, and technology would be regulated by Heart City. Peace and growth would now be ensured for all time. No more threats would bring down what had been built. With Natio the future we would remain strong.

"To this day there is still no cure for Bloodfire," boomed the video's narrator. "The domes were constructed to keep the citizens of Natio safe from the virus and the Reapers. Still, even with all that Natio has done to keep its citizens safe, Bloodfire still emerges from time to time, forcing us to purge those infected out into the wild to spare the rest of the Section from falling ill. Only on rare occasions has this had to happen, but together with the support of Heart City and loyalty to Natio, the human race will survive and grow stronger."

The video ended. I rubbed my eyes, trying to refocus on what I had just seen. It was the first time I had seen such an in-depth history of what had led to Natio.

I felt a sense of duty to Natio. I also felt conflicted. Part of me still believed that the government was tyrannical, controlling, and deceitful. However, now a part of me believed we, the Chosen Ones, were responsible for the rise of Natio. My eyes kept seeing flashes throughout the video, and now those images were burned into my mind. I couldn't explain it, but I knew I had to protect Natio, whatever the cost.

We were ushered back out the way we came in, then directed through another set of doors that were followed by a long corridor. Numbered doors started to appear on both sides of the hall. The first door said thirty-two, with thirty-one across the hall. In descending order the numbers dropped all the way to one. At the start of the numbered doors our escort addressed the group.

"Your room is the one that matches the number on your uniform," he said. "Inside you will find everything you need. Make your way to your room and head inside. Get some rest, training begins at zero six hundred tomorrow."

Halfway down the hall, my door was situated on the left side with the other odd numbers. As I reached for my door handle, a body collided with me. The hit was hard and forceful, causing me to spin. I searched for my attacker, but at first I couldn't focus. That's when I saw him. Eleven looked over his shoulder at me, still moving down the hall. A small smile emerged on his face as he reached his door. He opened it, stepping inside without breaking my gaze.

What's that guy's deal? I shrugged it off, stepping into my room. The place was very plain. A toilet, shower, and stainless steel sink were situated to the right. In the back left corner was my bed. There was a small dresser next to the bed with a lamp positioned on top of it. No windows. No chairs. Just very plain. In the dresser there were several uniform shirts with the number fifteen on them. Inside the second drawer were pants. The top drawer had undergarments.

As I dropped down onto the bed, the lights in the room turned off. The room was so dark I couldn't see my hand in front of my face. There was a sliver of light shining in from under the door, so at least if I had to use the bathroom I could fumble my way to the door, then hopefully find the toilet. I stood up from the bed and the lights shot back on. I was blinded by their brightness.

I rubbed my eyes. *Of course: automated lights.* I washed up while there was still light, slipped out of the clothes that I felt like I had worn for the last three days, and climbed into bed. The lights flipped back off. I stared at the ceiling as I had done so many nights before in Section Eight. Thoughts of home were jumbled with thoughts of protecting Natio. The confusion caused my head to ache. I closed my eyes, trying to stop the argument going on in my head. *Tomorrow is going to start early.*

CHAPTER 6

An alarm rang out throughout the room. I wasn't sure of the time, but it felt early. I sat on the edge of my bed as lights flashed and the alarm echoed off the walls. I rubbed my eyes, trying to shake the cobwebs. *Good God, I'm awake already! Shut up!*

I looked around the room, searching for a button or something to push. There was nothing. No button or switch or any sign of where the noise was coming from. I covered my ears and rose to my feet. The lights shot on and the alarm disappeared.

Of course. I hate this place already.

On my dresser a cup with a green liquid in it that was delivered by a mechanical arm that came down from the ceiling.

The drink appeared to be thick and there was a note next to it: DRINK THIS. I grabbed the drink, tilting the cup from side to side. I'd seen honey move more quickly. I tilted the cup back, half chewing, half swallowing the drink.

It was awful. The smell reminded me of something the horses in Section Eight left behind. The taste wasn't much better. I gagged, almost vomiting it back up.

Why am I drinking this?

Because the sign said to. You may not get any more food; just force it down.

I continued to force down the green goop. The beverage was finally gone, yet I still chewed on the remains. Swirling my tongue around my mouth, I tried to rid myself of every last bit.

I moved to my dresser to grab my uniform for the day. I had just finished getting dressed when a second alarm sounded, this time accompanied by the door to my room flying open. Lancaster stood in the doorway across the hall. I guessed this meant it was 06:00 and time to start training.

I moved into my doorway, looking down the hall to the right, then the left. Other heads began to peer out, trying to figure out the next step. Then, just as quickly as the alarm started, it stopped. A man at the far end of the hall to my left began to speak.

"Good morning, everyone. Training begins now. Please come this way and we will start Phase One." The man turned as everyone flowed out of their rooms.

Walking in two even lines, we proceeded through the doors at the end of the hall. Back in the great hall we slowly moved to a set of doors we'd never been through. On the other side we filed into place, stopping just in front of a massive indoor obstacle course. Ropes, walls, water, and mud were a few challenges that I could make out close to the start.

"Welcome to The Course," said the man who had guided us into the room. "Each pair will start when directed. You will move through The Course, completing each obstacle along the way. Move as quickly as possible. Your time will be kept based on your starting position. We will begin momentarily!" He directed the first team to the line and then said something to them that I couldn't hear.

A second man appeared with something in his hand. I couldn't quite make it out, but when he raised his arm, pointing it straight up, the object flashed and a boom rang out. It looked like a pistol, but instead of a bullet, a red glowing ball streaked from the end of it. The noise echoed through the room and caused every person in the hall to cover their ears. The first group took off racing toward the first obstacle. Both guys moved up over a twelve-foot wall, disappearing onto the other side. The next team stepped into position, waiting for the sound to mark their start. I tried to watch as the first group moved further into the course. I could feel the anxiety and excitement start to build.

Eleven was at the starting line awaiting the horn. As it sounded, he darted at the twelve-foot wall full speed, and with ease he was up and over it, not even using the rope for assistance. The other person from his Section was not so graceful. Number Twelve, a tiny excuse of a man, grabbed the rope, fighting with all his might. He walked up the wall slowly, moving hand over hand. He was almost over the top when he slipped, slamming into the wall and falling back to the bottom.

Number Twelve finally fought his way over the wall as the gun sounded, releasing the next group. Lancaster and I stepped up to the line, watching the Chosen Ones from Section

Seven work their way over the wall. My heart started to pound, anticipating the shot that would send us into the course. I looked over my shoulder, finding Goby. He nodded his head. I returned the nod and then turned my gaze to Lancaster.

I reached over, hitting him on the shoulder. His eyes shot up to meet mine. "You got this!" I told him. "One obstacle at a time."

He nodded, looking a little reassured to know that I had his back. Still not saying anything, his focus returned to the wall. My eyes returned to the wall as well. Twelve feet wasn't going to be much trouble for me. I wasn't sure how athletic Lancaster was, though. I debated whether to get to the top and then help him or to move through the course as fast as I could. There was little instruction other than to finish quickly. That and don't be last!

The gun blasted. I took off in a full sprint at the wall. Without breaking stride, I jumped off of my left foot, driving my right foot into the wall and then upward. I reached for the top of the wall, grabbing it with ease. I held tight with my left hand, turning back to see where Lancaster was. He was just reaching the wall. I reached my right arm down, extending it out to him. He jumped, grabbing hold as I threw him up to the top of the wall, and together we were over the first obstacle.

We landed on the other side, looking out over the course. The next obstacle was about fifteen feet ahead. It was a metal set of parallel bars, about eight feet off the ground and twenty feet long. Underneath it was what looked like muddy water. The consistency wasn't right, though. One of the earlier contestants was still trying to get through the stuff after falling from the bars. He was stuck chest deep, fighting forward at an extremely slow pace.

Grabbing onto the bars, Lancaster flew out in front. His light body weight was an advantage on this obstacle as he threw one hand over the other with complete ease. He reached the end of the obstacle before I was halfway across. I wasn't having too much trouble with the drill; it was just that I was too big to move quickly. I passed over the kid who was stuck in the thick mud soup below as he reached up, trying to grab my legs. I lifted my knees, scooting past him to reach the end of the second obstacle.

When I dropped to the ground, Lancaster was halfway to the next station. I took off running to catch up. The next spot had a rope ladder that traveled up twenty feet. At the top, there was a small platform just big enough for one person at a time. There was a set of parallel ropes, one on top and one below, that was designed to be crossed by walking. I passed Lancaster on the rope ladder, reaching the platform first.

I reached overhead, grabbing the top rope. Placing my foot out on the bottom rope, my heart skipped as the rope dropped a good three inches under my weight. I gripped the hand rope tight, digging into the braiding. The lines shook back and forth as I wiggled my way out toward the second platform. When I was halfway across, the bottom rope dropped even lower. I stopped, looking back at the start. Lancaster was stepping out onto the line. *Can this thing even support two people?*

I continued forward, trying to pick up my pace, placing one foot right in front of the other, hand-over-hand, moving quicker now. I had about six feet left. My right foot slipped, sliding off the rope. My body twisted and both feet dangled. I was being held up only by my grip on the top rope, but it sunk under my weight, throwing Lancaster off-balance and causing him to slip as well. The foot rope was now about chest high, which made it impossible for me to get back up onto it. I dangled, fingers clenched around the braiding. A slow trickle of blood ran down my forearm. I needed to move.

I slowly slid my hands across the rope. *Only six feet. You can do it.* I inched closer to the platform. The blood from my hands had reached my elbow. My hands burned with each move. *Only three feet now.* I threw my foot up onto the platform, sliding my hands along the rope. I lay motionless except for my chest rising and falling. I looked at my mangled hands as I attempted to catch my breath. Lancaster! I rolled onto my stomach, looking back at the obstacle. He still hung tight to the top rope, unable to move.

I stepped back onto the foot rope. It sank a couple of inches, but it wasn't enough. Placing both hands on the hand rope, I pushed up as hard as I could. Lancaster slowly lifted himself upward, finding his footing on the rope once again. I stepped back off of the rope and onto the platform. I turned to find the next obstacle, but there wasn't anything.

I scanned in front of me. Behind me. Around the entire platform. Nothing. There was no next step. I looked down to the ground, twenty feet below, and that's when I saw it. There was a large tank of water with what looked like a circle and an X on it, indicating the next spot. I took a deep sigh and jumped off the platform. My feet kicked and arms flailed as I fell to the ground. Just before impact, I managed to pull my arms across my chest and put my feet together.

I sank into the water, coming up near the wall where I could climb out. The next station was right out of the pool. As I stepped forward, a splash made me turn my head. Lancaster thrashed in the water, finding his way to the side. Climbing out, he joined me in front of the next station. This wasn't like any of the other obstacles. There was no physical challenge here, but some sort of puzzle.

The numbers twenty-five, twenty-four, twenty-two, nineteen, and fifteen were at the top. Then there were four buttons illuminated under the set of numbers. Each button had a number next to it. The numbers were eight, twelve, ten, and fourteen. I studied the puzzle as Lancaster joined me. When I glanced over at him I could see his brain piecing the parts together. He pointed to the ten, looking over at me. We both pounded the button as two doors opened up, leading us into a narrow hallway.

Lancaster was no longer with me. He must have been directed another way. I took a step forward. The space was small enough that I could touch the walls on either side of me without fully extending my arms. This seemed like an odd obstacle, so I continued to move cautiously. I took another step forward. There was a clicking sound, causing me to freeze. I looked down as the floor started to pull apart. I tried to retreat, but there was no going back.

The whole hallway floor was disappearing. I jumped, slamming both of my feet into the wall to hold myself up. The floor was almost completely gone now, revealing a hole with large, spear-like spikes sticking upward. There were three skeletons in the pit. I didn't know if this was just for effect or if I fell I would actually die. I wasn't about to check to find out.

Placing my hands on the walls, I jumped my feet forward, slamming them into the walls. My hands started to bleed again as I slowly inched my way along. The hall wasn't too long. *Only another five feet to the end.* I pushed hard, propelling myself forward a few more times. As I jumped down onto the platform at the other end, the floor slammed back together, hiding the spikes. A door opened, releasing me back onto the obstacle course.

I could feel my pulse throbbing through the cuts in my hands. I reached for my shoulders, ripping my sleeves from my shirt. Wrapping the cloth around my hands, the pressure eased some of the pain and slowed the bleeding. I finished bandaging my hands. Still no Lancaster. It looked like I was on my own from here on out. I moved forward quickly, reaching the next station. Each step felt heavier as fatigue set in.

I dove onto my stomach, sliding through the mud-filled ground, pulling myself along under barbed wire that hung above my head. The mud was thick, making it hard to move without raising up from my stomach. However, each time I did I found my back being pricked by the barbed wire. I felt the soft trickle of blood mark my shirt. Reaching the end of the obstacle, I found myself lost on how many stations I'd completed. My body was starting to ache all over. My heart pounded and my body throbbed.

The next station was another puzzle. This time no Lancaster to bail me out. I studied the wall. This time it was objects, not numbers. There were four images. Each one looked like it was angled in a different direction, but there was nothing that made any sense. I looked closer.

It was a large square divided into nine equally-sized squares. Each of those had a tenth little square centrally located and protruding off the main square. Each pointed in a different direction: A pointed up, B pointed down, C pointed right, and D pointed left. Inside the large box, three of the smaller boxes were filled in black in a diagonal pattern. A moved from bottom left to upper right. B moved from bottom left to upper right. C did as well, and D moved from upper left to bottom right.

Above the pattern a question asked: WHICH OF THE FOLLOWING FIGURES IS THE ODD ONE OUT?

I looked closely. I turned the images so that all the boxes faced the same direction as A. This was hard at first so I slowly tried to compare two at a time. A and B, if facing the same way, were the same. A and C, if facing the same way, were reverse. *OK, so C, maybe?* A and D, if facing the same way, were the same.

I reached out, pressing the button with C on it. The door slid open, this time leading into the next station, which was still on the course. No more hallways. There was a short strip of land twenty-five feet long and then a large pool. The obstacle was tricky, as the pool had a lid on top of it that covered a large stretch in the middle. I was going to have to swim underwater most of the way.

I wasn't a great swimmer, but I considered myself lucky to have actually had some time in the water since every year they'd use the snow melt to fill one of the old swimming pools in our Section. There really wasn't time to play in the water, at least in Section Eight, so I found it hard to believe that anyone here was a good swimmer. I studied the obstacle, looking for a way around the water, but there was no way for me to get on top of the pool cover; it was too thick coming out of the water. It was such a big block I could barely see the other side of the pool, but there was definitely a place to get out of the pool on the other side, assuming I could make it there without drowning.

I was going to have to swim. Or at least try to. I drove my feet into the ground with everything I had left. I dashed forward, reaching the end of the land strip. Then I dove forward, like my father had taught me when I was young, as far as I could, reaching for the pool with my hands. I glided through the air, entering the water head first. Sliding through the water, I kicked my feet as violently as I could while holding my breath and reaching forward.

Air forced its way from my lungs. I opened my eyes but couldn't see the end of the pool. I could feel my heart pound as my lungs started to burn, craving air. I could feel panic starting to set in. This was going to be it. All this way to die in a small pool of water. My kicking slowed and I reached upward, trying to find the air above me. I wanted air so badly. I fought with all I had left to keep from sucking in a large gulp of water.

There it is! The wall to the pool. Just out of my reach. I kicked hard three more times, stretching forward. My hand reached the wall as I fought with my feet to climb to the surface. My hands burst through the top of the water, grabbing for the ledge. Pulling myself up, I gasped, sucking in as much air as I could, savoring every large breath like it had been years since I'd felt oxygen in my lungs.

I pulled myself from the water, flopping onto my back, now coughing from trying to consume too much oxygen. I choked on the air. I stayed on my back until I felt my body start to return to normal and then forced myself to my feet. Still feeling weak and slightly lightheaded from oxygen deprivation, I surged forward. I had to be getting close. I had been fighting through this course for what felt like hours. I was physically and mentally exhausted. I didn't know what I had left.

Up ahead the course turned left. I pushed on. My feet no longer felt light and swift. Instead, they dragged and stomped forward. I made another turn. I could finally see the finish line. I studied the remainder of the course, which appeared to be only four more stations, and felt a renewed energy. The knowledge that I was almost done sent my feet moving swiftly once again.

I reached the next station. It was a series of hanging swings that had to be maneuvered over another pit of thick mud. There were four swings in total. The first one was attached to a pole at the top of a small platform. I climbed the three steps to the top, grabbing the swing and propelling myself out over the mud. I swung twice, kicking my legs to try to generate some momentum. I launched myself airborne, flying forward, reaching for the next swing. My hands outstretched, I grabbed the bar and sent the next swing flying.

Pain surged through my body as I felt my hands rip open again under the cloth bandages, almost causing me to let go. I forced my grip tighter as my bandages started to show red. I kicked my feet again, not wanting to waste too much time. The longer I tried to hold on, the less strength I'd have in my hands. I kicked hard, sending my body moving quicker now, forward and back. I launched forward again.

This time, I caught myself on the swing under my armpit. I swung free, slowly reaching for the bar with my hands. *Only two more.* I repeated my steps: kicking hard, creating a strong swing. At the peak of my swing I let go, free from all restraints for a couple of seconds as I floated to the next swing. Crashing into the next bar, my armpit serving as my hands, I grabbed hold of the swing. I reached the final platform, swinging onto it, and in one fluid motion I was down the other side.

Three stations left. The next station came up fast. I flew over the first two small walls. This station was easy. Pressing forward, I slid under the next hurdle. Two more walls to go. I was up over the first and then back under the last one. That station passed by without much effort at all. I sprinted forward, lungs starting to burn, legs and body aching. I only had a little left; it was time to dig deep.

Two stations! There were four large boxes laid out in front of me. They were staggered, spread across a space about a hundred feet long. The first box was on the right. I couldn't figure out what their purpose was. *Just keep moving.* I dug deep, pressing forward, about to pass the first box when I saw it. On a platform roughly thirty feet in the air, a man was controlling some kind of launching device. It fired a flurry of balls in my direction. I dove to the right, sliding behind the box as the array of balls banged off the floor.

The sound they made on impact indicated that they weren't soft, possibly made of some kind of metal or wood. I peered around the edge of the box. Another flurry of balls flew at me. I pulled my head back just as the balls ricocheted off the box. I took a deep breath. *Now what?* I listened as the shots popped out of the machine. There was a brief pause, then the shots continued.

That was it. Every ten shots the gun needed a short second to regroup before it fired again. That was my window. I was going to have to time it just right. I peered back, trying not to be too exposed as I looked for the next item of cover. I could see it as another round of balls crashed off the floor near my position It looked like there was another box maybe thirty feet away. If I could get a jump start on the next round of balls and make a dive for the box I might be able to make it.

I let another round of balls fly by, listening for the reload. I just had to time my break right. The reload period wasn't more than a few seconds. *Eight, nine, ten: GO!* I took off, head down, sprinting toward the next station. I was halfway across the space when the pop from the launcher sounded again. Two balls slammed into the ground just behind my heels. I took one more hard step, diving forward off of my left foot.

I went airborne as one of the balls slammed into my right leg. I hit the ground, sliding to a stop behind the box. I let out a grunt. My leg throbbed as I tried to gather myself. I was lucky. I looked at my leg where the ball had hit, realizing that it had just glanced off of me. If it would have been a direct hit I didn't know if I would be able to run. I took a few deep breaths as more shots caromed off the floor and box. The next station was about the same distance away from me as this box was from the last one. However, now that I had been hit I wouldn't be as fast.

I slid to the edge of the box, taking a peek up at the gunman. He stood waiting for me to make a move. The shots had actually stopped. I pulled back behind the wall as the next surprise happened. An object the size of a tree trunk was soaring down at me, attached to a rope. I dove onto the course as the object collided with the box, leaving a huge dent where it had made contact. I had escaped that hit, which might have been enough to kill me. However, now I was exposed.

I jumped to my feet as the next round of shots popped from the platform. I watched the launcher as balls came at me with a fury. I jumped, ducked, and somersaulted my way forward. I was elusive enough to avoid the round of shots. I jumped forward, rolling over the last shot and landing on my back. I continued my somersault, getting to my feet as the gunman was forced to reload. I wasn't going to waste too much more time at this station. I didn't want to be here when the next surprise happened.

I took a couple of deep breaths, composing myself, then darted in the direction of the last box. I watched the platform, eyeing the balls being shot at me. I stopped sharply as two balls passed in front of me. Continuing my run, two more balls passed just behind my head. I jumped, hurdling the next one, then dove forward to reach the next box. Another ball slammed into me. This time it was a direct hit. My ribs cracked as the air was forced out of my lungs. I collapsed to the ground with a thud, curling into a ball.

My left hand reached for my ribs, then pulled away quickly. The pain was too great to touch. The world became fuzzy as the edges of my vision began to narrow. Everything was clouded. I couldn't catch my breath because every time I attempted to inhale a sharp pain cut me short. *I think I cracked a rib or two.* I rolled onto my back, lying flat on the ground. The pain slowly started to subside and my breathing slowed closer to normal.

I reached for my ribs again, this time pressing my hand to the area of contact. The ribs felt swollen. A large puffy area rested over my ribcage in the shape of the ball. I ran my fingers along the contusion. I gritted my teeth, trying to fight through the pain. I took another breath, this time able to take in the full amount of oxygen. *Maybe they aren't broken.*

I rolled left, away from the injured ribs, placing my right hand on the ground for support. Still holding my ribs with my left hand, I climbed to my feet. I didn't hear any more shots being fired. Still, I moved cautiously, afraid if I stepped back out I'd be bombarded with more shots. This time I'd be unable to evade them. I peered around the edge of the last box. The platform was empty: no more gunman. I continued onward.

Only one more station! I told myself I was almost done. I just needed to grit my teeth and finish this thing. After another twenty feet, I came to a table. On the table there were various weapons: knives, swords, bows and arrows, axes and hatchets. I looked over the numerous choices, unsure of what was to come. The instructions were written just below the row of weapons:

GRAB THREE WEAPONS OF YOUR CHOICE AND
MOVE TO THE LINE.

I reached down, grabbing two axes and a hatchet and
moved forward to the line. Lights illuminated a course of targets.
There were three that were flashing, which I assumed meant they
were my targets. I watched as one target sat perfectly still, about
twenty feet away. Another was twelve feet away but moved side
to side as if it were on a pendulum. The last target bounced up
and down as well as side to side but was only roughly eight feet
away.

I grabbed the hatchet first. I gripped it with my right
hand and raised my arm above my head. Pain shot through my
entire body, originating from my ribs. I lowered my arm,
grimacing. I took a deep breath, feeling the pressure in my ribs
from the blow I had taken earlier. My hands throbbed, my leg
ached, and my ribs screamed as I eyed my final three targets. I
closed my eyes, attempting to block out as much of the pain as
possible.

I focused downrange. The farthest target stood perfectly
still. Rearing back, I let the hatchet fly with all I had left. The
small ax flew strong, spinning violently before slamming into the
target, lodging into the second rung from the bullseye. I grabbed
my ribs, wobbling over to my axes. Grabbing my first ax, I toed
the line. The longer handle and weight required a throw that
used both hands. I reached both arms over my head, aiming for
the pendulum target. I ripped my arms downward, and the ax
spun twice after flying out of my hands, striking the target dead
center.

Only one more target to go. I grabbed the second ax. I
toed the line, watching the final target dance all over the place.
The bandages on my hands were completely red now. My vision

was starting to blur again. I could feel myself getting weaker the longer I stood there. I pushed away the pain, but it was back before I had even a moment of peace. *This is going to hurt.* I let the final ax fly and then stood watching as it smacked into the board, sticking into the farthest point from the center. I grabbed my ribs, limping to the finish line.

At the finish line there was only one man waiting for me. He was dressed in an all-white jumpsuit. He had jet black hair and black eyes, which only looked darker in contrast to his pale skin. No one else was anywhere to be seen. *Am I the first to finish?*

Am I the only one to finish?

The man stepped forward, placing a hand on my shoulder as he led me away from the course.

"Congratulations, Number Fifteen," he said. "You did an outstanding job on the obstacle course. Let's get those ribs checked out and then you are to return to your quarters to get cleaned up. Lunch will be served as soon as the others finish the course. Right this way."

The man led me to a small table where another man in an identical jumpsuit waited for me. This man was also very pale. However, his grey hair and glasses made him appear distinguished and highly educated. I sat on the table as he lifted my shirt and pressed his fingers into my ribs. I grimaced as tears welled up in my eyes. *If they're not broken yet, you're on your way to getting them there.*

The man finished his poking around as he stood in front of me. "Well, good news. No breaks, just a nice bruise. I have some ointment here that I want you to put on your ribs right after your shower and then at least twice a day. My recommendation would be first thing in the morning and before lights out. It will help you perform better in the morning and sleep better at night."

The doctor turned away, grabbing a small tube of something from a tiny tray. He turned back, smiling at me as he handed me the tube. I looked at the tube and then back at the doc.

"Thanks." I said as he gestured for me to leave the area by pointing to the door. I slid down off the table, limping my way toward the door, where our original morning guide waited for me.

He opened the door. "Go clean yourself up," he said. "Feel free to rest for a while. You will be informed when to go up for lunch. You will have a little time to yourself now. Good work, Number Fifteen."

In my quarters, I climbed into the shower. I let the warm water run down my head, across my face. Placing my arms on the wall to support myself, I watched as the mixture of blood and dirt washed down the drain. My hands burned as I washed them out. I hadn't had a warm shower like this in my life, so I just let myself soak in the water. When I finally finished I felt a lot better, but the fatigue hit me hard.

I rubbed the ointment on my ribs, which were already turning black and blue. There was instant relief as the cream soothed my ribs. I gently dropped down onto my bed, causing the lights to turn out. *How will I ever survive this? How many of the others made it through? What happens if …*

I was asleep before I could finish my last thought.

CHAPTER 7

It felt like I was only asleep five minutes when an alarm sounded. A voice echoed through the room announcing it was time for lunch. I threw my feet off the side of the bed and rubbed my eyes. Rising to my feet, I was once again blinded by the lights coming on. My ribs ached, but not nearly as badly as they had before lying down. I shuffled across the small room to the door, but before I could grab the handle it shot open. Across the hall, Lancaster stood in his doorway looking like I felt.

He had a bandage on his right forearm and a few visible bruises. He also seemed to be standing slightly more awkwardly than normal. He shuffled his way into the hall, giving me a forced smile. I nodded my head, acknowledging his greeting. Neither one of us had much energy for more than that. Once in the hallway, we were directed to our right this time. I reached out, patting Lancaster on the shoulder.

I whispered, "It's good to see you made it. I was worried about you after the puzzle station."

He looked up at me. "Yeah, things got a little interesting after that. I'm sure you know what I mean. Those lasers really messed me up."

I was confused; I hadn't seen any lasers. "What lasers? My hallway after that station had a floor that disappeared."

Lancaster gave me a wide-eyed look. "Mine had a series of lasers that I had to maneuver. That's why I'm wearing this; one caught me on the forearm. Hurt like hell, too."

I wondered what other obstacles were different after the puzzle station but figured it didn't matter at this point. We were both here, so that was the important thing. We moved through the hall into our first gathering area. Once there, they moved us to a door that was on the far side of the room. I had never even noticed it before now, since it blended in with the wall until it was opened. We traveled through the door in groups of four.

Lancaster and I passed through the door with the two from Section Nine, which I knew because of what Goby had told me about the numbers on our shirts. *I wonder if Goby made it through.* I tried to scan the faces of the other groups, but we were being ushered forward too quickly. After passing through the door, we stepped into a small, square room. The door slid shut behind us as our guide pushed a button marked "T." The floor shook and we started moving upward. I reached for the nearest wall, not knowing what to expect.

When the room finally stopped moving, there was a brief pause before the doors opened and sunlight rushed in, causing everyone to shield their eyes. Cool air swept into the room. The fresh air felt good. We stepped into what looked like a garden. There were green plants and colorful flowers everywhere. Wood tables were set up with different foods on each one. Our group was guided to our own table on the far side of the garden. Four others were already sitting there when we arrived.

"Why hello, Dantin and Lancaster." Goby smiled, welcoming us to the table.

"Well, isn't this a nice surprise," Lancaster said, having a seat across from Goby.

The four people sitting already were from Sections Ten and Eleven, making our table a grouping of Sections Eight, Nine, Ten, and Eleven. I scanned the remainder of the garden. There were a few other tables set up with a variety of groups. It was strange, though, as our table was the only one in numerical order. Also, it appeared as if there were four kids missing. I was sure this would be addressed, but it was definitely becoming clear that not everyone was going to make it through training.

As we all got situated, introductions were made around the table. The two from Section Nine were a nineteen-year-old boy named Brock and an eighteen-year-old girl named Brantley. The two from Section Ten were both boys. A twenty-year-old boy, Rook, and a twenty-one-year-old boy named Demps. Then there was Goby, who was nineteen, and an eighteen-year-old girl from his Section, Carina.

Goby started talking as food was dropped onto the table. "So, now that we all know each other, how did everyone do on the obstacle course?"

I looked around. Nobody seemed eager to talk, so I started in. "Did they give us a score? I mean, I was just happy to finish."

Everyone at the table shot glances at each other. I wasn't sure what was going on until Goby said, "You finished?"

This was the first I'd talked to anyone, apart from my brief conversation with Lancaster in the hallway, so maybe that wasn't the case for everyone. "Yeah. Didn't all of you finish too?"

Everyone at the table shook their heads. That explained why they told me I had done such a good job. I didn't realize that most people didn't complete the course. I just figured you kept going until you finished. Maybe there was a cutoff point. This had me curious as to how everyone else did.

"When did they stop you if you didn't make it? I ... I just kept pushing forward until the last station told me to exit."

Goby started first. "I was stopped in the hallway where the floor disappeared. I couldn't get across, and when I fell I thought I was going to die, but it was just a hologram. I fell into a pit of mud where I was stuck until everyone finished the course."

Lancaster spoke next. "I didn't make it across the long pool that we had to swim. Not much time for that back in Section Eight. I think I actually drowned before they pulled me out 'cause there's some blank spots in my memory."

Brock couldn't get past the first puzzle. He said that each time he got it wrong they replaced it with another question until they finally dropped the floor out from under him. He landed in a pit of that thick mud, where he waited until everyone was done to get dragged out. Rook and Demps both failed to get past the series of swings.

Brantley smiled, listening to Rook and Demps talk about their failure on the swings. They were quite humorous together. Almost like they were brothers arguing over who did better.

"I couldn't get past the station with the ball launcher," Brantley said. "I got hit three times and blacked out."

For the first time, I noticed the bandages that Brantley had. Her left shoulder was wrapped up, pressed tightly to her side. She had a cut under her left eye where she wore a skin-colored bandage. She was also starting to bruise under her right eye. Under other circumstances I would say she was quite beautiful; however, the events of this morning's obstacle course had ruined that for the time being.

The only person who didn't speak was Carina. Everyone now looked at her, wanting to know where her course had ended. She sunk into her chair as if all the eyes on her made her extremely nervous. Goby leaned over and whispered in her ear. She nodded her head and then whispered something into Goby's ear. He listened and then turned to the group.

"Carina doesn't like to talk in groups. She said she fell off the swings too. The last one was just too far to reach." Goby turned his attention back to me. "So, Dantin, seems like we should take some notes on how to do things from you."

I smiled, trying to hide my embarrassment. "I don't know about that. I just got lucky is all. I almost didn't make it through the pool. I can hardly use my hands. Not to mention the station that shot the balls all but knocked me out of commission. Just lucky is all."

Lancaster burst into the conversation with a tinge of anger in his voice. "Don't give me that crap, Dantin. He made it all the way through while helping me get over the first wall. His hands are ripped up because he had to help me get past the parallel rope stage. Not to mention you made it through the rest of those obstacles 'cause you're one of the toughest guys here."

The group clapped in approval of Lancaster's rant. Brock from Section Nine patted me on the back. "Way to go," he said. "You did good, man. Be excited."

I'd never liked being the center of attention. It was never something I aimed for. I could feel my face flush with embarrassment, but I forced a smile. I quietly mouthed "thanks" and then nodded my head slightly. I was hoping that was the end of their attention.

I tried not to talk much for the rest of lunch. I watched as the others carried on telling jokes, sharing stories from home, and discussing what they thought was going to happen next. Meanwhile, I just picked at the food on the table. I enjoyed the meal as well as being out in the sun. I didn't realize how different it was being underground all day. The breeze, the smells, and the heat all made me miss summertime in Section Eight. Then, just like that, our mealtime was over and we were herded, like cattle, back onto the small moving boxes, Goby called them elevators.

Once back underground, we were placed in the main assembly hall, where a man wearing all white stood on a small pedestal, ready to address us.

"Congratulations," the man said. "You are the twenty-eight candidates moving on. You will begin training shortly and be able to spend time in all areas necessary to be successful here. Your training groups will be composed of the people at the tables where you just ate. You will continue to work together as we move forward. Someone will be by shortly to direct you to your instructor. Again, congrahlations."

The man stepped down. I turned to our group that was already gathering. A small man cut through the crowd, appearing in front of us. He cleared his throat, gaining everyone's attention.

"Ladies and gentlemen, you will follow me to weapons training."

He led us out of the assembly hall and through a series of corridors. After what felt like an oddly large amount of turns, we arrived at a door labeled: FIRING RANGE. I could only assume this was our final destination as we all patiently stood waiting for something to happen. After a brief delay, the man knocked on the door, and it cracked open. Our small guide slipped his head in the crack, exchanging words with whoever was on the other side of the door.

The door slowly creaked open and our guide turned to us. "Right this way."

The group filed into the room. There were a number of stations set up, waiting for our arrival. Each station consisted of two different types of bows and a sheath of arrows. Our guide gestured toward the various numbered stations, and everyone moved cautiously toward them. Nobody really knew what to do since there hadn't been any instruction up to this point.

Everyone settled into their own station and began to look around at each other for what we were to do next. A man started to speak, causing the group to turn in unison.

"Good afternoon, group," he said. "You may be wondering why we would be working with bows and arrows. I'm sure at this point you have many questions that don't pertain to weapons at all. We will get to all of your questions in time. For now, all you need to know is that I am your firearms instructor and it is my goal to make you proficient in as many weapons as possible during your stay here. In combat situations, you may not always have control over what weapons are available to you.

"Today we will focus on a few different types of bows. I'm sure a lot of you are wondering, why not just shoot something with a gun? There are a number of situations where a bow may be a better alternative. For instance, there is a great amount of stealth that can be attained with a bow. Guns have a tendency to give away your position. As for this weapon, it is just as deadly, yet much quieter."

Our instructor grabbed a bow, drawing the string back and letting it go. The soft sound of the string snapping whipped through the air. He set the bow back down, surveying the group, sizing everyone up as he paced by. After a short study of everyone, he pointed us toward the shooting stations. Each station had two bows, but I noticed that the size of each bow varied with each person.

Our instructor moved behind the group where he could see everyone. "I want everyone to grab the smaller of the two bows. Hold the bow with your non-dominant hand."

Brock leaned back, looking over his shoulder. "Which hand is my non-dominant hand?" he asked.

"I don't know." The instructor seemed perturbed by the question. "Which hand do you throw or write with?"

Brock nodded. "OK," he said, picking up the bow with his right hand.

By now the instructor was right behind Brock. "It's the opposite of that."

Brock frowned slightly, switching the bow into his left hand. "Got it."

The instructor crossed his arms and continued his lesson. "Take an arrow with your free hand. Place the notch onto your string, resting the end of the arrow just above your grip. The hand that is holding your bow is your sight. You will use it to aim. Wherever that arm points, your arrow will go. Straighten it out and point it downrange. Now, using two fingers, one above and one below your arrow, pull the string back to your face. Release."

The group released, sending arrows flying downrange in all directions. If we were supposed to hit something with those arrows, we all just failed. The instructor seemed pleased enough, though, so I assumed we did something right. I looked out over the range, noticing that my arrow had traveled the farthest. I wasn't sure that meant anything; it was probably because I was the biggest of the group.

The instructor started in with the next portion of the lesson.

"Very good. Now that you have the basic mechanics to fire your weapon, it's time to learn how to aim. When you pull your arrow back, bring the string to your face and stare down the arrow where you're attempting to shoot. Then take a deep breath in and release the string."

I reached for my next arrow. This time as I loaded the arrow on the string I noticed a target about fifty feet downrange light up in the shape of a man.

Why does it look like a man? Why not an animal? Aren't we practicing to hunt? I guess they never did say anything about what we're using the weapons for.

There were target points that were highlighted as kill zones. I pulled my string back, looking down the arrow, locating my target. I took a couple of controlled breaths. Holding my breath, everything steadied, I released. The arrow soared, striking the target in what would have been their shoulder.

"Not bad, Fifteen. Keep working on it. Make your adjustments and go again. That's a pretty good non-kill shot. You would have taken down your target with that shot. Now work your way into one of the kill zones," the instructor said, moving down the line, watching the others shoot.

I reached for my next arrow as Carina drew back her bow. She stood tall, making her look very long and lean. Her hair, dark as night, fell just past shoulder length. Her bronze skin showed her muscle tone as she stood frozen with her arrow drawn. She let the arrow fly. I watched it strike the target center chest. Right in the middle of a kill zone. She smiled, pleased with herself. Goby nodded approval and then shot his own arrow downrange. It soared high and right, sailing past the target and clattering harmlessly to the floor.

The instructor patted Carina on the shoulder, making her look very uneasy. "Nice shot, Twenty-two. Excellent work." Shifting his focus to Goby, he spoke again. "Better keep working on your accuracy, Twenty-one."

It took a couple more shots before I felt comfortable aiming at the kill zones. It appeared that Carina, Brantley, and me were the top shooters in the group, each of us having hit the kill zones several times during this part of the practice. Brock was lucky to have his arrow fly forward and not back at him. Rook and Demps would hit the target pretty regularly but had very inconsistent groupings. Goby and Lancaster seemed to be making progress but would hit the kill zone one time and then send an arrow soaring way off-target the next.

The instructor clapped his hands, stealing our attention from the targets. "OK, group, nice work getting familiar with this first weapon. Tomorrow we will begin using your larger bow for longer-range targets. Be prepared to use this weapon tomorrow morning for your challenge. Nice work. Tinker will lead you to your next station: hand-to-hand combat."

The man from earlier reappeared. He waved us to the door, leading us back out through the maze of hallways. I was so turned around from all the different tunnels by now that I didn't know where I was being led. I thought we were headed back to the main assembly hall when we suddenly arrived at the door labeled COMBAT.

Tinker pushed the door open, and we followed behind him into the room, where the other group was still finishing their training. Two of the trainees were being highlighted; one held a gun while the other was unarmed. Number Eleven was the unarmed person in this scenario, but I couldn't see the number of the gunman.

Eleven had his hands in the air as the gunman approached, placing the barrel of the gun almost in contact with him. Then, faster than I'd ever seen another person move, Eleven punched the gun with his left palm while kicking the gunman in the chest with his right foot. The gunman collapsed to the ground, leaving Eleven holding the weapon. Eleven looked down at the fallen kid, then raised the back end of the gun and slammed it into his face.

Number Eleven raised the gun again for a second blow but was stopped by the instructor. The kid had started to bleed instantly from his head. A group of people rushed in, escorting the injured kid from the room while the rest of the group was dismissed. Eleven rejoined the group, and they were led out of the training room.

"That dude is an asshole," I whispered to Lancaster.

Lancaster laughed. "Yeah, but I'm not going to be the one to tell him."

I smiled at Lancaster as we gathered around our new instructor.

"Today, we are going to be learning to disarm an enemy," the instructor said. "With this, it obviously requires close-range movements and precise timing and speed. I'll pair you up to start, but we will rotate partners as we go to get a feel for different styles. OK, Fifteen and Seventeen: station one. Sixteen and Twenty-one: Two. Eighteen and Twenty-two: Three. Nineteen and Twenty: Four."

I was paired with Brock. We moved over to station one, where we waited for further instructions. This was the first time I noticed just how large Brock was. He was slightly taller than me but probably outweighed me by thirty pounds. His short blond hair was shaggy, falling in all directions, while his blue eyes looked gentle, unable to hurt a soul. Everything about him was intimidating until you looked into his eyes. He was exactly what I'd imagine my grandfather meant when he called someone a gentle giant or giant teddy bear. I didn't know him well enough to confirm that this was true, though.

The instructor began his lesson.

"We are going to start with a frontal disarmament. One person will play the attacker while the other will prepare to disarm."

I grabbed the fake gun, which was a rifle..

"Attacker will point the gun at the chest of their enemy," the instructor said. "To disarm, we must first move the barrel away from our chest. This is an important detail in all of our actions today. If you're going to attempt to disarm someone, you must clear the line of fire before any other movements can occur.

"Throw your hands up and to the right, grabbing the barrel, pushing it away from your body. While doing this, begin to step past your opponent, behind one of their legs. Drive your shoulder forward, sending them over your leg to the ground. Maintain your grip on the gun, yanking it away as they fall."

Our instructor rolled through the actions he just spoke about, demonstrating on an assistant who held the gun. He moved so fast and confidently that the disarming looked effortless.

After disarming the assistant he looked back at our group. "Any questions?" he asked. After a short pause, he said, "OK, begin."

I pointed the fake gun at Brock's chest. He stood there, arms up, looking at the barrel as if unsure what to do. I was about to ask if he wanted me to go first when the gun deflected away from his chest. Before I knew what had happened it felt like a sledge hammer had hit me in the chest, and I was on my back. I coughed as the wind escaped my lungs. Then I started to laugh, trying to shake off the pain.

Brock stood over me with a big smile on his face, extending a large paw down to me and helping me to my feet. "Did I do good?" he asked, so childlike.

I coughed out a few words: "Yeah, big guy, you did good."

He seemed very pleased. "Your turn?"

I shook my head. "Yeah, just give me a second. You hit harder than a bear."

After regaining my breath I found myself staring down the barrel of Brock's fake gun. His face was serious and almost stern. I cleared my head, preparing to make my move. I pushed the gun to the right, sliding my right leg behind his left, driving my shoulder forward into what felt like a cement wall. I found myself off-balance and exposed with my hands on the gun. Brock threw his hands forward, shoving me back on my heels and to the ground.

I didn't even have time to decipher what had just happened before I was being pulled up off the floor faster than I had just fallen. Back on my feet, I tried to think what I could possibly do to disarm a man of this size.

The gun was back at my chest, ready for another go. I wasn't going to be able to overpower him. I needed to use my quickness to throw him off-balance.

I swung both arms up from left to right, hitting the gun with my forearm. In the same motion I jumped around behind Brock, passing him on his right side, swinging myself up onto his back. I threw my weight backwards as I wrapped my arms around his neck in a chokehold under his throat. We both fell backwards and Brock landed on top of me. All of my remaining air wheezed out of my lungs, and it felt like I might pass out. I squeezed tight around his neck, hoping I could hold on just a few more seconds. My vision was beginning to narrow as the black inched in; I was on the verge of blacking out when I felt Brock tapping my arm.

I released the pressure and he rolled off of me as we both gasped for air. The instructor knelt down beside us. "Very nice improv, Fifteen. He's not an easy one to disarm. Be careful losing hold of the weapon, though. If you fail to choke him out, you're dead."

Our instructor got back to his feet and had us rotate to our next partner. Brantley stood in front of me. She really was quite beautiful, even with the bruises from the obstacle course the other day. She was fairly tall, probably 5'8" or 5'9". She had lightly tanned skin. Her green eyes bore right into mine. She had longer, sandy-colored hair, not quite brown or blonde. It was pulled back into a tight ponytail.

I started with the gun, aiming the rifle at her head. Brantley stood with her hands up just about ear height, elbows bent, looking defenseless but relaxed. Then, in one fluid motion, she lowered her body, grabbing the barrel of the gun with both hands and thrusting it upward. I fought to regain control of the weapon as she drove her knee into my gut while pulling the gun out of my grip. The air coughed from my lungs as I dropped back onto the floor.

"You all right there, big guy?" Brantley asked with a satisfied smile.

"I'll be fine," I said as I tried to smile back.

Tinker entered the room, indicating our time in hand-to-hand was over. Gaining everyone's attention, he moved us to the door. As we walked, he talked over his shoulder. "Next stop: weight training and conditioning." He smiled, perhaps thinking that this was fun.

If I was being honest, it hadn't been that bad. I felt like I was learning something, which was better than being forced to work in the Lumber Yard. And I had always enjoyed physical activity, whether it was on the playground with friends or our rec class in school.

We moved quickly through the corridor and back through the assembly hall. Passing by our quarters, we found ourselves back by the obstacle course from the other morning, where there were a few different stations set up.

Tinker smiled again. "Have fun. See you all in a little bit." Then he disappeared back out the door.

There were six stations set up for our training and conditioning. Station one was a rope about thirty-five feet high connected to the ceiling. The instructions were to climb without using our feet. There was a station with a small buggy filled with weight that we had to push a hundred feet. Then, there was an over-under wall station like the one from the obstacle course. Fourth on the list was a fake tree with minimal branches that we had to climb. The fifth station was fake tree trunks that were fifteen feet tall that we had to lift and flip over. Last was a set of parallel bars we had to climb across hand-over-hand.

It was similar to what we had to deal with during the obstacle course. I assumed we would have to do the course again at some point, especially considering that there were fewer people in the group now than there had been only a few hours ago. There were only so many ways to eliminate people from the group. At least that's what I was guessing.

The physical challenges were definitely my strength. All the years living in Section Eight and performing the physical labor of moving lumber, climbing trees and chopping them down had built up my upper body. Even before I was sent to work beyond the wall, I was asked to split wood as a regular part of my day since I was 12. I moved through the course with little difficulty, though the climb without my feet was slightly challenging as my hands started to bleed again. I had a feeling that by the time I was done here, my hands would be so hardened nothing would hurt them.

Rook and Demps moved swiftly through the majority of the climbing stations. Their smaller stature hurt them in the cart push and tree trunk flip. They found a way through them, but it was obvious that it was a strain. Goby and Lancaster were definitely the two weakest in the group. They both struggled with the climbing and lifting sections. However, I already knew that they were also the two smartest. I'm sure there was going to be a balance between how smart and how strong we were, otherwise people like them wouldn't have been chosen for The Conscript.

Brock was strong on the weighted challenges but he, too, struggled on the climbing portions, not having ever had to lift his own body weight. Carina and Brantley were extremely fluid in their movements when it came to the climb, making it look effortless. Unfortunately, their lack of size hurt them in the weighted challenges, Carina more so than Brantley.

There was only one more stop for training today, and I was starting to get a feel for what each individual's strengths were. It wasn't hard to see that the girls were very athletic and swift with their movements. Carina was the best shooter, Brock was the strongest, Goby and Lancaster were the smartest. I didn't feel like I was overly poor at anything, but I didn't really have a specialty. I didn't know if that was good or not. I guessed time would tell.

Tinker dismissed us from weight training, taking us to our final room. "All right, group, last station, then dinner. Time for some problem solving."

The room had three tables with three seats at each table, two spread apart from each other on one side and one on the other. We were each directed to a table.

"This will be your work packet today," our instructor said, placing a packet of paper facedown in front of each of us as he moved around the room. "When you flip it over there will be a couple of questions, which you will be asked to answer as quickly as possible. When you're done, flip your packet back over and set your writing tool down. You will be graded on speed and accuracy. Any questions?"

The room was silent as everyone waited for the go-ahead. The instructor scanned the room. "Good. Begin."

I turned over my packet. Page one had a word question on it with a small picture.

You have a 3-gallon jug and a 5-gallon jug. You need to measure exactly 7 gallons of water. How do you do it?

Huh? I reread the question. I looked up to see that everyone had already started writing. Everyone except Brock and me.

OK, so both full equals eight. If I fill up the three-gallon, dump it into the five-gallon and refill the three-gallon, that's six. Oh, what the hell? I scratched my head. I looked at the pictures of the three- and five-gallon jugs, which didn't help me at all.

OK, I think I got it. I wrote on my page: *Fill the five-gallon jug. Pour the water into the empty three-gallon jug. That leaves two gallons in the five-gallon jug. Dump out the three-gallon jug, pour the two gallons from the five-gallon into the three-gallon jug. Then fill up the five-gallon: seven!*

I turned the page, looking around the room as people turned another page ahead of me. Goby and Lancaster had already finished. They had their arms crossed and were looking around the room as everyone else worked. I turned my attention back to my page, knowing that I was going to have to continue to focus to get through this section. I was so worried about what everyone else was doing that it distracted me from the task at hand.

The next question read:

In this puzzle, three numbers — 16, 14, and 38 — need to be assigned to one of the rows of numbers below. To which row should each number be assigned? Hint: This is not a

mathematical problem. The numerical values are irrelevant.

A: 0, 6, 8, 9, 3

B: 15, 27, 21, 10, 19

C: 7, 1, 47, 11, 17

If this isn't a math problem then why are there numbers? I examined the rows. Row A, moving left to right had zero, six, eight, nine, and three. Row B had fifteen, twenty-seven, twenty-one, ten, and nineteen. Row C contained seven, one, forty-seven, eleven, and seventeen. *So where would sixteen, fourteen, and thirty-eight fit?* I stared so hard at the question I felt myself going cross-eyed. I looked up from my page. Brantley and Carina were done. So was Rook. Demps, Brock and I were still working. *Focus, Dantin!*

I shook my head, turning to the last question. *I'll come back to that one.* The last question sat on the page:

A man is trapped in a room with only two possible exits: two doors. Through the first door, there is a room constructed from magnifying glass. The blazing sun instantly fries anyone or anything that enters. Through the second door, there is a fire breathing dragon. How does the man escape?

Well, I know what I would do. Wait until nightfall, then exit through the magnifying glass room. It couldn't be that easy.

I thought about it. Were there any other options? I was sure there were, but nothing came to mind. I was so far behind everyone at this point that I just wrote down my first thought. *Hopefully that is right.*

Turning back to question two, I saw that Demps had now finished, leaving only Brock and me. Brock looked completely confused. It appeared he was still on page one. *At least I'm not going to finish last.* Then I felt bad for Brock. I'm sure he was so frustrated. The gentle giant of our group was definitely not a genius. Not that I had much room to talk.

I studied the second question again, trying to find anything at all that would make sense. Nothing seemed to work. I finally decided to guess. I wrote fourteen goes to A, sixteen goes to B and thirty-eight goes to C. I put my writing utensil down on top of my packet and sat back in my chair. The instructor came over, grabbing my work.

He scanned the pages, nodding, shaking his head, then nodding again. He turned to the middle page, setting it on the table. "Why did you choose these columns for the numbers?"

I paused. Should I tell him I guessed? "Well, to be honest, sir, I didn't know so I guessed."

He nodded, then pointed to the paper. "Watch!" He began to trace the numbers from Row A, making large, round movements for zero and six. Then using two circles joined to make the eight. Then swooping through the nine and three. He did the same motion over the thirty-eight. "All the numbers in row A are rounded shapes. See?"

I did; it clicked. I could see the pattern. I nodded. The instructor turned back to the page, pointing to Row B. "What goes here?"

I traced the numbers from B, then pointed to the sixteen. The instructor nodded. "Why?"

I looked up at him from my chair, "Because row B has a numbers with a mixture of curves and lines and so does sixteen."

"That's right." The instructor paused. "In the future during our practice sessions I'd rather you leave a question blank than guess. If you were to guess right, we would assume you know it and wouldn't spend time teaching you. These sessions are designed to keep you learning, and if you pretend to know something you'll only set yourself up for trouble later."

I nodded, a little embarrassed. "Yes, sir!"

The instructor stepped away from the table, addressing the whole room. "Very good job today. Please remember as you continue to train that you will not only need your physical abilities if you are to survive this training, you will also need your brain. I suggest you spend as much time challenging your mind as you do your body. We will continue tomorrow. You are dismissed for dinner now; Tinker will lead you up."

Survive? What did he mean by survive? Did he mean life and death or did he just mean making it through training? What happened to those who didn't advance in the training? Where did they go?

I needed to figure out how to solve these problems if I was going to make it through this. I knew I had what it took physically, but I always doubted my intelligence. My sister was always the smart one. I wondered what Micca was doing right now; I missed her and the rest of my family. I was worried I would never see them again.

It was the first time I feared what was to come.

CHAPTER 8

At dinner, I sat with the group. The night sky was clear and crisp. The fresh air felt good, even though it was slightly cool. Small lights were strung throughout the garden. It was a dim light, yet somehow it still felt bright, which didn't make sense to me. But my mind wasn't worried about the lights. I was still battling with the words from our last instructor. Everyone else seemed less concerned with his remarks, but I couldn't let it go.

"What do you think our instructor meant by 'survive'?" I asked, eager for some feedback.

Goby shook his head. "Well, we know not everyone makes it through training; he probably just meant completing the program."

"No, no that can't be it. I mean, why would he word it that way? You know, 'survive' indicates if we don't make it we're dead," I argued.

Brantley chimed in next. "There's no way they'd kill us all off during this. Why would they do that? They probably just get reassigned. What value would it provide to kill us?"

I shook my head, frustrated that nobody else could see what I saw. "What would they have us do? Nobody ever returns home from The Conscript. So, if we don't make it through training, why hasn't anyone ever returned home?"

Goby looked frustrated with my comments. "Even if we don't complete the training they can't afford to have us return to our Sections and tell others what happens here. It's in their best interest to reassign us and give us a life within Heart City. Just calm down and relax: getting chosen is a blessing."

I put my head down. *How can everyone feel this way? Why would he use "survive" if he didn't know something we don't?* "Is that how you all feel? That I'm overreacting? Brock?"

Brock looked up at me with a confused look on his face. "Huh? I dunno … maybe."

What? Maybe what? He's dumber than I am; why even ask him? I stopped thinking about it, putting my head down and ignoring the rest of the group while I ate dinner. The food was very good and put me a little bit at ease. I still didn't trust what was happening right now. I knew there were already four people no longer with us. If I could find out what happened to them, maybe I'd feel more comfortable.

Tinker arrived, dismissing us from dinner. "OK, everyone, back downstairs we have a movie and then bedtime." He led us back to the elevator.

I tapped Tinker's shoulder. "Tinker, what happened to the four kids who didn't pass the obstacle course this morning?"

Tinker's eyes showed some discomfort with the question, but his answer was confident and to the point. Almost as if scripted. "Those of you who do not progress during the training, we find a position for you that utilizes your strengths for Heart City."

Something felt off about his answer. I couldn't place it, so I decided not to question him anymore. I just nodded my head. He looked relieved that his answer was enough for me. For the time being it was enough. But I still wanted to know more. I needed to know more.

Back in the auditorium, another video illuminated the big screen in front of us. The film showed a number of the highlights of Heart City. Their science division, educational standards, advancements in cleaner fuel. All of these things that weren't shared with any of the Sections. Throughout the video, there were brief pauses in which images flashed on the screen. I couldn't tell what the images were or even if they were actually images. Just that the film was interrupted for a short moment.

After the video, I felt a little less upset. My curiosity over what happened to us if we failed training had subsided. I felt a renewed sense of purpose to serve Natio. Natio and Heart City needed us. They wouldn't discard us like garbage if we failed. Goby and the others were right. I was being irrational.

In my quarters, I prepared for bed. I showered again, getting myself cleaned up. After my shower, my ribs started to ache again. I found the ointment, applying a good amount to my ribcage. I also decided to rub some into my hands. If it was able to reduce pain in my ribs maybe it could help with my hands as well.

I finally finished prepping for bed and moved slowly across the room, where sitting on the side of the bed turned into more of a fall. After I crashed onto the bed, the lights flipped off, and the fatigue from the long day finally consumed me. I rolled onto my back, closing my eyes. I didn't even have time to think about anything before I was asleep, dreaming of my role within Natio.

*****

The next six days were the exact same. Every morning we would wake up to a disgusting drink that was our breakfast. After that, we were directed to the assembly hall to join our training groups. My group would go through morning sessions in the same order every day: weapons, hand-to-hand, weightlifting, and then problem solving.

Shortly after problem solving ended, we were directed above ground to lunch. We were left alone during lunch, free to relax and be ourselves for one hour. Then, we were pulled back underground and into our afternoon sessions. Same order as the morning, only advancing what we had worked on that morning. By the end of the first week, I felt as if we'd covered more in training than most people learn in a lifetime.

Every day ended with dinner outside followed by a video of some kind. They almost always showed the various ways that Heart City had saved us and advanced our people through their innovations, although there were two videos to show the dangers of old America and what could happen if we let Natio fall. By the end of the week, I felt my affection for Heart City and Natio growing stronger. I couldn't quite understand what had caused these feelings. We weren't treated all that great and they definitely worked us to the bone. My feelings were always strongest after our evening video.

On the morning of our seventh day, things changed. The routine that had become so comfortable was abandoned—well, not completely. There was still that nasty breakfast sitting on my dresser like clockwork. I had actually started to get used to its taste. It was hard to believe that I could get used to eating garbage. Apparently if you do anything long enough it becomes second nature.

After my morning rituals, we were led down the hallway to where the first day's obstacle course had been. The twenty-eight contestants stood bunched together, waiting for instructions. There was a small obstacle course laid out in front of us. It didn't seem to be nearly as large as the one from day one, and there were a few other changes to the course.

The same man who made all the announcements appeared in front of the group. "Ladies and gentlemen," he said. "Today is Challenge Day One. Today you will be asked to use all of the skills that we have been training you on to maneuver the course. You will be partnered up with someone from another training group. Scores will be recorded, so perform your best. You will be given a minute to prepare yourself, then we shall begin."

OK, competition day. I shook my head and arms while bouncing up and down on my toes. I did this when it was cold out in Section Eight to get my blood flowing. I figured it would work the same now to help wake me up. I needed to make sure my performance was strong. As curious as I was about those who didn't "survive" training, I wasn't ready to find out about it yet.

I was partnered up against Number Twenty-five. He was just a little shorter than me. He was very muscular with dark skin and eyes and hair that was cropped short. As we both stood in line waiting for our turn, we were able to watch those ahead of us move into the course. This was different from the first obstacle course, where we didn't know what was coming next.

I was able to make out four of the six stations without too much difficulty. There was an archery station first. It looked like after hitting five targets we would be able to move on. Next was a rope climb, exactly like in training. Then it appeared to be some problem solving, but that was one of the stations where I wasn't really sure what to expect. After that was a tree climb and parallel rope cross. Station Five was a weightlifting station, but I wasn't able to see what exactly was happening there. The last station was hand-to-hand combat.

That was the station everyone in line could see the best since it finished right next to the group as we waited. There was a huge advantage to being the first to finish the course. The fight began as soon as both contestants entered a circle that had been drawn on the floor, meaning the person to finish the course first could catch their breath and then use that to their advantage. It appeared that the goal was to complete a submission on your opponent.

Two groups left to go and I was up. I cleared my mind, trying to calm my nerves. I knew I was going to have to be physically and mentally sharp today. The more my head was cleared, the less likely I would be to lose time during the problem solving, which I already knew was going to be my weak spot. I believed it would be the difference between getting to rest before the hand-to-hand combat section and losing out on that recovery time.

One group before we were up. That's when I noticed Eleven waiting in the hand-to-hand zone. He hardly looked like he was breathing heavily. I looked through the course, trying to find who he was waiting for. It was Brock. He must have gotten held up during the problem solving. Or the archery. Neither were his strong points.

Brock finally entered the combat circle, breathing heavily from trying to make up time on Eleven. He bent over, hands on his knees, trying to compose himself. Eleven didn't give him a second to breathe, coming at Brock full bore, shooting in low and grabbing Brock around the waist. Brock grabbed Eleven, throwing him to the side like he was a rag doll.

Eleven hit the ground rolling, sliding to a stop. He didn't waste any time before he was back up on his feet, this time throwing punches, landing two to Brock's face: first a right cross to his cheek and then a left hook to his jaw. Brock stumbled back, putting his hands up in defense. Eleven was relentless, throwing body shots below Brock's guard followed by another left-right combo to Brock's face. Brock continued to retreat.

Brock was backed up to the edge of the circle as Eleven moved in on him again. Brock reached out with both of his large hands, clasping down on Eleven's shoulders. He picked Eleven up over his head and slammed him onto the ground. Eleven let out a gasp as the air left his lungs. *Yes! Kick his ass, Brock!* Eleven laid curled in a ball on the ground as Brock advanced. Brock had bent forward to deliver a second blow when Eleven struck Brock on his right knee.

The shriek that followed was terrifying. The sound echoed through the open space, causing those who weren't already watching to turn their attention. Eleven got to his feet as Brock was down on one knee grabbing his right leg. Eleven twisted to his right, winding up, then let a huge right hook fly. The shot sent Brock to the ground, landing face-first. The combination of the pain from his knee and the hit from Eleven left him unconscious.

It took three people to drag Brock from the combat zone. He was starting to come to, but there was still no getting him to walk on his own. I closed my eyes, shaking my head. Poor Brock, just didn't have enough to outlast him. I turned my attention back to the start of the obstacle course.

Twenty-five and I toed the starting line, waiting for the signal to start. The horn sounded, sending us racing forward. Twenty-five was extremely quick, reaching the first station before me. I reached for the first bow, loaded an arrow and then looked downrange. The first target swung back and forth on the same plane, roughly fifty feet downrange. I let my first arrow fly: direct hit.

I reloaded the bow. The next target was the size of an apple sitting on a pole. It appeared to be the same distance downrange as the first target, and it was a stationary object. This helped. I pulled the bow into the loaded position, letting the arrow go. It soared straight and true, piercing the second target. *Two for two*. I moved quickly for my third arrow. The target, which was about twenty feet away, bounced up and down and moved laterally.

I set my sight, aiming at a single height. A common mistake was to follow the target up and down. That was entirely too many planes to try to focus on. I moved from side to side, anticipating the target's drop. With the target at the bottom of its bouncing path, I released the arrow. Perfect contact. Another center impact.

I placed the bow on the table, glancing over at Twenty-five as I reached for the larger bow. He was still working on the second target. I had earned myself a small lead. I knew it would be important to extend that lead before reaching the problem-solving station. I quickly refocused on the remaining targets.

The next two targets were both over a hundred feet away. There was a stationary target first, roughly the size of a pumpkin. I pulled the bow back, aiming upward to allow for the distance. I released my fingers, holding my finishing position for a second as I watched the arrow arch across the range at my target. The arrow struck the target, landing in the very top zone.

I let out a small sigh. *A hit is a hit.* The last target moved slowly from side to side at the same distance. This target was a little bigger, about the size of a man's torso. I watched it float across the ground. The speed wasn't extremely fast, but at this distance it would be enough. I took my stance, pulling the bow into place. I angled up as well as in front of my intended target.

I released the arrow. It whistled through the air downrange. The target slid across the ground from left to right. Impact. The arrow met the target about halfway through its route, sticking into what we had classified in training as a kill zone. I let out a small smirk, then realized I had more stations to attend to. I put the bow back on the table, racing forward to Station Two.

I grabbed the rope, pulling myself up hand-over-hand, my fingers gripping into the twisted twine. My body moved swiftly up the twenty-five feet. After ringing the small bell at the top, I looked back at the archery station. Twenty-Five was just now moving to the long-distance targets. To save time I slid down the rope about ten feet and then let go, falling the last fifteen. I hit the ground, catching myself, then was off running forward to Station Three.

Station Three: problem solving. I reached the table, looking at the problem written on the table. There were four possible solutions. I shook my head. *Look at the question first, you idiot!* I scanned up to the top of the table:

Y is to the east of X which is to the north of Z. If P is to the south of Z, then in which direction of Y, is P?

The possible answers were:

North, South, Southeast, or None of these.

This question was perfect for me. It was one of the few areas of problem solving I was actually good with: direction. This was thanks to my father sneaking me around the dome, teaching me how to find my way around. *OK, so Y is east of X which is north of Z. That makes Z southwest of Y. Then P is south of Z, which only adds to the southwest direction. Southwest!* I looked for the answer: None of these! I slapped the button, changing it to green.

I sprinted off to Station Four just as Twenty-five arrived at the table. I climbed the fake tree quickly, as I had done so many times at home with real trees. Reaching the top, I stepped out onto the parallel ropes, sliding my hands and feet along the line. I reached the tree on the other side and began my descent. I was halfway down when Twenty-five began his climb of the first tree. He had answered the question quickly as well.

At Station Five, I found five fifty-pound bags of grain. I had to lift each bag and throw it twelve feet onto a platform. I grabbed the first bag, tossing it over my shoulder, then moved close to the platform and tried to push the bag upward. It was no use. I didn't have the strength to throw the bags like that. I took a few steps away from the wall while grabbing the corners of the bag. With my back to the platform, I slid the bag between my legs and then, jerking forward and upward, I swung it from between my legs and over my head.

I released the bag at the top of my swing, arching my back. The bag flew upward, landing on the platform. I grabbed the other bags, performing the same maneuver: Positioning myself at the edge of the platform. Sliding the bag between my legs. Rocking twice, swinging the bag to eye level and then letting it gain momentum with each swing. I let out a yell as I launched the second, third, fourth, and finally, fifth bag. Each bag landed on the ledge, meaning each throw had to surpass the last.

I was breathing heavily as I exited the lifting station. Twenty-five had almost caught up to me as I made my way into the combat arena. He had two bags left to throw as I passed into the circle. I put my hands on my knees, trying to catch my breath. Every second I had to breathe was an added bonus at this point. I knew once Twenty-five entered the arena I would have to move quickly and not let him catch his breath.

Just a few moments later Twenty-five entered the arena at a full sprint, moving right at me. He was determined not to let me catch him off-guard while he tried to catch his breath. He came at me quickly, lunging forward at my right leg. I lifted my leg, trying to avoid the takedown, and caught Twenty-five on the head with my knee. It was unintended yet very effective. The blow knocked him onto his back.

I could see he was disoriented. I moved into an advantage position on top of him, throwing punches at his face. I was punching rather wildly, landing one out of every four to five hits. My right landed on his forehead. Then, three punches later, a left to his nose. Twenty-five's eyes watered as blood started to run from his nose. He tried to retaliate, throwing a right cross that missed its mark.

The punch caused him to roll, giving his back to me. I clamped down around his mid-section with my legs, forcing him onto his stomach. He threw a wild right elbow, then a left. I avoided the major blows, allowing his shots to glance off me. I slid down on top of him, my arm locking under his neck. I felt my elbow slip under his chin; gripping my wrist with my left hand, I flexed. I could feel my arm dig in deep under his throat.

Twenty-five fought hard, trying to hold off blacking out. I was in deep, though, with my chokehold. I squeezed tight, shifting my weight forward, driving with my hips. The choke went deep and I could feel his fight slowly dissipating. A couple more seconds and there was a tap at my shoulder. He had submitted. If this were a real life-or-death battle I would have continued to squeeze, but today submission was the ultimate goal.

I stood up as Twenty-five rolled onto his back, gasping for air. Blood ran from his nose. His eyes were red from fighting for oxygen. I reached my hand down to him, helping him to his feet. He stood there next to me, bent over, still trying to get a grip on his breathing. I patted his back as I exited the combat arena and made my way into the viewing area with the rest of the trainees.

The groups that had already completed the course stood watching as the next set of combatants took off into the arena. Goby and Lancaster joined me on a bench in front of Station Five. Most people waited by Station Six to see who would win the fight. I didn't care to see the fights at this point, though. I was just happy to be done with my challenge for the day.

"Hey, Dantin, nice work in there," Lancaster said, patting me on the back. "You got through the problem solving really quick."

I smiled, knowing that however fast I was, it was nothing compared to Goby and him. "How did you do?"

Lancaster shook his head. "I did really good with all the challenges except this one," he said, gesturing to Station Five. "I just don't have enough strength. I was pretty spent after the rope climb. I won my fight, though."

I patted him on the back. "Way to go, buddy. I guess those tips in training paid off. How about you, Goby? How did it go?"

"I think I did OK. Definitely still need more work on my strength as well. I guess Lancaster and I are very much alike."

I smiled. As smart as Goby was, I'd known this after three seconds of talking to him. They could have been brothers they were so much alike. "Yeah, I would agree with you there. Very much alike!" I smiled up at him, letting out a soft chuckle.

I looked away from our conversation as Rook made his way to Station Five almost dead even with the guy from Section Sixteen. Rook made his way to the bags, dragging them over to the platform one at a time. He then utilized the same technique that I had, swinging the bags and launching them over his head onto the platform. It took him a couple of tries to get three of the bags, but he still made good time, pulling a little ahead of his opponent.

I moved my attention back to Lancaster and Goby. "Have any of the others finished the course besides Brock?"

Goby nodded. "Yeah, all of the others are done except Brantley. She still has to go."

I looked around the crowd, trying to find the rest of the group. "Well, where is everyone else? Is Brock OK?"

Lancaster shrugged his shoulders. "I'm not sure where Brock is. He was taken to get fixed up after his fight with Eleven. Demps and Carina were over by Station One earlier. Oh, there they are." Lancaster pointed at the two of them as they walked over to us.

Demps smiled as he closed in on us. "Hello, gang. Resting up, are we?"

Goby pointed to the combat arena. "Rook just entered the arena."

Demps' smile faded as he moved quickly to Station Six. Carina sat down on the bench between Goby and me. She smiled at me. "Nice job in there, Dantin. You looked better than anyone else I've seen. I was the first to go, so I've gotten to see everyone else go too."

"Thanks," I said shyly. I'm not sure why I didn't feel comfortable taking praise, even from friends. Maybe it was because I didn't get a lot of it back in Section Eight. "How did you do?"

"I did OK, I think. I passed all of the stations without too much difficulty. The combat zone was tough. I found a way to get a submission, though, so I hope that was good enough."

I looked at Carina, and her dark eyes locked with mine. "I'm sure you did great. I think if you completed all of the stations well and won your fight you did real good."

Carina smiled. She looked much younger than eighteen. It was sad to think that someone like her was forced to be here. Not that life back in the Sections was any easier or better, but to be ripped away from your family like that, it just wasn't fair.

Especially for someone as sweet as Carina. This place didn't feel like a place for someone like her.

I looked back to the course. Brantley was entering Station Five. She had pulled ahead of her opponent by quite a ways. I looked back along the course, trying to locate her. The girl was still on the problem solving station. Brantley didn't waste any time flying through the bag toss, her muscles flexing, showing her definition with each toss. It still amazed me each time I saw how muscular she was. She was probably the most athletic of all the female trainees.

Brantley was so far ahead that by the time her opponent made it to the combat arena, she had fully recovered. It was a quick and almost effortless fight. Brantley's fluid movements and size were all too much for the girl from Section One. The fight lasted all of thirty-five seconds. As Brantley left the arena a loud horn sounded, causing the entire group to turn.

"Great work this morning, everyone," said the man who had given us our pre-challenge instructions. "You all are dismissed to your quarters to clean up. Please make your way back to your quarters the way we entered. After you finish getting cleaned up you are welcome to return upstairs for lunch. We will resume training following lunch. Again, good work. Thank you!" The man scurried off the stage as the group migrated back to the entrance.

I moved slowly once back in my room. The challenge took more out of me than I'd initially thought. I must have been riding high from the adrenaline. It took me several minutes just to get my shower going. If it weren't for the announcement every five minutes counting down to lunchtime, I probably would have fallen asleep. But there wasn't time for that today. Only five more minutes before everyone was to report to the surface for lunch.

Up top it was another beautiful day. The sun was shining and the air was moderately warm. It was a comfortable day with a soft, cool breeze. I loved being outside. It was disappointing that we only got two times a day in the fresh air.

At our table, Goby and Carina were already eating. Lancaster and I joined them. More food arrived as Brantley and Demps pulled up seats.

"Where's Brock and Rook?" I asked them.

Brantley and Demps looked at each other and then back at me. Demps shrugged. "I don't know," he said. "The door to his room opened with the rest of ours, but he wasn't inside. I assumed he had already come up."

Brantley's eyes met mine. "Maybe they're still in the infirmary?"

Lunch passed quickly and more quietly than usual. The group seemed concerned with the absence of two of its members. I wasn't hungry. The missing group members combined with the re-emergence of my "what happens to those who don't complete training?" question made the food taste bland. I picked at a piece of bread, forcing down a little food since I knew I wouldn't eat again until dinner.

After lunch ended, we were gathered together in the assembly hall. The Training Speaker, as we had started to call him, addressed the group. "Congratulations, Chosen Ones, you have completed the first week of your training. You twenty-four will continue with your training as scheduled. Keep up the good work!"

So we're down to twenty-four. Four more gone. There was a small stir this time among the crowd at the announcement of four more trainees being dismissed. Perhaps it was because now we had begun to get to know each other. I looked around the group as others seemed to have looks of concern. I still needed to know: *What happens to those who don't make it? Where are the four who were eliminated this time?*

The remainder of training that day went by without much excitement. Brantley and Demps were distracted during most of the drills. The loss of Brock and Rook affected them the most. The rest of the group performed with a lackluster level of enthusiasm and effort as well. This was the first time the group seemed to be at odds with our situation. At dinner, everyone was on edge.

I leaned over the table. "So, does anyone else want to question what happens to us if we fail to complete the training?"

Brantley reached across the table, punching me in the face. "They're fine, just reassigned!"

"Damn it, Brantley," I said, covering my eye where she hit me. "Listen, I'm upset about the loss of Brock and Rook too. I just think it's time we consider that there is no reassignment."

The table almost seemed to be in agreement with me when Tinker appeared. He handed letters to Brantley and Demps, saying, "These are from Brock and Rook."

Brantley ripped open the letter, scanning it quickly with her eyes. A small smile started to form. "Brock is fine! He's been reassigned to a manual labor position to accentuate his strengths."

I looked at Brantley, confused. The timing of this letter was too perfect. "Did Brock use the word 'accentuate'?"

"Yes, it's right here in the letter."

"I'm not trying to be disrespectful"—I was also not trying to get hit again—"but do you think Brock would ever choose to use that word?"

Brantley looked back at the letter, considering my words, then glared at me. "I don't know. Maybe they helped him with the letter. It's in his handwriting, though. What more do you want?"

"Look, I hope Brock and Rook are alive as much as the rest of you," I said. "I'd just like to see them is all. That letter doesn't prove anything." I was frustrated by how much trust everyone was showing that their friends were OK.

"They're OK, Dantin. Just be happy for them!" Brantley's eyes were filled with tears masked by rage by this point. "What does your letter say, Demps?"

Demps looked down at his letter. "It says that he has been reassigned to the science division to test the new products. This is definitely something Rook would be good at—he has no fear of anything, always willing to try something once." There was a tinge of doubt in Demps' voice.

I decided not to press the issue. "I hope you're right. I really do."

Brantley slammed her fist into the table. "We are right!"

"OK." I put my doubts aside and ate my dinner.

Maybe they all just need some hope to hold onto.

CHAPTER 9

The week passed and so did some of the tension. The group slowly started to get back to a normal routine, which was probably partly due to the increased intensity of training. Weapons training shifted away from bows to throwing knives, axes, and pistols. The presence of guards also increased during weapons training. During combat training, we learned advanced takedowns, sword fighting, and how to use staffs. Problem solving was still a point of struggle for me; however, I continued to excel in strength training.

It was the night before the next challenge event, and while the group tried to present an appearance of being relaxed, you could tell there was tension building as we ate. The groups tried to keep things light, but the impending challenge loomed large, stealing everyone's attention.

"So, what do you think we'll be asked to do tomorrow?" Goby asked the group.

Lancaster spoke up first. "I'm not sure, but training sure has picked up this week."

Brantley chimed in next. "I overheard one of the other kids saying they think there will be more people in the groups competing tomorrow. I'm not sure how many, but from what the people I was talking to said they are going to try to put you against other people of similar skill."

Goby looked at me. "If that's true, you'll have to go up against Eleven, Dantin. You two have been the top performers so far."

I shrugged. "I guess so. I guess we won't know until tomorrow."

Brantley's eyes narrowed. "What's your problem?"

I was taken by surprise by Brantley's attack. "No problem; I'd just rather spend our dinner talking about other stuff than what's going to happen tomorrow. This could be our last night together. Wouldn't it be nice to just talk, enjoy the evening? While we still can."

Carina smiled. "I agree with Dantin. I didn't have many friends back home, and you guys have become better friends than I've ever had. We spend every day together, and I don't want to spend my last night talking about things we can't control. I mean, if it is my last night."

Lancaster, as if reading our minds, started in: "What do you think everyone is doing back home?"

I smiled. "Well, I know what's going on with my family. Mom's cooking or cleaning, trying to keep her mind off everything else happening around the dome. Micca probably has her face buried in a book, and Grandpa is probably throwing a fit about something!" I laughed a little at the thought.

Lancaster let out a little laugh as well. "Yeah, your grandpa always did seem fiery."

"Fiery is an understatement," I laughed.

Demps smiled a little. "Sounds like you have a nice family back home. I have two little brothers. The weather is starting to change back home so they'll be out stirring up all kinds of trouble. I swear I was saving their butts every other day."

The thoughts of home had everyone at the table smiling. The mood had shifted from doubt and dread of things to come to memories of better times. I scanned the table as everyone seemed to be enjoying the brief moment of happy thoughts. All except Brantley. She sat staring at the table, face long and almost sad.

I stood, moving around next to her. "Are you OK?" I asked softly, trying not to take away from everyone's moment.

Brantley's eyes looked up at me filled with tears. "Yeah, I'm OK."

"What is it?" I asked, placing my hand on her back.

She spoke, her words shaky. "When I was taken, my father and brother tried to stop them. My brother even tried to volunteer himself in my place. Things got out of control and ..." she looked away, eyes welling up with tears. "They beat them and then dragged me away. I don't even know if they're OK. I don't know anything and there's no helping them from here. I'll never see them again."

I moved my arm around her shoulder. "You're not alone, Brantley. We're here with you, and I'm going to tell you what my Grandpa told me before I left. Do what you need to do to survive and find your way home! If we get through this, we can find our way back. We can be the first."

Brantley smiled through the tears. "Do you think so?"

I smiled back at her. "I know so."

Brantley grabbed me, wrapping her arms around my neck. Tears fell from her face, landing on my shoulder. She sobbed quietly as a spot began to soak through my shirt. She squeezed me tight and I matched her intensity. It felt good to hug. I hadn't hugged anyone since my last night in Section Eight. I was used to getting at least a couple of hugs a day back home. In this moment, I felt my mind drift away and I was back in Section Eight.

Brantley sighed slightly. "Thank you."

Still hugging Brantley I responded, "You're welcome. That's what friends are for."

We pulled apart to find the rest of the group now watching us, wondering what had just happened.

Goby looked at me. "I want a hug now!"

Just as soon as he finished his sentence, Carina grabbed him, wrapping her arms around him. Their eyes squeezed shut as they held each other tight for a second before pulling apart. Demps seemed to be feeling the love as well as he turned to Lancaster with his arms extended.

Lancaster shrugged his shoulders. "Why not?" He pulled in tight, giving Demps a hug.

The entire table laughed as the two guys hugged each other. The mood was definitely lighter for the remainder of dinner. There was a renewed sense of hope that had been gone all week following the loss of Brock and Rook. Everyone ate until their bellies could hold no more. After dinner, we were led to the theater room for our evening movie and then sent to bed.

In my quarters I lay on my bed in the dark. I felt exhausted, but I couldn't sleep. My mind wandered, thinking of home, the group, and things to come in training. I gazed at the ceiling in the darkness. I wished I had my ball. I'd throw that thing at the ceiling for hours. It always helped to calm me down. Right now that would be helpful. I knew I needed to get some sleep; tomorrow was another Challenge Day. I had to be on my game.

My mind continued to wander until I drifted off to sleep. The night flew by in what felt like mere minutes. Unfortunately it didn't feel like a restful sleep. I was quickly startled awake and it was time to get my game face on. The morning routine had become automatic. Same thick beverage breakfast. The doors flying open. Lancaster standing across the hall. Then the short walk to the training arena. Today was a little different, though. As we entered into the arena we were directed into one of four groups. I was directed to the right, and Lancaster was pushed left.

As the remainder of the trainees entered the room, I started to notice the groups were equal in size: six contestants in each. Lancaster and Goby were together in one group. Carina and Brantley were together in another. Demps and I were alone in our respective groups. The groups quickly became silent as the Training Speaker took his position.

"Good morning, everyone," he said. "As you can see, today you have been divided into four distinct groups. The challenge today plays to your particular area of weakness. We all have weaknesses, and today we will challenge you in yours."

I stopped listening as the Training Speaker continued with his speech. I already knew what my group would be asked to do: more problem solving. This meant all my physical strength would count for nothing against my group. The only thing I could hope for was that it was as much of a weakness for everyone else.

I looked around at the other groups. Lancaster and Goby were in the hand-to-hand combat group. That was appropriate. The only other group they would fit into would be weightlifting, but there were others weaker than they were. I could have used a little of their brains today; too bad there was no group help there.

Carina and Brantley were in the weightlifting and conditioning group, not because they weren't strong in their own right, but because they didn't give the girls much help when it came to changing the weights they were required to lift. That made the majority of the weighted objects a large challenge for the girls, which explained why four of the six members of that group were girls.

Demps was in the weapons group. This was definitely his weakest point, but he was very well-rounded when it came to his skills: not really one to stand out in any department but also not too weak in any area. I felt like he was going to be fine in that group. I had seen some of the others with weapons. They would be better off throwing their bows at the enemy instead of trying to shoot them. At least Demps could hit a target.

The Training Speaker finished his morning monologue, dismissing us. They had the course set up so the groups could watch the others while they attempted to complete the challenge. I'm not sure why they wanted to take the extra time to allow us to watch when they could have been done with the day's challenge quicker if they just let us all go at one time. I wasn't too upset, though; I was curious to see how my friends would do.

The first to go was the weapons group. Demps took his position on the range with the five others in his group. Each person had a lane with three weapons to use. First weapon up was the bow. Then a pistol. Last was what looked like throwing knives. The group was ordered to the ready, there was a short pause, and then the horn sounded.

Demps picked up his bow, loading an arrow. A target appeared downrange, sliding side to side on the same plane. Demps pulled the bow back, letting his first arrow fly. Contact! The number one flashed up above his position on the range. The rest of the group had a number above them as well, indicating the number of hits.

After four targets with the bow, it was on to the pistol. Six targets snapped up. Demps fired slowly, lining up his targets, hitting the first two before the remaining targets disappeared. It was timed. I hoped he realized he was going to have to shoot faster. The next set of six targets appeared. Demps started firing, trying to adjust his shots on the fly. This time he hit four before the targets disappeared.

Demps moved quickly, dropping the clip from his gun, grabbing another and slamming it in place. The gun clicked just as the next round of targets appeared. Wasting no time, he opened fire. Four out of six again. That was the last round with the pistol. Demps placed the gun down, grabbing the knives.

I scanned the scores: Demps had thirteen. A kid from Section Three had fourteen, but other than that there was some terrible shooting going on. The other scores were eight, four, four, and three. Demps was not going to finish last even if he didn't hit any more targets. The three kids battling to not be last had better focus on this final part.

Demps finished strong, hitting three out of five targets with the throwing knives, finishing with a score of sixteen. That was good enough for second place in the heat. A kid from

Section Two finished last with a final score of four. He was unable to hit any targets with the throwing knives. He was escorted off one way while the rest of the group was brought back to the viewing area. It was interesting to see how quickly they moved the last-place person away from the rest of the group.

Weightlifting and conditioning was next up. Carina and Brantley moved slowly into the arena. Brantley definitely stood out in this group. I looked over the course, trying to see what challenges they would have to complete.

The course wasn't overly long. There was a weight pull or push, depending on how you wanted to move it. The small carriage was to be moved fifty feet. Then there was a tree climb followed by a set of swing jumps. After that there was another tree climb to get down. Then a cargo net climb with a parallel rope cross. At the platform on the other side it looked like they were supposed to jump down into a pool. Last was a rope climb for twenty-five feet.

I knew Brantley was going to be fine, but I was initially concerned about Carina. Luckily, this course was actually suited to her strengths. While her overall strength wasn't great, she did move her own body weight well and was an excellent climber. This was about as good a setup as I could have hoped for for her.

The course was set up to have everyone go at the same time. It was going to be a race. The horn blared, sending everyone into a sprint to the first station. Brantley pressed her back to the carriage as the wheels turned. She created a little momentum then quickly turned, putting her hands on the carriage, pushing it the fifty feet without too much difficulty. She was already twenty feet out in front.

Carina struggled getting the carriage started, but once it started rolling she seemed to pick up speed. She finished third behind a boy from Section Fifteen. Two girls, one from Section Thirteen and one from Section Five, were behind Carina. A small boy from Section Six brought up the rear. I wonder how he'd even survived this long.

Carina started her tree climb as Brantley was coming down the other side. Brantley had opened up her lead even more during the swing portion. Carina moved swiftly to the top but hesitated before starting out onto the swings. This was where she had struggled during the opening day obstacle course. As she paused, the girl from Section Thirteen passed her, grabbing onto the first swing. She swung twice before flying to the second swing.

Carina grabbed the empty swing, rocking back and forth. She kicked hard, letting go. Flying forward, her hands grabbed the second swing, but her momentum was too much to control. Her hands slipped as she lost her grip, falling back to the ground. Luckily they had padded the landing zone. Even though they were trying to eliminate people, they didn't want them to go out like that.

The small boy from Section Six was now ahead of Carina as the fall had sent her all the way into last place. She made her way back to the tree, climbing quickly to the top. The boy from Six wasted no time flying across the swings. I guessed that was how he'd survived this long: he was very fast using his own body weight. Carina took a deep breath and swung out on the swing again, this time maneuvering across the section with little difficulty.

Brantley was already jumping off of the platform into the pool as Carina exited the tree climb. Carina had made up a little time from her fall by the time she reached the cargo net. The girl from Section Five was about halfway up. The boy from Six was just starting as Carina reached for the net. The boy from Six was fast, flying up the net, passing the girl from Five. Carina fought, reaching the top just after the girl from Five. There were four sets of parallel ropes to cross so each person could have their own if multiple people were at the top at the same time.

The boy from Six was starting to pull away now. He moved quickly and with little difficulty across the parallel ropes and onto the next platform. If Carina was going to avoid finishing last she was going to have to pass the girl from Five. They were just about even at the halfway point of the rope cross. The girl from Five seemed to know this and, trying to move quicker, she slipped and lost her footing. Carina moved quickly just ahead of her.

Brantley finished the course in first place as Carina reached the platform. Carina wasted no time moving to the edge, jumping off into the pool. A short swim to the other side and she was out of the pool. The last obstacle was the rope climb. The boy from Fifteen had finished just behind Brantley, and the girl from Thirteen was done as well. The boy from Six was halfway to the top of the rope as Carina started her climb. The girl from Five was right behind her.

The two battled next to each other on their ropes, struggling with wet hands to get a grip as they fought their way up the climb. Carina held a small lead but it wasn't nearly enough to feel safe. For the first time, you could see the determination on her face as she pulled with all her might. There were only five more feet to go. Then Carina's hand slipped, causing her to slide down a couple of feet. The race was deadlocked now.

The two pulled at their ropes, propelling their bodies upward. Only two feet left and the girl from five began to reach for the bell that marked the finish. She swiped with her hand, but she had started her reach too soon. She wasn't close enough and the miss caused her to lose her grip a little, opening a window for Carina as she made two more strong pulls and slapped the bell. The horn sounded as the two competitors slid back to earth.

Brantley gave Carina a big hug as she reached the ground. Then they made their way with the rest of the group back to the viewing area as the girl from Section Five was taken off in the same direction as the kid from the earlier competition. The next group up was problem solving. Go time. I moved forward into the arena. There were six tables set up for each of the contestants.

I looked around, not recognizing any of the other kids except Eleven. He was in the same group as me. I didn't want to assume that he struggled with this as much as I did, just that it was his weakest area. There were no girls in this group. I should have known that. The girls in Section Eight were always more educated because the guys were often forced to work even before placement at eighteen. I assumed this was probably true in the other Sections as well.

I pulled up a seat at one of the tables where I could see all the other contestants. This way I could know if any of the others finished. I didn't know if this was a good idea or not. It could cause me to freeze up or to rush through the packet. I needed to know, though. I pressed my fist into my hand, cracking the knuckles on my left hand, then my right. I turned my head side to side next, cracking my neck. I was ready.

The horn sounded as I pulled the first page back, revealing the first question:

Each of the following questions is based on the following information: Six apartments on a floor in two rows facing north and south are allotted to P, Q, R, S, T, and U. Q gets a north-facing apartment and is not next to S. S and U get diagonally opposite apartments. R is next to U and gets a south-facing apartment and T gets a north-facing apartment.

There were four questions using that information. I drew a map on the page indicating that the apartments of P, R, and U faced south while S, T and Q got north-facing apartments. Question one:

If the flats of P and T are interchanged then whose flat will be next to that of U?

OK, so if you switch P and T then P faces north and T south, but that doesn't change that R is next to U. I scribbled "R" on the page. Moving on to question two. The questions for this section weren't too difficult. I completed all four relatively quickly and turned to page two. I looked up to see how everyone else was doing. It was hard to tell where anyone else was, though, as they all had their faces buried in their work.

Page two. The next question was number reasoning:

Look at this series: 7, 10, 8, 11, 9, 12, ... What number should come next?

This is a weird series. Small number, big number, small number, big number ... seven to ten is plus three, ten to eight is minus two. That's it! The next number should be twelve minus two which is ten again. I scribbled down ten.

I was moving well so far. I felt good about my pace. I moved on to the next question:

Choose the correct alternative that will continue the same pattern and replace the question mark in the given series. 589654237, 89654237, 8965423, 965423, ?

Oh, hell. I hate big numbers. I felt my eyes cross trying to look at the numbers. I blinked hard, trying to regain my focus on the task, trying to find a pattern. *Each number is definitely smaller. And it looks like the majority of the digits are still the same.* I looked over the numbers again. They were all the same, minus one number. First from the beginning of the sequence and then from the end.

I got it! I wrote down 96542. Taking off the three in the last sequence gave me the answer. Only one more question on this page. I began reading the numbers:

In the series 2, 6, 18, 54, ... what will be the 8th term ?

Eighth term? What's wrong with knowing the fifth term? Stupid question.

I put my elbows on the table, pressing my hands to my head. My brain felt like it was in overdrive. It was about to overheat from all the use.

I'm not a thinker. I never will be.

Shut up! Focus.

It didn't help; all of this problem solving was making me go crazy. I honestly didn't know what to do anymore. I just sat there, looking at the numbers as they blurred in and out of focus.

Focus, stupid! Let's go; you can do this.

I ran through a number of different scenarios coming up empty for a solution. *What if two times three is six, then six times three is eighteen and eighteen times three is fifty-four. That's it! OK, so fifty-four times two is one hundred eight plus fifty-four is one hundred sixty-two. Oh, hell, this is getting hard. One hundred sixty-two times two would then be three hundred twenty-four plus one hundred sixty-two is four hundred eighty-six. Only two more to go; great!* I scribbled on the paper, multiplying the next two numbers by three. 1,458 multiplied by three was my answer: 4,374.

I turned the page, revealing the next set of questions. *Last page.* I looked up, checking the room. There were three people done. They sat with their arms crossed, watching the rest of the group. A kid from Section One, Eleven and I were still working. I looked back to my page, trying to regain as much focus as I could. I knew I was cutting it close with my struggles on the last page. I took a deep breath—*time to focus up*—only a couple more questions.

The next question contained a combination of numbers and letters in boxes. There were three boxes across and five boxes down. The top line of boxes had 3, P, 8. The next four rows were: 9, G, 11; 2, U, 4; 3, W, 1; 7, ?, 18. The far left column and far right column were numbers. The middle column was letters. The question mark represented a missing letter.

I wrote out the alphabet A-Z, circling the letters that were already being used. P is the sixteenth letter, G is the seventh letter, U is the twenty-first, and W is the twenty-third letter.

There is no way to make the numbers match up.

I looked at the numbers and letters again. *OK, the U and W have small numbers, so maybe it's reverse value. So, Z equals 1; Y: 2; X: 3; and W:4. Three and one, added together equals four. YES!*

I rearranged the values of the letters, listing them in reverse from Z to A. *Adding seven to eighteen equals twenty-five so the answer would have to be B!* I wrote down the B, moving on to question two on the page. *Only two more to go.* I looked up and saw that Eleven had finished. It was down to me and the kid from Section One. I had to bear down. *Only two questions left.*

The next question had a similar setup. The left column was all letters, the middle was numbers and the right was letters: N, 252, R; T, 500, Y; Y, 400, P; K, 132, L; and G, 182, ?.

I looked at the letters and numbers, starting with the two spaces that had the Y. I looked at my letter values from the last question starting with the "A equals one" table. *T equals twenty, Y equals twenty-five and P equals sixteen. The middle numbers, five hundred and four hundred. Twenty multiplied by twenty-five is five hundred and sixteen multiplied by twenty-five equals four hundred. This one is easy.*

I moved to the bottom of the page: *One hundred eighty-two divided by G, which equals seven, will give me my answer.* I wrote out the division problem on the page and got twenty-six. The answer was Z, which I wrote down before moving quickly to the last question. I had to keep moving. I didn't even bother to look up to see where the kid from Section One was.

The last question had six triangles lined up on top of each other. Starting from the top and moving down, the numbers were three, five, eight, thirteen, and twenty-two, and the last triangle had a question mark. I looked over the values in the triangles. It seemed simple at first: *three plus five is eight and eight plus five is thirteen, but then eight plus thirteen is not twenty-two.*

I looked back to the top, trying another pattern. I doubled each number: *Three doubled is six. So if I subtract one, that's five. But then five doubled is ten. Well, if I subtract two, that's eight. So if I double eight and subtract three that should be thirteen —which it is.*

I found my pattern!

I took the final number, doubling it and subtracting five. That gave me thirty-nine, which I wrote down on the page quickly. Slamming my writing utensil onto the page and pulling away from the table, I looked up. The kid from Section One sat watching me with a small hint of a smile on his face.

I was last. I was about to find out what happened to those who didn't complete training.

I felt my heart drop. I pulled my chair back toward the table. Placing my elbows on the table, I buried my face in my hands. I felt a rise in emotions beginning to build. I didn't want anyone to see me start to lose it so I leaned back in my chair, taking a deep breath. I tried to steady myself as I sat, waiting to be directed through the door with the losers of the first two competitions.

Six men entered the arena, each moving to a table. They each grabbed one of the booklets on the tables, flipping through the pages. The guy at my table sifted through the pages and chicken scratches, then put the packet back on the table, giving a thumbs-up. I watched as the men put down the other booklets, all giving a thumbs-up. The guy looking over the work for the guy from Section One was last. He set down the booklet and then shook his head.

The five other men joined him at the table, each looking at the booklet. Then in unison they all turned, shaking their heads as well. *He must have missed a question.* The boy from Section One was escorted out as we were told to head into the viewing area. I didn't realize how hard my heart had been pounding, thinking I had been eliminated. But now as it calmed down, I could feel myself starting to relax as I moved, still in a daze over what had just happened.

I was, luckily, still in the group. But that was so much closer than I wanted. I honestly should have been eliminated. If it weren't for a mistake from the kid from Section One, I would have been. I took a deep breath, trying to calm myself down as the horn sounded to start the next group. I snapped my head up just in time to see the six kids facing off with each other. Goby was lined up across from a kid from Section Seven. Lancaster was against a girl from Section Seven. Then the guy from Section Twelve faced off with a guy from Section Two.

The horn sounded as the contestants began to fight. Goby moved quickly, taking out the kid from Section Seven. Goby was actually bigger than him, which was a rare scenario for him.

Lancaster had a little bit more trouble with his opponent. Knowing him, I think part of the problem was he didn't want to hit the girl from Section Seven. She didn't share Lancaster's reservations. It wasn't long before she had him in a chokehold, causing him to tap out.

The guy from Section Two was a little bigger than his opponent from Section Twelve. That didn't slow down the kid from Twelve one bit, though. He landed multiple combos on the kid from Two and controlled the tempo of the fight from the onset. After a few more punches, the kid from Twelve threw his fist into the right knee of the kid from Two, taking him down. That's when he maneuvered himself into an attack position mounted on top of his Section Two foe. The kid from Two didn't fight back. He just lay there with his hands over his face.

The horn sounded, ending the first round of fights. Goby, the girl from Seven, and the guy from Twelve were escorted from the arena. Lancaster was asked to fight the kid from Two next. Lancaster pushed in on the kid, pressing the action. The kid from Two was banged up pretty good from his last fight, and Lancaster used that to his advantage. He attacked the kid's already cut eye, working the left side of his face.

The kid went on the defense really early in the fight, allowing for Lancaster to control the pace. He pressed in on the boy, moving at his banged-up eye, taking him to the ground with a leg sweep. The kid fell, rolling onto his stomach. Lancaster quickly dropped on top of him, landing an elbow to the back of his head. Then, slipping his arm under the kid's chin, Lancaster finished him off with a chokehold. Two tapped Lancaster, signaling defeat. Lancaster let go and quickly hopped to his feet. The boy from two just lay there, completely exhausted from two defeats.

Unfortunately, the kid from Two wasn't done yet. He had one more fight to go, against the boy from Section Seven. It didn't matter at this point; he was already mentally defeated. He carried himself with no confidence: head down, shoulders sunk forward, barely defending himself. He seemed to know his time was close to an end. The kid from Seven knew this too. He moved quickly on the offensive, wasting no time taking the kid from Two to the ground.

There was little fight left in the kid from Two, just a punch here or an elbow there, with no accuracy. The kid from

Seven moved to avoid a flailing elbow and then caught the smaller boy from Two with a stiff jab. That was it: the kid from two stopped moving. The accumulating blows combined with the accuracy of the most recent hit were clearly enough. He was unconscious. The kid from Seven stood up, leaving the boy from two lying motionless on the floor. As the Section Seven fighter left the arena, two men entered, picking up the kid from Two and carrying him out the door with the others who had lost today.

The Training Speaker took his place up on his pedestal. "Congratulations, winners of today's challenge. There will be a short break for you to clean up, then lunchtime. Keep up the good work and strong performances. The final twenty has been set!"

CHAPTER 10

At lunch, everyone smiled and laughed, enjoying the successful morning. Some of the other tables were not so jubilant. Table one, which consisted of the people from Sections One, Two, Three, and Four, were down to three members: a guy from Section Two and both Chosen Ones from Section Three, a boy and a girl. None of the three seemed overly thrilled to be there. It was interesting how much of a toll the training appeared to be taking on the other tables.

Table two, which consisted of those from Section Five and Section Six as well as Section Fifteen and Section Sixteen, had six of their original eight left. A boy from Section Five, both trainees from Section Six—including Eleven—two boys from Section Fifteen and a girl from Section Sixteen. Although they had the majority of their group still intact, this table had not become friends like ours. This didn't surprise me. How could anyone become friends with someone like Eleven there?

My group was at Table Three, and we still had six of our original eight. Then there was Table Four, which had a boy and a girl from Section Seven, a boy from Section Twelve, a girl from Section Thirteen, and a boy from Section Fourteen. They had taken the second-biggest hit among the groups, being down to five left. This table was the only other table that was even talking to each other. Tables one and two weren't talking at all.

This was the second time I'd noticed the breakdown of the tables. It still didn't make any sense how the groups were divided, with two tables in order of Section and two intermixed. Just as I was examining the groups, Tinker arrived. I looked around and noticed there was a member of the capital's escort team at each table.

Tinker told our group, "There has been a group realignment to allow for better training during the week. Number Twenty, you will move to Table One."

I wanted to protest., but what use would it be? There really wasn't any negotiating. I looked at the rest of the group, and it appeared they all wanted to speak up as well. Instead, we all sat silently as Demps got up and made his way over to Table One. I looked around to see what other moves were being made. Only one other person moved; the girl from Section Sixteen got up, meeting up with Demps at Table One. Table Four remained the same.

Tinker walked off as Brantley started to talk. "Why didn't you say anything?" she asked, looking at me.

I shook my head in surprise. "Me? You all could have spoken up as well. Besides, what could I have changed?"

"Dantin's right," Goby said, trying to calm Brantley. "There was nothing any of us could do."

I wasn't sure why everyone seemed to be looking to me for some kind of answer. I didn't have one. All I really knew was that I wasn't going to be able to change anything. I had no power here; I was exactly like the rest of them. If anything, I was the luckiest one to still be here. After almost losing my challenge this morning I could have been long gone by now.

"Sorry, Dantin, I didn't mean to blame you. I … I just, I don't even know what anymore," Brantley said, sounding completely defeated. This transfer had affected her almost as much as if Demps were lost permanently.

"It's OK," I said, trying to reassure her. "Demps isn't far away. He's just forced to eat and train in a new group. Doesn't mean we won't see him anymore. Right?" I shot Brantley a smile.

"Yeah, you're right," Brantley said, trying to convince herself.

I'm not sure I totally believed myself either. He might as well be placed into a different Section, because up to this point we never saw any of the other groups except during the transition between training stations.

I needed to change the conversation, something to help lighten the mood. I looked at Goby and Lancaster. "So, how about getting lucky that guy didn't get all the questions right?"

Lancaster smiled. "Yeah, it's a good thing he's dumber than you are."

Yes! That's what I was hoping for. Half laughing, I shot back, "Easy now, I may not be the brightest but I'm smart enough to know you lost to a girl in a fight today."

By now the whole table was laughing at us jabbing into each other. It was the perfect distraction for all that had just taken place. Lancaster laughed, shooting back, "My mother always taught me to never hit a girl. I let her win."

I honestly believed him when it came to that comment. However, I wasn't about to let that win him this battle. "Uh-huh, I'm sure that's it. Is that why you were tapping out crying for help?"

Lancaster shot me a crooked smile. "OK, Dantin, you got me. ... Oh, what's two plus two?" Before I could shout out the correct answer to stop his point, he was talking again. "Don't worry, it will come to you eventually—or you could just wait for the other person to get it wrong."

I smiled. No more words to combat that comment. The horn sounded, ending lunch, and we all returned to the assembly hall to get our day's directives. We would continue training, but every day it was a slightly different order. It was going to be another long week. It was important as a group that we prepare for the things to come. There was no telling what the next challenge would hold.

*****

The week progressed quickly. There were great efforts to pick up our training intensity, and we made a lot of advancement in weapons mastery, combat, and physical training. There was a heavy focus on stealth training in combat.

I still struggled with the problem-solving section, especially with the more advanced questions. Goby and Lancaster were completing very advanced equations now. It all looked like a foreign language to me.

It was strange without Demps around. His sarcastic humor that seemed to break the tension at just the right time. His ability to keep even the most intense training days feeling light. We could have used him during a week like this. It appeared as if they were preparing us for the next phase of training, prepping everyone for an increased training load.

At dinner that night, before the next challenge, the group was in a fairly good mood. Goby and Lancaster talked about some equation they had been working on all week. Brantley played with Carina's hair, talking about girl stuff. I couldn't follow what they were talking about; however, I enjoyed seeing everyone at ease. It felt like a group of friends getting together on a spring evening rather than a group of inmates stuck together. I couldn't help but smile watching everyone talk.

"What?" Brantley asked, snapping me out of my daze.

"Oh, nothing."

"Why are you smiling?"

"This just feels right. This moment. It feels like a group of friends just getting together after a long day of work to enjoy a dinner together. I … I'm just happy to be a part of this moment is all." I smiled, scanning everyone's face.

Brantley smiled, noticing what I saw. "We do look rather chummy, don't we?"

Goby smiled. "I'm glad to be a part of this group. To have the chance to know you. And I want to thank all of you for making this time away from home not completely terrible."

The group smiled, knowing he meant that as a compliment. Lancaster looked over at his new friend. "Yeah, you're not so terrible either!"

Goby laughed,. "I guess that didn't sound right, did it?"

I looked at him. "We knew what you meant. From all of us, you're welcome."

Carina started to tear up. Then the tears started to flow down her face. She buried her face in her hands, pulling her hair away from Brantley. Brantley, realizing that she was upset, leaned in close and grabbed Carina's hands, trying to pry them from her face.

"What is it, sweetie? Why are you crying?" Brantley asked softly.

Carina wiped her eyes. "I'm scared. I don't want this to be the last night I'm here. I'm scared of what happens if you lose a challenge. I don't want to be reassigned. That training is getting harder. I know the challenges are going to be tougher and tougher. I don't know how much longer I can make it. It just seems like I'm swimming into the current, not actually getting anywhere."

Carina started crying again, covering her face. Brantley wrapped her arms around her. There were few words for a situation like this. Nobody really knew what the next challenge would be. Nobody knew how long they would be around. The group watched as Brantley hugged Carina tight, rocking her back and forth.

I got up, moving around the table to Carina's side. I knelt down next to her. "Hey. Look at me." Carina's head emerged from her hands, eyes red and puffy from the tears. "You are strong. You have the strength to make it through this. Do you hear me?" Carina nodded her head. "You are the reason that I make it through every day here. Did you know that?"

Carina shook her head. I didn't think she believed me.

"I watch how brave you are, how strong you are, and it gives me strength to push through each day. So you can't stop being that. I need you to stay positive and keep being strong. Do you think you can keep motivating me?" I finished, placing my hand on her back.

Carina wrapped her arms around my neck, almost knocking me onto my back. She squeezed hard and I returned the hug.

"Thank you," she whispered into my ear, her voice still a little shaky from the emotions she was battling,

I didn't say anything. I knew she was going to be stronger now. I could feel it. Her fear, at least for the moment, had subsided. Brantley grabbed my arm, smiling at me, thanking me without a word. I smiled back at her, giving her a slight nod. I let go of my hug, kissing Carina on the forehead. She felt like a little sister to me even though we were the same age.

It felt like I had just helped Micca with some great problem. It felt good. I felt at peace. Just another moment of gratitude for this day. The problem was that I knew the moment would pass. Soon, there would be another challenge and others would be gone. I just hoped I had given the group enough strength to survive the next stage. This was an individual challenge, but we had clearly become stronger together.

Dinner ended, but for the first time, instead of our usual evening movie, we were ordered off to bed early. I guess I didn't mind too much since it seemed like they had started showing the same films over again. There was only so much "love Natio, give thanks to Heart City" that I could handle. I was OK with having a little extra time in my room. Time to prepare myself for tomorrow's challenge.

In my room, I paced back and forth, trying to allow myself a little time to think with the lights on. I knew that once I touched the bed the lights would switch off, leaving me alone in the dark. *I wonder what kind of challenge we will have to do tomorrow?* I thought about what we'd already had to face.

Honestly, there really couldn't be too many more surprises at this point. *Could there?*

The horn sounded, indicating five minutes until lights out. I finished washing up, quickly getting myself ready for bed. I reached the edge of the bed as the lights flipped off, leaving me in the dark. I felt around the edge of the bed, making my way under the covers. I only lay awake for a couple of minutes. The last thoughts of the evening passed through my head: *"Be stronger than the others. Be faster. Be smarter. Outlast everyone and find your way home! When it's all over, always remember one thing! Remember we enter as one into the Kingdom of Lions!"*

*****

My grandpa's words still echoed in my head as the morning horn sounded. In the training room, the Training Speaker began his usual Challenge Day spiel, talking about how much hard work we'd put in, how much our country appreciated us, and how much of an honor it was to be a Chosen One. I stopped listening after he welcomed us. We were already divided into groups. It wasn't hard to tell that we would be doing another challenge in a similar format to last week's.

There was one thing that didn't seem to add up quite right, though. The groups weren't even in number. The first group consisted of the remaining girls. There were six of them: one each from Sections Three, Seven, Thirteen, Sixteen, and then Brantley and Carina. Group two had the small boy from Section Six, the guy from Section Twelve, Lancaster and Goby. Demps was the only person I knew in group three. He was joined by a group of guys from Sections Two, Three, Five, and Fourteen.

I was in group four with Eleven. Also with us were the two kids from Section Fifteen and the guy from Section Seven. The groups were slightly different, but it appeared that we were grouped based on our skills again. I finished examining the groups, listening to the last part of the Training Speaker's speech.

"Today you will face off against those similar to you in what we consider your strongest attribute," he said. "Get ready to perform; we will start shortly."

I wonder what they consider to be my strongest attribute? I watched as the girls were getting prepped to enter into their challenge. It appeared to be a weapons challenge. *I guess that's pretty fitting.* I remember on day one how accurate both Brantley and Carina were with the bows. They had picked up on all of the weapons well during training. I don't recall ever seeing any of the other girls shoot, but it wouldn't surprise me to think they were good shots as well.

It looked like it was going to be a pistol and bow challenge. I didn't see any other weapons. Once the girls took their places in their shooting lanes, three targets popped up fifty feet downrange. They looked like human bodies. There were two small red spots on the targets about the size of strawberries, one in the middle of where their head would have been and the other where their heart would have been.

I watched Carina as she pulled back her first arrow. She released it, letting it fly downrange. It struck the middle of the heart-positioned strawberry dot. Her next two arrows hit the other two targets as well, the first in the head and the second in the chest. I scanned the targets quickly, trying to get a feel for how everyone else was doing. Brantley and the girl from Section Three also hit all three targets. The girl from Section Sixteen only hit one.

All the girls set down their bows, grabbing the pistols. Only one target popped up— concentric circles spreading outward from a center dot—a hundred feet downrange. It looked as if each outer circle had a smaller point value. The guns exploded as the group sent shots at the targets. Each girl fired until all you could hear was the hollow clicking of the empty clip.

The girls reloaded a second clip as the scores were tallied. Each girl had ten shots on her targets. The max score was one hundred. Brantley scored just that, each shot landing inside the bullseye. Carina scored ninety-seven, getting seven center-mass shots and three in the ring just outside the bullseye. The girl from Section Three also got a ninety-seven. The girl from Section Sixteen continued to struggle, scoring an eighty-nine.

The next target popped up. It was seventy-five feet downrange with the same scoring rings as the last target. This target added a new dynamic to the competition by sliding side to side. The girls took aim, firing at a much slower rate this time as they lined up each of their shots before pulling the trigger. The focus on each of their faces was unmistakable. As the last shots were fired, the girls placed their guns back on the platform in front of them.

The scores popped up above each of their stations. Brantley shot another perfect score, which was fifty. I knew Brantley was a talented shot, but even I was amazed to see a second perfect score. Carina was the second-best shot in the group. She scored a forty-eight on this round. I was pleased. The two girls from my group were safe and moving on. The same couldn't be said for the girl from Section Sixteen, who was grabbed and escorted out of the arena.

Lancaster and Goby were next up. After watching the last performance and how good it was, I knew this group would be doing something with their intelligence. All that meant for me was that I really wouldn't know how they were doing until the end. Each of the contestants took a seat at their own table. A timer on the wall showed ten minutes. A horn sounded, the timer started counting down, and each person ripped at their packet.

Lancaster studied the first question in the packet, smiling while he read the directions. It must have been a question he was familiar with. He scribbled a few things down and then moved quickly onto the next page. Goby whistled a tune while he looked over the set of questions on his packet. It amazed me how fast the group answered questions and turned the page. The efficiency of these first two groups was impressive.

The time ticked away as pages turned with regularity. Lancaster and Goby almost laughed at the problems as they turned the pages. The same couldn't be said for the kid from Section Twelve, who by now was starting to sweat. Drops had formed on his forehead along with a small ring on his shirt around his neck. The kid from Section Six appeared to be deep in thought, but not having too much trouble.

When the timer hit zero, the horn sounded. The group set their writing utensils down as a group of men entered the room, one for each table. The men examined the questions, flipping through the pages. There was a short consultation among the graders, then they grabbed the kid from Section Twelve, removing him from the room. The rest of the group returned to the viewing room.

The next group was called forward. Demps was in this group. He moved into the arena last, following the kids from Sections Two, Three, Five, and Fourteen. Once in the room they were instructed to pick up a staff. Each grabbed one of the long wooden weapons that was situated in the corner of the room. This was going to be a combat group. I knew then that I would be running the obstacle course.

Each of the guys in the group had their weapons ready. Two numbers lit up, indicating who was fighting: Twenty vs. Four. That was Demps and the kid from Section Two. The two guys entered into the arena, circling each other, staffs at the ready. Three quick strikes by Four parlayed beautifully by Demps. They continued to circle. Three more strikes; Demps retreated, deflecting each blow.

Demps quickly turned on the offensive: three high strikes followed by a low sweep. The crack of the wood echoed through the arena as the kid from Section Two blocked the three high blows. Then, jumping over the sweeping move by Demps, Four swung downward in one motion. The strike caught Demps on the left collarbone before he could get his staff back up in defense.

The blow disabled Demps' left arm. It looked as though it may have even broken the bone. Demps held the staff in one hand with his left arm dangling at his side. Three more attacks. Demps slid the staff back and forth, blocking the first two blows before the third caught him on the side of his face. Demps spun, losing his balance, collapsing to the floor. He pushed hard with his feet, sliding across the floor.

When he tried to push off of the floor with his good arm to get back up, the kid from Section Two advanced at him, catching him in the ribs with a sweeping blow as he rose to his feet. A crippling scream escaped Demps's mouth as he crashed to the floor, unable to catch himself. He pushed up onto his knees, his right arm planted on the ground for support. Four wound up for a final blow, staff raised overhead, ready to strike. Demps threw his staff upward with his right arm, catching the kid in his right eye.

Four wobbled backward, grabbing his eye. Demps was still fighting to get to his feet when the kid regained his composure. Four pressed forward again. Demps swung the staff, sliding it across the ground at his feet. Four saw it coming, deflecting the blow, sending Demps off-balance. The kid raised his staff over his head again, this time swinging downward before Demps could gather himself. The blow slapped across the left side of his face.

Demps spun down the remaining couple of inches to the ground. He lay motionless. The kid moved around him, looking to take another shot at him when the horn sounded. Demps was unconscious. Two men entered the arena, placed him onto a stretcher, and removed him from the room. After Demps' removal I didn't pay too much attention to the rest of the fights.

The next thing I remembered was being ushered into another section of the arena, where the obstacle course laid out in front of us had a number of new challenges. We were told to toe the starting line. It was apparent now that we would be racing each other through the course. The horn sounded as the group raced toward the first obstacle. During the start, Number Eleven, who was to my left, punched one of the kids from Section Fifteen, causing him to fall.

At the first obstacle there were four logs floating in water. The kid from Section Seven was the first to arrive. I was right behind him, followed by Eleven and the two from Section Fifteen. I watched as the kid from Section Seven ran out onto the logs. He reached the second log before it spun out from under his feet, sending him splashing into the water.

I had been around logs my whole life. My father used to take me to the Lumber Yard, where Grandpa worked, inside the dome back in Section Eight. It was where I would work from time to time before I was placed into the lumber detail outside the dome. I knew how to maneuver myself across them. However, I hadn't spent much time on floating logs. I knew speed would be the key here, and I hoped that my familiarity with logs would help me navigate this challenge.

I moved swiftly, barely making contact with the top of each log before I was on to the next one. I crossed the four logs without any difficulty. I smiled at my brief success, but I didn't bother to look back to see who else made it across. I pressed forward, reaching the next obstacle. There were three consecutive walls, each standing about twelve feet in height.

I sprinted, jumped, and pressed my foot off the wall, grabbing for the top. Hoisting myself up and over the first wall, I landed in stride, moving quickly toward the second. Again I pushed off the wall, reaching for the top. Grabbing the wall, I pulled myself up. As I crossed over the second wall, I caught a glimpse of Eleven making it over the first wall. I pushed forward, wasting little time scaling the third wall.

Still moving quickly, I reached the next part of the course: a rope climb to a platform about forty feet high. I was three-quarters of the way to the top when the rope began to shake violently. I looked down at the ground as Eleven whipped the rope back and forth. I fought through the shaking, reaching the platform. *I wish I had a knife right now; I'd cut this rope and be done with him.*

The next part of the course was a parallel rope cross. Grabbing the top rope, I started sliding across to the other platform. I reached the other side as Eleven reached the first platform. I thought about staying to shake the rope as he tried to cross, but I figured it best to keep moving. I leapt onto the swing, generating momentum before launching myself to the next swing.

There was something exhilarating about jumping from swing to swing, forty feet in the air. After three more jumps, the final jump presented itself. I hadn't noticed when I started that the last jump was from the swing to a cargo net. I swung twice, generating a little extra momentum. One more kick and I was airborne, soaring for the net. My arms slid into the spaces in the rope, ripping my skin.

The tearing of flesh sent a shot of pain through my arms. I felt the warm trickle of blood start to flow from the wounds as I fought to regain my position on the net. Getting myself situated, I moved downward. I reached the ground relatively quickly and ran again for the next obstacle. As I approached, I realized this was another new challenge: a series of poles, each higher than the other.

The poles formed a peak and then descended after reaching about fifteen feet or so. The tops of the poles were about half the size of my foot. The poles formed a triangular shape. This was going to be a speed and balance test. I sprinted, jumping upward as I pressed off of the tops of the poles. It was similar to running on logs, but the change in height did a number with your balance. As I reached the top, I felt myself waver.

The movement coming down was going to be more challenging. I began slowly hopping down, landing on each next step. Eventually, I picked up my pace. The last part of the race lay just ahead of me. As I got closer to the ground, I regained confidence in my footing, speeding through the last three steps, hitting the ground in full stride. The last part of the race was a sprint to the finish line. My lungs now burning, my legs throbbing with each step, I sprinted forward.

Moving swiftly now, I felt a second wind come over me, and the pain in my lungs and legs subsided. I was only twenty feet from the finish line when I saw it: the final obstacle, which appeared to be hidden from the end of the previous challenge.

There was a gap in the floor at least fifteen feet in length. I was going to have to jump. I did my best not to lose speed as I approached the opening. I planted hard with my left foot, driving my right knee forward and upward, taking flight. My arms and legs swung violently as I soared through the air.

I hit the other side of the gap, catching myself on my forearms. The pain from the cuts I got on the rope earlier was almost too much to bear. I slid backward, but only for a moment. I felt my teeth grind as I drove my forearms into the ground and pulled myself up onto the ledge. Rolling twice, I crossed the finish line. I lay on my back as out of the corner of my eye I saw Eleven go airborne, making his jump at the space. He vanished into the hole; only his fingers on the ledge could be seen.

After a couple of seconds he fought his way up and through the finish line. I stood, waiting for the next instruction, watching as the kid from Section Seven crossed, then one of the kids from Section Fifteen. Finally, Number Thirty found his way across the finish line. He wasn't with us long before he was escorted out the door with the others who'd lost today, including Demps. I took a deep breath, knowing that it was over.

The horn sounded, ending the challenges as the Training Speaker stepped back up to his little pedestal. "Congratulations on another great Challenge Day. Those of you needing medical attention, proceed to the infirmary. Lunch will be served in one hour. Everyone else, report back to your room to clean up. Thank you."

I returned to my quarters to clean myself up for lunch. The soap burned my cuts as I showered. The blood had stopped flowing by now. The cuts weren't too bad, but they were definitely going to leave a mark. I had several on my forearms now. As I finished cleaning up, the horn sounded, indicating lunchtime.

The sun was warmer today than it had been the last few weeks. The light breeze that blew through the eating space felt nice. At the table, the group sat grabbing at the first round of food. I joined them, pulling up a seat next to Carina. Lancaster and Goby were discussing some of the problems from their challenge.

I put my hand on Carina's back, smiling at her. "I told you that you were going to be great today!"

Carina smiled. She didn't speak, but she didn't have to. She just kept eating, but her demeanor was unmistakable. I could tell she felt good about her performance today. So did I. I was happy that she had proved me right. I was happy that all of us did well today during the competition. Well, most of us. I looked over to Table One. No more Demps.

Lunch passed with little conversation. Challenge days were always so draining. I think everyone was just happy to have made it through another day.

After lunch, back in the assembly hall, the Training Speaker addressed us all: "Congratulations, you are our final sixteen. You will no longer train in your groups. As we get started, your group guide will direct you to your private training rooms. This is the beginning of your advanced training. You will be assigned a mentor to help you with your greatest weakness. Good job today, and good luck."

The remaining trainees all looked at each other. I could see the fear and sadness in everyone's eyes.

Tinker appeared, smiling brightly. "Right this way, everyone. Follow me."

Tinker led us through a door and down a few different hallways. We finally reached a row of doors where he slowed, studying the signs. He stopped in front of a door, turning back to the group. "OK, Number Fifteen, you're through here," he said.

I wanted to say something to my group, but the words didn't come. I offered a smile as I stepped past everyone to the door and opened it, leaving the group behind. The door shut behind me and I paused momentarily. I wondered if I would see them later for dinner or if that was the last time I would be with my friends.

As I passed into the room I stopped suddenly. I could feel my jaw drop, but I was unable to control it. Sitting at a table in the middle of the room was the most beautiful girl I had ever seen. Dark brown hair and lightly tanned skin. Toned, muscular body that sat with great poise. Her green eyes watched me thoughtfully as a smile crossed her lips.

"Hello, my name is Gaia. I will be your tutor," the girl said.

CHAPTER 11

I stood, eyes wide, unable to move or speak. I felt myself try to snap my jaw shut. I stuttered through my introduction. "Dantin, I'm Dan … my name is Dantin."

Gaia showed no emotion. "It's nice to meet you, Dantin. Come in, have a seat." She said, gesturing to the chair across from her.

As I pulled myself into my seat, I started again, this time with more confidence, having had time to process the situation. "So, you're my tutor?"

"Yes," Gaia said, looking over a chart on the table in front of her. I'd never felt like this before. She had me totally befuddled. "I've been assigned to help you with some of the problem-solving questions as well as to challenge you intellectually. It will be important for your advancement in the program to learn some of these processes."

"Yeah, I would agree. It's definitely the area that I need the most help. Have you tutored before?" She didn't look much older than me so I was wondering how many others she'd helped.

I could tell the question caught her a little off-guard. "Why do you ask?"

"I just have a lot of questions. I thought maybe you could help me understand what's going on here."

Gaia looked almost upset with my words. "I'm not here to be your friend. I'm not here so you can feel good about what's happening. My one goal is to prepare you for the next challenge and make sure you continue to improve intellectually."

"Well, a good way for you to help me with the next challenge is to tell me what to expect next. Don't you think?"

"Listen," she said sternly. Now I knew for sure that my line of questioning was starting to get Gaia upset. "I don't know what's going to happen next. I don't know anything other than what they told me, and that is that you need help with problem solving."

"So I'm your first." Gaia's eyes narrowed as I quickly tried to finish my statement. "First student, I mean."

She pressed her lips together and then formed a thin smile, trying to blow off the awkwardness of the statement. "I'm completely capable of helping you."

I sure hope so, or you won't see me for long. I nodded, showing my trust and approval.

Gaia gestured to the paper in front of me. "Are you ready to begin? Open your packet and we will start to work our way through some of the questions."

As I worked my way through the first couple of problems, Gaia got up from her chair and circled around the table to watch me work. It was the most distracting thing I'd ever dealt with. *Is this part of her job?* I finally finished up the first page of questions as she leaned over my shoulder to look at the packet.

As Gaia looked over my work, I studied her face. I shook my head, looking back down at the paper after realizing that I was staring.

"Very good, Dantin," she said, touching my arm, her voice sounding warm for the first time.

My heart quickened at the soft touch of her fingers on my skin. I felt my skin crawl a little and then ripple with tiny bumps. I tried to hide my discomfort, but it seemed Gaia had picked up on it, pulling her hand away. As she pulled away there was a sweet smell that wafted past my face. It was similar to the flowers I used to smell in Section Eight that bloomed in the spring, but there was something different about it. I looked up at her, sending her a shy smile. She nodded slightly, but didn't return the smile.

The rest of the training session went pretty smoothly. We worked through a few more problems. Gaia helped with a couple of questions, showing me some shortcuts to allow me to be more efficient.

At the end of the training session, a horn sounded, dismissing me to my next station. Gaia stood at the door and, shaking my hand, said, "I'll see you tomorrow. Good work today." She smiled as she opened the door.

"Thanks. I'll see you tomorrow." I put my head down, rushing quickly past her.

The remainder of training that day was done by myself. The group was completely broken up. I went first to the shooting range, working through a number of different weapons. Then combat training with just the instructor and me. I liked combat training in this setting. I was able to get more focus on the areas I wanted to improve. Last, I worked through a small workout circuit that had a number of obstacle course exercises.

At dinner, I was reunited with the group at our table. This was a pleasant surprise. Goby and Lancaster were already there talking when I pulled up my usual seat. Then Brantley and Carina joined the group.

The group was gnawing on the bread that was already on the table when I started in with the questioning.

"So, how was everyone's mentor?" I asked.

Carina answered first. "My mentor was mean. All he did was yell at me. They said that my physical strength was my weakness, so I worked on strength and obstacle course work the whole time. I don't even think I caught his name. I don't want to go back. I'm not sure I'm going to be able to lift my arms to eat."

Brantley nodded with understanding. "Yeah, my mentor was pretty brutal, too. He made me do a lot of the same things. I worked on lifting heavy rocks and logs and then had to run the obstacle course. My guy was really old. I wanted to tell him to lift the weight! I don't think he could."

The table laughed. Lancaster went next, still laughing a little as he started to talk. "My mentor was great. We worked on hand-to-hand combat and some of the weapons training. I feel like I learned so much more about self-defense in that one session than I had this whole time."

Goby nodded. "Yeah, I worked with a guy on shooting weapons. I, too, feel more comfortable after one session with this guy than I have after … How many weeks have we been here now? I can't even remember anymore. What about you, Dantin? How was your mentor?"

She was beautiful. Even with her cold demeanor, Gaia was amazing. *She's probably just being cold to protect herself. She seemed to open up at the end of the session.* Then I realized I was just sitting there smiling, thinking about her.

"She was incredible. Absolutely stunning. I'd never seen anyone like her before. She's going to help me with my problem-solving abilities. It's hard to focus on the questions, though, with her in the room."

Brantley interrupted me. "What do you mean, 'Never seen anyone like her before'? Does she have, like, three eyes?" she said sarcastically.

"Oh, Brantley," Goby chimed in. "No need to act like that. Tell me, Dantin, what was her name? Did you talk about anything else besides your problems?"

Brantley crossed her arms. "Yeah, are you guys in loooove?" she said bitterly under her breath.

I wasn't sure what was going on with Brantley, but I started to answer the questions. "Her name is Gaia. We didn't talk about much other than problem solving. She was actually a little cold at first, but I think she will open up. And, no, Brantley, we're not in loooooove. I've got enough love right here at this table." I smiled at her, trying to get her out of her pouty state. She didn't budge, but the corners of her mouth did curl up slightly.

I looked around the table and saw that everyone was still looking at me to talk more. "She did touch me, though."

Just then, Brantley smacked me in the back of the head. "Ouch!"

"Now you've been touched twice today." Brantley was smiling now.

"Yeah, but the first touch felt good." I smiled back at her, rubbing the back of my head.

"Well, guess I'll have to work on that part. Besides, I'm not the stunning one, remember? I'm just a dirty trainee." She stood up from the table, grabbing Carina by the arm. "Come take a walk with me."

Carina stood up, and the two of them disappeared into the garden.

I looked at Goby and Lancaster. "What was that all about?"

Goby smiled. "Well, it appears that someone might have a little affection for you."

I felt my brow curl. "What, Brantley? No … since when … I mean …. why?"

Lancaster laughed at my attempt at a sentence. "I can tell you this much, buddy: she's had her eye on you for a little while now. Obviously, you've noticed that, right?"

Goby and Lancaster laughed as I thought about Brantley. *Why hadn't I noticed? I don't think of her like that. She's like a sister. Isn't she?* I looked back up at the two guys who had become good friends of mine over the last couple of weeks. They were enjoying my struggle.

Goby, still laughing, said, "It's about time you had a tough time with something. This has all been too easy for you so far."

I shook my head. "What am I supposed to do with this information? I mean, we don't even know if all of us will be here next week, or the week after."

I could feel my confusion replaced by anger. *Why does she have to like me? Why couldn't she just have been like everyone else and be a friend?* Brantley's newly exposed feelings toyed with my head. My thoughts bounced between Gaia and Brantley. I knew Brantley better, from the way she acted when she was mad to her smile. I hardly knew Gaia, but there was no mistaking what I felt today when I entered that room. Or when she touched my arm.

What's wrong with me? I have a job to do.

The horn sounded, ending dinner. Brantley never returned to the table. Goby, Lancaster, and I made our way down to the assembly hall. I couldn't find Brantley or Carina anywhere as I looked around the room. I could see Tinker standing near one of the doors.

The Training Speaker made his way to his usual podium. I stood up on my tip-toes, trying to peer over the crowd.

"Before we have our movie, I have a couple of announcements," the Training Speaker started in. "I need Chosen Ones Ten, Fifteen, Twenty-six, and Twenty-nine to report to the front. Your mentors have requested an extra training session with you."

Fifteen. That's me. I knew this was going to send Brantley into a complete tizzy. She probably wouldn't talk to me again for a week. Assuming we were both here in a week.

I weaved my way through the crowd to the front. Tinker stood by the door, arms crossed, waiting for me. He smiled, grabbing my arm, leading me through the door. We moved quickly back through the hallways to the training room.

"OK, I will be back after the movie ends to escort you back to your room," Tinker said, disappearing back down the hallway.

I took a deep breath, pushing the door open. Gaia sat at the table, waiting for me to enter the room. She was behind the desk again. Her legs were crossed. Both her elbows rested on the table and her hands were positioned under her chin, holding up her head. Her head was down, looking at a paper as her hair fell over her eyes. I took another step into the room as her eyes shot up at me.

"Dantin, please come in." Her voice caught me off guard for some reason, and I froze briefly before continuing into the room.

I reached the chair, grabbing the end of it. "I was told you wanted to see me again."

"Yes, I feel like we might have gotten off on the wrong foot. Plus, I wanted to go over a couple more problems with you. I feel like we didn't cover as much as I wanted to today. I didn't want to wait until tomorrow to see you again—I mean, to get these problems in."

Her words played with my head. I could feel myself trying to read into what she was saying, attempting to make more of this situation than was there. I didn't exactly understand why I was summoned to train again tonight. I did know that it wasn't what I was thinking it was.

Maybe this is part of my mental training? She's going to play with my head and see if I can still make sense of things.

"I also wanted to apologize for earlier," Gaia continued.

I shook my head. "For what?"

Gaia shook her head, her eyes piercing but sad. "I just felt like maybe I gave you the wrong impression about me, maybe. Just … I'm sorry."

I wasn't sure what she was sorry for, but this conversation was more than confusing. I couldn't understand any of what was happening in this moment. I didn't know what she was apologizing for or why I was here. Or what exactly we were trying to accomplish during this time together. Everything was messed up. Maybe I was struggling with this because of the new information I learned about Brantley. It was all too much, and my brain was all over the place.

"It's OK. I didn't get any wrong impressions. You're my tutor. Your job is to make me smart enough to survive training. Nothing more, nothing less." I looked at her as she shook her head.

"Exactly." She smiled at me. "You know, you're smarter than you realize. I think it's just lack of practice that is your biggest problem with these questions. Which is why I figure if we meet twice a day you will begin to work more quickly through them. You didn't miss any questions. You just take a long time to analyze the information. Do you see what I'm saying?"

I nodded. "I'm not that smart. My sister is the smart one in my family."

Gaia smiled. "You have a sister. One of these days I'd like to hear about what she's like, but I promise you, you're smarter than you realize. I'm going to help you with this."

"Sounds good to me," I said, sitting back in my chair. "I'm afraid if I don't get better with this, I won't make it through training."

Gaia came around the table, bringing her chair with her. She slid up next to me as we opened up the packet of questions. We started by going over the questions that I had answered earlier. We worked through the problems again, and she pointed out where I had taken unnecessary steps.

Over the next hour and a half we worked through a number of additional problems to make sure the concepts were starting to stick. The time passed by so fast. Gaia was brilliant, making the questions make so much sense to me.

"Great job, Dantin. You're really starting to get the hang of this," Gaia said, her hand landing on my elbow. I could feel my pulse quicken again. I looked up, meeting her eyes as the door swung open behind us.

Tinker stood in the doorway. "Time to report to your quarters. Lights out is in thirty minutes."

Gaia pulled her hand away as I rose to my feet. I pushed my chair back in and took a couple of steps toward the door. I turned back as I reached the door.

"Thank you, Gaia," I said. "This was really helpful; you're a great tutor."

Gaia smiled as I turned to head out the door. I wound my way through the maze of hallways, making my way back to my quarters. In my room I prepared for bed, getting all of my things together.

Lying in bed I found myself comparing Gaia and Brantley. They were both so different, yet tonight I finally realized that I did have feelings for Brantley. I'm not sure how I missed them before, but they were definitely there. All the time we'd spent together. The looks, hugs, jokes, and her incredible skill as a Chosen One.

I was also extremely attracted to Gaia. Initially it was just her looks. She was so beautiful, like nobody I'd ever seen before. There was something about her that drew me in. Perhaps it was just because everyone here in training was always so banged up and Gaia looked like she'd never had to lift her finger for anything in her life—not in a bad way, just that there weren't any cuts and scrapes to distract from her looks. Then tonight I saw her caring side. I saw her intelligence and kindness.

But none of this mattered. I had a job to do. I needed to stay focused. Maybe someday I'd be able to explore these feelings, but for right now, I needed to be about the work.

*****

Morning came quickly. The alarm sounded, snapping me from another dreamless sleep. I lay on the bed staring at the ceiling. My eyes were heavy; it didn't feel like I had slept for more than fifteen minutes. This situation with Brantley and Gaia was going to get me all messed up. I was losing sleep over something I didn't have any say in or any time for. I couldn't get the conflicting thoughts out of my head. This was the last thing I needed to worry about right now.

Getting to the final sixteen was good, but if I was going to do what Grandpa told me, I needed to stay focused.

I fumbled through my morning routine. Today was going to be long. I didn't want to train; I just wanted to hide away in my room and sleep. The horn sounded: fifteen minutes until the door would open.

My day started with Gaia and problem solving. I sat staring at a problem on the page. Every time I tried to start reading the question, my eyes would cross and the words would blur together. I decided to pretend like I was working through the first problem, but Gaia wasn't fooled. She circled around, sitting next to me.

"Is everything all right, Dantin?" She touched my shoulder as she spoke.

"Yeah. I just didn't sleep well last night," I told her. "Do you mind if we don't do problem solving right now? I promise I will be better in the afternoon. My brain just can't handle any extra thinking right now." I rubbed my eyes as I tried to refocus.

Gaia smiled a little. "Then what do you suggest we do for your training?"

I can think of a few things we could do.

I shook my head, trying to force out those thoughts. *You're an idiot, Dantin.*

"Tell me a little bit about yourself?" I finally said.

Gaia looked at me. "Well, what would you like to know?"

I hesitated, trying to think of a good topic. "Your name is very interesting. Does it have any special meaning?"

Gaia nodded. "Actually, it does. My name originated in Ancient Greece. Gaia was considered the mother of all the gods. She was the goddess of earth. It was from her that the Titans were born, as well as the gods of the sea and air. The mortals were born of her earthly flesh."

"That's amazing," I said. Gaia smiled. "They didn't teach us much Greek mythology where I'm from. I wish my name had a cool story like that. I don't even know if there is a reason for my name."

"You've never studied ancient mythology?" Gaia asked.

I shook my head. "No, we don't have any books on that where I come from. At least not that I know of. They definitely didn't spend any time teaching us that in school."

Gaia looked confused. "Interesting. That's too bad. I always enjoyed learning about the different parts of our history. They say history is the key to our future, because if we fail to learn from our past, we are ultimately doomed to repeat it."

Gaia paused a moment as I reflected on her words. "Well, you may not know the meaning of your name, but it is a good name," she said. "A strong name. Besides, it's not what your name used to mean that matters. It's what you make your name mean with your actions of now. That's what really matters."

I smiled. I liked that way of thinking. She was right. *Who cares if my name has a special meaning? All that matters is making a name for myself now.*

The hour of training passed quickly. The horn sounded and Tinker appeared to escort me to my next training post. The rest of the morning went by in a blur. I felt myself go through the motions. What a waste. I needed to do better.

When the horn sounded again to send us to lunch, all I could think about was getting Brantley to talk to me. I wasn't trying to make any confessions of my feelings. It was still much too early for that. However, I valued her friendship and didn't want to lose that either. I also felt like we still needed each other. All of us. Finding a way to hold onto that connection was what had made our group so strong. I needed her to know how much I valued our relationship. Besides, if there were any girls who could make it through this training, it would be her.

Lancaster and Goby sat pulling at the bread that had already been placed on the table. Carina arrived just as I did. I looked around for Brantley, but she was nowhere to be found. I turned my focus back to the table. "Where's Brantley?"

Goby looked up from picking at his bread. "She said she was going to eat in the garden today."

I immediately got up from the table and moved into the garden. I needed to talk to her. This couldn't go on anymore. *I didn't even know she had feelings for me. I don't understand how this could be my fault. She totally blew this out of proportion. There's no need for her to act like this. There's no reason we can't be friends. I mean, maybe someday more, but not now. We've got training and competition to worry about. Right?*

"Brantley?" I said as I entered the garden.

Brantley sat alone on a bench, facing some of the flowers. She didn't even bother to look up at me. She kept picking at some of the bread that she had pulled from the table. I moved in closer —slowly, mostly because I knew she had it in her to hit me if I wasn't careful. I finally reached the bench where she was sitting. I sat down beside her, facing the other direction. Looking over my shoulder, I started to speak again.

"Brantley, I'm sorry if I hurt you," I started.

She didn't even let me get another word out. "You didn't hurt me," she snapped.

"Well, I … Then why are you eating in the garden?"

"Because I didn't want to be around someone like you." She looked at me, tears in her eyes masked by the anger on her face.

"What did I do? I don't understand." I was hurt and angry myself at this point.

"You're just so blind, aren't you?" she responded.

"Listen, I'm not sure why you're so angry with me," I said. "I'm not sure what I did, but there's a few things I want you to know. I value you as a friend. You are one of the few people who I've ever felt knew who I was. We've been through a lot together in a short period of time. We are going to go through even more in the weeks to come, and I need you in my life. I know I've upset you even if you don't want to admit it. I also know that I have feelings for you, and I'm not entirely sure what that means. But I think that maybe you have feelings for me, too."

Brantley was now looking right at me, her eyes shining and beautiful. I paused a moment to stare into her eyes.

"I don't know what to do about those feelings right now," I told her. "All I know is that we need to be on the top of our game from here on in if we're going to make it through training.

I don't want to be a distraction for you, and I can't allow you to be a distraction for me."

Brantley's shining eyes narrowed. "So I'm a distraction, huh? I'll just help you out and stay away from you so I don't distract you anymore. I wouldn't want to be the reason you fail the training." She got to her feet and stomped off out of the garden.

"Wait!" I tried to stop her, but it was too late.

Way to go, idiot. Pretty sure you made that worse! I didn't know how to fix things this time. *Maybe it's better this way. Now you won't be a distraction for her.*

That's not at all true. You're making excuses for things that don't make any sense. Things were so much easier back in Section Eight.

Why'd you call her a distraction, dumbass?

Brantley had never been a distraction. She had always been a helpful and motivating friend. I needed to get her back. I needed to get back on speaking terms with her again. That was all that mattered. I didn't want this to be something that threw her focus off, either. Brantley was always someone who could keep me on track. She wasn't afraid to tell me exactly what she thought—which was obvious from this current situation. I knew deep down that if I was going to survive training, I was going to need Brantley.

CHAPTER 12

Brantley continued to eat in the garden throughout the week. I was frustrated with the way things were, yet trying to fix things had only made them worse. I had clearly discovered something I was worse at than problem solving. I sat with Goby and Lancaster at dinner two nights before the next challenge, trying to figure out a possible solution. If I was going to make things better before the next event, I was going to have to move quickly.

"What can I do?" I asked as I nibbled on some bread before dinner was served.

Goby shrugged. "I don't know. I'm not really good with girls. Although, apparently, neither are you."

Lancaster laughed. "You did try saying you're sorry, right?"

"Of course I tried that," I said angrily. "It only made her more mad."

"Hmmm … interesting," Goby said, rubbing his chin. "Perhaps this is one of those situations you're just going to have to let run its course."

I shook my head. "I need her in my corner. I need all of you in my corner. You're the closest thing I have to family here, and I want all of you with me during this process. It's the only way I'll be able to make it. It's the only way we all make it. I'm not sure I could handle losing one of you at this point."

Lancaster looked at me. "Have you told her that? That sounded like a pretty good apology to me."

I shook my head in frustration. "I tried to, but I think my words came out wrong. Do you think you can tell her that I'm really trying here? Maybe she would listen to you guys."

"I'm sorry, but I'm not getting in the middle of your little love triangle," Goby said, smiling across the table.

"I don't want a damn love triangle. I just want to get through training and then maybe I can figure out what's going on here. She doesn't seem to realize that if we don't make it through training, it doesn't matter how I feel about her—or anyone, for that matter." I was really starting to lose my patience.

Goby and Lancaster were no longer looking at me. They were staring over my shoulder. I turned my head, seeing Brantley and Carina standing behind me. Carina passed me, touching my shoulder as she pulled up a seat. I stood up, turning around as Brantley attempted to leave.

I reached out, grabbing her elbow. "Please."

Her head turned, her eyes fixed on mine. "Fine, but not here."

We walked into the garden and found a bench to sit on. I looked down at the grass. "How much of our conversation did you hear?"

"Enough," Brantley said shortly.

I didn't know how much was enough so I decided to start from the beginning. "Listen, I don't know what I feel for you, or Gaia, for that matter. Honestly, I don't care to be more than friends with either of you at this moment. My only concern is finding a way for all of us to make it through training. I need you on my team for that to happen. I don't know what the future holds, but I know that there is no future if we don't all make it through training first. I need all of you with me. I'm not willing to lose one more person."

I looked up as Brantley looked down at her feet. "I understand. I know what you mean."

"So, can we start over? Can we still be friends? You are the strongest person in this group, and if we're going to make it through, we all need you."

Her eyes met mine. "Yeah, we can be friends. I'd like that," she said, smiling a little.

I smiled back. "Good." I grabbed her shoulders, pulling her in for a hug. "Thank you."

It was nice to have her in my arms. She smelled sweet like the flowers in the garden, and even though she'd become extremely toned and hardened by the training, she felt soft in my arms. I didn't want to let go. I slowly pulled back and gave her a smile. I threw my arm around her shoulder as we returned to the group, taking seats next to each other at the table.

The remainder of dinner went well. There was still a little tension that I'm pretty sure everyone felt. Saying we were just friends was easy, but we both knew there was something more there that we were simply burying for the moment. However, it was nice to have everyone back at the table together. It was only a few days before the next challenge, and things were really starting to pick up around the facility. I had a feeling the trainers had something big planned.

That evening, I was called away to do more training with Gaia while the rest of the group attended a movie. I felt a new focus on my work, and Gaia noticed.

"You're doing really well tonight," she said. "What's brought on this sudden surge of effort? I haven't seen this from you all week."

I smiled. "I fixed a problem that I was having. It was distracting me and taking away from my full focus on these problems."

"What kind of problem were you having?" Gaia asked, leaning across the table.

"There's a girl in my group that was upset with me. I think we worked it out for now, though."

Gaia's eyes searched mine for more answers. "Is this a girl that you like? Or ..." Her voice faded..

Gaia's questions perplexed me. "No. I mean, I don't know. I like her, but she's a friend. And I need as many friends as I can get right now. I don't need the kind of distraction that comes from trying to be more than that. Do you know what I mean? I ... I don't know; it's just a lot right now. Plus, she was mad at me for something silly." I didn't want to talk about all of this. I tried to go back to my problems, but Gaia had different ideas.

"Why was she mad? What did you do?" she pressed.

I sighed. "I didn't do anything. She was just mad," I said, my voice snapping more than I wanted it to.

Gaia looked at me, knowing there was more to it than that. "There had to be a reason. Girls don't just get mad."

"Sure they do," I said, smiling.

Gaia didn't find my joke very funny. Her eyes narrowed, and my smile faded quickly.

"Fine," I said. "She was mad because of you."

"Me?" Gaia pulled back, pressing her hand to her chest in defense. "What did I do? I don't even know her."

I shook my head, looking down at the table. "She was mad at you because I said you were pretty. That I thought you were attractive. I know, it's stupid. You're my mentor and my tutor. I was just telling everyone about you and I guess I described you in a way that led to Brantley getting mad."

Gaia blushed a little. "You think I'm pretty?"

"Of course I do. You're beautiful."

Oh, great. This is not going to end well. Why can't you just keep your mouth shut?

"Thank you. Nobody has ever told me I was pretty before." Gaia smiled at me from the other side of the table.

No way. Back in Section Eight, someone who looked like she did would be so sought after she would probably stop liking boys all together. "I find that hard to believe. You are very pretty."

Gaia blushed again. "I mean, I've had a number of suitors, but the men of Heart City aren't exactly good communicators. It's all about status and advancement. What someone like me could do for their position within the government or how I could help their career. Nobody spends time getting to know people here. I guess that's something we've lost along the way. Everything is about your place in the order of things. How can you move up the fastest?"

"I'm sorry to hear that. You deserve better," I said. "But, like I told Brantley, I need people to be on my side to help me make it through this training, so I can't be more than your student."

Gaia frowned, shaking her head. "Oh, of course. We are forbidden to have relationships with the Chosen Ones. So you're safe there. Friends—or, I mean, student-teacher. That's … that's what we are."

I smiled at her attempt to reassure me. "I'm OK with friends. Assuming that's allowed?"

Gaia smiled as the horn sounded, ending our session. The movie must have ended. Tinker appeared in the doorway to lead me to my quarters. I looked back at Gaia as I was leaving the room. "I'll see you tomorrow. Goodnight."

"Goodnight, Dantin." Gaia smiled as the door shut.

In my quarters, I found myself on my bed in no time at all. The lights out. The room pitch black. My mind finally felt at peace for the first time all week. It was a good day, and before I had any time to fill myself up with my inner dialogue, I was asleep.

It was the first night all week that I slept well. I dreamt of a time years from now. I was free. I didn't have training, I didn't work in the Sections, and I was happy. I had friends with me. It was beautiful. It was the best dream I'd had in years.

The horn sounded, tearing me from my utopia.

One day until the next Challenge Day. I moved with a renewed vigor as I prepared for the day. My steps were lighter than they had been in weeks, my mind clear and focused. I finally had things back in order. Brantley and Gaia were on my side. I had my team back. I was ready for anything. I finished dressing as the door swung open. Men stood in the hall, directing us into the challenge arena.

We were herded like sheep down the hall. In the challenge room the arena was set up with the obstacle course from the first day. *This can't be right. The challenge isn't supposed to be until tomorrow.*

The group finished filing in as the Training Speaker took his place in front of us. He cleared his throat.

"Welcome, trainees. Today is a special event challenge. Every year we have an unscheduled challenge to test your abilities to adapt to the unknown. Today is that day. You will be running the Day One obstacle course. However, I wanted everyone to be made aware of one significant change. You must finish! This is where we start to weed out the weak. This is where we see who has what it takes. Good luck and press on!"

When I looked at Goby and Lancaster, I could see the concern in their eyes. I was concerned, too. Not for myself but for the rest of my group. They had all failed the obstacle course on the first day. I knew we had all gotten stronger, but this was going to be a true test of exactly how much we'd improved. I searched the crowd for Carina and Brantley.

Our group gathered together as they lined people up at the starting line. They were launching people based on their training number, so we had some time. I took a good minute to look at the group, studying all of their faces. I feared I would not be seeing all of them again after today. I saw tears forming in Carina's eyes. Concern covered the brows of Goby and Lancaster. Brantley stood strong and confident, but I knew she was worried as well.

Brantley was the only person I was confident could make it to the end. I knew how strong she was. Plus, she almost completed the course the first time. I wrapped my arms around Carina, pulling her in close. I felt her trembling arms wrap around me. I felt her sob as she pushed her face into my chest, her tears soaking through my shirt.

I grabbed Carina's shoulders, pulling her back from our embrace, and looked into her eyes. "I want you to listen to me. No matter what happens today, this won't be the last time you see all of us. Do you understand? I know we all have a hard challenge ahead of us. I know this is designed to knock some of us from the training. Remember that reassignment isn't the worst thing."

Carina nodded her head. She even tried to smile a little. I grabbed her again, giving her a big hug. She whispered in my ear, "Thank you. You make all of us stronger." She kissed me on the cheek and turned away, going to the group and hugging each of them.

Brantley appeared by my side. "You know she looks to you like a big brother, right?"

I nodded my head, not taking my eyes off of Carina. "Yeah. I'm worried about her."

Brantley threw her arm around my shoulder. "We all are."

I turned my head to look at her. "Just stay focused, all right? You can do this!"

Brantley nodded. A crooked smile formed at the corners of her mouth as she winked at me. "We got this." She walked forward, heading toward Carina.

I turned my gaze to the starting line of the course. The first couple of groups had already launched. Lancaster and I would be up in two more groups. I grabbed Lancaster's sleeve, dragging him to the starting line. I smacked him on the back, sending him jerking forward. He smiled as he shrugged his shoulders. I reached out, grabbing his left shoulder with my right hand.

"Just keep moving. Don't stop, no matter how much it hurts or how impossible it seems," I said, trying to sound like the inspirational leader I felt he needed right now.

Lancaster nodded as the group in front of us started on the course. I watched as the two disappeared up over the first wall. The rest of the course was hidden again, just like day one. Only this time I knew what to expect on the other side of that wall. I knew I would be able to help Lancaster through some of the first obstacles, but we would get separated once again about halfway through the course.

It was there that I would be on my own. I would have to keep my focus and not worry about the rest of my group until I completed the course. Only then could I let those thoughts enter my mind.

I closed my eyes and took a deep breath through my nose, holding it for a moment, then slowly let the air escape through my lips. I felt my heart rate slow and my mind clear. I was ready to go. I toed the line, preparing for the horn to send us into the course.

The horn sounded and I raced forward toward the wall. I jumped, pressing up off the wall and grabbing the top. I hoisted myself up and sat at the top waiting for Lancaster so I could help him scale the wall as I did the first day. But when I started to reach down, Lancaster pulled hard twice on the rope and quickly climbed up next to me. He shot me a smile as he flipped his legs over the top, landing on the other side.

It was my first time seeing just how much Lancaster had improved. His strength and speed from the first day to now was night and day. I smiled as he ran forward into the course. I hopped down, racing to catch him. I, too, felt lighter on my feet, flying through the course together, moving quickly between physical challenges. Soon we reached the middle of the course where the brain teaser was.

I reached up, giving Lancaster a high five as we answered the question. The rest of the way I would be on my own. I moved quickly between challenges. I felt as if I was in a dream. I never fatigued. My heart never pounded. It was nothing like the first day. I was in complete control of myself as I flew between obstacles. I raced forward, finishing the course with little difficulty. I had never felt so dialed-in before.

Even the section with the ball cannon was not nearly as difficult. I didn't know how to explain this improvement. Apparently having regulated meals every day mixed with all of the training really did make us stronger. However, I didn't think that this amount of improvement was completely due to our training. People don't move like I was today.

After completing the course, I was sent back to my quarters to clean up. I didn't really feel like I was overly dirty, but I knew the protocol by this point. I made my way back to my room. I cleaned myself up and waited for the horn to send us up to lunch. That was when I would find out what was going on with the rest of the group. It felt like an extra long wait this time before the horn sounded, releasing me to the surface.

Up in the garden I made my way to my table. I was the first to arrive. I sat, waiting for the rest of the group to start making their way up. A few minutes passed and nobody else had shown up yet. I was starting to get nervous. Some of the other trainees had arrived and were starting to eat their meals. Eleven was there; so was the girl from Section Seven and the boy from Section Fifteen.

Finally, Lancaster arrived. I sighed; at least I wasn't alone. Shortly after Lancaster, Goby made his appearance, and then Brantley. We all sat waiting for Carina to pop her head around the row of bushes and flowers. The other tables were digging into their meals, but our group was too worried about Carina to start eating.

I counted the people at the other tables. There was the boy from Two; the girl from Three; the boy from Five; of course, Eleven; the girl from Section Seven; the boy from Fifteen; and our group of Lancaster, Brantley, Goby, and me. That left us with ten trainees. This is when it hit me that Carina wouldn't be joining us. Unless somehow there were two more people making their way up, it seemed we had reached the final ten.

I looked at my friends as their eyes still searched for Carina. "I don't think Carina made it," I said.

Goby shook his head. "No, she's coming. She's just running late is all. She will be here."

Brantley's eyes started to fill with tears. I could feel my eyes starting to water as well. The sweetest one of us, the one who didn't belong in this place, was gone.

Goby was fighting, hanging on to hope, thinking that she would still be here, that she was just running late. It was a fool's dream, one that nobody wanted to try to wake him from. Lancaster had his arm around Goby, trying to comfort him.

Lancaster shook Goby lightly. "It's OK, buddy, she's better now. She doesn't have to deal with all of this stuff anymore. She can be reassigned. We will see her again soon when all of this training is over. Right?"

Goby sniffed, wiping the tears from his eyes. "Right."

I really wished I could believe that was the case. For some reason, I found myself always doubting what happened to those of us who didn't survive training, ever since the day when our instructor used that exact word: "survive." People don't need to survive if they get reassigned.

I sure did hope the group was right, though. I couldn't bear to think of Carina not being alive.

The horn sounded, ending lunch. I grabbed a piece of bread from the table and shoved it into my mouth, trying to get at least a little food into my system before training. We were gathered into the assembly hall. There was a lot more space in this large room now.

The Training Speaker took his place as he always did after a challenge.

"Congratulations, final ten," he announced. "You have made it to the final stages of training. We will continue forward as usual. However, the challenges will continue to become more difficult. You will be tested to the limits of what you're capable of. There will be a final weeding of the weak until we reach our four victors."

Four. This was the first time hearing how many people would complete training. Four. That meant Goby, Lancaster, Brantley, and I could make it through training. This was the best news I'd heard in a while.

I knew what I had to do now. I needed to make sure my group survived. There was only one thing I cared about now: get through the rest of training with my group intact.

CHAPTER 13

"Dantin, are you OK? You seem distracted." Gaia looked at me across the table. The concern in her eyes was unmistakable.

"I'm sorry. It's been a tough day so far. Someone close to me didn't make it through the last elimination. I guess I am a little distracted," I admitted.

"I'm so sorry. They are just reassigned, though, so you will see them again." Gaia eyes fixed on mine as she smiled.

I felt hope for the first time in a while about what happens if we fail. But part of me still wasn't convinced. "You know this for a fact? You've seen this?"

Gaia's eyes dropped, fixating on the table. "No." She looked at me with renewed confidence. "But that's what they told us. Why would they lie? They told us that if your trainee does not complete training they would be reassigned and no longer need our services. Why would they tell us that if it wasn't the case?"

I raised my eyebrows. Shaking my head, I said, "I don't know."

"It has to be true." She reached across the table, grabbing my hand. "You're still here, though, and that's all that matters right now. All you can control is what happens to you in this next moment."

I felt my heart flutter at the soft touch. I looked from Gaia's hand up into her eyes. "Thanks."

Gaia smiled. "You're welcome. Now, let's make sure you're ready for whatever they throw at you next and get some of these problems done."

I nodded, returning to my work. She was right. I couldn't keep dwelling on things that were out of my control. I needed to stay focused on what I could do to make sure I was completely prepared for whatever came next. I couldn't help my friends if I got eliminated in the next challenge. There was only one way to make sure that I was able to help them. I needed to survive myself. *Focus, you idiot, you need to learn something.*

I trained hard the remainder of the day. I had a renewed focus fueled by my feelings about losing Carina. I was sad she was gone but didn't want to lose anyone else. I buried the feelings of worry, instead focusing on hope that I would one day be reunited with her. I put together the best day of training I'd had since I arrived. I finished the day feeling very confident and proud of what I had accomplished.

Somehow that wasn't enough to stop my mind from wandering that evening. In bed I found myself drifting between thoughts of what Carina might be doing now and what the future after training looked like. I knew I needed to stay focused on the present, but I couldn't help thinking about what things might be like after this was all over. The last thing I remember thinking before drifting off to sleep was how we might all be back together once this was over.

*****

The morning horn startled me. I was deep in sleep when it echoed through the room. The lights blasted on, causing me to shield my eyes. I rubbed my eyes, trying to shake the morning cobwebs. After a few moments, my eyes finally adjusted to the light and my breakfast smoothie appeared on the dresser top. *Yum, more green stuff.* I actually enjoyed the drink now, taking it down with little difficulty.

The door slid open. Lancaster stood in the doorway of his room. People were moving the wrong way down the hall, in the direction of the challenge arena. We just had a challenge the other day. Why would we be going back there again already?

I worked my way into the crowd as it pushed to the challenge arena, where the ceiling had been removed and light from the morning sky trickled into the room. A huge rock wall shot up from the ground into the sky. It had to reach several hundred feet high. The ten remaining trainees stood at the base of the huge wall, heads tilted back, trying to see the top. I'd never seen anything so tall in my life.

The clouds moved past the top of the wall, making me feel like I was swaying. The illusion was dizzying. I forced my attention back to the ground and felt my body regain its balance. Searching the crowd, I made my way over to Lancaster and Goby. Brantley joined us shortly after.

"What do you think we'll have to do today?" I asked, trying to take their focus off the wall.

Goby smiled. "Looks to me like we'll be climbing."

I scanned the group. "Don't you think it's a little odd to have another challenge so quickly?"

Lancaster shook his head. "Do we really know what to expect? This is all a mystery to us."

He was right. We didn't have anything to judge the future on. They could have a challenge a day from here on out for all we knew. There was no telling what they wanted us to do or when they wanted us to do it.

The ten of us were beginning to grow restless. A number of the people paced back and forth looking at the ground. I could feel the anxiety growing in me as well. I just wanted some direction. Some kind of clue as to what we were here for.

As if reading my mind, the Training Speaker took his position. He cleared his throat and said, "Today marks the start of the final challenges. Each challenge will require mastery of a different skill set. Today we test your strength and endurance. Climb!"

The speech ended and the horn sounded. The group rushed to the wall, grabbing hold of the different grips moving upward. I hesitated slightly, reaching the wall last. Number Eleven was already about fifteen feet up the wall as I reached for my first hold. Wrapping my fingers over the top of the rocklike grip, I stuck my feet onto the wall. I moved quickly, using my long legs to reach for various holds, propelling myself up.

I was quickly even with Eleven on the wall. We had scaled about forty feet. My forearms were starting to burn a little from the various small holds. I found a large grip, squeezing in with my right arm. I took my left arm off the wall and shook it out then switched, giving my right hand a good shake. Eleven never slowed, still moving up the wall. I knew eventually he would need to rest. It was too high of a climb not to.

As I let my arms recover I searched back down the wall. Goby, Lancaster, and Brantley were in the middle of the pack. *That's good*, I thought as I returned my attention to the next phase of the climb, reaching over my head for a grip. I dug my foot into another hole, pressing my weight upward. I slid along the wall, moving quickly again. I flew past Eleven as the fatigue started to catch up to him, gaining about a fifteen-foot lead. The grips at the beginning of the wall were larger, but over the last thirty feet they had slowly started to decrease in size.

I was starting to have trouble finding good holds. I found a good spot to wedge my body in, stopping again to survey the wall. I scanned the various grips to my right and left. That's when I saw my next move: a crack in the wall about three inches wide that ran from just above and to the left of my current location the remaining hundred or so feet to the top. I worked laterally to my left, sliding into position. The crack was now directly above me.

I was just a couple of feet from the start of the crevice. There was a nice piece of rock sticking out of the wall slightly above me to the left, just out of my reach. I repositioned my feet, giving myself a little extra leverage. Hoisting myself upward, I grabbed for the hold. The rock ripped from the wall. I lost my balance and began to slide down the wall as my right hand squeezed the grip it was on as hard as I could. The rocklike grip flew down, whipping past three of the other trainees, including Eleven.

My right hand and foot were all that kept me on the wall. My left leg and hand swung as I tried to regain control. Though it was probably more like a few seconds, it felt like minutes passed as I tried to regain my balance against the wall. I finally regained control and began reaching for a hold with my left hand. That's when I felt something pulling at my left leg. I looked down. Eleven had caught up—he was right on my heels now—and was grabbing at my shoes. I pulled my left foot up out of his grasp. I searched the wall for a grip, something that I could get ahold of to pull myself up and away from him.

Eleven lifted himself up, grabbing at my foot again. He hooked onto my left foot, but I kicked downward, causing him to lose his grip on me again. It was almost enough to send him off the wall. He had a good hold with his right hand and both feet, though. I frantically scanned the wall for my next hold, grabbing at a spot just up to my left. It was right below the crack. If I could get there I would be home free and out of danger.

I looked down between my body and the wall at Eleven. He was repositioning himself for another grab at me. I put my left foot up onto another ledge. I was just out of his reach. I reached upward with my right hand, finding just enough of a grip in the crack in the wall. I wedged my fingers inside the crack, pulling to the right, and hoisted myself up using my legs. I wedged my left hand into the crack just above my right.

My hands, both in the crack now, pulled in opposite directions like I was trying to rip the wall apart. I moved slowly. I was finally completely into the crack, my toes wedged into the small crevice and my hands pulling to keep me tight to the wall. This was a good path to the top, but it was also a very vulnerable position. If I were to slip now I wouldn't have enough strength to hold myself up. I needed to create leverage with my feet and then find some grips outside the crack.

Firmly wedged into the crack, I began my search for holds for my hands. I saw a few spots to grab, sliding my hands away from the crack while keeping my feet pressed tightly into it.

Putting all of my weight on my right foot, I slipped my left foot into the crack just above it. Perfect. Now I was wedged in tight. With my feet in position I could now slide along the crack as I climbed the remainder of the wall. I positioned my hands on various grips outside the small crevice as I slowly walked one foot over the other up the crack. It was slow going, as I had to make sure one foot was secure before moving the other into position.

I peered over my right shoulder; seeing that I had regained space between myself and Eleven, I felt a little more at ease. He was still trying to find a way up the wall using the smaller holds. I guess he didn't feel as comfortable as me using the crack. I had about twenty feet left to the top. I continued to shimmy my way up the crack, reaching the summit first. I placed both hands on the top of the wall, dragging myself over and onto my back.

I slid my feet onto the floor at the top of the wall, positioning myself to look back over the side. Brantley was right behind Eleven, almost even with him on the wall. She was a good ten feet to the side of him, though, which made me feel a little more comfortable. I wouldn't have put it past him to throw her off the wall if he could. Goby was still in the middle of the pack. Lancaster had fallen to the back.

Lancaster was one of three at the rear of the group. It was the boy from Section Five, the boy from Section Fifteen, and Lancaster. I watched as he moved slowly and deliberately, struggling to find holds. Brantley and Eleven reached the top as Lancaster fell a little behind the boys from Section Five and Section Fifteen. Goby was only about thirteen feet from the top now. If Lancaster was going to make it through this challenge he was going to have to pick up the pace.

Goby pulled himself up over the ledge right next to where I was positioned. I returned my focus to Lancaster. "Come on, Lank, you're almost there!"

Goby and Brantley flanked me on either side as we watched the last three fight their way to the summit. I could see the fatigue on Lancaster's face. I knew he was running out of steam. The boy from Section Fifteen reached the top, pulling himself over. Only the boy from Section Five and Lancaster remained. Lancaster had slowed practically to a halt. He squeezed the wall, pressing himself close to it. He didn't have anything left.

The boy from Section Five grabbed the top. I closed my eyes, knowing Lancaster had lost. I leaned my head back, knowing that when we got down he would be taken off to be reassigned.

A scream tore through the silence. My eyes shot open. I looked back over the edge of the wall. My eyes met Lancaster's just before his body hit the ground hundreds of feet below.

Did he let go? What happened? I watched as blood started to pool up around his motionless body. I looked back at the wall. It was flat, straight, and as sleek as a floor. There were no more rock-like grips. They had all vanished. Even the crack that I had used to scale the wall was gone. There was nothing. I looked at the others as the shock on their faces said it all. Even those who weren't in our group looked terrified.

They had made him fall. This wasn't an accident. There was no reassignment. This was exactly what I had feared all along. Everyone stood quietly, unable to take their focus off of Lancaster's lifeless body.

Goby was pale. He pulled away from the wall and vomited. Then he crouched down, covering his face. He and

Lancaster had grown so close these last few weeks. I knew this loss was going to be hard on him. It was going to be hard on all of us. I didn't have any words to comfort him this time. I sat down next to Goby on the floor. Brantley sat down next to me. I didn't want to move.

An elevator appeared and Tinker motioned everyone onto the platform. I slowly climbed to my feet, pulling Goby from the ground. Helping him to the elevator, we made our way back to the arena floor. By the time we arrived back at ground level, Lancaster's body was gone. All that remained was the bloodstain from where he'd hit.

The Training Speaker cleared his throat, getting the group's attention. "Congratulations to the final nine. You will have thirty minutes in your quarters and then proceed to lunch."

That's it. That's all he's got. They just killed a kid. A brilliant and talented kid and that's the statement he's got. Anger surged inside of me like I had never felt before. I wanted to kill him. Jump up on his little platform stage and rip his heart out in front of the group. But what would that solve besides probably getting me killed too? It wasn't going to bring Lancaster back. Instead, I put my head down and wandered back to my room.

In my room I lost my composure. I let the anger out, yelling, throwing anything I could get my hands on. I ripped the drawers out of the dresser. Threw the sheets and pillows off the bed. I slammed my hands on the top of the counter by the sink. After a five-minute rage-fueled outburst, I finally started to calm down. I turned the shower on.

I put my hands on the wall of the shower, letting the hot water run off my head and down my back. I closed my eyes, listening to the sound of the water trickling down my body. I slowly started to calm, and my breathing gradually returned to normal. I didn't move for about three minutes as images of Lancaster flashed through my memory. I couldn't believe he was gone. I slowly started washing up. I finished my shower and changed into clean clothes.

By the time I reached the surface for lunch, everyone else was already at the tables eating. Goby and Brantley sat quietly, each picking at a piece of bread, the majority of their lunch sitting untouched on their plates. I took a seat next to Brantley, across from Goby. His eyes were red as he looked at me. He shook his head and then returned to his bread.

I took a deep breath, letting it out slowly. "Listen, guys, we need to block out what happened today."

"Forget?" Goby's eyes narrowed. "They killed him, Dantin. How do you block that out?"

I shook my head. "I don't know"—I paused for a second, trying to gather my thoughts—"but we have to find a way. It's up to us to honor the rest of the group that's no longer with us."

Goby shook his head. "They're all dead. Everyone is dead!" Goby's voice echoed through the silence, causing everyone's heads to turn. "Soon I'll be dead, you'll be dead"—he gestured at Brantley—"and you'll be dead." He looked at me.

Everyone was watching our table now. Even some of the capital guards were looking our way. I reached across the table and grabbed Goby's hand, urging him to calm down. The last thing we needed was for him to be taken away before even doing a challenge.

Still holding his hand, I spoke softly. "We still have each other, and we still have a long way to go until the final four. Don't lose focus now. I know today was terrible, and Lancaster will be greatly missed. But I still need both of you. Lancaster wouldn't want you to quit fighting. I can't lose you too. We've still got too much to fight for."

I could feel the tears beginning to well up in my eyes again. Brantley wrapped her arms around me, resting her head on my shoulder. She whispered, "I'm still with you."

"Good. Together we can still make it to the end," I replied. I looked over to Goby. "Are you still with us?"

"Of course. I just didn't think you were right about the reassignment. I never would have thought that they would kill us all off," Goby said, wiping the tears from his eyes.

He was right, though. I thought the reassignment situation was bogus, but killing all of us off … even though I had thought it, I'd never really believed it. Not until I saw Lancaster lying at the base of the wall, bleeding onto the floor. That was the moment that let all of us know what the people of Heart City were capable of.

Lunch passed quickly. Instead of training, we were all gathered into a movie. It had something to do with why the government had to be more controlling than old America. I didn't actually watch. I stared at the floor watching my feet kick for the majority of the movie, lost in thought. I couldn't stop wondering why we were chosen. What is our purpose in all of this? What does the government expect from us? What does it mean to make the final four?

The movie was long. Several hours passed. After the show, everyone was sent to their mentor for training. Tinker stopped at the usual door, leading me inside before disappearing back down the hall. As I entered the room, I met Gaia's eyes. She stood up from her seat, welcoming me into the room.

I felt the sadness inside me. "You were wrong!"

Gaia frowned slightly. "What do you mean?"

"About reassignment. There is no reassignment. They killed Lancaster today. He lost the challenge and they killed him. Why did you lie to me? Why?" I let all of my hurt and betrayal show, even though I knew she didn't know anything about what really happened to people who were "reassigned." Or at least if she did, she was good at hiding it.

"What? I'm so sorry." Gaia moved around the table. "Are you OK?"

I shook my head. I could feel the tears coming on again as I pictured Lancaster's scream and motionless body. "No. No, I'm not."

Gaia grabbed me, wrapping her arms around my neck. "I'm sorry, I didn't know. I was told that if you didn't complete training you were reassigned." She squeezed my neck tight.

"Get off me!" I pushed her arms away angrily. "What else aren't you telling me?"

Gaia looked at me, eyes wide with shock and hurt. "I wasn't lying. Everything I told you was the truth. At least as far as I knew, it was the truth. You have to believe me."

I stood, shaking my head, trying to get a grip on everything that was happening. I wanted to believe Gaia, but she was one of them. Or was she in the dark about all this like us? I didn't know what to think anymore. This was all too much to handle right now. Gaia moved back next to me. She wrapped her arms around my neck again.

I didn't move. I let her hang around my neck as I tried to calm myself. After a few moments, I slowly brought my hands up around her lower back, hugging her back.

"I need to get smarter," I said. "Fast. I don't know if I will make it through a problem-solving challenge. I … I'm not ready to die."

It was the first time since starting training that I had thought about dying. It was strange to open up like that in front of someone, especially since Gaia was from the capital. I didn't know if I could trust her. I wanted to, but there was part of me that felt like she was just another part of this system designed to control us. She didn't know what it was like in the Sections. She didn't know me, what I'd been through these last few weeks. Why was I opening up to her anyway? I pulled my hands back, pushing her away from me again.

Then I saw the tears in her eyes. She really did care.

I brushed the tears away from her cheek. "I need you now. Can you help me?"

She sniffled softly, rubbing the tears from her eyes. She nodded her head. "Yes."

Training that day was very productive. Each problem produced a different challenge, yet I worked my way through them. I was starting to get the hang of these problems. I still worked too slowly at times, but it was rare that I missed an answer. Hopefully, that would be enough to make it through the next problem-solving challenge.

An hour passed, then Tinker appeared, dismissing me from training. It was dinnertime. Back on the surface the night air was comfortable. There was a light breeze that blew through the garden. I gazed up at the stars, hoping Lancaster was looking down over us. I hoped that there was at least someone looking over us. We could use all the help we could get right now. There was no telling when the next challenge would be.

"How are you guys holding up?" I asked as I pulled up a seat at the table.

"I'm OK," Brantley said, looking over at me. "I think Goby is still out of it a little."

"I'm OK; it's necessary to have casualties when trying to find those capable of defending Natio," Goby spouted off, almost as if being instructed.

I looked at him, confused. Then I looked over at Brantley, who was nodding her head. "He's right, Dantin. There will always be casualties during war."

"War? What war? What are you guys talking about?"

Goby looked at me. "Like the movie said, we have been chosen to protect Natio and the government. It's sad, but war is always sad. To avoid more bloodshed there must be small battles to protect the larger population."

"What?" I replied, confused.

I didn't know what to make of any of this. Then I remembered I hadn't watched the movie earlier, just listened to the words a little. I knew what the movie was about, but I must have missed something by not watching.

There was something about those movies. I wasn't sure what, but there had to be a reason for them.

Brantley put her hand on my shoulder. "We just have to be stronger than the others," she said. "Like you said, Dantin, only four of us survive, so let's make sure it's us."

I nodded my head. It was the first thing they had said that made any sense. "That's right, let's be the ones to survive."

Chapter 14

The rest of the week passed without any challenges. It was back to the usual routine. Breakfast smoothie. Training protocols, lunch, more training, dinner, and while the rest of the group attended a movie, I trained some more. The odd behavior that Goby and Brantley had displayed had subsided slightly. They still seemed to be oddly comfortable with the current situation, but I chalked it up to just trying to move forward.

It had been five days without a challenge. I knew it was only a matter of time before the next challenge presented itself. In these last five days, while consistent with what I had grown used to, one thing was different: Lancaster wasn't there to greet me each morning. I was finding it hard to get used to; I kept waiting for the door to slide open and to see him standing there, ready to start the day.

I knew he was gone, but his loss had definitely hit me hard. I did the best I could to keep focused on the tasks at hand. I focused my energy on the work. This morning's training session had gone well with Gaia. I was starting to feel very confident in my ability to problem-solve. My other training sessions were successful as well. I was dialed-in during target practice with all of my weapons and I had a strong workout before lunch. Despite all the distractions, I was feeling good.

The sun was hot today at lunch. As I sat at the table, sweat started to form on my brow and I could feel beads of sweat forming on my back. There was little talking today. Maybe it was the heat. Perhaps it was because we knew there would be another challenge soon. Either way, we didn't have much to say.

The food—some kind of chicken dish—was good. I couldn't stop shoveling it into my mouth. I think I went through two full plates before cutting myself off. I'm not sure where the hunger surge came from, but I wasn't alone. Everyone seemed to be shoveling in their meals.

When the horn sounded to end lunch, Tinker came up to escort the group down the elevator. We didn't go to the assembly hall, though. Instead, we were passing by our quarters to the challenge arena. This was the first afternoon challenge we'd had. They really were trying to keep us off-balance by changing the challenges. The times, the days—everything was random now. There was no telling what was coming next.

In the room there were nine tables. I knew instantly what the challenge was going to be. I was going to have my recently honed problem-solving skills put to the test. I felt my heart quicken. A lump formed in my throat. A cold sweat broke out on my back. I was coming unhinged. I needed to relax. I closed my eyes, but visions of failure filled my mind.

I shook my head, trying to shake the thoughts. Then I remembered a technique my grandpa used to use with Micca to calm her down when she was starting to get worked up. He would say, "Your breath is the key to your control."

I remember watching him teach Micca to control her breathing. I closed my eyes and drew in a large breath through my nose, filling my lungs with as much air as I could. I held the breath there and then tried to inhale again on top of all the air I already had. Then I let everything leak out through my mouth in one long exhalation. I repeated this act two more times. I felt my heart start to slow. My mind became clear and I began to relax.

The Training Speaker addressed the group. "Ladies and gentlemen, please take a seat at one of the tables. Today's challenge will begin shortly, once everyone is settled in. Good luck."

I made my way to a table situated along the outside where I could see the rest of the group. I needed to make sure that I could see when people started to complete the challenge. I knew that seeing people finish before me wasn't going to speed me up or help me answer the questions in any way, but I felt it did let me know whether or not I was making good time. I took another one of Grandpa's deep breaths, trying to calm my nerves. It was almost time to start.

A horn sounded and an image appeared on the desk, as if it were some kind of projection screen. It was a seven-by-seven box with a bunch of arrows in it. I focused on the image for a moment, trying to get a sense of what it was. It was a maze! In the lower lefthand corner there was a box marked START. It was lit red with an arrow pointing up and to the right. Toward the upper righthand corner was a green box with the word GOAL. Each choice led to another set of arrows. The arrows pointed in all directions. I assumed only one way led to the goal.

I studied the possible choices, choosing to go right first. I touched the box to the right of the start point. The box illuminated, turning red. *Is red good?* I had three choices now. I studied the options; I could move up, diagonally to the right, or straight right again. I pushed the button diagonally right. The box turned red. *I hope red is good.* I pushed right three more times, positioning myself closer to the goal.

I was now at a point where I could go up or right. I chose up the next two times. I now was forced to move diagonally right again. This time it pushed me back left. I was starting to run into boxes that left me no choice but to follow their direction. This didn't feel right. I moved a few more spaces, finding myself stuck in a circle. There was no way out.

I reached up and pushed the reset button at the upper right of the table. The START box relit red. I looked up, checking the progress of the rest of the group. There were already three people done. *I'd better figure this out quick or I'm in trouble.* I retrained my focus on the board, trying to block the growing anxiety. I could feel the sweat starting to run across my forehead again. I changed directions, this time pushing the button just above the start button.

Now I could go up or diagonally right. I figured I needed to make my way to the goal, so I chose the diagonally right path, then I moved right. This time I was at a three-way junction: up, right or down. I didn't want to go down; that would be the same path I was on before. I looked right, quickly seeing my options. I had a feeling that up was the right way, so I went with it. The box lit up. I pushed up again.

I was on the same level as the GOAL now. I could move right or left. I looked right and saw that it was a trap. I chose left, and the box lit up. I pushed upward two more spaces. I was at the top of the maze now. Only one real way to go, so I pushed right. As the next box lit up I glanced at the group. There were only three people still looking at their mazes. I quickly switched my gaze back to the maze.

The next spot led me downward at an angle to the right. Another three-way junction: left, right, or down. I studied my options, taking a quick peek at the GOAL. Down was a trap. So was right. I pushed left. Then up diagonally to the right. I was closing in; I could feel it. I moved right again. Only a few more moves. I looked up. Only one person still had their head down.

I snapped back to my maze, pushing the button to the right and then down. Last two moves. Diagonally down to the left, and I was there at the GOAL. I glanced over at the kid who had his head still down, trying to figure out his next move. Suddenly his eyes shot up from the maze. Wide. Filled with fear. Dark as night.

His body began to shake and contort in his chair. I couldn't help but watch as he shook violently, foam forming at his mouth. His eyes went from wide and dark to rolling into the back of his head. Foam spilled from his mouth, and his body shook several more times. Two more shakes as the tremor passed. Then the kid's head fell forward, limp on his chest, the weight forcing him facedown onto the table.

The whole group watched in terror, unable to avert our gaze. I kept waiting for him to regain consciousness even though I knew there was no coming back for him. He had been eliminated. It was the boy from Section Fifteen. Facedown in a pool of vomit and foam.

I felt a surge of relief as I realized I had survived again. Then I felt guilty for being thankful that it wasn't me. My emotions battled with each other before my attention was torn away from the dead boy by the sight of the Training Speaker.

"Congratulations," he said. "You have survived yet again and are now part of the final eight. There will be a short recess to go to your quarters and then dinner will be served." The Speaker smiled as he stepped down and disappeared out of sight.

Two men entered the room, removing the boy from Section Fifteen. That's when I noticed the small needle in the bottom of the chair. I looked back at my chair noticing the small hole as the rest of the group silently scurried out of the room. Nobody spoke as we made our way to our quarters where we could calm our nerves. I stood in front of the mirror looking hard at myself. That was the second time I barely escaped the problem-solving challenge. I was still cutting it too close. I took a deep breath, letting it out and splashing water on my face.

The stress of the challenge made the time in the room fly by. The horn sounded, releasing us to dinner, and I took the elevator to the surface. The rides up were a lot less crowded than they had been earlier in training. With only nine—eight, as of a little while ago—of us left, most of the time we rode the elevators alone or with just one other person.

On the surface, the night air felt significantly cooler than earlier. I moved through the garden to the table. Brantley and Goby were already there again. I apparently took more time in my quarters than most.

Brantley jumped up from the table, wrapping her arms around my neck. "I was so worried when there were only two of you left working on that puzzle."

I squeezed my arms around her. "Me too. Me too."

The sight of the boy shaking violently flashed through my head. That could have been me. Shaking uncontrollably to my death. I let my arms relax from Brantley, pulling up a seat at the table.

Goby smiled at me, looking up from his food. "Glad you made it, buddy."

I smiled. "Yeah. You think you could share a little of that brain of yours? I saw you were done before I realized I had gone the wrong way."

Goby laughed a little. "Only if you can share a little of all the other skills you have on me. I think that'd be a fair trade. Some of your height, strength, speed, shooting ability, and combat skills for a few problem-solving abilities."

Brantley chimed in, "Goby, you could also give him a little of your good looks to sweeten the deal." She winked across the table and then punched me in the arm.

Goby chuckled. "Yeah, sure, I think that works. Anyway, I don't think they'll do any more mental challenges. I find it hard to believe they would risk losing some of their better talent on a challenge like that. They can always continue to work on problem-solving abilities. They can't teach size, strength, or physical abilities. So, I think you're in the clear from here on out," he said, looking at me.

"I don't know about in the clear. But if there aren't any more mental challenges I don't think I'd protest." I smiled, reaching for some of the dinner that was piled on the table.

Goby smiled. "It's hard to believe there are only four more challenges left. We're so close, but it still feels so impossible."

Brantley and I nodded. It was hard to believe we were getting close to the end of the training process but with each challenge potentially being the end of one of us, it didn't feel like we were any closer. It actually made it feel impossibly far away.

"I agree, the pressure to survive makes it seem like this will never be over. Like we're not actually getting any closer to the end of this all," I said, looking at Goby.

"But we are closer," Brantley insisted, trying to inspire us to stay positive. "Just a few more challenges. We've made it this far; we can finish this together."

I smiled at Brantley. "You're right. We can do this."

There was little talk after that. As dinner ended, the horn sounded to send us back down to the assembly hall. I watched the group disappear into the theater as Tinker led me back down the corridor. I had taken this walk so many times now that the twisting hallway system was no longer confusing. I could find my way on my own, but I had a feeling that was something that would be frowned upon.

Gaia met me halfway across the room as I entered. She jumped into my arms, wrapping her arms around my neck. This was my second nice hug today. I wasn't sure what this one was for. She held me for what felt like minutes. Slowly, she released her grip, backing away from me. She continued to hold her gaze as she smiled at me.

"I heard there was another challenge today. After what you told me last time I was worried. I didn't know who got eliminated," she said softly, a slight tremble in her voice.

I nodded. "Yeah, it was a close call. I think I should be thanking you for all your extra help with me. It was a problem-solving challenge. A maze. I finished second to last. I don't know how close the other kid was to finishing, but it scared me."

"Well, all that matters is that you did finish. That, and …" —Gaia paused for a moment—"and you're still here. Do you want to do some problems today or just relax? I can understand if you don't feel up to doing more problems after what you went through earlier."

I moved to the table, pulling up a seat. "Let's just hang out for a little bit, then we can do some problems. I could use a friend right now. I want to talk about anything except what I'm dealing with here. It's been a lot."

Gaia pulled her chair around the table to the same side as me. "I can do that. What would you like to talk about?"

I wasn't really sure. I thought for a second, then asked, "How about we start with what did you do today?" I smiled at her. "Then maybe you can tell me some of the hobbies you like?"

"Well, today started early. I had to get up to get ready for train—" She stopped short, took a breath, then continued, "Actually, I went into the park this afternoon and spent most of the day under a tree. I listened to music and soaked in the sun."

Why did she stop? Is she hiding something? What isn't she telling me? What train? I decided not to push it and instead decided to ask about the music. "Listened to music? Was there a band playing?" I wasn't sure how she was able to listen to music. In Section Eight we only heard music if someone was singing or during the Remembrance Day celebration.

Gaia reached in her pocket, pulling out a small device. It had lights on it and a couple of buttons. She pushed one and sound burst into the air. "See? Music."

I was amazed that something so small could produce a sound so great. "What is that?"

"It plays our music. Don't you have these in the Sections?" Gaia asked.

I shook my head. "No, the only music we have is the kind we have to play. We don't even have lights. We use candles and fire. Although it did appear that this year they were beginning to introduce some of the string lights for us. All of this stuff here is so foreign to me."

Gaia looked sad, trying to find her words. "You don't have anything like this?"

"No, everything in the Sections is very controlled," I said slowly. "They regulate everything from our clothes, to food, to job—everything. It's a pretty simple life."

"I didn't know it was so bad." Gaia's sadness seemed genuine. She truly didn't know what it was like in the Sections, and it upset her.

"It's not all bad. It's just simple. We aren't being tortured or anything. Maybe someday it will be like this place. Besides, the government says it's in our best interest to not have such things. It's what led to the Bloodfire in the first place."

Gaia smiled at my optimism. "So, tell me, Dantin, is there someone special back home?"

I shook my head. "I mean, there's my mom, sister, and grandpa. I don't think that's what you mean, though, is it?"

"Not exactly," Gaia said shyly.

I looked down at the table, then back at Gaia. "No, they don't really give us much time for romance back home. It's a lot of work, work, and more work. In that way it's kind of like it is here for training. But, truthfully, I never really made an effort. A lot of times marriages are arranged by the parents. Families try to strengthen their position by marrying their children to those they think will improve their standing. Besides, I had my family to look out for, so that always came first. What about you? Is there anyone special here?"

Gaia shook her head. "No, not really. The guys here aren't like you."

I felt my heart flutter at the comment. Cold chills ran down my arm, leaving small bumps behind. "What do you mean like me?"

Gaia blushed a little. "Well, the guys here are weak and fragile. They are into themselves and are all very flamboyant. They're all about moving up in the government and their status. They aren't able to talk. Where you—"

The door opened, interrupting her comments. Tinker stood in the doorway. "Time for bed, Number Fifteen."

I smiled at Gaia as I stood from my chair. "Goodnight, Gaia."

"Goodnight, Dantin," she said softly with a smile.

In my room I lay awake on my bed. *Guys like me? What did she mean by that? Does she like me?*

No, there's no way. Not a guy from the Sections. She was just intrigued by my differences. She could have any guy she wanted here in the capital. That's what it is: it's a trap. It's another game or a part of the training. They are trying to trick me by having her pretend to like me.

Stop it, stupid. You're being paranoid.

I shook my head, breaking my thoughts. This place had really done a number on my ability to trust people. My mind was always trying to convince me of the worst in people. But I still wanted to believe in the good.

I felt my head start to ache from the confusion. I rolled over onto my stomach, burying my face into the pillow. I yelled. The muffled sound was barely audible through the thick pillow. I rolled back onto my back. Stars danced above my head from the yell.

I rubbed my eyes, trying to calm myself. This day had been the most stressful day yet. My emotions ran wild. I tried to close my eyes, clearing all of my thoughts. The stress of the day had me struggling to fully grasp all that was happening around me. I needed to regain my composure. There were still a number of trials I would have to complete. Final eight. Four more would be eliminated before this was over. I still needed to focus if I was going to survive.

*****

The morning horn sounded, raising me from my sleep. The lights shot on and the door to the room ripped open. This wasn't the usual morning routine. The horn sounded again as I strained to see, my eyes not yet adjusted to the light. Tinker stood in the doorway on the other side of the hallway, directing people into the challenge arena. A few trainees walked by as I finally got to my feet.

Another challenge? They must be trying to weed us out quickly. Not even a full day between challenges. I fumbled my way across the room. I threw my uniform on and pushed out into the hall. Everyone was moving through the door into the challenge arena. I followed, still trying to shake the cobwebs from being jarred awake. It felt extremely early, like I had only been asleep for an hour at most. I yawned and shook my head as I joined the group in front of the Training Speaker.

"Good morning, Chosen Ones," he said. "Today we will continue to find out which of you will have what it takes to make the final four. There are spots on the ground behind you with your number. When I dismiss you, make your way to your spot and prepare for the challenge. You will travel across the parallel bars until the horn sounds. Good luck."

This seemed like an odd challenge. All we had to do was cross the parallel bars until the horn sounded. Seemed easy enough to me. I turned, finding my number on the ground. In front of the number there was a set of steps leading up to the parallel bars. Each person had a small area to start from that was all their own. After a few bars everyone merged onto one set of parallel bars.

I guess this is where things could get interesting. It could get quite crowded with eight of us working our way across the bars. I climbed the steps leading up to the bars and waited for the next set of instructions.

The horn sounded. No instructions. I watched everyone else climb the stairs in front of them and grab onto the bars. I followed suit and slowly worked my way onto my private section, letting a number of people move farther onto the shared section.

Number Eleven jumped out in front. I finally reached the portion that was shared by everyone, finding myself next to Brantley. I moved forward as she swung next to me. I was only a couple of bars onto the shared portion when a sound distracted me. Two walls shot up from the ground, one blocking where we had entered the parallel bars and one at the far end, preventing an exit. I stopped my progress, swinging slightly in place.

The floor rumbled, pulling apart. I looked down as the ground separated. As the space below us became wider, I noticed that in the space was a kind of bubbling liquid. It appeared to be extremely hot, yet there was no steam coming from it. I looked closely at it, trying to figure out what it might be. It continued to bubble and gurgle. It had a silver tint to it. I wasn't sure what it was, but I knew I didn't want to be the one to find out.

Seeing that there was no use moving I held my ground and tried to clear my mind of what was going on around me. I felt myself go calm as my body became lighter. I opened my eyes, watching the people around me begin to panic, swinging around the bars, wasting precious energy. There was no use trying to move; there was nowhere to go. The girl from Section Three screamed as Eleven pushed his way past her. She almost lost her grip moving away from him to let him pass.

I watched him move closer to the middle, then stop, hanging alone. Nobody would dare go near him. He'd knock anyone off the bars who went near him. I changed my focus. The bars at the far end had started to turn red. I squinted, trying to see what was happening. I turned my head, looking back to the start. The bars there were also red.

Every couple of seconds, the next set of bars began to glow. They looked as though they were starting to heat up. People closest to the edges began to move in closer to the middle. Goby was situated behind Number Eleven, close to the middle. Brantley was still next to me. I looked at her; she was really starting to struggle. I turned myself on the bars, facing her.

"Hey, we need to move to the middle. The edges are going to start getting hot. Are you able to move?"

Brantley shook her head. "I don't think so."

I looked at the red bars as they started to close in on us. We still had several bars between us and the heat, but we couldn't hope to wait it out where we were. I needed to get her to move at least a couple of bars just to be safe. I looked over at the other end as the bars began to close in on a couple of people on the far side. I couldn't make out who they were, but they were beginning to move to the middle as well.

"I'm right here with you," I told Brantley. We need to move, just a few bars. OK? You can do this."

Brantley nodded her head. She swung slightly, throwing her right hand forward to the next bar. She quickly grabbed it. Her left arm joined it so that she was hanging on with both arms again. She began to swing again as I moved laterally next to her. She reached again, grabbing the next bar with her right hand. She pulled her left off, reaching for the bar in front of her.

Brantley screamed as her left hand slipped, sending her body forward. She hung with one arm as her fingers started to slip from the bar. I moved quickly forward, grabbing a bar next to her. Her right hand slipped, sliding from the bar as she let out another scream. I threw my left hand down, grabbing her wrist as she fell, and gripped tightly to the bar above me with my right hand.

Sweat beaded across my forehead. My right arm screamed a burning sensation began to build up in my forearm as if the muscle was on fire. I squeezed my fingers tightly around Brantley's wrist as she dangled below me. We swung ever so slightly back and forth, creating more tension in my right arm. I stared into Brantley's eyes as we hung there.

"Don't let go!" she screamed up at me.

"Grab onto me with your other arm," I said, gesturing to her free hand.

"I can't," Brantley wailed.

"You're going to have to. I don't know how much longer I can hold on. You need to get your other hand on me. I will help."

Brantley began to reach upward, grabbing at my midsection with her free hand. I pulled upward at her wrist, lifting her slightly higher. Her hand gripped onto my shirt, then around my waist. I pulled on her arm again, getting her up a little higher. I wrapped my legs around her just under her hips. Crossing them, I held her tightly in place.

"Brantley, you're going to have to let go of my arm and wrap around me. I have you with my legs. If I don't get my other arm back, we won't last much longer." I could feel my fingers starting to slide from the bar.

Brantley nodded. "OK, I'll try."

"Don't worry, I have you. On three. One. Two. Three." I pulled hard at her arm, lifting her up again slightly as I reached behind my back before letting go of her hand. She slapped her arms together around my waist. I could feel her squeeze, locking into place. I reached up for the bar and grasped it with my left hand, releasing some of the strain on my right arm.

The burning sensation in my arms grew with every passing second. There was no moving at this point, so my only hope would be for someone else to fall before us. Brantley gripped my waist tightly, her head pressed against my stomach. I still had my legs wrapped around her for extra support. I felt my hands start to rip again, fingers sliding slowly from the bar. This was it: we were going to go down together.

I looked down at Brantley, and our eyes met. I think she knew I didn't have much longer to hold on. She mouthed the words "thank you" to me. I looked back at my fingers; all I had left were a couple of fingertip holds. A scream echoed through the arena as my grip failed, sending us hurling down toward the pit below. Brantley squeezed me tightly as we fell.

Suddenly, we stopped falling, floating a few inches from the liquid.

Screams filled the arena. I looked down to my waist, thinking it was Brantley. She squeezed me tightly, eyes clenched shut, but she wasn't screaming. Another bloodcurdling wail echoed through the challenge arena. I looked at what held us up. It was some kind of invisible shield. That's when I saw the girl from Section Three sinking into the liquid, her flesh being torn away by it.

She was bright red, bleeding as her skin melted. The bones in her hands were already starting to show as she screamed again. I looked away. Another scream, this time more muffled, as if she were gargling water. It was the last sound. I looked back to where she had been. All that remained were bits of flesh and hair floating on the surface. Then that, too, was gone.

I tapped Brantley on the back of her head. She opened her eyes and looked up at me. "We're OK. We made it," I said.

"I didn't want to look. I thought the screams were you. How are we OK?" she stammered shakily.

"I think maybe the girl from Section Three fell just before we did, activating the shield to prevent more than one person from being eliminated. It doesn't really matter, though: we are OK."

Brantley slowly loosened her grip as we got to our feet. We walked slowly across the invisible shield, making our way back to solid ground. Goby joined us there, wrapping his arms around both of us. The group was now down to seven. Somehow the three of us were still a part of it. I kept my arms around Brantley and Goby as the Training Speaker took his position.

"Congratulations, everyone," he said. "We will take a short break to allow you to collect yourselves and then meet on the surface for breakfast. The rest of the day will be yours. There will be no more training today. There will be shuttles to take you into the city to enjoy a little of what Heart City has to offer. Great work, everyone." The Training Speaker finished and exited the arena.

"We get a day off," I said, squeezing my arms around Brantley and Goby.

They both smiled. I could sense excitement from them for the first time in weeks. I, too, was relieved. A day with no more stress and pressure. It was greatly needed. We made our way back down the hall to our rooms. I jumped in the shower, prepping myself for breakfast. When I got out of the shower, clothes were sitting on my bed. There was a note on them:

For your day on the town, wear this.

It was a pair of blue pants and a shirt that was a rusty orange color. I threw the clothes on, looking at myself in the mirror. I didn't feel like a number. I felt comfortable. These were the most comfortable pants I had ever worn. This outfit was nicer than anything I had ever worn before. For Heart City, I was sure it was simple, perhaps even cheap; however, for the first time in weeks I felt like a person. Today, I wasn't a slave to The Conscript.

CHAPTER 15

I was the first to arrive on the surface. I sat at the table in my usual spot, picking at some of the bread. Goby joined me next, patting me on the back as he moved around the table. He was wearing similar pants to mine with a dark blue shirt. There was a slight pattern on the front that seemed to move as he did. It was an extremely interesting effect. As he sat down, his eyes widened, staring beyond me.

I turned my head as Brantley came around the corner. It was as if time slowed. She moved gracefully around the last of the hedges, her hair flowing off of her shoulders. She wore a yellow dress. The tiny straps on her shoulders revealed her beautiful muscle tone. The dress hugged her body then became looser, flowing softly off of her, finishing about mid-thigh.

I couldn't take my eyes off her as she approached the table. As she closed in, I blinked myself back to the moment, shaking my gaze free of her. She strolled in next to the table, calling out to us, "Hey, boys! How are you guys doing?"

We were both speechless at the non-uniformed Brantley. She was like a completely different person than the one we'd been partnered with now for weeks.

Goby finally choked out, "We're good. You excited to go into the city today?"

Brantley smiled, nodding excitedly. "Yes, very much so."

I finally found some words. "You … you look beautiful," I sputtered.

Brantley blushed a little. "Thanks. You guys don't look half bad yourselves."

After a quick meal, we were taken back below. Tinker led the group through a series of hallways to the front of the building. As we exited the training facility, the sounds of the city crashed into us like a wave in the ocean. People moved quickly in all directions. Cars passed us, speeding to their destinations. The signs on the buildings showed pictures of different things that I had never seen before. Three vehicles waited for us on the edge of the walkway to take us into the city.

Goby, Brantley, and I entered the first car. Closing the door, we squeezed in next to each other in the back seat. The man in the front looked over his shoulder. "Where to?"

We all looked at each other, not sure what to tell him. I looked back at the man. "What do you recommend? We've never been here before."

The man smiled. "OK, I know the perfect place to start."

The vehicle surged forward effortlessly, soaring smoothly across the ground. We sped down the street, passing other vehicles. We swerved through traffic, turning left twice and then taking a right. After what felt like ten minutes we came to a stop. The man in the front looked back over his shoulder and smiled. "Start here. I think you'll like it. I'll be right here when you're ready to see the next place."

We filed out of the car. My eyes scanned our current location. We were in the middle of a large, open square with people moving in all directions. Buildings rose around us on all four sides. In the middle of the square was a beautiful fountain. The group made our way to it. Standing at the base, we tilted our heads back to see the top.

Water poured out of the top of the fountain, falling gently down several tiers before collecting in a pool at the base. The fountain was amazingly white. Small figures were carved with intricate detail into the sides of the centerpiece. The different tiers had small pools, and as the water traveled down from the top, each basin got larger. Its shape looked similar to one of the old pines from back home. I had never seen anything like it.

"It's amazing!" I said, still studying the details of the fountain.

"It sure is," Brantley sighed.

I took my eyes away from the fountain, scanning the square. People gathered in different places throughout the open area. There appeared to be things going on in all directions. It was too much for me to take in at once. I was overwhelmed by the size of the space and the number of people here. I scanned the area once more, my gaze stopping on a woman kneeling on the ground next to a white board.

"Over here," I said, taking off toward the woman. Goby and Brantley chased after me.

"Dantin, where are you going?" Brantley called after me.

I took a few more steps, stopping just in front of the woman, watching her work. "Right here."

The woman was using different colors to draw an image on the board. I watched as each swipe of her hand brought the next part of the picture into focus. It was incredible to watch as her hands created vivid imagery on the once completely blank white board. I moved around the board behind the woman to see what she was drawing. I tilted my head, mimicking the artist. It was beautiful!

The green flowing hills. The flowers blooming on either side. The river flowing between the hills. A man and a woman sitting on a blanket having a picnic. The colors and scene were the best I had ever seen. As the woman put the final touches on her work, I looked closely at the people in the picnic. The guy was dressed in blue pants and an orange shirt similar to mine. The woman had on a yellow dress.

She was drawing Brantley and me. I looked up at Brantley and she saw it too. As she continued to watch the artist add the final strokes to her work, a smile formed on her face. "You're amazing," she said to the artist.

"Thank you, Miss. Would you like to buy?" the artist asked, looking up at her.

Brantley frowned. "I don't have any money. We're not from here."

Then, as if the woman knew who we were, she pulled away a little and frowned to herself. "I'm sorry for your losses," she said, rolling up the picture. "A gift. I hope you have many days to enjoy it."

The woman handed the picture to Brantley, placing her hands on Brantley's. "Thank you." Brantley said, softly.

Just like that, the woman packed up her things and was gone. I stood watching as she disappeared into the crowd. Apparently, people knew about The Conscript here. Or they knew something. I wasn't sure what all was public knowledge, but there was definite remorse in her eyes and in her voice. I looked back to Brantley, who still hadn't moved, staring at the rolled-up picture in her hands. I think she shared my realization.

Goby started moving quickly across the square. "Guys, this way. Check this out!"

We followed quickly in pursuit of Goby as he weaved through the crowd. I couldn't see what he was moving toward; he was moving too quickly. I watched him pass between several people. Then, as quickly as he had taken off, the crowd split, giving me a clear view of what he had seen. It was a long row of tents lining the edge of the square. Each tent had various items in it.

It was some kind of market. There was everything a person could imagine: clothes, food, jewelry, gadgets, art, and so much more. The first two tents were women's clothes and various paintings. Brantley went straight to the clothing tent. I watched as she touched the different fabrics, running her fingers across everything. Her face changed with every touch, smiling and then scrunching up as she shook her head. I watched her, imagining what she was saying to herself.

Brantley continued to investigate the different items. So many colors and styles. The colors were so beautiful: brilliant reds, greens, and blues. Everything in the Sections was always so simple and dull with little color, if any.

Brantley smiled as she moved through the tent. She was so happy and free of fear. It was hard to believe that no more than a few hours ago we were hanging on for our lives. She seemed so at peace now. So filled with joy. It made me so happy to see her this way.

I didn't want to interrupt her pleasure, but there was a lot to see. "Brantley, let's go see what else we can find."

Brantley turned, moving through the market, almost skipping. It was a side of her I'd never seen. It made me imagine what she was like back home. She was probably always like this. Filled with happiness. Cheerful. I wished there were a way for her to be this way again. It seemed so natural for her. We turned, exiting the tent, then moved slowly down the path, taking in the various vendors and their goods.

Goby walked just ahead of us before turning and disappearing into a tent. Brantley and I followed, wondering what had caught his eye. We pushed our way into the tent, looking for where Goby had gone. I scanned the area, seeing him in the back of the tent fiddling with something. I tapped Brantley on the shoulder, nodding toward Goby. We slipped deeper into the tent, coming up next to him.

When we arrived, Goby was holding a small wooden object. "Isn't it amazing?"

I couldn't tell what it was, just that it was about twice the size of both of his hands. "What is it?" I asked.

He turned, showing me the front of the object. There was a tiny glass door framed in wood. A pendulum swung back and forth through the glass. A small face numbered one to twelve sat above the window. That's when I recognized what it was. It was a miniature grandfather clock. We didn't really tell time anymore since everything ran off the horns and whistles, but I remember my grandpa showing me one before. It had been passed down from his grandfather.

"It's a handmade clock. I've only seen old pictures of these. It's so fascinating," Goby said.

The store owner appeared behind us, watching us admire his work. "Do you like it?" he asked excitedly.

We all jumped, turning around quickly and facing the man. He was an elderly gentleman with grey hair that looked as if it were fighting to become white. He wore small glasses. His clothes were faded. The man stood staring at us, smiling slightly, showing his off-white teeth. I noticed a small walking cane in his right hand as he hobbled forward, limping slightly. He was a tiny man.

Goby looked at the man. "It's incredible. Did you make all of these?"

"Sure did, son. Spent a good portion of my life working on these things. Don't get too many people from around here coming through my tent. My guess is you're not from around here?" the old man asked, inching closer.

Goby shook his head. "No, we're not. Do you get many visitors that aren't from here?"

The man looked at the ground and then back at Goby. "Just once a year. I didn't realize it was that time already. How many of you are there left?"

I looked at the man. "There are seven left. What do you know about us?"

"Oh, not much. Just that they bring a group of you in every year. Only a few of you ever visit. Usually when they start getting down to the end. Last year when they came by there were only six. Where are you from?" he asked, pointing his cane at Goby.

Goby replied, "I'm from Section Eleven." He pointed at Brantley. "She's from Section Nine, and he's from Section Eight." He finished by pointing at me.

The man nodded. "I see. And you all have become friends? By this point I rarely have more than one of you in here at a time. This is a pleasant surprise. I sure do wish you all the best of luck. If you get a chance, I'd love to see you guys again. I hope you can stop by some other time. You go ahead and take that clock there. I can see how much you enjoy it; I hope you have many more days to appreciate it."

Goby smiled, pulling the clock in closer to his body. "Thanks!"

That was the second time someone had given us something, wishing us many days to enjoy it. I had a feeling that the people of Heart City knew more about our situation than even we did. Or perhaps they'd been around long enough to know that people came to visit once and never returned. That would be enough to think that something bad might have happened. Especially if any of the past Chosen Ones talked about what had been happening.

We exited the tent, continuing back through the path of storefronts. We made our way all the way to the end of the row. The last two stores were a clothing store and a jewelry store. Brantley and Goby entered the clothing store as I ventured on my own into the jewelry store. I peered at the items as I moved slowly through the rows. There were items of gold, silver, and beautiful colored beads.

I was looking over a number of gold pieces when I saw it: a small charm at the end of a small gold chain. It was a round gold disk with a lion's head on it. The lion looked majestic, mane full and powerful looking. It reminded me of my father and grandpa's saying about the Kingdom of Lions. I held the charm closer, studying it. There were two rings, and on the outer ring there was something written along the edge:

We Enter as One into the Kingdom of Lions.

"Do you like it?"

I jumped, dropping the charm as it swung on its prong.

"I'm sorry, I didn't see you there," I said. "Yes, I like it. It reminds me of home. Where did you get it?"

I turned, catching my first glimpse of the woman who ran the store. She was just a little older than my mother. Long auburn hair ran down to the middle of her back. Her skin was pale from lack of sun. Her body was still in relatively good shape as though she got more exercise than most people in the city. Her blue eyes studied me as I stared back at her. She leaned sideways, looking around me at the piece I had been admiring.

"That thing there, let me see … Oh, yes, I got this from a man in Section Eight many, many years ago. My guess is before you were born." Her eyes narrowed as she looked at me.

"I'm from Section Eight," I said with shock at the piece's origin.

"I see. So I guess you are here for the training?" Her eyes still studied me. She looked at me as though she knew me.

"Yeah, I am. Do you know about the training?" I asked, hoping that maybe I could learn a little more about everything that went on inside the city.

The woman shook her head. "No, not much, just what the others who visit tell me. However, I feel like your visit here today was fated. This piece here," she said, grabbing the lion charm, "was destined to return to a person from Section Eight. Today is that day. Take it. May it bring you luck."

The woman reached past me, grabbed the charm, placed it in my hand, and closed my fingers around it. "Find a way to get it back to Section Eight. It's where it belongs, just like you."

Before I could respond, the woman turned, disappearing through the back of the tent. I whispered under my breath, "Thank you." I put the charm around my neck, sliding it under my shirt.

Outside the tent, Brantley and Goby were waiting for me. "I think it's time we make our way back," Goby said, gesturing back to the square.

I nodded. "Yeah, I'm sure there are some other places to see. Assuming we still have time."

We regrouped back at the vehicle, which still sat where we had left it several hours ago. The driver had fallen asleep. He snapped awake at the sound of the door opening, fumbling through a number of words that didn't make any sense before registering where he was. He looked at us through a mirror in the front and then turned to face us.

"Back are we. What did you think?" he asked.

Brantley smiled at the man. "It was amazing."

The driver nodded. "I thought you would like it. Where to now? We don't have to be back until dark. That gives you about six hours still. Perhaps we should get some food before our next stop?"

I was getting hungry. I nodded, looking at Brantley and Goby as they, too, nodded in approval. "Let's eat."

The driver turned back around, looking out the front of the vehicle. "I know just the place."

The vehicle surged forward, rejoining the flow of traffic. I watched the various buildings pass outside my window as we traveled further into the city. It was a short ride. We turned right, coming around a corner and then quickly coming to a stop. A number of people sat along the street at tables in front of a building. It appeared to be a popular spot, as most of the tables were taken.

The driver turned back to us. "We're here. When you get inside, ask for Benzie and tell him that you're friends of Holland. He will take care of you."

I nodded, following Goby out of the car. We walked up to the building, going through the door. Inside there were double the number of people that sat in front of the building. Servers scurried back and forth, racing between tables. The sound inside was deafening as so many people attempted to carry on conversations. There was a woman standing at a small podium smiling at us. As we approached, she welcomed us.

"We were told to ask for Benzie. We are friends of Holland," I told her.

She nodded and then turned, disappearing from sight. After a few moments she returned. "Right this way," she said, grabbing a couple of menus and leading us into the restaurant.

The woman weaved through the tables, taking us toward the back of the building. We weaved through the crowd right behind her. There didn't appear to be anywhere to go ahead as all the tables were full. The woman turned right sharply, reaching the back wall of the restaurant. She grabbed at the wall, turning a piece that stuck out slightly, then pushed it open. It was a hidden door, designed to look like the back wall of the restaurant.

We passed through, entering a large room. There were several tables situated throughout the space. However, unlike in the rest of the restaurant, these were empty. The woman directed us to the table in the middle of the room, setting down the menus. After allowing us to sit, she disappeared without saying a word. I surveyed the room, trying to take it all in.

The room looked very elegant. Polished wood floors. Red curtains hung from the walls, accenting the paintings. The room was dimly lit. Along the wall small lights lit the paintings. Little chandeliers hung over each table. A silk tablecloth covered the table. It was unlike anything I'd ever seen. Everything about it felt like it was designed for luxury.

A medium-sized man appeared in the doorway. He moved swiftly to our table. He wasn't dressed like the rest of the servers inside the restaurant. He wore dark pants, a white shirt, and a dark jacket that matched his pants. The man had bronze skin and black hair. As he got closer, he smiled, revealing a set of extremely white teeth.

The man bowed slightly, then greeted us. "Hello, my name is Benzie. Welcome to my restaurant. I was told that you are friends of Holland, which means you must be part of the training. How have they been treating you?"

We all looked at each other, but nobody answered. Benzie continued, "That well, I see. Today I hope to change all that. Whatever you want is on the house, so please enjoy all that you can. Can I start you with a drink while you continue to look at the menu?"

I'd never had a choice of what I could drink. It was always water or nothing. "What kind of drinks do you have? I've only ever had water with my meals."

Benzie looked at us, appalled. "Oh, you poor thing. I know just what to bring you all. I will return shortly."

Just like that he turned, scurrying out the door. I turned to the group. "Do you find it odd that everyone knows about us?"

Goby smiled. "Not as much as it does that they wish us many more days. It's like they know most of us die."

I nodded. "Yeah, that is true. Anyway, what do you guys think you'll have for lunch? I don't even know what half of this stuff is."

Brantley shook her head. "Maybe he can just surprise us with that too. That way I don't have to guess at something."

The table laughed a little. It really was a foreign land to us. The names of foods. The multiple drink options. Even the feel of the restaurant. There was nothing like this back home. No places that people went to eat just for fun. Besides, even if there were, nobody had any money to purchase a meal like this. We simply traded our work for our survival. It was sickening just how good the people in Heart City had it.

Still, there was something about their kindness. Their constant caring and concern. Even with all the benefits they had, they seemed to care deeply about us, who had little. If it weren't for that, I don't think I'd be able to look at them without disgust. Everyone in Heart City seemed to be good people, and even though they had an abundance of things, they were very caring. In Section Eight people never had enough to share with others; it was barely enough for ourselves. But here, each one of us was given a gift today because of who we were. Now we were getting a free meal. It truly was the nicest we had been treated since coming to the city.

Benzie entered the room holding a tray with three red, bubbling drinks. Two servers followed behind him carrying sizzling trays of food. It looked like Benzie had taken it upon himself to pick out our lunch portions after all. Benzie sat the drinks in front of each of us, then directed the servers to put the food in the middle of the table. We were each given a plate and utensils to eat with.

Benzie bowed again. "Enjoy. I will return momentarily to see if you need anything else."

The smell from the food invaded my nostrils. My mouth started to water. I could feel my stomach churn, begging for a piece. It was the most intoxicating smell I'd ever experienced. I reached across the table, throwing a little bit of everything onto my plate, filling it to the point that I didn't think it would hold any more.

I took the first bite. It was incredible. The moist food melted as it touched my tongue, sending numerous sensations across my taste buds.

"Oh man, that's fantastic." I let out a moan of enjoyment as I let the food slide down my throat. I closed my eyes, trying to take in all the flavors as they lingered on my lips. It was too good to be real. I was dreaming. Except I wouldn't even know how to dream up something like this.

I opened my eyes, watching Brantley and Goby go through the same routine: eyes closed, lips locked to hold in all the flavor. They swallowed, licking their lips to try to capture all that was left. I smiled, knowing what they were experiencing. I took another bite, and again I was mesmerized by the taste. I didn't want to swallow, just hold the taste in my mouth permanently.

I picked up my drink and held it in front of my face, watching the tiny bubbles float to the surface. The red liquid fizzled as I tipped the glass to my lips. I could feel the bubbles on my tongue. As I swallowed, the liquid danced down my throat with a burning sensation. Then the taste followed, and even with the discomfort the beverage created I was driven to take another sip.

Nobody talked for the rest of lunch. The only sounds that could be heard were the tapping of silverware on the plates and the slapping of lips followed by the occasional moan of satisfaction. When I had finished as much food as my body was capable of holding, I sat back in my chair, placing my hands on my belly. I watched as Goby attempted to fit more food into his body, which was full ten minutes ago.

Benzie returned. "So, my friends, how was everything?"

Goby, mouth still full, responded, "Words would not do it justice."

Benzie smiled. "Thank you. You are too kind. I am very pleased that I could serve you fine young people today. May your stay with us be long and fruitful. If there is anything else you need, please do not hesitate to ask. Farewell."

Benzie turned, exiting the room. We sat motionless for a few minutes, trying to muster the strength to lift our overstuffed bodies. After a short moment, we fought our way to our feet, making our way back through the restaurant. At the car, Holland had fallen asleep again. The sound of the door opening startled him awake, and he turned to face us.

"It's good, no?" he asked, smiling back at us.

"It was fantastic," Brantley said.

"OK, very good. We still have time; where to now?" Holland asked, excited to continue our tour.

I looked at the group, then at Holland. "Take us where you go when you want to get away."

Holland smiled at my suggestion. "Very good, sir. I have just the place; you will love it!"

It was a short drive to our next destination. After only a few blocks we came to a stop. I looked out the window, completely unimpressed with Holland's choice of places. The buildings in this section of the city lacked the brilliance of the rest of the city. There were fewer people and lights. It looked more like an area of the city for poor people than a place to get away.

"Holland, is this it?" I asked, raising my eyebrows.

Holland shook his head. "No, no, you must take the elevator right there. It's on the surface. Go, enjoy. You will like. I promise."

We got out of the car, moving to the elevator that sat on the edge of the street. It was a public elevator to the surface. After we pushed the button near the door, a light shot from the ceiling down to the ground within the tube. The elevator door slid open and we entered. The doors slid shut and we were shot upward to the surface.

When the doors opened again, I felt my jaw drop. The scene before me was beautiful. The colors were more brilliant than anything I had ever seen. Flowers bloomed all around us. The green from the grass and trees was incredibly vibrant and more alive than anything I'd seen in the woods of Section Eight. A small stream flowed through the middle of the garden space. A path branched off, going right and left.

The sun was shining brightly and a soft breeze floated across my face. I watched as the grass danced and the trees waved. The sound of running water was peaceful as we walked closer to the creek. The path next to the creek branched off again, leading through a small archway. On the other side of the archway were rows and rows of flowers and plants. It was amazing, just like Holland had said.

Brantley smiled from ear to ear. "It's beautiful."

Goby nodded. "Yes, yes, it is." Then he ran off, disappearing into the garden.

I laughed slightly. "Where do you think he's going?"

Brantley shook her head. "I don't know. Maybe he wanted to enjoy the flowers alone." I looked over at Brantley, catching her eyes. She sure did look beautiful today. She smiled at me. "What?"

"Nothing, I'm just taking everything in. It's just all so beautiful," I said.

"It sure is," Brantley agreed.

We continued to walk, moving along the creek. After a while we came across a large boulder. I climbed on top of it and helped Brantley up so we could sit together. The boulder overlooked the creek. I watched the water flow. Listened to the wind blow. I wanted to take in everything about this moment. Brantley tilted her head, resting it on my shoulder. The moment was perfect.

We sat next to each other not saying a word for over an hour, just watching as life passed before us. Nowhere to be. No responsibilities. It was peaceful. I wished it could last, but I knew this was just a moment, and a brief one at that.

We finally rose to our feet. Hopping down from the rock, I reached up, helping Brantley back down to the ground. As she landed in front of me, our eyes locked again. Then, without any warning, she leaned in and kissed me.

Her lips were so soft against mine as our mouths pressed together. It felt as if time slowed and the seconds were drawn out. As she pulled away, the taste of her lips lingered on mine. I felt my eyes open slowly, bringing Brantley's face into focus. She smiled, then wrapped her arms around my neck.

She whispered in my ear, "I know you don't want to deal with this kind of distraction right now. I get that. I just realized that our time here is not guaranteed anymore. I almost died today. I just wanted to make sure that I did that before my time was up. I didn't want to miss my chance. Also, I wanted to thank you for saving my life. You didn't have to do that today, but I'm glad you did. Please, I know you want to say something, but don't. Not now, anyway."

Brantley slid by me, walking back up the path. I turned and watched her walk away, my heart still pounding, my mind still not right from the kiss. It shook me, rocked me in a way that I never would have expected. I didn't know what it meant. I didn't know how to respond. There were no words; nothing could have prepared me for this. I blinked, trying to bring myself back from my daze.

My head spun and my mind raced. I knew these feelings were already there, but now this complicated things. Complicated things in a way that was great and awful at the same time. I was unsure what to do or where to go from here. I knew only two things: that I liked Brantley a lot and that I needed to stay focused to make sure we both got through training, whatever the cost. I needed her more than I realized.

The moment her lips touched mine, everything changed.

CHAPTER 16

The next few days returned to normal, rolling by with little distinction. There were no more elimination challenges. Training resumed and so did the stress of when the next challenge would begin. Brantley and I had not spoken about the kiss. I assumed now that she wouldn't. Part of me didn't want to either, but still I found myself wishing she would bring it up. I couldn't stop thinking about it. I didn't know what she wanted, and there was still too much at stake to dwell on it.

Every moment I wasn't training I found myself thinking about Brantley. I had never been this conflicted about a girl. I wanted to tell her how I felt, but I also didn't want to say something now only for it to be a distraction during the next challenge. I also didn't know if she kissed me just so that she could clear her mind or if it was her way of telling me that she liked me as more than a friend. I thought I knew, but when we don't have time to talk about it, the mind has a funny way of playing games.

Then there was Gaia. In the past few days there had been a shift in our training. The problems we worked on were still very challenging, but she was starting to treat me as more of a friend. Being with her each day was a break from the stress and strain of the everyday grind. We talked about everything from food, hobbies, and her favorite place in the capital to what she thought about The Conscript. We spent as much time talking about each other as we did training my problem solving. It was a nice reprieve from daily events, even if it did distract from my learning time.

Today, training took a turn toward the strange. During weapons practice they introduced a new style of training target. They were holographic projections of real people. Some were just regular-looking people. Some looked like some of the other trainees that had been eliminated. We were put into a crowded area similar to the marketplace we had just visited, and then a picture would appear and we were required to shoot that target.

It was strange to pretend to kill someone. Even though they were just holograms, it felt like killing all the same. It wasn't something I was fully prepared for. There was a new element of stalking that was added in as well. The target would move behind cover, around corners, and away from me. I would have to pursue them and take the shot at the appropriate time. I started with using the bow and then progressed to the guns. My range with the guns had increased greatly over the last couple of weeks.

I was now relatively deadly from over a hundred yards and, depending on the setup, even farther.

The other disturbing part of the training was in the hand-to-hand combat. We had to fight against the holographic projections as well. They were so human-like, I could feel the contact when I landed a blow. It was just like fighting a human opponent. The holograph even bled. In the final part of my training, I delivered a blow that would have killed a man. The holograph reacted exactly as I would have imagined, even spitting out fake blood.

I was quite shaken up when I reported to Gaia's training. She sensed it the moment I entered the room.

"Are you OK? Something seems off."

"Training this morning was odd. I … I'm just a little shaken is all." I tried to brush her off.

I sat down at the chair in front of the table. Gaia pulled her chair around, joining me on the same side of the table. She bent forward, grabbing my hand. "It's OK. You can tell me."

I looked at her, still trying to shake the final image of my earlier training. "They had me pretend to kill people today. It felt so real; it just threw me is all."

Gaia's eyes widened. "Kill people? Why? How did they do that?"

I shook my head. "I don't know why. They didn't say. The targets during practice were exactly like people, though. They walked, looked, even felt just like real people. They were some kind of holograph, but they had mass. It was so real."

"I'm so sorry, Dantin. What can I do?" Gaia asked, her eyes showing concern.

"Let's just talk about anything but training." I looked up at her. "I know they're preparing me for the next challenge. It's been too long to assume that they wouldn't have one soon."

Gaia nodded her head. "OK, so, let's talk about something non-training related." Her eyes left mine, landing on my chest. "What's that?" she asked, pointing.

I looked down to where her finger directed me. My medal had slipped out of my shirt during the combat training. The gold lion's head rested in the middle of my chest. "Oh, it's a gift I got when they let us tour the city. A jeweler gave it to me. It's from my Section. It has a saying on the back that my dad and grandpa always used to say to me."

Gaia grabbed the medallion, placing it in her palm. She leaned in close, studying the lion. As she leaned in, her scent wafted across my nose, smelling of fresh fruit. I closed my eyes, taking in the scent. It was intoxicating. I opened my eyes again, looking down as Gaia flipped the medallion over, studying both sides.

"It's beautiful. We Enter as One into the Kingdom of Lions. What does it mean?" Without pulling away she looked up at me, her face no more than a few inches from mine.

"I'm not sure. I always believed it to be a saying relating to the afterlife. We all enter the afterlife as one to receive our fate. Something like that," I said, but the truth was I wasn't sure why my grandpa always used to say it.

Gaia smiled. "I like that."

She sat back in her chair and I was finally able to breathe. "Thanks," I said, tucking the medallion back into my shirt.

I stood up from my chair. I knew there was only a little time left in our session, so I prepared myself to leave. Gaia stood, wrapping her arms around my neck. The force shot me back a couple of steps before I was able to plant myself. The smell of fresh fruit invaded my nostrils again. I wrapped my arms around her lower back, squeezing her close. I could feel her chest rise and fall with each breath.

She turned her head, whispering in my ear, "I wanted to do this before Tinker showed up. I want you to know I am hoping for your safety every day. I have really enjoyed our time together. Being that there aren't any guarantees that I'll see you tomorrow I needed you to know … just what you mean to me."

She kissed me on the cheek and then continued, "You be safe. Good luck. I know there are only so many challenges left, and I know you have what it takes to make it." She squeezed me one last time and then pulled away.

Just as she did, Tinker pushed open the door. "Right this way, Number Fifteen. The group is being summoned."

It's time. Another challenge. I could tell by the word choice. My suspicions were proven right as we passed through the assembly hall. Walking down the hall by my quarters to the challenge arena, I wondered what they had in store for us today. It had been several days; I was sure they could have thought of something clever by now. At this point it could have been anything.

As I was led through the door into the arena, I stopped. My eyes widened at the sight. It was home. Everything about it was exact. The color of the buildings. The look of the streets. The stones and dirt roads. The people moving through the streets as if they were heading to work. *How could they do this? How did they bring my home to the capital?*

I scanned the room. Goby and Brantley were already here. Their eyes looked exactly as I imagined mine did, wide with total amazement and recognition. Their Sections must look the same. If this was the case then all the Sections must be relatively the same. Three of the four other trainees gawked and pointed at the little city with amazement. Only Number Eleven seemed unimpressed, standing with his arms crossed.

The Training Speaker took his position and announced today's challenge.

"Welcome back, everyone," he said. "Today we will test a combination of the skills that you have learned since coming to us. You will each have a target that you must locate, track, and then eliminate without being seen. Before the start of the competition, an image of your target will appear before you. Study it for the brief time that you have, then move quickly. Remember, don't get caught. You will be armed today with your knife and a compound bow. Make sure to conceal it under a jacket or other article of clothing. Good luck."

That was the most instruction for a challenge that we've received in weeks. I felt my nerves sharpen, preparing for the start of the challenge. I made my way to the platform with my number on it. I grabbed my knife, sliding it into a holster on my belt, then grabbed the handle of the compound bow. The weight felt perfectly balanced in my hands. I placed the bow across my shoulders then grabbed a jacket, sliding it on over the bow.

I looked into the challenge area. I watched the people as they moved through the street. It looked as though the city went on for several blocks. *Amazing.* I would have to locate my target quickly, then find a place to complete the attack. It would be impossible to eliminate a target on the main street without drawing attention to myself. A light flashed, and an image of an elderly man appeared in front of me. The holographic head was three-dimensional and spun, giving me a chance to see him from all sides.

My target had a birthmark on his neck about the size of a plum. This could prove to be useful in trying to locate him in the crowd, especially since the number of people moving through the street had appeared to pick up. Once I located my target I needed to follow him to a less populated area. If he didn't move to one I wasn't sure what I was going to do. That was a problem I'd have to attack later.

When the horn sounded, everyone moved into the street. I walked slowly, letting the group get ahead of me. I made my way down the main street through the town, staying to one side, away from the middle. I leaned up against a building, watching as people passed moving left and right. A mother with two children scurried across the street and around the corner of a building. A young man rushed forward with his head down. I caught a glimpse of a couple of elderly men, but neither of them matched my target.

Number Eleven walked right down the middle of the street, no more than ten feet behind the person I assumed was his target. His eyes were fixed on the man. He was closing the distance as the man turned into one of the side alleyways. *Well, that was convenient.* Eleven followed him, closing in behind him. He reached for the man, placing his hand across his mouth, slitting his throat with the knife. The man fell to the ground and then vanished as the holograph stopped projecting.

A beam of light shot down, trapping Eleven in place. Number Eleven fought, shaking from side to side with his arms and legs pinned together. The beam didn't allow him to move at all. It looked like once your assignment was completed you were removed from the equation. I looked at the beam, then saw a second beam appear. That meant two of the seven had completed their assignments. I needed to locate my target.

I scanned the crowd, looking for the grey hair of my target. After two false alarms, I finally spotted him talking to a group of people. I noticed the birthmark on his neck. He had his back to me. The group he was talking to seemed to be very interested in what he had to say. I wasn't going to be able to kill him while he was talking to them.

I moved across the street to get a better angle on my target. Halfway across the street, another beam shot from the ceiling. That was number three. There were four of us left. I positioned myself against a wall, close enough to hear the man talk. He was going over some kind of treatment process for the crops they were growing at work. He must have been the project manager of the produce department or something. The detail was incredible; the holographs were even programmed with realistic dialogue.

I leaned against the wall, arms crossed, as the man continued to talk. I was beginning to grow impatient. I was also starting to become nervous. If he didn't finish up, everyone else was going to have their kill before I would even get a chance. Another beam shot down. *Three left. Let's go, guy, get on with it already.* I listened closely as the man appeared to be finishing up his orders.

He gave the first two guys assignments and they rushed off. He turned his attention to the other two gentlemen, explaining what their part would be. I couldn't tell what he was saying, exactly. Not that I would understand anyway—I wasn't much of the farming type. Nor did any of that actually matter. The two men nodded as another beam shot down from the ceiling. I didn't have much time. I began to slowly move closer to the man.

The two men nodded again as my target finished his instructions. They both moved away as I reached my target. I took my knife, sliding it just between his spine and rib cage, piercing his heart. I didn't even slow down as I kept walking past the man. I heard him fall to his knees and collapse on the ground. A woman screamed, and I was trapped in place. The beam had shot down, holding me still.

I must have succeeded, then. They wouldn't trap me if I were caught, would they? There was still one of the other trainees out there trying to track their target. I shifted my eyes from side to side as best as I could, trying to locate anyone who was trapped. Most of them were probably behind buildings or in what appeared to be alleyways. That's when I saw Number Four. He was moving slowly, eyes fixed on someone in front of him.

A holograph of a younger man moved away from Number Four. I shifted back, watching Number Four pick up his pace, closing in on the man. I couldn't move my head, so I shifted my eyes as best I could, focusing in on the man. He was almost out of the range of my vision when he froze in place. Number Four paused too, seeing that his target no longer moved. The holograph turned, pointing a gun at Number Four.

The sound of gunfire exploded. I flinched but was held perfectly still by the force field. Number Four's head shot back as he crumpled to the ground. Blood began to pour out of his head as the beam disappeared along with all of the holographs. I turned my head from side to side then shook my arms, testing to make sure I was fully released. Number Four lay motionless, a pool of blood all around his head. He had been shot by a hologram.

How is that even possible? I should have learned by now that nothing was impossible here in Heart City. I looked at

Number Four one more time. I no longer felt sorry to see these people die. It was strange, but I only felt relieved to know that it wasn't Goby or Brantley. This new numbness was unsettling to me. I had always been someone who cared about others. Put them before myself. Now, there were only two people I cared about; everyone else was expendable.

It was the only way to ensure Brantley and Goby survived with me. Others would have to die for this to happen. For the first time, I was OK with it. I was truly starting to change. I turned, walking to the front of the city where we had entered from. Goby and Brantley were already there waiting for me. I shook Goby's hand and gave Brantley a half hug. The rest of the group stood at attention as the Training Speaker started in.

"Very good. Some of you have greatly impressed us today. Your skill and precision is exemplary. We will take a short recess to allow for everyone to clean up and then meet up in the garden for dinner. This evening we will continue with our usual routine. Congratulations to the final six."

At dinner, the mood was relatively light. I think it was due to the slightly less stressful challenge. I had come the closest to being eliminated. I was curious about their targets, though.

"Did you guys notice the force field beams before you took out your target?"

Brantley shook her head. "No, it scared me when I couldn't move."

"I saw the first beam come down, but I didn't know what it was until I took out my target," Goby said. "Did you know about it?"

I nodded. "Yeah. I saw Eleven take out his target and then get trapped behind it. I knew what it was. It's also how I tracked how many people had gotten to their target."

Goby smiled. "Very smart, Dantin. I'm impressed. I guess your tutor has been paying off."

I hadn't thought about it, but she must have been. I was surprised that nobody else had figured out to count the beams. "Do you remember how many beams there were when you took out your target?" I asked Goby and Brantley.

Goby looked up, thinking for a moment. "I think there were two when I got to mine."

"There were four when I took my target out," Brantley said.

Good. Neither of them had been in relative danger of being the last one left. That made me feel better about the way the challenge happened. "What was your target like?"

"Mine was an old lady," Brantley said. "It was hard for me to take her out. I actually waited until she was far down one of the alleys and shot her with an arrow. I wouldn't have been able to stab her, I don't think."

Goby and I nodded with understanding. "My target was a young man," Goby said, looking down at the table. "I got to him back behind a couple of the old buildings away from everyone else. I think I was the furthest from the main street. What about you, Dantin?"

"Mine was an old man. I didn't even find him until two people had already taken out their targets. He wouldn't leave the main street, either. There were five beams up when I stabbed him right in the middle of the street," I explained.

Goby's eyes widened, "And nobody saw you?"

I shook my head. "At first I thought somebody did 'cause a woman screamed, but it was only because the man fell dead. I timed it just right, I guess."

Brantley shook her head, pointing at me. "You need to be more careful. They could have easily seen you and then you wouldn't be here."

"Trust me, I wanted to be," I said, "but the guy wouldn't leave. And, like I said, there were already five beams up. I didn't have much time to wait."

Goby took a bite of food. "Well, we're both just happy that you're OK," he said with his mouth full.

I was glad everyone was OK, too. *We only need to survive two more challenges.* We were getting very close to the end. It was only a matter of time before the final four would be revealed. It was the first time I had thought about it. After all the training, it was almost over. *Then what? What happens to us when it's all over? Why are they training us like this? There has to be a purpose.*

Only time would reveal the true nature of what they were trying to prepare us for. After all that had transpired over the last few weeks and today, it was clear that we would be around death. First, letting us see our friends die in front of us. Then, today, eliminating a target. They were trying to prepare us for what it would be like to take a life. That's why they made the holograms so real. Perhaps we were training to become some kind of soldier.

Then it hit me. I knew what they were training us for. We were assassins!

CHAPTER 17

It made so much sense now. The hand-to-hand combat. The weapons training. Learning to problem-solve and adapt to different environments. Plus the new holograms and simulating taking someone's life. I didn't know how I hadn't seen it before. At the same time, there's no way I could have known. We could have been training for literally anything. But it was so obvious now: we would be weapons for the capital to use.

This realization of what we were was hard to take. I found myself having trouble sleeping that night. *I'm not a killer. I don't want to be a killer. Better yet, what does the government need with a bunch of assassins? Who are they targeting?* The thoughts invaded my mind, keeping me from being able to relax. The next morning came without getting any sleep. I knew today was going to be a rough day without the proper rest.

I dragged myself to my first training station with Gaia. It was the first time I'd seen her since she'd given me the hug and kiss for luck. I didn't know what to expect during this visit. The whole thing kind of took me by surprise. Gaia met me halfway across the room, wrapping her arms around me again. We hugged each other for several seconds; it was so nice just to be held.

"I'm so glad you made it. I honestly couldn't think about anything except whether or not I would see you again," Gaia said as she held me close.

I pulled back, looking into her tantalizing eyes. "Looks like you're stuck with me for at least one more day."

Gaia pushed me. "Don't say that. Why would you say that?"

I looked at the floor, ashamed of what I was being trained to do. "Do you know what they're training me for? Why I'm here?"

My head rose back up to meet Gaia's gaze, and her eyes filled with concern. "No. What are they training you for? You know?"

I nodded, then looked back at the floor. "They're training me to be an assassin."

"WHAT? No way. Why would you think that?" Gaia stepped back, turning away from me angrily. "There's no way."

I followed after her, grabbing her arm, turning her around. "For the last challenge they had us track people and kill them as a simulation. Why else would they do that?"

Gaia shook her head. "Maybe they're training you for the army and they want to make sure you can kill without too much remorse. I don't know. Why would they need you to be assassins?"

"I think it's because all of the Sections are the same so we have insight into how to get around each one. Plus, we look like the others from there so we can blend in. You know we can pretend to be from the different Sections because we know how it is to live there. I don't know. But it sure feels like that's why we're getting trained at this point. They're letting us watch the other trainees get killed right in front of us. They're desensitizing us. Something just doesn't add up," I pleaded with Gaia.

Gaia shook her head again. "Like the fact that they want you to be an assassin. How can they possibly control you to kill other people from your own Sections? Why would they need that anyway?"

I looked away. "I don't know." For a moment I doubted my own logic, but something seemed too real about the way I felt. "I'm not sure why, but I know I'm right."

Gaia shook her head. "Well, I don't think you are. There has to be a better reason. I won't believe it."

"Fine, don't believe it," I said, my tone getting short as I felt my anger begin to grow. "I hope you're right, but you're not the one facing death every day. Training in how to kill people. How to shoot weapons. Just remember that."

Gaia turned, tears in her eyes. "I just don't want to believe that's what they're turning you into. I'm sorry, I don't want to fight with you about it. I just don't want to see you change."

I sighed. "I'm not going to change. I'll still be the same person you've known. I promise. I'm not going to let them turn me into something I'm not."

We didn't talk much after that. Gaia thought it was best to focus on work, so the remainder of the session was spent going over various problems. The whole conversation had gotten both of us a little riled up, but I felt myself calm as the session continued. The rest of the session I actually felt quite focused. It made the time fly.

The horn sounded and Tinker entered the room. "Time to change training stations."

I turned, walking to the door. I was only a couple of feet away from the door when I turned, looking back at Gaia. "I promise!"

The rest of training that morning went by with little variance from our normal day. I worked on my weapons proficiency, I worked more on hand-to-hand combat, and I had a light workout. The workouts had become progressively easier as the challenges had become more difficult. It felt as if they were saving our energy and strength for the challenges. They didn't want us too worn down when we were asked to try and kill each other.

I was the first to arrive at lunch. I sat contemplating whether or not to reveal my theory to the group or keep it to myself. I argued over and over in my head whether it was something that needed to be shared or not. I finally came to the conclusion that it was important. I needed to share it with the group. If not for them to know, at the very least to see what they thought about it. To see if I really was just being crazy.

Brantley and Goby arrived together and sat down at the table. I took a deep breath. "Guys, do you know why they're training us? What this program is all about?"

Goby looked up at me. "We're going to be assassins. What's this all about, Dantin?"

I paused, taken aback by Goby's calmness. "How long have you known?"

Goby looked at Brantley and then back at me. "Several weeks now. Are you just figuring this out? Maybe they shouldn't have let you skip all those movies. They've explained everything."

I looked at both of them as they just peered back at me like there was no problem with this. "And you guys are OK with this?"

"Of course, Dantin," Goby said, sounding kind of irritated by my concern. "We are responsible for stopping the threats against the government. Without us, another war could break out, another Event, or worse. We're doing a very important job."

I put my hands on my head, not fully able to process all that had just been said. How could they feel like killing people from our Sections was the answer? I didn't understand. They said the movies had told them everything. I remembered the first couple of movies, but I couldn't stay focused because of all the flashes throughout the film. They were so distracting and I always felt funny after.

That was it: the flashes. They had to be the reason Goby and Brantley were acting so strange. I remembered a while back, after the first death, we all watched a movie and then suddenly things weren't so bad. That had to be it. They must have been using the movies to do something to our minds and our emotions. That's why that day following the challenge I felt better —and suddenly had the desire to serve Natio—after watching the film. They had hidden messages in the movies.

"You guys have been tricked. The movies have secret messages to trick you into believing this is the right thing to do," I tried explaining to them.

"No, Dantin," Goby said. "It is the right thing to do. Without us there could be war."

I shook my head. "What if it is someone you know? What if the movie said I was the target? Would you kill me? Just take me out?"

Brantley shook her head. "Dantin, you would never be the target. You are one of us. Besides, these people that we're assigned to kill are real threats. Some of them have already caused major damage. I would never kill you."

I pulled at my hair. I felt like screaming. I buried my face in my hands, putting my head on the table. A soft hand caressed the back of my head. I felt my heart slow and my breathing start to return to normal. The hand rubbed along the back of my head and down my neck. I took a deep breath, letting my feelings begin to subside slightly. I raised my head back up, locking eyes with Brantley.

"It's going to be OK, Dantin. We will be in this together and we will get through this together. It's for a good cause, a worthy cause. Trust us." She smiled, doing her best to put me at ease.

I still didn't believe it was the right thing to do. I didn't want to kill anyone. Yet I also didn't want to put either of my friends in danger. Or allow for a war to break out. There must have been more of a threat in the Sections than I had realized. More importantly, I didn't want to give the Overseers or Natio a reason to eliminate me. It was probably in the best interest of everyone if I just let this go for now. Besides, there really wasn't anything I could do; I was still trying to survive training.

"OK. If you guys believe in the cause, I'm with you," I lied, trying to sound reassuring.

Goby and Brantley both smiled. "It's going to be fine. We are simply here to help keep the peace," Goby said, returning to his food.

The rest of the day passed with little out of the ordinary. I skipped the movie, again, meeting up with Gaia instead. I still had my doubts about what they were telling us. Besides, like Gaia said, there were no guarantees as to how many more times I'd get to see her. I could die in the next trial or be assigned somewhere else. I was going to take advantage of the time I had left. I had a feeling the final challenges wouldn't be too far off. Something about the escalation of events had me believing the final four would be revealed sooner than later.

I was exhausted by the time I reached my room. I skipped my evening routine, heading straight for my bed. I hit my pillow and was out before the lights flipped off. I slept like a baby, not waking once before the morning. When the horn blasted to get us up, I was so dead asleep it made me jump. I tried to shake the haze from my head as I pulled myself together.

I slogged through my morning routine of green smoothie, brush my teeth, and get dressed, finishing just as the second horn blasted. The doors opened and everyone was being directed to the training arena. *Challenge time.* I stepped into the hall as Brantley and Goby joined me. We walked together down the hall to the arena. When we passed through the door the final challenge was towering in front of us.

Fifteen-foot-high metal walls encased the normally open training arena. A massive doorway stood open with arrows painted on the back wall of the entryway directing us where to go next: right or left. After that, I couldn't see anything else. The walls were too tall to see what else was behind them. The entrance was very intimidating, though. The smooth, shining metal was neatly polished. The entrance looked like it was built for a giant. I could only imagine what creative threats waited for us behind the walls.

The Training Speaker took his place. Clearing his throat he began, "Welcome. Today we will find out who the final four will be. The challenge that lies before you is a labyrinth with hidden paths and obstacles. The first four to reach the middle of the maze will be the victors. Those who fail to reach the end will be eliminated. Good luck—and beware, as things are ever changing."

I guess there aren't going to be two more challenges after all. My heart pounded as the horn sounded, sending the six of us racing into the maze. I was the last to pass through the massive doorway. After I passed into the maze, the wall slammed shut, sealing us in. A large sliding piece of metal shielded where the entrance used to be. *Well, apparently there's no leaving the way we came.* I moved into the labyrinth, going to the right.

Half the group chose left while Brantley, Goby, and I moved to the right. We had decided to stay together for as long as we could. I was sure they would find a way to separate us at some point. For the time being, though, we would travel as one. As we moved deeper into the maze, I ran my hands along the metal wall. It was smooth and cool to the touch, polished so much that I could see my reflection in it. The floor was the same way, as if we were walking on mirrors. This made seeing the upcoming turns difficult as the reflections made things seem as if they went on forever.

There was no way to know what was the right way. The walls were too high to see over. Every choice we made was a guess. We kept moving, taking a right and then a left. As we approached another fork I turned to see which way we should go. "Right or left?"

"Right," Brantley said, pointing down the path.

It was amazing how quickly Brantley could transform from the friendly girl next door to this focused huntress. Her eyes changed from wide and beautiful to narrow and intimidating. Her soft features hardened with intense focus. It was almost as if she was someone else. Not the sweet girl I knew from all the days of lunch and dinner, but an alternate version of herself. It was truly amazing to watch.

I turned, leading us forward. There was a long path in front of us. We wouldn't have to make a choice to turn for several hundred feet. It looked like there was something up ahead, just before the split in the path.

"Guys, do you see that?" I asked, moving forward. I had just passed through another turning point when a large rumble shook the ground.

I froze, trying to keep my balance. The sound had come from behind me. I turned, then backed up in fear. My reflection stared back at me: the walls had changed. The long path was now broken up into different paths. That's what the Speaker meant by "ever changing." I pounded on the metal, yelling, "BRANTLEY! GOBY!"

I put my head against the cold metal, listening for any response. I couldn't hear anything. I was on my own. I turned back around, looking for the thing I had seen up ahead. There was nothing there. A new wall blocked the place where it had been. The whole maze had changed. This was going to be a much harder challenge than I had originally thought; there was no telling which way to go.

I moved forward to the next left turn and looked down the path, turning my head back and forth, trying to see what my options were. *It doesn't matter, stupid, you don't know where you're going.* I shook my head and decided to follow whatever my gut told me. It said go left. It was strange now without the group. The only sound was that of my feet pinging off the metal floor.

The path turned right after about two hundred feet. Even after all these weeks it still amazed me how large these obstacles were while still fitting inside the training hall. As I turned the corner, my right foot landed on a square piece on the floor, causing it to give way beneath my shoe. The piece sunk into the ground, clicking into place. I looked at the floor, studying the square, but snapped my eyes up as a large explosion shook the ground. *Are we shifting again already?*

My eyes widened. A flash of light forced me to squint. Two large fireballs roared down the hallway, barreling toward me. I slammed onto the ground, smacking my chin on the metal floor as the two fireballs flew over me. The heat as they passed was blistering, but just for a moment. I felt my temperature rise instantly. The fireballs crashed into the wall behind me, exploding, sending flames flying over my back.

I screamed as my shirt burned, sticking to my flesh. I could feel the skin melt away instantly from the heat. I rolled onto my back, attempting to put the flames out. I crawled forward, trying to get out of the range of the remaining fireballs. Their heat had started to make the floor extremely hot. I could feel my hands start to burn as they touched the ground. Crawling forward, I clenched my teeth, trying to fight off the pain. I finally found myself out of the range of the heat and back on the cool metal flooring.

I looked down the hallway, preparing for another wave of fireballs. Nothing seemed to be coming. Perhaps it was only the two this time. I took a few moments, trying to regather myself. Every move I made sent pain through my back. My shirt was burnt into my flesh. Every time I pulled on it I could feel it tearing some of my skin away. Tears ran down my cheek as I tried to pry some of it loose.

The pain was too much. It felt like I was going to pass out. My vision blurred and narrowed. Black spots invaded my sight. I stopped trying to free my shirt from my body and pulled myself up to my feet, placing a hand on the wall for balance. I closed my eyes, trying to block out some of the pain. When I reopened them my vision was starting to return to normal. I needed to press on.

I took another step forward as the ground started to shake again. Instinctively, I fell to the ground, preparing for another blast. The rumbling continued as I looked down the hall. The walls were shifting again. The path ahead of me was now several hundred feet longer. Again, there was something in the distance. I couldn't quite make it out, but it was on all fours. It appeared to be covered in hair. *What could that be?*

I narrowed my eyes, trying to focus on the object. The thing turned to face me. *Oh, my god!* It was a wolf. I had only seen a few back in Section Eight, but this was most definitely a large wolf. The wolf took a step forward, head down, eyes fixed on me. I knew there was no staying here anymore. I pushed myself up onto my feet, sprinting forward and taking the first turn I came across. The wolf was now racing toward me as I turned right down the first hallway.

I looked over my shoulder as I made another turn, this time going left. The wolf slid by the turnoff, unable to stop himself on the slick floor. That was my only advantage. I needed to take as many turns as I could to try to lose him. Plus, in a straight-line race he'd have me in no time. I turned right again. The path ahead was over three hundred feet long, with no possible turns. I thought for a second about going back, but that was not an option with the wolf behind me.

I sprinted forward into the long hallway. I was fifty feet in when I noticed the holes in the wall. I didn't know why they were there, but I knew there had to be a reason for them. I took a step back, trying to analyze the situation. As I did, I stepped onto another block, forcing it into the ground. I shot my eyes back down the path, preparing for the worst.

The wall opened up ahead on both the right and left sides of the path. *Maybe I gave myself a way out.* Moments later, a huge ball attached to a long arm swung through the opening. Then another. There were three in total swinging at completely random paces. The balls that were attached to the pendulum device were about the size of a man. I turned back as the wolf slid into the hallway.

I didn't have much choice; I sprinted forward. The air whistled behind me as something was shot through the holes at me. I didn't slow down. I pressed forward, only fifty feet from the pendulum devices. The wolf was right behind me. I didn't turn to look, but I could hear the clicking of his feet on the metal. He growled as I reached the pendulums.

The first pendulum swung, passing just in front of me. It was so close I could feel the air as it flew by. I kept sprinting, preparing for the next ball to pass. Coming from the opposite side, the ball was bearing down on me. I could see its path as I jumped forward just in front of it. The ball swung just behind my heels. Only one more. I kept my pace, not missing a step.

The balls looked to be much closer together than they actually were. There was at least fifteen feet or more between each arm. As I neared the next ball, I could see that the wolf was now extremely close to me. I could see the next ball swinging down toward the pathway. I was again right in line with its timing.

Or not. It looked like it was going to hit me; I hadn't timed it well after all. I wasn't going to make it.

I lowered my body, diving forward. I hit the ground.

A yelp sounded out from behind me as the ball swung by. I turned my head to see what happened. The wolf lay motionless, bleeding from the impact of the ball. He had to be dead; I couldn't imagine any creature surviving a hit like that. I slid backward on my butt, watching the hallway. *I made it.* I reached the back wall and leaned up against it. The cold metal, along with the pain from my burns, sent chills down my body. I leaned forward as the hallway closed back up, removing the swinging pendulums.

I still didn't know where I was. I didn't know which way I needed to go. There was no clue as to where the final goal was. It was like trying to shoot a mouse with an arrow with your eyes closed.

I pushed myself back onto my feet. The ground shook as the walls shifted yet again. I turned my head back and forth, trying to see where the changes were happening. To my right the walls slid to reveal a new pathway.

That's when I saw it. For the first time, I had a direction I needed to go. No more than five hundred feet away, a small light shot into the sky. Underneath it, there was a domed structure which appeared to be made from the same material as the force field that had kept Brantley and me from falling into the skin-melting liquid during the challenge a few days ago. It looked like there was a small table in the middle.

Just as quickly as it appeared it was gone as the maze shifted again, hiding the finish. At least now I finally had a direction to go.

I worked my way left, right, and then left again, trying to continue in the direction of the finish line. I had just taken another right when suddenly the ground shook. A loud rumble echoed off the walls and through the arena. I was knocked off-balance, landing on the floor, which was no longer smooth and metallic. Now, it was stonelike. It appeared that the entire maze had changed from metal to stone in an instant. *How is that even possible?* I laid still as the rumbling subsided, the path now lined with stone pavers, bits of gravel, and an uneven surface. I climbed back to my feet and continued forward.

I came to a gap in the maze. A large pit blocked my path, at least fifteen feet wide, spanning from wall to wall. *This has to be the right way.* At the bottom of the pit, large spear-like spikes stuck up from the ground. Three skeletons lay in the pit, just like in our first challenge so many weeks ago. This time I was sure they were real. The brutality of everything I had witnessed was enough to confirm that. I backed up several feet, preparing myself for the long jump.

As I sprinted forward, the stones shifted under my feet. It was harder to get up to full speed than I had anticipated. Each stride resulted in a small slip of my plant foot. Still, I continued forward, driving hard to reach top speed. As I approached the edge, I pushed hard off of my left foot, flying upward. I could feel my weight starting to return to earth as I neared the other edge.

I leaned forward, hitting the ledge hard. My momentum caused me to slide across the stone ground. My body skidded to a halt as pain shot through my knees and elbows. I rolled over onto my back, looking at my left elbow first. I was bleeding. I reached over, pulling the tiny stones out of my arm, trying to clean my wound. After picking the rocks from my elbows, I sat upright. My knees burned and ached.

I crouched forward, looking at my legs. My left knee wasn't too bad: a few small stones and a little blood. My right knee had a grape-sized rock stuck just above my kneecap. I picked the smaller pieces of rock from my knee before taking another look at the larger stone. I pressed my fingers around the rock, causing pain to shoot all the way down to my ankle. Closing my eyes, I pried the rock from my knee.

Surprisingly, it wasn't too bad. I looked down as blood began to ooze from the wound. I quickly grabbed the sleeve of my shirt and pulled on it several times, causing it to tear free. I stretched the fabric as far as I could then tied it around my knee, pulling it tight to try to stop the flow of blood. I fought my way to my feet. Limping forward, I continued to move in the direction of the finish line. *It can't be too much farther now.*

With each step my knee throbbed and I could feel myself wince. I turned right again, and as I did the ground began to shake again. The rocks on the walls rumbled as small fragments began to drop, smacking against the ground. The space before me began to shift, revealing the finish line yet again. I gritted my teeth, trying to increase my speed. A boulder broke free from the wall, crashing to the ground behind me.

I stopped, looking back at the large rock that now lay on the ground. My eyes searched the walls as another rock came free. I jumped forward, avoiding the falling rock. Moving into a hobbled run, I accelerated toward the finish line. Rocks began to jump off the wall, smashing into the ground just off my heels. I continued to sprint as best I could, each stride now followed by a hobbled hop. I was fifty feet from the finish when the walls began to shift again. I could see my opening starting to close.

I yelled, mustering all the strength I could. I was moving faster now. A rock fell from the wall, landing right in front of me. I hurdled it, not losing momentum. I was almost to the finish; the wall was now halfway shut. I dove forward, flying past the wall just as it slammed shut behind me. I dragged myself through the field of light into the domed finish area. I looked up, seeing Goby's outstretched hand.

"Glad you could join us, buddy," Goby said, helping me to my feet.

I looked at the other trainee, noticing that it was Eleven. He stood by himself by the small table in the middle of the dome. Brantley still wasn't there. I turned, looking out into the maze. All I could see were walls. There was no telling who was close to the finish and who wasn't. I looked back at Goby; he was bleeding about as much as I was. His elbows were banged up. He had a cut over his right eye. His forearm looked like it had been bitten.

"When did you get separated from Brantley?" I asked him.

"It wasn't long after you got pulled away from us. We ran into a wolf and were forced in separate directions."

I could feel my eyes widen with fear.

Goby read my mind. "Brantley was fine; the wolf followed me and then got pinned behind a different set of walls when the maze shifted."

I felt myself breathe again. "Good. She better hurry, though. There's only one more spot."

Goby nodded. "I know."

We both turned, looking out at the maze. The walls started to rumble again, shifting. It was happening more frequently now. Maybe they were trying to get more people to make it close to the finish line. As the walls opened up fully, I could see the boy from Section Five. He wasn't very far from the finish. As I scanned the other openings, Brantley came into view. Her head turned and, even though she was several hundred feet away, I could feel our eyes lock.

"BRANTLEY! Run!" I yelled, trying to get her attention.

Her arms swung violently as she propelled herself forward. My eyes darted back to the guy from Section Five. He, too, was in an all-out sprint. The ground was still shaking as the walls shifted. In the far distance behind the guy from Section Five, I could see the girl from Section Seven. She was so far behind there was no way she would be able to catch him unless he were to fall. I turned my attention back to Brantley. She had evened the distance between herself and the guy from Section Five.

The race was on. Each pushed forward, driving hard for the shielded dome. The first to reach it would activate its reflective abilities, preventing the other from entering. My eyes darted back and forth between the two. They were within a hundred feet now. It was still neck and neck, too close to tell which one of them was actually closer. I felt my pulse quicken. A lump formed in my throat.

I choked out a few words: "Come on! Just a little further, Brantley. You're almost there!"

I positioned myself at the edge of the dome, waving Brantley on. My arms frantically turned circles, encouraging her to keep moving. Both she and the boy from Five entered the final few feet. The boy from Section Five appeared to have a slight lead.

Brantley, only five feet away now, dove, flying through air. Her hands reached through the dome as she crashed into my outstretched arms. The boy from Section Five had started to enter as well, but the speed of Brantley's dive carried her through first, activating the outer shield. The boy's arm dropped to the floor and his body smashed into the outer wall, falling back onto the ground. The momentum of Brantley's dive had carried her right into me, throwing me off balance, causing us both to fall to the ground with Brantley on my chest as I squeezed her tight.

She buried her face into my chest as I wrapped my arms around her. Her breathing was deep and strained from the sprint. I held her close. "You made it. It's OK! You made it."

Brantley pushed herself up off of me and then helped me to my feet. The arm of the boy from Section Five lay on the ground in a small pool of blood. Brantley, Goby, and I stood in the middle of the protective dome as the boy from Section Five pounded on the walls, screaming in agony, blood running down his side from where his arm had been severed. I looked up as a green gas began to fall over the maze. It draped over the walls, spilling into the open areas. The guy from Section Five began to grab at his throat. He appeared to be gasping for air. He curled up, turning away from the dome.

I watched, waiting to see what would happen next. The boy turned, slamming himself up against the shield. The skin on his arm and face were starting to be eaten away, peeling from his body. The boy smacked his hand against the wall, leaving a bloody handprint with each blow. He coughed as blood spilled out of his mouth, falling onto the rocky floor. Falling to his knees, he looked at his hand as the flesh eroded.

The girl from Section Seven ran in from the corridor, screaming hysterically. Her body, too, was being eaten away by the gas. She sprinted, not slowing down as she collided with the side of the force field. The force of the impact along with the frailty of her body killed her. She collapsed to the ground, motionless, her body still melting away. I squeezed my eyes shut, trying to block out what was happening in front of me.

The boy's screams slowly dissipated, turning into muffled gurgles. I opened my eyes as the boy twitched on the ground. His eyes were dead but the nerves in his body still fired, trying to fight off the poison. After a few more moments, his body fell silent. No more shakes or twitches. A huge blast of wind flew through the maze, pushing the remaining green gas from the arena. The shield relaxed and the walls shifted, revealing the way out.

We walked down the pathway in silence, Eleven out in front. As we reached the entrance to the maze, the Training Speaker stood waiting for us. He smiled widely, welcoming us out of the labyrinth. His white teeth showed through the grungy beard that had been growing for the last couple of weeks.

"Congratulations," he said. "You are this year's survivors. I trust that this year's group will do great things. Please, take a moment to go and gather your things from your quarters. The horn will sound in thirty minutes and you will receive further instructions. Again, congratulations! Victory!" He raised his arms, fists clenched.

CHAPTER 18

I stood in my room staring aimlessly at the floor as the words echoed in my mind: *"You are this year's survivors."* I didn't know how to switch my brain out of survival mode to celebrate. Instead all I could do was stare. I scanned my room, trying to trigger some kind of internal response to move, but I didn't even know where to start. They said to collect my things, but everything I had that was my own was left behind in Section Eight. The only thing that was mine now was the medallion that I wore around my neck. I wanted nothing to do with my numbered training uniform or anything that would remind me of this place.

I mustered the motivation to move across the room and sit on the edge of my bed. The lights went out. I tried to shake the images of the last two trainees that flashed in my head, to think of anything that would dull the sight of their mutilated bodies.

Brantley's smile came to the forefront. Her heavy breathing as she lay on my chest after the last challenge. Her soft lips when she kissed me in the garden inside the city. I felt myself smile at the thought that we had made it. We had survived together.

I kicked my feet up onto the bed and closed my eyes. Gaia's plea to never change flashed through my mind. Her beautiful smile and soft skin. Her touch when I needed it most. Her hug telling me that she cared for me and hoped to see me again. If it hadn't been for Gaia's constant ability to make me forget I was fighting for my life, I was sure I would have perished by now. Both she and Brantley had saved me.

Then there was home. Were Micca and Mom OK? Did Grandpa know what was going to happen here? Is that why he told me to outlast the others and to survive? He must have known something about the training, something about what happened here in the capital.

I recalled his words: *Find your way back. Remember, we all enter as one into the Kingdom of Lions*"—the same words that were inscribed on the medallion from Section Eight.

This all echoed through my mind. What did it all mean?

The horn sounded as the lights flipped on. The door to the room slid open. Tinker stood in the doorway. He smirked slightly, then waved me into the hall. "Not bringing anything, I see."

"What is there to bring?" I asked.

"Well, not to worry. You will have all new things soon. You get placed today. This is a good day. You will see." Tinker marched down the hall as Goby and Brantley joined me.

Eleven brought up the rear as we followed Tinker. We weaved our way through the series of long corridors. After several turns, we exited through the front of the building. A large vehicle waited for us just outside the doorway. We crossed the stone entryway down to our ride. Tinker popped open the door, ushering us into the car. Brantley and Goby got in first. I paused at the door, looking back at the training facility one more time.

"You going to miss this place?" Tinker asked.

"Not at all," I replied. "But I can't say this place didn't change me."

Tinker nodded, then ushered me into the car. He slid into the car last, closing the door behind him. Settling in, he turned his attention to the driver.

"Driver, take us to Freedom Row." Tinker turned to us, smiling.

The name of where we were going did sound nice. But it didn't mean anything to me at the moment. I watched Brantley and Goby as they gazed out the windows of the vehicle. They both smiled as the city rolled by. Everyone seemed to be intrigued by what was about to happen and where we were going. All except Eleven. He glared right at me. I caught his gaze but turned away from him quickly. I glanced back and saw that he continued to stare right at me, not moving at all. I looked out the window, trying to ignore him, yet I could still feel his eyes bearing down on me.

Even though the ride was relatively short, I was uncomfortable the entire way. The car turned onto Freedom Row, a tiny neighborhood with small houses lining the streets. We passed several houses then pulled to a stop outside a one-story home. It wasn't overly large, yet even with its one story it was still bigger than my place back in Section Eight..

"Dantin, this is your place," Tinker said, opening the door. I froze, not sure I was ready to leave the car. "Come on, go check it out."

I was shocked. I didn't know what to do. I never expected to be given a home. Brantley and Goby gently pushed me toward the car door. Once outside, I stood on the sidewalk staring at my home as Tinker handed me a key. I held it in my hands, staring at it. I took a step forward and then paused. Tinker's hand pushed on my back and I started forward again.

I heard the door close and the vehicle scoot off as I reached the top step of my porch. There were two rocking chairs to the right of the doorway, each made of wood. A small table sat between them. They looked out over the neighborhood. I turned around, enjoying the peacefulness of the neighborhood. All the homes appeared to be empty. However, three of them had their own elevator to the surface, which made me believe they were still occupied.

I turned the key in the door and pushed it open, stepping into the entryway. The one-story home had massively high ceilings. It was larger and more open than any home I'd ever been in. The place was fully furnished. To my left were a small couch and a chair. The floor had a rug on it. There was a stone fireplace. As I stepped into the room, lights automatically turned on. I paused, thinking someone else was there with me. Then I realized it was the same automated system that had been in my quarters during training.

To the right of the entryway was a common eating area. A large table sat in the middle of the room with six chairs lined up around it. When would I ever need six chairs for dinner? The wood tabletop looked heavy and solidly built. I ran my fingers over it, feeling the smooth warmth of the wood. Then I turned my attention back down the hallway.

On the left side of the entry hallway was the kitchen. To the right was a bathroom, complete with shower and tub. Back home in Section Eight all you ever saw was a tub. It would be nice to take a bath to help remind me of home. At the end of the hall there were two more doorways. The room on the right was a bedroom that connected with the bathroom. The room on the left was empty.

The house was nice. Everything was already in place for me. Everything worked and looked new. I went into my bedroom, opening up some of the drawers. They were filled with clothes—regular clothes. No more uniforms. No more numbered shirts. I was now able to look and feel normal again. At least to some extent. The clothes were still very different from what I was used to back home—more colors and brighter. I stood looking in the mirror.

"Hey, neighbor!" a voice said from behind me.

I turned around, seeing Brantley standing in the doorway to my bedroom. "Hey there. Is your place like mine?"

Brantley smiled. "Exactly. Same empty room and everything. It's a little big for me, though."

I nodded my head. "Yeah, I agree. I don't really need all this space. Did you see where Goby is?"

"Yeah, he's across the street, not far from us. I'm sure he'll find his way over here before too long." Brantley said, moving into the room.

I ran my fingers across the dresser as I looked over at her. "So, what do you make of all of this? Do you think we're finally safe?"

"I don't know what we are just yet. But it does feel good to be out of those quarters. They were a constant reminder that any day could be the last. At least now we don't have that to worry about." Brantley sat on my bed, looking over at me.

I sat next to her. "Well, I'm just glad we both made it. That was my only concern. Finding a way to get us both through," I said, tossing my arm around her shoulder.

Brantley leaned her head, resting it on my shoulder. "Yeah, I agree. At least we still have each other. No matter what comes next, we won't have to face it alone."

I held her close, sitting in silence as a smiling Goby entered the room. "Hi there, neighbors. Pretty nice places we got!"

"Sure are, buddy. You get all settled?" I asked.

Goby laughed. "Settled? What have I got to settle? All I have of my own is that clock the man from the market gave me. I set it on my fireplace."

Brantley and I both nodded. We didn't have much of our own, even in this new place. Everything had been provided for us, not really ours. Everything that was once ours was left in our Sections. All we truly had anymore was each other. Even through all of the death and struggles of training, we held onto that.

"Well, buddy, at least we all have each other!" I smiled.

Suddenly, a voice echoed through the house: "I hope you all are finding your new living accommodations adequate. Take a few more moments to explore, then a vehicle will be by to bring you back for Phase Two of your training to ensure that all of you are fully prepared to carry out your individual assignments. You will have one full afternoon of training and then you will be given your assignments. We are excited to have you on our team."

I didn't recognize the voice. It wasn't the Training Speaker. I stood up from the bed and made my way to the front of the house. On the porch, Goby and Brantley joined me. I locked the door and slid the key into my pocket as our ride pulled up. It was a short visit at home, that was for sure. We all climbed in and were taken back to the training center. The ride felt significantly shorter going back.

Back in the training building, we were escorted into separate rooms. The room had a single padded table in it. I was told to sit on the table and wait for the doctor. Almost as soon as I sat down the doctor entered the room. His white robe swayed as he moved across the room. He took a bright light, checking my eyes, then ears. Finally, he had me open my mouth. After completing that task, he tallied something on his chart.

He returned in front of me. He took a small mallet, tapping me just below my knee. My foot shot out involuntarily. He continued to poke and prod at me as he moved behind me. The doctor felt along my spine and then ran something down the middle of my back. My shoulders pulled back and I sat upright. He proceeded to snap his fingers next to each of my ears. I ducked away at the sudden sound.

Again, he returned to his paper, marking a few things down. He grabbed a syringe from one of the drawers before returning to me. The doctor then grabbed my right arm, turning my palm face up. He tied an elastic band around my bicep then tapped at the corner of my arm twice. He quickly removed the syringe from its wrapper and slid it into my arm. He pulled a piece off the back, leaving just the needle sticking out of my arm, and then took a glass tube and connected it to the syringe. I watched as the blood began to fill the small vial.

He removed the tube and then the needle, placing a small piece of gauze on the puncture. He nodded at me to hold it there and then returned to his notes. He still hadn't said a word. The doctor removed a sticker from his clipboard, slapping it onto the vial, and placed it on a tray next to the file. He then opened a box and removed three more syringes from it. This time each one contained a different colored liquid. He moved back in front of me.

"Lift your sleeve," he said as I pulled up my shirt sleeve on my right arm. He slid the first needle into my arm, driving the liquid into me. "Now, give me your left arm." I pulled the sleeve down on my right arm. Switching hands, I extended my left arm. He grabbed my wrist and proceeded to drive the next syringe into my arm, pressing the next set of liquid into me. "Now, stand up and drop your pants." I slid off the edge of the seat, turned around and pulled down my pants. A sharp prick stabbed my right butt cheek as the third needle was emptied.

The doctor returned to his file as I pulled myself back up onto my seat. He scribbled down a few more notes as I waited for more instructions. The doctor turned to me. "OK, now hang tight. I will return shortly."

Just like that, he was gone, file in hand. Several minutes passed. I grew impatient as I lay staring at the ceiling. Finally, the doctor returned, standing in the doorway. "Very good, you can continue to training." Then he disappeared again through the door.

What was that all about? I pulled myself back onto my feet. Moving through the door, I found my way to the next training space. It felt more like a classroom. There were several tables and chairs. I grabbed a spot next to Goby. At the front of the room was a board with a few things written on it: *Identify, Monitor, Eliminate,* and *Invisible.*

An extremely tall man entered the room. He had to be near seven feet tall. He had long blonde hair and wore glasses. He used two walking canes to brace himself as he moved across the room. The canes were designed with a forearm support and a handle to hold about a quarter of the way down. He positioned himself in front of the small group. Bracing himself against his supports, he looked over the group then turned and, looking over his shoulder, pointed at the board with one of his braces.

"Do you see these words here? These are the words you will now live by. Everything we do is supported by these four words: Identify, Monitor, Eliminate, and Invisible. If you were to ask me, the last word is the most important. Each word, however, carries significance to your mission."

He looked over the group, studying each of our faces. "Does anyone know the meaning of the first word?"

Goby started speaking. "We must identify our target. Make sure they are who we are tasked to locate."

"Exactly. Make sure your target is who you think they are. We have intel on a number of threats within the various Sections. We relay that information to you. It is then up to you to make sure that you target the correct person." The instructor spoke slowly and clearly, pausing slightly between every word. "There have been several people who have used doubles now that they are becoming more aware of us. You must be aware of this as well."

The man pointed to the second word. "Who can tell me about the word 'Monitor'?"

Brantley raised her hand as she spoke. "After we locate and identify our target, we are to monitor them for several days to determine if there is any suspicious behavior."

"Very good," our tall instructor praised. "It is very important to monitor the actions of your target over several days. Our goal is to make sure that we gather as much information about the other people they are in contact with as possible. Also, we want to make sure we have the correct target. So, use your skills to track them, be sure that they are a threat. Identify more people involved if possible. Very good!"

I looked at the words as they started to become more clear as to what they were designed for. The next word was *Eliminate,* which I could only assume meant to kill. It was the second time that I felt in the dark. This was probably another thing that was explained in the movies I had missed. I was sure that was how everyone seemed to know what these words meant before the instructor explained them.

The instructor continued. "Next word: 'Eliminate.' Who can tell me about this word?"

Eleven chimed in for the first time. "We kill them!" That's all he said.

The instructor smirked slightly. "Well, not quite as poetic as I had hoped for. However, yes. There will come a time when the threat must be removed from the various Sections. We are to do this however possible, but then are asked to stage the death to make it appear as an accident. Or perhaps of natural causes. Don't leave your knife or arrow sticking out of their head. Find a way to stage the scene. This leads us to the last word: 'Invisible.'"

The instructor looked at me as if expecting me to give an explanation. I looked to my right and left as the entire group waited for my response. "Don't be seen. Get in and get out without being noticed. Be a ghost," I guessed.

The instructor smiled. "Very good. That is exactly what we're looking for. You were only imagined to have been there. You were in and out without being noticed. Nobody could describe you. Our goal is to always go undetected. This is the most important thing. If you are exposed we lose you for that Section, which limits your usefulness. Be a ghost!"

The lanky instructor hobbled forward. He leaned in over the tables, looking back and forth at each of us. "If you follow these four words you will be very successful in completing your tasks. Stick to your strengths and, no matter what, always be a ghost. The next stage in training will be through that door," he said, using his cane to point at the door that he had entered through.

I rose to my feet and with Brantley, Goby, and Eleven right behind me, made my way to the next room. It looked like an arena from one of the challenges. Perhaps we were going to do one more round of training before receiving our assignments. We gathered near the first area in the arena. It was a shooting station, exactly like the range we had practiced on.

The new instructor appeared behind us, startling the group. "Welcome," he said. "Today we will perform a final assessment of all of your skills with weapons and hand-to-hand combat before determining your target. Based on your result here, you will be assigned your first target. We will start on the range, bow and arrows first. An image will pop up in front of you, then you will be required to locate and eliminate. Without hitting any of the other targets."

The new instructor was slightly shorter than me. He had brown hair and brown eyes. His face lined with several scars, he appeared to have had combat experience. The man carried himself as if he knew how to handle himself. I wouldn't question it. He stood with his arms behind his back, clenched together, revealing his broad shoulders and large chest. As I looked at him he nodded at me, instructing me to get ready without a word.

The group toed the line of the shooting range, arming ourselves with our bows. An image of a middle-aged man appeared floating about fifteen feet in front of us. The image rotated, allowing us to see everything about the target. This man had a scar on the back of his left forearm. *I don't know if this will be helpful at all, but the birthmark last time was.* The horn sounded as several images of people appeared downrange.

I studied the crowd of people as they weaved in and out of each other. I saw the target about two hundred feet away. He was passing between people, moving from left to right. I drew my arrow back, letting it fly downrange. The arrow soared as the man passed two more people. My arrow struck the man in his ear, dropping him to the ground as a second arrow whistled over his head. I looked to my right as Eleven became furious.

My arrow had hit just before his. A new image appeared in front of us. This time it was a woman, no more than thirty years old. She had dark hair and wore similar clothes to that of Section Eight. I looked for any other signs to make her appear unique but couldn't find any before her image vanished. A new set of people appeared. I looked through the crowd, trying to locate her. *There!*

I drew my arrow, preparing to fire as the target dropped. Again, a second arrow flew by, missing, as Eleven started to cuss under his breath. I looked to my left as Brantley smiled at me. I smirked, knowing that her arrow had hit the target first. Eleven heard me laugh and shot daggers at me with piercing eyes. I could feel his gaze without looking. The third image appeared; it was an older gentleman.

The man had grey hair and a full beard. He appeared to be shorter and carried a satchel over his right shoulder. Maybe that would be enough to give him away. The image vanished and the new group of people appeared. I saw the old man instantly, drawing back my arrow. I released it, and as it traveled I looked over at Eleven; he, too, had shot his arrow. I returned to the target as my arrow passed between two innocent people's heads, slamming into the old man's eye.

The image of the man vanished as Eleven's arrow missed for the third time. I was pleased with my performance, especially because it infuriated Eleven, the man who at every turn had attempted to make things harder for me. From pushing me on the opening day to trying to pull me off the wall, the man was a constant bully through all of this. It didn't surprise me that he had survived training, but if I could make him look bad now, I was all for it.

The instructor cut us off. "Very good. Now, place down your bows and grab the pistols. There will be three more targets. Get ready."

I set down my bow, grabbing the pistol from the table to my left. I checked the clip and loaded a bullet into the chamber. It was ready to fire. All I needed was to locate the next target and squeeze the trigger. The rest would take care of itself on this one. A new image appeared, rotating before me. I studied the woman. She was old, at least seventy. That was enough to be able to locate her.

The image vanished as the next group of people appeared. They were a good distance away. The majority of the group was over a hundred feet away and moving. I located the old woman weaving through the crowd. I raised my pistol, tracking her movements through the rows of people. She cleared the group, giving me enough space to squeeze off a shot. I pulled the trigger as the gun exploded, sending a bullet flying downrange. The woman flew back, then vanished.

My target acquisition felt smooth. I was quick on the trigger. Everything about this training felt strong. I was more focused and my senses felt heightened. I didn't know how to explain it, but everything was coming easily to me. The only thing that had changed today from the last few weeks was the lack of pressure of death.

The next target appeared, and I studied the image again. This time the images appeared downrange and I located and eliminated the target within ten seconds. I smiled at my accuracy and success. I glanced to my left as Brantley and Goby looked at me with amazement in their eyes. Even they were impressed with the speed and skill I was displaying. I glanced over to my right as the anger continued building within Eleven. His face was red and his brow was furrowed.

There was one target left. I turned my head back to the range as the next image appeared. It was an old man who looked like my grandpa. I studied the image, staring at it closely. Everything about this man reminded me of my grandfather. The image vanished and the next group of people appeared. I searched the crowd, finding the man. I raised my gun, preparing to fire. I could feel my finger starting to squeeze the trigger—and then relax.

I couldn't do it. I tracked the man with my pistol, unable to squeeze the trigger. The explosion of a gun fired to my left. The image disappeared and the room lit up, indicating the end of this part of training. I continued to stare downrange. Eventually I closed my eyes, shaking the image from my head as I placed the gun back on the table. I rejoined the group, who had already turned to face our instructor.

The instructor addressed the group: "Very good, everyone. We will now proceed with a combat scenario that will test your skills. Right this way."

The instructor moved us past the firing range to an open area. It was laid out just like a city street would be in one of the Sections: Narrow gravel streets with buildings running down either side. Trash and debris lining the street. There was a small curb and tiny sidewalk, though most of the time people just walked in the middle of the road.

"You," he said, pointing at me. "You will go first. Enter the street."

I entered the arena, moving down the middle of the gravel road. The buildings on either side stood still, looking vacant. I felt my heart start to pound. A nervous anxiety swept over me. I didn't know what to expect. As I reached the middle of the small-town layout, I bent down, picking up a broom that had been left in the debris. Stepping on the head of it, I snapped it off, creating a small spear. Moments later, a scream from behind me caught my attention.

I turned just in time to duck, avoiding a blow from an attacking hologram. The hologram wielded a shovel, swinging it over his head and down at me. I raised my broomstick, stopping the first blow. I dropped to a knee and slapped the stick against the assailant's knee. His feet shot out from under him, forcing him down onto his back. The point where I had snapped the broom head off made for a nice, sharp edge. I raised my arms over my head and slammed the stick into the hologram's chest.

A small gasp left the hologram, then it vanished. Two more appeared the moment the first was gone. They entered from opposite ends of the street and positioned themselves on either side of me. I opened my body up, pointing one shoulder at each of them. This allowed me to see each without turning too much. The hologram on my left attacked first, swinging wildly at me with a broken tree branch.

I deflected the shot with my broomstick, then kicked the man into the second hologram. Now they were both in front of me. The two came at me at once, swinging violently at me with their weapons. I deflected a shot to my left, then back to my right, moving so fast now that instincts were driving me. I was moving before I even saw the next blow. After deflecting several shots from the two holograms, I swung hard from right to left, slapping both men across the face with a single blow.

The hologram to my right collapsed to the ground. I moved quickly to him, stabbing him in the throat. By the time I had turned around, the second hologram had regained his composure. It was amazing how humanlike these images were in the way they reacted and moved. The hologram attacked again, swinging low to the left and then high to the right. I dropped the stick, blocking the incoming blow. I deflected three more shots after that.

We circled each other. Another overhead attack. I pushed my arms up, stopping the blow from landing. The force of the swing snapped my broomstick in half. I held each piece in my hands, realizing my biggest defense was gone. I pushed in on the man, swinging rights and lefts. He deflected the first couple of shots, but I finally got through, slapping him across the right side of his face and then landing another blow to his ribcage.

The man backed on his heels, retreating. I pressed forward. I slapped one of the broomstick halves against his right wrist then his left, forcing his weapon from his hands. I fired my left hook across his collarbone. I pulled back both pieces of my broomstick and shot the jagged edges at the man. One entered each of his eyes. The hologram flickered slightly then fell to his knees, vanishing.

I was watching the hologram disappear when something crashed into the back of my head, forcing me to the ground. I collapsed onto all fours, looking up over my shoulder in time to see the second blow bearing down on me. I rolled right, avoiding the shot. I rolled a second time, pulling myself up onto my feet. My eyes searched for my attacker. I finally regained my senses and found myself looking directly into the eyes of Number Eleven.

He stood, holding a wooden staff. Blood dripped from the middle of it. I reached back, touching the back of my head. Warm and moist, I brought my hand into view. The red blood dripped between my fingers. I wiped my hand off on my shirt as Eleven swung his staff at me. I dodged back, leaning to the left as the staff crashed into the ground. He followed with a backhand shot that I dropped underneath. Still moving backward, I dodged another shot, sliding to the right.

I felt my back press up against the wall of one of the buildings. Eleven fired the end of the staff at my midsection. I sidestepped the blow, grabbing the staff as I lunged forward at him, my elbow colliding with his jaw. He dropped the staff as we tumbled over one another. Crashing into the ground, I rolled over the top of him, landing back on the gravel road. I tried to turn over, but it was too late. Eleven had mounted my back and slid his arm under my throat.

I felt him clamp down, blocking my airway. I gasped for breath, prying at his arm. I tried to move my body but it was no use. He had me locked down. The edges of my vision started to fade, turning black. I swung my right elbow up and back, catching him on the side of the head. I didn't have enough force to jar him loose. My body was weakening. I was almost blacked out; there were only a few moments left before I would be unconscious.

I swung my arm again as it flew back weak and soft, falling short with zero damage. I tried again, but I had zero strength left to fight. There was only one final thing I could do. I reached up, tapping Eleven's arm, trying to get him to let me free. He had won.

No response. I tapped again.

I felt another violent squeeze as the world turned completely black.

CHAPTER 19

Everything felt hazy. I strained to open my eyes. Shadowy figures moved in front of me. I could hear voices talking, but I wasn't able to make out any words. I blinked, opening my eyes again. The figures began to take shape. They were still not sharp images, but I could make out the silhouettes of Brantley and Goby. I strained my eyes more to try to focus, finally creating a clearer picture of the room. Brantley and Goby stood to the left of my bed. A doctor stood on the right, checking a machine I'd never seen before.

I swallowed. An apple-sized lump stuck in my throat. I tried to take in a deep breath; that, too, was difficult. Brantley leaned over the bed, touching her hand to my forehead. Her hand ran back over my hair, landing on my cheek. She smiled at me. I attempted to smile back, but I wasn't sure if it actually formed through the pain. Goby's hand dropped down, landing on my shoulder.

I opened my mouth but was unable to form any words. I tried again, forcing out a whispered, "What … hap … happened?"

Brantley's face turned angry as she looked off past me at nothing. "Eleven attacked you during your final training session. He put you down, choking you until you blacked out. The instructor had to pry him off of you. I don't know why, but he snapped."

I swallowed again; this time it was a little easier. I took in a breath. "I remember that now. Is training over?" This time the words seemed to come out a little easier. However, they were still no louder than a whisper.

Goby laughed a little at my question. "Yeah, buddy, training is over. We get our assignments tomorrow."

"When can I get out of here?" I asked, still straining to generate any volume.

The doctor stopped checking the machine and turned to me. "As soon as I check a few more things and give you some medicine to help with your throat. Open wide; I'll administer a dose now."

I opened my mouth as he squeezed several drops of liquid from a tiny dropper into my throat. The liquid instantly cooled my burning throat, giving it immediate relief. It was amazing. I could feel my throat healing. The doctor shined a light into my open mouth. He checked several angles before allowing me to close my mouth. I swallowed again. This time there was only a lemon-sized lump.

"This will help with the swelling and pain. You will do the same thing I just did at least every two hours. You should be good as new by morning. Do you understand?" the doctor said, handing me the small vial of medicine.

I nodded as I took the tiny bottle from him. He turned back to his machine as I returned my attention to Brantley and Goby. "So, what do we have left to do today?"

"Nothing," Goby said. "We're done until tomorrow when we get our assignments. Then, after we get our assignments, we ship out within twenty-four hours." He turned, leaving my bedside.

Brantley rubbed my forehead again. "Just rest up. You'll be out of here soon. We're going to go grab some breakfast, but we will see you later."

"Breakfast? Was I out for a full day?" I asked, shocked.

"Yeah, training finished up yesterday." Brantley leaned forward over the bed, kissing me on the forehead. She smiled and then turned, disappearing from the bedside.

I closed my eyes, trying to relax. I took another deep breath, feeling my throat fight the air in and out of my lungs. When I opened my eyes I was greeted by Gaia's smiling face. She leaned over the bed, looking down at me. She looked beautiful, her hair pulled back, eyes glowing at me. She grabbed my left arm, her eyes searching my face. I reached across the bed, grabbing her hand with my right hand and flashing her a smile.

"Hey! How are you doing?" Gaia asked.

"I've been better. I've also been worse." I laughed, causing myself to cough.

Gaia moved her hand to my chest, trying to ease my coughing. "Stop joking; you need to rest. Getting all worked up isn't going to help you get better."

"I know. I'm sorry." I smiled at her. "How did you know I was here?"

"I asked who made the final four. They told me that you had along with number Eleven, Eighteen and Twenty-one. So I asked if I was still able to see you now that training was over. They told me that you were being integrated into the capital and then you were going through training. That's when I found out that you had gotten hurt and were here."

I smiled again. "Checking up on me, I see."

Gaia pulled her arm away from my grasp. "No!" She turned away but looked over her shoulder at me. I could see the smile forming on her face. "OK, so I wanted to make sure you were OK. What of it?"

I reached out and grabbed her hand. "I'm glad you did. I was hoping I would be able to see you, too."

She leaned forward, kissing me on the cheek. "Well, you get better, then we can talk. They told me where you live, so I will make an effort to stop by and see you before you leave. If not, I will see you when you get back. Now that you're considered a citizen there are some really nice places I want to show you in the city."

Gaia smiled, turning to leave the room. I watched as she turned the corner and disappeared through the door. I reclined my head back, staring at the ceiling. It was something I had done for so many years now when I tried to think. *Those two girls still have me twisted.*

I truly didn't know what to make of them. They were both amazing in different ways. It was hard to determine which one was more amazing. I was just glad to have both of them in my life. For however brief it may be.

Moments later, the doctor returned to the bedside. He pulled at the sensors that were attached to me. "OK, you are free to go."

I sat up, throwing my feet over the side of the bed. The sudden movement caused me to become slightly disoriented. I could feel my head spin as I placed my feet on the ground. I kept contact with the bed for a minute, trying to collect my bearings. I didn't want to give the doctor any reason to make me remain in bed. After a moment, my head returned to normal. I made my way out of the room and out to the street.

It was closing in on lunchtime and I was feeling quite hungry. I needed to get some food. At the curb, a vehicle waited for me. I did like the constant transportation service. I hadn't had to walk anywhere of great length since arriving at my new home. As I climbed in and positioned myself into the back seat, the driver looked over his shoulder. He smiled, revealing a large gap in the middle of his front teeth.

"Where to, sir?" he asked.

I needed some food. That's when I remembered my house was stocked with food. "Freedom Row, please."

"Yes, sir," the driver said, whipping back around.

After the short ride through the city the driver arrived at my door. I climbed the steps to my new home. Lights flipped on as I moved through the house to the kitchen. As I had expected, there was plenty of fresh bread and meat to make a sandwich. I gathered up a few other snacks and made my way outside to the rocking chairs on the front porch. As I rocked, watching the street for signs of life, I felt my eyes start to get heavy. I reached in my pocket, pulling out my medicine. I dropped a few drops in my throat and then drifted off to sleep.

Several hours later, I awoke to Brantley coming up my porch steps. She hopped up onto my porch. "Hey there. You still tired?"

I rubbed my eyes, wiping away the last remaining sleep. "No, I think I'm good now. What are you up to?"

"Nothing. Do you want to have dinner together?" Brantley asked as she leaned up against the porch railing.

I stood up from my porch chair. "Yeah, that sounds nice," I said, opening the door to escort Brantley inside.

We worked our way to the kitchen. Brantley grabbed a number of food items, preparing dinner like she had worked in the kitchen her whole life. I watched from the doorway with amazement. She moved around the kitchen like my mother did back home, her movements quick, precise, and confident. I leaned against the doorway watching Brantley work as the meal came together. She made a few final preparations and then turned on the stovetop.

The fire from the stove began to heat the pan. Brantley grabbed the food, tossing it into the pan, which sizzled as the food began to cook. Steam rose from the pan, and an incredible aroma filled the air. I could feel my mouth start to water. Brantley looked over her shoulder, smiling at me as I continued to watch her work. Turning back to the food, she began to flip it around, stirring it frequently. After ten minutes she turned the fire off, removing the pan.

Brantley divvied up the food onto two plates. She turned around, steam rising from each plate, and set them on the kitchen table. I moved into the room, pulling up a seat across from Brantley. The food looked great. There was a mix of chicken and vegetables cooked together. A light sauce glistened off the food.

"Where did you learn to cook like this?" I asked, putting the first bite of food into my mouth. The taste was excellent. The chicken and vegetables melted in my mouth as I chewed, and the light sauce added a sweet and spicy flavor.

"Back home I cooked for my family, so I always spent my days in the kitchen. Never with this many resources, though." Brantley smiled. "Do you like it?"

"It's amazing. Absolutely delicious!" I said with a mouth full of food.

Brantley smiled, blushing slightly. "Thank you!"

I put another bite in my mouth, closing my eyes as I took in all the flavor. "So good."

I shoveled the remainder of the food into my mouth. Before I knew what had happened, my plate was empty. I looked at my plate and then over at Brantley's. She still had half of her meal left. I glanced up as she put a small bite of food into her mouth. She smiled while she chewed. Swallowing the bite, she pushed her plate toward me. "Would you like some more?"

"I don't want to take yours," I said, shaking my head.

"It's OK, I don't need as much food as you," Brantley said, moving around the table and pulling her chair next to me. "Here, we can share."

We sat next to each other, finishing the rest of the food. When we were done I wiped my mouth, grabbed both of our plates and took them to the sink to rinse them. When I turned around, Brantley was still sitting at the table. It was nice having company. It was nice being free to move around and do what we pleased. It was a rare and new feeling.

"Want to go sit by the fireplace?" I asked as I finished cleaning the plates.

"Yeah, that sounds nice," Brantley said, climbing to her feet.

In the living room Brantley took a seat on the couch as I tossed a few pieces of firewood into the fireplace. I worked the set of matches that sat on top of the hearth. After a couple of moments, I got the fire started and it crackled to life. The heat rose, filling the room as I sat next to Brantley on the couch. We sat silently, staring at the fire. Brantley dropped her head slowly onto my shoulder. I wrapped my arm around her.

The moment felt nice. Comfortable. With all that was happening around me, this was a safe place. For the first time I was completely free of the chains that had held me down all my life. I watched the fire dance as I wondered what it would be like to have a life like this full of relaxed, happy moments where there was no fear of what the next day would bring. How nice it would be.

If only this moment were truly real, not just a small fraction of time. A false sense of hope. A tease of what a normal life could be like. It wasn't my life. I knew that tomorrow I would be given an assignment that could result in the death of another human. Brantley would as well. After tomorrow, my life would change forever. In just a moment's time, I would no longer be an innocent young man, but a killer. I wished for a way to freeze this moment. Live the rest of my days like this.

"Can I stay with you tonight, Dantin?" Brantley whispered. My eyes shot down at her as she gazed up at me. "I don't want to be alone tonight."

I could see that she was feeling as I was, wanting so desperately to hold onto this moment for as long as possible. "Yes," I whispered to her. "Stay."

We sat in silence for another hour, watching the fire burn down. The heat of the room kept us comfortable. The only sounds were that of the fire crackling as the wood split and burst. After the hour passed, the fire was all but burnt out. Only the red embers remained. I rose to my feet, reaching my hand down to help Brantley to her feet. As she rose she wrapped her arms around my neck, squeezing it tightly, pressing her head to my chest.

"I don't want to get assigned tomorrow. I don't want to leave," Brantley said softly.

I sighed. "I don't either."

"I'm tired. Let's go to bed," Brantley said.

We made our way down the hall to the bedroom. I pulled the covers back as Brantley climbed in. I tucked her in then made my way over to my side, sliding in next to her. Brantley curled up next to me, her head near my shoulder and her hand on my chest. She breathed softly, her eyes closed and her body close to mine.

"Do you think we will be the same after this?" she asked softly.

She didn't have to explain what she was talking about. I knew she meant after killing someone. Would we be the same? I didn't have an answer.

"I don't know. I hope so." I brushed the hair from her face and kissed her forehead. "I don't see you ever changing in my eyes."

There was a pause and then a soft whisper: "Goodnight, Dantin."

"Goodnight."

*****

It was the best night's sleep I'd had in several weeks. By the time I woke up, Brantley was gone. I rolled out of bed, rising to my feet. I searched the house, but there was no sign of her. I wasn't sure why she felt she had to leave so quickly. I was making my way to the kitchen when the internal speaker system beeped, alerting me of an incoming message. An announcement blared through the house.

"You are asked to report to the training facility for your assignment. Please proceed to your designated areas immediately. That is all." The voice disappeared as fast as it had arrived.

A vehicle waited out front to take me to the Training Center. As I arrived, two men greeted me, directing me to my assignment group. I followed them down a series of winding corridors to a large room. In the middle of the room was a large wooden table. There was a large monitor on the back wall with several smaller monitors lining the side walls. There were already two men sitting in the room when I arrived.

The man on the left was an older gentleman. His silver hair was cut short. He had bronze skin, which was rare for people in the capital being that most of their days were spent underground. The second man was younger, probably ten years older than me. He had medium-length, sandy-colored hair. He was the proper amount of pale for a capital citizen. He wore glasses and a white lab coat.

The older gentleman greeted me as I entered the room.

"Good morning, Dantin, I am Captain Barnes. I will be your commanding officer from here on out. You will report on all missions to me. If you have any questions, please feel free to ask me at any point. This here," he said, gesturing to the other man, "is Ratchet. He's our chief science engineer. He will make sure you're properly armed for each mission."

Captain Barnes pointed to the chair at the far side of the table facing the monitor. As I sat down, Barnes pointed a remote at the screens, which flickered and then illuminated. The large screen displayed a color-coded map of Natio with each of the distinct Sections laid out.

The majority of the map was green. Including Section Eight. There were four sections that were yellow and one that was red. The red section—Section Fifteen—blinked, flashing repeatedly. The yellow Sections consisted of Four, Six, Eleven, and Twelve.

Captain Barnes went over to the large monitor. He pointed at the screen with his back to me, then turned.

"Have you ever seen a map of Natio?" he asked.

I shook my head. "No, sir, not one like this, anyway."

The map displayed the outline of old America as I had seen many times in textbooks. However, the old outlines of states had been removed. The only city now showing on the map was Heart City. Instead of territories, states, cities, lakes, rivers, and oceans, there were small circles indicating the locations of the domes. The various domes were numbered One to Sixteen, starting in the south along the Gulf of Mexico and moving clockwise around Heart City along the border.

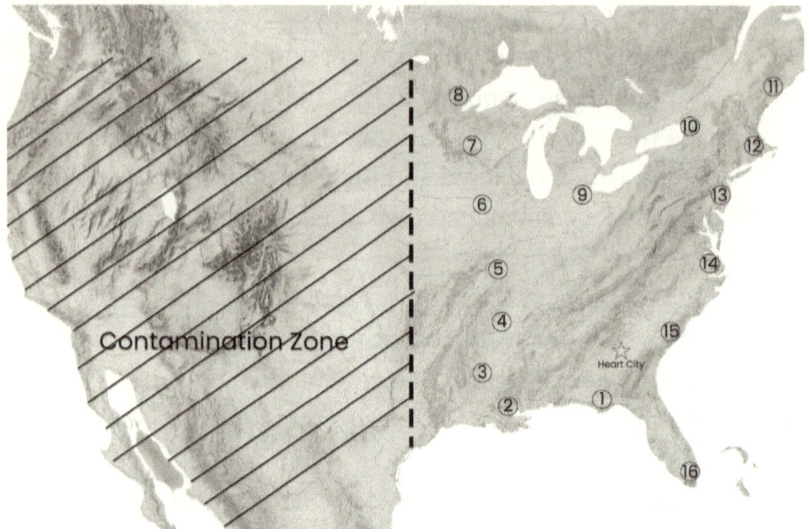

The largest concentration of domes ran along the Mississippi River, starting at the sea near what was once New Orleans, working all the way up to the north where the river ended. Section Nine sat in between the cluster of Great Lakes and Section Ten along the Canadian border just east of the lakes. The rest of the domes bordered the Atlantic Ocean.

West of the Mississippi River was an area of the country that was deemed "Contamination Zone." This portion of the county took the brunt of attacks during the Canadian-Mexican War. Nuclear bombs destroyed all that was habitable, and all that remained was a scorched wasteland. It was said that entering that portion of the country would lead to radiation poisoning and certain death.

Captain Barnes turned back to the map, talking to the screen. "This map indicates the status of each Section. Green means that there is peace and the people are working as told. Yellow indicates areas of minor concern: potential risks have been spotted. Red means danger. As you can see right now, we are relatively at peace."

"Yes, sir," I acknowledged.

Barnes reached up, tapping the screen as the map zoomed in on a layout of Section Four. It was exactly how I would have imagined Section Eight would look like from the air. A small blinking light flashed in the northwest sector of the Section. I studied the street map as Barnes turned, moving closer to the table. He placed his hands on the table and leaned forward.

"Your assignment is within Section Four. There have been rumors of secret meetings and potential for dissension." He turned back around. "Your target will be this man."

He pointed the remote at the table, pressing a button. A holographic image of the man appeared, rotating in the center of the table. He was an older gentleman, roughly the same age as my grandpa. I studied the man as the image rotated. Captain Barnes pressed another button to zoom in on the image. Now only the man's head was visible. This gave me a good chance to see his face. His white hair and wrinkled face stared right back at me.

Barnes continued, "This man has been reportedly holding secret meetings after curfew. He is also believed to be a member of a secret group of rebels who threaten our peaceful way of life. There have been reports of this group now in several of the Sections. Your assignment is to locate and monitor this man's movements. Report back anyone he has contact with, anything that seems suspicious. If you perceive the threat to be real, eliminate the target."

I looked at the map and then back at the image of the man. Finally, I turned my attention to Barnes. "Yes, sir."

"Very good," Barnes said. "Ratchet here will now go over some of the gadgets you will have for this particular mission."

"OK, so what we need to start with first is …" Ratchet spoke fast, then trailed off, making it hard to follow him. He paced back and forth while fidgeting with his hands. Then he stopped momentarily, grabbing a small device from the table. "… this. This is your communicator. It will allow you to make contact with Captain Barnes while you're in Section Four."

The device fit into my palm. There was a small red button on the top left of the piece. I turned the communication device over in my hand, studying it closely. I was amazed that something like this would allow me to communicate with Barnes all the way back here in the capital. I pressed the red button, and the communicator beeped.

"When you push that button you open up communication pathways with Barnes. After you finish your statement, release the button and he can respond." Ratchet had started to pace again. He paused slightly before speaking again. "OK, the other thing you will need is this pair of glasses. You will be disguised as an Overseer during the day, so you can use these glasses to hide your eyes as well as protect them. When night falls, you push the button on the right side of the frame and they will help you see in the dark."

Ratchet handed me the glasses, and I put them on. The room fell dark as I looked through the lenses. These must be meant for during the day. It would be nice to not have to squint through the sun. My eyes had become more sensitive to the light having been underground for so long. I reached up, touching the button on the right side near my temple. The lenses switched and the entire room burst into light.

I quickly pulled the lenses off; the brightness was too much to bear having come from such darkness. "I assume the change won't be so drastic if it's completely dark out?"

"Correct," Ratchet said, shaking his head violently. "The two other pieces aren't anything all that exciting. First is your bow, which as you can see here on the table doesn't look like a bow."

Ratchet reached down, grabbing a metal grip off the table. It looked like the handle of a compound bow, but without the rest of it. He held up the small piece and pressed a button with his index finger. The grip snapped open, expanding in his hand. My eyes had to be bulging out of my head. In his hand was a full-sized bow. Ratchet smiled at my amazement.

On the table next to where Ratchet had picked up the bow was a quiver of arrows. They were also crafted of extremely light, durable metal. Ratchet grabbed one of the arrows from the quiver. He looked at me, holding it up. There was no arrowhead on it. I wasn't sure how effective this would be.

As though reading my mind, Ratchet said, "Each arrow has an option of three different heads. There is your normal lethal arrowhead. Then there is a shorter, duller head that carries a small electric charge to disable your target. Last, and my favorite: the explosive head. In case you really want to send a message."

Ratchet smiled, pleased with himself. He put the arrow back in the quiver as he collapsed the bow back into its original state. Both the bow and quiver were quite small, which would make them both very easy to conceal. After setting the bow and quiver next to each other, he looked up at me.

"This way you can carry your weapon with you at all times without drawing attention to yourself. It's only a little click away," he said. "The last weapon is your knife. It has no special features other than I've built a holster into your Overseer's uniform to conceal it. Otherwise, it is just a knife. Do you have any questions?"

I looked at all the gadgets as they lay on the table in front of me. "No, I think I'm good."

Captain Barnes stood up from his chair. "Very good! You leave first thing tomorrow morning. You will report to the train depot. An alarm will sound in your home to indicate when you must leave. Good luck!"

I stood up from my chair. "Thank you, sir." I turned, making my way back to the door. The two men who had escorted me down to the room led me back up to the front of the building, where the vehicle waited to take me back to my home.

After being dropped off, I stood on the porch of my home staring down the street at Brantley and Goby's houses. They didn't appear to be home yet. I entered the house, tripping over a large duffle bag that lay in the middle of my entryway. I looked around the place, trying to find someone. There was nobody there. I zipped open the bag, finding my Overseer's uniform, communicator, and weapons.

I should have known that even though I'd been given a home within the city, I wasn't the only person with a key. I grabbed the bag and set it in the living room. I scanned the rest of the bag for anything else. I had one pair of black pants and a black long-sleeved shirt. Three Overseer uniforms. My bow, a quiver of arrows, and my knife. The quiver was built in a way that it could rest against my back under my uniform undetected.

Everything was designed to be invisible. Nobody would have a clue that I was not an Overseer. It made me wonder: how many times when I saw a new Overseer in Section Eight were they actually an assassin? I tried to think back to how many different Overseers I had seen during my time in Section Eight. Perhaps some of those accidental deaths weren't actually accidents. There was no way to know.

A knocking behind me pulled me from my thoughts. Goby and Brantley stood looking at me. "Hey, buddy, did you get your assignment?" Goby asked.

"Yeah. How about you guys? Where are you off to?" I asked.

Goby nodded. "I'm off to Section Six. There's a man there who is believed to be harboring rebels."

"And I'm off to Section Twelve. There's a woman there who has been organizing small uprisings within the Section," Brantley said. "What about you?"

"I'm headed to Section Four. There's an old man there who they feel is a threat. Fun stuff, huh? Do you leave tomorrow morning too?"

Brantley and Goby both shook their heads. "No, we leave in an hour," Goby said. "That's why we stopped by. We wanted to wish you luck and say goodbye before we had to head out." He extended a hand toward me.

I moved past the hand, giving him a hug. "You be safe. Good luck, and I'll see you when we all get back."

"You too. Be safe," Goby said, turning and heading out the door.

Brantley stepped forward, wrapping her arms around my waist and resting her head on my chest. "Do you think we will see each other again?"

"Of course we will. Why wouldn't we?" I said, resting my cheek on the top of her head.

"I'm just afraid that with all of the missions they will be sending us on, we won't ever see each other." She looked up at me as I pulled my head back.

"We will see each other again. I promise," I said, trying to sound as sure as I could.

Brantley smiled. "Thanks, I needed to hear that." She pulled away from me, stepping into the doorway. "Be safe. I will see you soon."

I smiled at her. "You too."

Brantley turned to leave but stopped suddenly. She whirled around and strode back into the house. She wrapped her arms around my neck, pressing her lips to mine. Time froze as the kiss felt like it lasted for minutes. I felt my heart quicken. My body ached for more. Then, just as quickly as it had started, she pulled away.

"Just in case," she said, smiling as she turned and bounded out the door.

I stood still, frozen by the moment in the doorway. I watched as she walked down the stairs, headed to the street, and turned left, disappearing from sight. I stood staring at nothing for several minutes before snapping back to reality. It was the second time she had sent my body into a tailspin. I wanted to chase after her. Hold her and not let her go. But I knew that wasn't an option. Instead, I turned, moving slowly back into the house.

I plopped down onto my bed. A replay of the day's events played out in my head. The new assignment. The beginning of my new future. Brantley.

Was it really goodbye or just a "see you later"? I wanted to believe I'd see her again, but the truth was, I didn't know. I did know that I would do everything in my power to see her again.

Will we be the same people next time we see each other? Is this the beginning or the end?

CHAPTER 20

I stepped out onto the platform at the train station, duffle bag over my shoulder. The sounds of the various engines filled the platform. There were four trains waiting to depart that morning. Mine was taking off from track four. Tinker stood waiting for me outside the train. I handed him my duffle bag, and he carried it onto the train. I looked back toward the city, getting one final look at the capital before my journey to Section Four.

As I placed my foot onto the first step of the train, my name echoed across the platform: "Dantin! Wait!"

I held onto the handle and leaned off of the train, scanning the platform to see where the voice had come from. My eyes landed on Gaia as she ran across the platform, racing toward me. I hopped off the train as she jumped into my arms, wrapping her arms around me so tight her feet came off the ground. Finally, she released her grasp, dropping to the ground.

"I was afraid I was going to miss you!" she said frantically.

"I didn't think I was going to see you either. I'm glad you made it," I said, surprised she came to see me off.

She smiled. "How long will you be gone?"

I shrugged. "I'm not sure. As long as the job takes. Hopefully not too long, though. As much as I'm looking forward to getting back into the Sections, I don't want to be there long."

"Well, I just wanted to come see you off. Have a safe trip. I'll see you when you get back." Gaia smiled.

I smiled back, placing my hand on her shoulder. "Thank you."

I started to make my way back to the train.

"Dantin!" I spun back around as Gaia grabbed my head, pressing her lips up to mine. Her hands were soft on my cheek. Her lips were full. She held me close and then pulled away, leaving her hands on either side of my face. "Hurry home!"

I turned without another word and climbed back onto the train, emotions bombarding my head. I was conflicted yet again as I made my way back to my cabin. I opened the door to my room and sat down as the train surged forward, leaving the station. A part of me felt as though I had betrayed Brantley, even though we weren't really together. Part of me argued that Gaia had always been the person who was there for me. I felt my head start to ache.

I looked out the window, trying to clear my head of these thoughts. The last thing I needed now was something distracting me from my task. Something that could lead me to make a mistake. We were out of the city now. The trees passed with regularity. The sun was starting to rise on the horizon. It was the very early moments of daylight. The train accelerated, causing the passing scenery to blur together.

The ride to Section Four was only a couple of hours. It wasn't long before Tinker appeared at the door to my room.

"We will be arriving in fifteen minutes," he said. "You might want to change into uniform."

I opened my duffle bag, grabbing the Overseer's uniform. I slipped it on, concealing my arrows under the white jacket. My knife slid nicely into the holster that Ratchet had created in the uniform. I grabbed my bow from the bag, just in case, holding it in my left hand. I threw the remainder of the duffle bag over my shoulder as the train began to slow. There was still a twenty-minute carriage ride to Section Four. None of the train depots went up to the Section gates.

The train stopped and I exited onto the platform, where the horse and carriage waited. Tinker stepped off the train behind me.

"These are your transfer papers," he said, handing me several sheets of paper. "Nobody will ask you any questions. Deliver these to the Capitol Building upon arrival and they will get you settled. Make sure you contact Captain Barnes once you're inside the Section. Upon completion of the mission, we will send another train to retrieve you."

Tinker disappeared back onto the train, and I climbed into the carriage. The driver slammed at the reins, jolting the horses into a light jog, and the carriage bounced forward.

The ride to Section Four passed relatively quickly. I could feel every crevice and bump along the narrow dirt path through the woods. By the time we arrived, my butt was sore from the wood seat and constant bouncing. It was quite the change from the smooth rides I had become accustomed to in Heart City.

The carriage dropped me off in front of the Capitol Building. I entered the building, which looked exactly like the one in Section Eight. The resemblance was almost scary. Everything about this place was exactly like home, except for the types of trees. That was the only discernible difference. The receptionist took my papers. She looked them over and then disappeared through a doorway. After a moment, an Overseer appeared.

"So, you're the new transfer I was told about," the man said, looking me over. "Right this way; I'll show you to your quarters and then you can get to work."

In Section Eight, the Overseers' quarters were within the Capitol Building. The same was true in Section Four. The Overseer who greeted me moved around the reception area, leading me up a flight of stairs. On the second floor there was a row of doors, each with a number on it. We moved down the hall until we got to room twenty-two. He slid a key into the door, shaking it open. It creaked as it swung into the room.

The Overseer handed me the key. "Here you go. This will get you in the front of the building if you're out after dark. It will also get you into your room, as you can see. Do you have any questions?"

I shook my head, setting my duffle bag on the floor next to the bed. "No, I'm good. Thank you!"

"Very good," the Overseer said, turning to exit the room.

After he left, I opened my duffle bag, grabbing my communicator. I pressed the red button on the side, causing the device to beep.

"Captain Barnes, this is Dantin reporting in," I said. I waited a minute with no response and then tried again. "Captain Barnes, this is Dantin."

The device crackled as Captain Barnes' voice boomed through the tiny speaker. "Very good, Dantin. Locate the subject and monitor his movements. Report back tomorrow morning. Good luck."

I placed the communicator back in my bag and made my way outside. On the street, people scurried in all directions. I moved across the square in front of the Capitol Building. On the far side of the square, an Overseer stood with his arms crossed, propped up against one of the buildings. I looked for a spot opposite him. Crossing another small street, I leaned up against a building where I could watch the people pass by.

The lunch horn would be sounding momentarily. It would be the best chance to locate my target. The old man would be eating with the rest of the Section. Like clockwork, the horn sounded and people emerged from all the work buildings. Lunch was a communal activity in the Sections. It was a chance to sit and talk to friends about things that were going on at home, work, and in their lives. With every Section having a curfew, evening get-togethers were rare.

I scanned the crowd as people moved quickly across the square. That's when I saw the old man weaving through the flow of people, heading away from the lunch meeting area, away from the Capitol Building. I popped off the wall, moving along the side of the building, following the man's movements. He continued through the crowd, then down a side street.

I worked my way to the end of the building, turning down the side street. The old man was about two hundred feet ahead of me. I wanted to make sure to keep my distance. I didn't want to draw any undue attention to myself. The man passed several work depots before walking between two buildings close to the end of the road. I sped up, trying to get to the end of the road before he got too far ahead.

I reached the last building on the street and placed my right shoulder against its old stone wall. I leaned my head forward, peering around the corner. The man stood back in the alleyway, about fifty feet away. I pulled my head back quickly, afraid I had stuck out too far.

I leaned up close to the wall, peering around the corner with just my left eye. A second man had appeared. The two men talked, but they were too far away and too quiet to listen in on. My target grabbed something from the other man, then turned, heading back up the street.

I whipped around the building out of sight. Hurrying back down the street, I turned down the first alleyway I came to. I hid behind a couple of broken crates as the man passed by. I needed to find out what had been given to him. It would be the perfect thing to report back to Captain Barnes. I climbed out from behind the crates, returning to my original corner post, waiting for the lunch horn to sound again.

The horn sounded and people began to return to work. I watched as the old man passed back through the square and entered the old building for woodworkers. Now I knew where he was going to be at the end of the workday. I headed back into the Capitol Building. I needed to write down what I had seen so far so I didn't forget any of the details, not to mention I had several hours until the next horn would sound. There was no reason to spend it out wandering about.

In my room I proceeded to take notes. Afterward, I decided to rest up; it was going to be a long night. I was going to have to track him home and wait to see if he tried to conduct an after-curfew meeting.

I climbed into bed, staring at the ceiling. The way the man moved around the Section reminded me a lot of how Grandpa used to conduct himself. He always did what he wanted, including attending those late-night secret meetings. *I wonder if he's on Natio's watch list?*

✳✳✳✳✳

My eyes shot open as a horn sounded. I threw the covers off me, jumping to my feet. I grabbed my bow, throwing my quiver of arrows on my back and covering them with my Overseer jacket. I raced down the hallway and through the entry of the Capitol Building. I slammed through the door and sprinted into the open square, my eyes immediately focusing on the woodworkers building. I scanned the area right around it, but there was no sign of my target.

I felt my heart start to pound as the adrenaline began to flow. I moved quickly, almost frantically, in the direction of the building. I forced myself to slow down and appear calm, moving with a purpose but without drawing attention to myself. The old man suddenly appeared in the doorway to the woodworkers building. He looked left then turned right, moving with the crowd to the living area of the Section.

I followed about a hundred feet behind the old man. He weaved his way relatively quickly through the throngs of people. His footsteps appeared much lighter than a man's his age should be. I watched as he made his way to the end of the first street of housing units, entering the last home on the left. I stopped, letting the crowd push on by, and continued down the next row of living units.

As the neighborhood became emptier, I positioned myself at the far side of the street, where I could see through the man's first-story window. I saw him move over to the kitchen table and kiss a young girl, who had to be his granddaughter, on the head. The little girl laughed and then went back to reading her book. The scene reminded me so much of home. In my mind I could see Micca at the table with her schoolwork.

I pictured what would be going on if I were home right now. Most likely, Mother would be attempting to cook with little to no food. Grandpa would probably be complaining about something that had happened that day. Micca would probably have her nose in a book. I would be sitting next to the fire watching everyone do their usual routine.

I pushed the memories out of my head, focusing back on the moment at hand. I had a job to do, and I needed to stay in the present.

I continued to watch as the old man made himself comfortable on an old rocking chair. Moments later, an older woman—the man's wife, I assumed—entered the room. She moved across the kitchen, pulling food from the stovetop. She yelled something to the old man while placing the food into bowls and setting them at the kitchen table. There was nothing suspicious about any of this behavior. It was just a family sitting down to dinner.

I positioned myself in the evening shadows with a clear view of the old man's home. I made myself comfortable, preparing my glasses for use as the sun dipped out of the sky. It was going to be completely dark within minutes.

I'd been sitting for what felt like hours, waiting for something to happen, when the mood in the house changed. The woman started yelling at the old man. I watched as she waved her arms around, gesturing at the man. This didn't seem to affect him any as he threw on a light jacket and exited the home.

As soon as I threw the glasses on, the dark streets suddenly became clear and well-lit. The glasses were incredible. Everything glowed with perfect clarity. The man appeared not too far ahead of me. I tried to remain in the shadows as I followed him. He weaved through the various streets, avoiding all the locations where the Overseers had positioned themselves. He knew exactly how to get through the Section without being seen.

He turned down a couple of different streets before cutting through an alleyway, I stayed within a hundred feet of the man without leaving the darkness of the shadows. It was so dark on some of the streets it would have been hard for someone without night-vision glasses to see their hand in front of their own face. He was nearing the edge of the dome when he turned down another street, disappearing behind a building. I hurried to the entrance of the alleyway.

I moved slowly around the corner and into the alleyway. The man turned right again, and I realized he was going in circles. Either he knew I was following him or he was trying to ditch anyone who might be following him. I still assumed he didn't know I was there. I moved down another alley when suddenly, the man slowed, staring at a wall. It was a dead end. I ducked behind a dumpster, waiting for the man's next move.

"You are here for me, aren't you?" the man said without turning around. I waited for a response, but nothing came.

"I know you're there; you've been following me."

I realized he was talking to me. I climbed to my feet, stepping out from behind the dumpster. The man slowly turned around to face me. I felt my hand grab onto the handle of my knife, pulling it from its holster. I watched the man through the glasses as he tried to make me out in the dark. He still couldn't see who I was or exactly where I was in the dark.

"Please come closer. I can't see you," the man said, squinting into the night.

I didn't move. I stood back, watching cautiously. I knew better than to reveal myself. I still needed to determine what this man knew. I also knew now that I would have to eliminate him. He was officially a threat because he knew about my presence.

Without saying a word, I slid my knife back into its holster. I grabbed my bow, snapping it to full form. I slid an arrow from the quiver. My heart quickened. I had pretended to kill so many people in training, but this was completely different. I knew this man wouldn't disappear after he died. He would just lie there and I would have to cover up his death.

I placed an arrow on the string, drawing back the bow. The man's eyes suddenly dropped, losing hope.

His gaze landed on my chest, and I could see the last glimmer of hope return.

"If it is time then it is time. We all enter as one into the Kingdom of Lions," the man muttered under his breath.

I felt my arm relax on the bow. *How does he know those words? Who is this man?*

Suddenly, the world went black. A hood snapped over my head, rendering my night-vision glasses useless. I swung wildly, missing everything. I swung again, and this time I felt a set of large hands clamp down on me right at the elbow, pinning my hands to my side.

I struggled to break free, but it was no use. I pulled again in an attempt to break free, but still nothing—the grip was too much. I stopped fighting, then as I relaxed I was hit over the head. The world around me disappeared into a muffled silence. I don't think I was fully unconscious because I could feel my body being dragged down the alley, but everything was a complete haze.

When I came to, I was tied to a chair, the hood still over my head. I shook at the ropes; they were tight. I wasn't going anywhere. I turned my head, trying to find a hole of any kind to look through. I needed to know where I was. I could hear a few men talking quietly on the other side of the room. It was hard to make out what they were saying, I turned my head toward them, trying to focus on their voices.

It was no use. The talking stopped. Then, just as quickly as it had stopped a voice boomed through the room, "Why are you here?"

Maybe this is another test. I wasn't going to talk. It was time to show how strong I really was. I just sat there as the next line of questioning began.

"What's your name?" There was a short pause. "What are your orders?" Another pause. "Tell me something, son. I don't want to resort to other methods to get you to talk."

The threat was real. I could tell by the sound of his voice that he had tortured before. I could also tell that he didn't enjoy it but was willing to do what it took to get answers. I took a deep breath, preparing for the next phase of questioning. The man walked toward me. I tensed up, preparing for an attack.

My chair flew back, lifting my feet off the floor as I crashed backward. I stopped before hitting the floor, reclined at an extreme angle. Water began to pour through the hood over my head. Every breath was contaminated with water and it felt as if I were drowning. I choked in as much air as I could. There wasn't much. The flow of water was steady, and my mind began to tell me that I was drowning.

The water stopped and I coughed, choking through the soaked hood. Even after the flow of water stopped, every breath I took was wet. I choked again, coughing up a little more water as the hood was ripped off my head. Finally, fresh air. I spit water across the floor, fighting for oxygen. My eyes watered as I finally gathered my breath.

The man grabbed the medallion from my neck, snapping it off. He held it in his hand. "Let's start with something a little easier. Where did you get this? Why do you have it?"

As I choked one more time, I debated whether to say anything or not. The man moved toward me, preparing for another attack with the water. "Wait," I gurgled out. "I got it from Heart City. An old woman gave it to me. It reminded me of home."

"Explain. How does this remind you of home?" the man demanded.

I hesitated, but what would it hurt? I wouldn't be telling them anything about my mission. "My grandpa always used to say that," I said. "We enter as one into the Kingdom of Lions."

The man circled around me. "Do you know what it means?"

"No," I said, shaking my head. "I was taken before he ever explained that part to me."

The man didn't seem satisfied with my answer. He grabbed my hair, pulling my head back. "Do you know what it means?"

"No!" I exclaimed as convincingly as I could.

The man turned away from me, looking at the wall. For the first time I realized that there was a mirror to my left. The man moved through the room, always making an effort to look at the mirror. Besides the mirror, the room was very plain. There was nothing on the walls, the floor was bare, and other than the chair I was sitting in, the room was empty.

There was one unique thing about the room, however, and I had only just now noticed it: there was a light, like the ones from Heart City. Not a candle or lantern, like the typical lighting from the Sections. *This* is *a test. I knew it.* I returned my gaze back to the man as he circled in front of me.

"Who are you?" I asked, looking up at the man.

"We are of no concern to you," he replied, eyes narrowed.

"We?" *Who is we?*

"It's not my place to say." The man threw the wet hood back over my head.

The cold, damp hood made it hard to breathe once again. I could hear the man walk across the room away from me. It sounded like a door opened and then clicked shut. The room was quiet. I listened closely, trying to hear any sounds that would indicate movement. It appeared that I was alone. I squirmed a little in my chair, hoping the water would have caused the ropes to stretch a little. No luck.

A new voice boomed through the room. "Tell me how our saying reminds you of home."

"I already told you," I said angrily. "My grandpa used to say it all the time."

"Is that all?" the man questioned.

"Well, my dad said it before him," I said, not quite sure why I was revealing this. "But he died. He died a few years ago now."

"Do you believe your grandfather was trying to prepare you for something? Why do you think he continued to say that phrase after your father died?" The man's tone had changed. It was much calmer now, and it felt as though he was genuinely interested in my story.

"I don't know. Maybe he said it so I wouldn't forget my father. I just know that I will never forget those words. I'll never forget my family or my home. And I am done talking now; do what you have to do to me."

I sat there waiting for the worst. I didn't know if he would continue to try to get more information from me or just kill me. Either way, I knew I wasn't going to be leaving this room. It was a shame to have survived all that I did to die here. I was ready, though. I could feel every part of me relax.

"I've got one last question for you," the man continued. "What Section did you call home?"

I thought for a moment. Would answering this change anything? "Section Eight. I'm originally from Section Eight."

The man moved toward me, his hand clasped onto the top of my head. I closed my eyes, preparing for the final blow, when suddenly the hood was ripped off. I squinted, peering into the room, trying to regain my focus. The man stood at arm's length from me, towering over me. His voice echoed off the bare walls.

"Welcome into the Kingdom of Lions, son!"

As my eyes finally adjusted to the shadows, the man's face came into focus.

"Dad?"

END OF BOOK 1

ABOUT THE AUTHOR

Charles Schultz grew up in Worthington, Ohio. He spent the majority of his youth playing sports with a dream of becoming a collegiate athlete. Eventually his love of baseball earned him a scholarship to play at Youngstown State University. As a college athlete Charles spent a lot of time developing his writing. First, it was as a tool to set goals, journal successes and failures, and clear his mind from the immense amounts of work it was being a college athlete. Charles spent a lot of time creatively writing poems and after his playing career ended he decided to try something different, writing his first book Hitman's Redemption.

Charles has spent the last several years expanding on his passion for writing. He has since written several other books, blogs, articles, and even contributed to a chapter to his professors coaching book. Charles loves being able to share insights, stories, and more through his writing. He also has a passion for coaching and speaking. He currently coaches several athletes as well as works with the Wooster High School Softball team.

Charles currently resides in Wooster, Ohio with his wife Erin and three children; Hunter, Sayler, and Charlie. He works as a strength coach, softball and baseball instructor, and coach. He loves talking about his passions and encourages anyone who might be on a journey for greatness themselves to reach out and connect.

Connect with Charles and follow what's coming next at www.charlesaschultz.com.